Exile as Challenge

The Tibetan Diaspora

edited by

DAGMAR BERNSTORFF
HUBERTUS VON WELCK

Orient Longman

ORIENT LONGMAN PRIVATE LIMITED

Registered Office
3-6-752 Himayatnagar, Hyderabad 500 029 (A.P.), INDIA

Other Offices
Bangalore, Bhopal, Bhubaneshwar, Chennai, Ernakulam, Guwahati, Hyderabad, Jaipur, Kolkata, Lucknow, Mumbai, New Delhi, Patna

First Published in German by
Nomos Verlagsgesellschaft, Baden-Baden 2002
This enlarged and updated English edition 2004
Reprinted 2004

ISBN 81 250 2555 3

Typeset by
Scribe Consultants
New Delhi

Printed in India at
Baba Barkha Nath Printers
New Delhi

Published by
Orient Longman Private Limited
1/24 Asaf Ali Road
New Delhi 110 002

Contents

Foreword

It is now more than forty-four years since we were compelled to seek asylum in a foreign country. I left my homeland for exile in India, followed by a steady flow of Tibetan compatriots, ready to embrace the life of a refugee. For many, the trauma of the upheavals that had already taken place in Tibet was sufficient to make the freedom of exile, with all its hardships, attractive.

In those early days we were indeed fortunate to receive tremendous help and support from the government and people of India. Initially they provided us with necessary food and shelter, but in the longer term we were offered land to create settlements, as well as the administrative expertise required to establish such communities and set up schools and other facilities for our children. Members of the international community too came to our aid with exceptionally generous support. In the early sixties, many members of our community, especially the school children, depended on aid supplied by Western voluntary agencies.

However, from my point of view, the purpose of coming into exile concerned much more than mere physical survival. In Tibet we were faced with a concerted threat to our identity. Our unique, rich and ancient cultural heritage was faced with imminent actual destruction as our way of life, our social structure and our monastic institutions, the repositories of our education and culture, were turned upside down. The task of those of us in exile was not only to alert the world to what was going on in Tibet, appealing for help to stop it, but equally important to set about preserving our traditions as best we could.

Over the decades since, we have achieved considerable success; stable settlements have been created and along with them schools, medical facilities and religious and cultural institutions have been established. In the monasteries and nunneries of all our spiritual traditions, educational and training programmes have been resumed and in many places improved and extended. Monasteries that were previously concerned only with rituals have introduced courses in philosophy to give their monks an integrated perspective on their practice. Likewise, philosophical training has been made available to nuns who had no such access before. Many monastic institutions also provide their students with some knowledge of modern subjects. In addition, artistic skills such as painting, metal work, wood-carving and sacred dance traditions have survived and are being passed on to new generations.

Within the Tibetan community in exile, we have taken significant steps towards introducing democracy and a modern administration. This culminated in the direct election of our political leadership in 2001. We are committed to continue taking vigorous actions to further promote democratic values among ordinary Tibetans.

In 1959, if they had heard of Tibet at all, many people had very confused notions about our culture, religion and way of life. Today, I can state with confidence that there is both a much better understanding of Tibetan culture, and a general appreciation of its value throughout the world. Although we have been successful in preserving our values and cultural forms in exile for the short term, in the long run we have to return them to Tibet. For this reason I have proposed a Middle Way approach to the Chinese authorities under which we acknowledge their interests in Tibet in the context of genuine autonomy for the Tibetan people that allows for the preservation of our unique cultural heritage and identity.

This book deals in some detail with what has taken place in the Tibetan community in exile. These years in exile have been a challenge, we have achieved much that we can be proud of and much that we can look forward to contributing positively to life in Tibet one day. We have not done this alone, but have received tremendous support from many quarters, and I hope we will continue to do so until our ultimate goal is realised.

Throughout our struggle and our own difficulties as refugees we have tried to keep the rights, welfare and freedom of our six million fellow countrymen and women in mind. I believe that an important aspect of being human is creativity and that to be able to exercise creativity, people need to be free. Those of us living in exile have experienced that freedom, and, even as refugees we have learned something of its value. We are free to speak out for the Tibetan cause and draw attention to the ongoing restrictions in our homeland. Because we continue to have this responsibility to our brothers and sisters in Tibet, I believe that it would be wrong for us to return to Tibet before all Tibetans enjoy the rights those of us in exile and much of the world at large take for granted. I hope that readers of this book will realise that what motivates and unites the Tibetan community in exile is the wish to preserve our distinctive identity, to promote our religious and cultural heritage which is based on a centuries-old philosophy that is of benefit even in the twenty-first century not only to the Tibetan people but to all humanity, and to protect the delicate environment of the Tibetan plateau.

Our struggle is based on truth, justice and non-violence and is not directed against China. We have been fortunate to receive increasing worldwide sympathy and support, even from some Chinese. While I am appreciative and grateful for the consistent generosity and friendship we have received, I sincerely hope that it will not slacken, but will increase until our final goal is won and the exile of Tibetans may come to an end.

1 September 2003 — Tenzin Gyatso, the XIVth Dalai Lama

we have tried to keep the rights, welfare and freedom of our six million fellow countrymen and women in mind. I believe that an important aspect of being human is creativity and that to be able to exercise creativity, people need to be free. Those of us living in exile have experienced that freedom, and even as refugees we have learned something of its value. We are free to speak out for the Tibetan cause and draw attention to the ongoing restrictions in our homeland. Because we continue to have this responsibility to our brothers and sisters in Tibet, I believe that it would be wrong for us to return to Tibet before all Tibetans enjoy the rights that we in exile and much of the world at large take for granted. I hope that readers of this book will realise that what motivates and animates the Tibetan community in exile is the wish to preserve our distinctive identity, to promote our religious and cultural heritage which is based on a compassionate philosophy that is of benefit even in the present-day context not only to the Tibetan people but to all humanity, and to protect the delicate environment of the Tibetan Plateau.

Our struggle is based on truth, justice and non-violence and is not directed against China. We have been fortunate to receive increasing worldwide sympathy and support, even from some Chinese. While I am appreciative and grateful for the consistent generosity and friendship we have received, I sincerely hope that it will not weaken, but will increase until our [illegible] and the future of Tibetans is [illegible].

[illegible] The Dalai Lama

Introduction

DAGMAR BERNSTORFF AND HUBERTUS VON WELCK

The Tibetan community in exile is one of the most resilient and successful refugee groups in the world. The Tibetan people who had lived for at least the last two hundred years secluded on the 'roof of the world' with hardly any contact with other societies and cultures, have in exile performed three remarkable feats. First, individual Tibetans and their families stand on their own feet economically and are able to maintain themselves. Second, a school system has been built up, which has transformed a largely illiterate society (as far as the lay people were concerned; the monastics were of course learned) into a fully literate society within two generations—a testament to political will. Finally, His Holiness the fourteenth Dalai Lama, the temporal and spiritual leader of the Tibetans, introduced democratisation and reduced his own power step by step, so much so, that in 2001 the prime minister of the Government-in-Exile (the chief kalon) is no longer appointed by the Dalai Lama, but directly elected by the Tibetan diaspora.

It has been rightly said that the success of the Tibetan refugee community is due to their culture of hard work. Another essential factor was that a part of the Tibetan society has been transplanted to South Asia with their own internal organisation, their culture, their leader. It was surely a wise decision to create settlements, (located on land leased to the community by the governments of the various states), where the refugees could rebuild their lives. This contrasts with other refugee groups who have lived in provisional camps for decades entirely dependent on assistance.

The Tibetans retained their organisational structure, however, with one important difference: the influential abbots of the major monasteries as well as the big landowners have lost their power and influence with their land. In the settlements, every adult, whether farmer, nomad, businessman or monk, was alloted half a hectare of land—a drastic change in a society dominated by monastics. The young Dalai Lama was thus able to bring in modernisation and democratisation without much resistance.

There is comparatively little systematic research on the Tibetan community in exile. Sociological enquiries date back to the 1960s, but almost ceased in the 1970s.

This volume, aims to fill this gap at least in facets and to encourage reflection and further research, and is a revised and enlarged English edition of the German publication *Tibet im Exil* (Baden-Baden 2002). The articles have been updated and three new chapters have been added: Ven. Sherab Gyatso writes on monks and monasteries, Maura Moynihan relates her experiences working with Tibetan refugees in Nepal and Alison Reynolds reports on Tibet Support Groups worldwide.

The editors of this book focus on two themes. First, how do the Tibetans preserve their culture? Second, how do they prepare for the return to Tibet, should an acceptable form of autonomy within the People's Republic of China emerge? These themes emerged from the editors' convictions that the rich Tibetan culture with its unique methods of mind training and knowledge of the human psyche must be preserved as an essential element of Tibetan identity and as a part of world culture. Further the editors condemn the atrocious human rights violations inflicted on the Tibetans by the communist government of China, and believe that Tibetan political self-determination must be restored. His Holiness the fourteenth Dalai Lama granted a long interview to the editors on the very theme of the preservation of Tibetan culture and his concept of the middle way for achieving autonomy based on nonviolence.

Section I of this book attempts an overview of the historical and political framework. Michael von Brück gives an outline of

Tibetan history and culture. He points out that Tibet has not always been secluded and cut off from the world; on the contrary, it has had intensive cultural and economic relations both with its northwestern neigbours, China and Mongolia as well as with Nepal and India. These relations were however not always peaceful. Another misunderstanding is addressed: Tibetan society was not as feudal as some authors and particularly the spokespersons of the occupying power maintain. Approximately 48 per cent of the population were nomads who were certainly not serfs. Another estimated 12 per cent of the Tibetans lived in towns engaged in commerce, crafts or government service, and around 20 per cent were monastics (see p. 324). The farmers were hereditary tenants, who handed over a part of their harvest to the landlords. They also worked part-time on the fields belonging to the monasteries and in return the monks performed rituals and gave advice.

Opinions vary greatly on the question of Tibet's independence before the Chinese occupation. Historically the two states were involved in a variety of relationships—from interaction between two sovereign states to a priest-patron relationship initiated by the Mongols, to some kind of protectorate and tribute relationship, to de facto independence of Tibet since 1911. Gerald Schmitz points out that the Tibetan state may have ceased to exist after the Chinese annexation, but the Tibetan people have nevertheless the right to demand self-determination, which can take a variety of forms. He quotes international law; a state which does not protect the lives and well being of its citizens—as is the case with the People's Republic of China vis a vis the Tibetans—has forfeited the right to rule.

The next three chapters seek to shed light on the perceptions of the major international players, namely the Indian and the Chinese governments. Gyaneshwar Chaturvedi explains Indian policies on Tibet in the context of India's relations with China. The government of independent India with Jawaharlal Nehru as prime minister and foreign minister gave priority to its China policy. Nehru had a vision of a new strong Asia entering the world scene, led by the two 'great Asian cultures'. He underestimated the potential threat of having Chinese troops at the Indo-Tibetan border and failed to realise that the Chinese neither shared his vision, nor perceived India as a friend. The Indian government had inheritated certain extra territorial privileges from the British in Tibet, but gave these up without asking for a political price. In 1954, with the signing of the Agreement on Trade and Intercourse between the Tibet Region of China and India, the Indian government tacitly recognised Tibet as part of China. The Joint Declaration of the prime minister of India and China after A.B. Vajpayee's visit to Beijing in June 2003, where 'The Indian side recognises that the Tibet Autonomous Region is part of the territory of the People's Republic of China' is therefore not a new departure, but reflects an old position, albeit this position is now stated clearly and unambiguously.

Joachim Glaubitz analyses the Chinese perceptions, which claim Tibet as part of China. He argues—and Schmitz agrees—that the history of relations between Tibet and China cannot be explained in terms of the categories of modern nation-states and contemporary rules of international law, since these relations were premodern in concept and practice. Unfortunately the Tibetan government did not understand the importance of establishing Tibet as a nation state by demanding international recognition and entering into diplomatic relations before the Chinese civil war was over.

Section II, Tibetan Society in Exile, looks at the structures and institutions the exiled community has developed. Tsewang Phuntso analyses the Central Tibetan Administration, recognised by the Indian government, the international donors and certainly by the Tibetans themselves as the only authority to speak for the refugees. This administration succeeded in developing a structure capable of managing the manifold crises refugees have to cope with and absorbing a never-ending stream of new refugees. Adaptation to very different conditions of life, be it the climate or the workplace, needed imagination and strength to tackle the ever new problems of rehabilitation. Dawa Norbu looks at the lives of the refugees from the other end, from the settlements. He points out that the settlers applied indigenous principles of leadership to their new existence, thus facilitating adaptation to an unknown environment and encouraging participation and integration.

A core chapter deals with the introduction of democracy into this traditional society practising unconditional faith in the spiritual and temporal leader. This is nothing short of a miracle. The fourteenth Dalai Lama himself insisted on democratic participation of the refugees as a model for a future Tibet and—unheard of in the history of democracies—voluntarily and without pressure gradually reduced his own power and prerogatives. Tsering Tsomo writes about the Assembly of Tibetan People's Deputies and how the members slowly gained confidence in taking decisions and checking the administration.

Media and freedom of expression is an essential part of democracy. Thubten Samphel traces the history of Tibetan media which for all practical purposes started only during the years in exile. The most striking aspect is the Tibetans' enthusiasm for the internet and their skilful use of this medium. Hundreds of websites connect the exiles living on different continents, and not only the exiles amongst themselves, but also Tibetans in Tibet or in China. Thus a 'Virtual Tibet' has been created.

A second miracle concerns education. Tibetan lay society was largely illiterate, but within two generations the literacy level among 15–24 year olds has risen to 97 per cent. At the time of the exodus from Tibet the Dalai Lama insisted on special schools for Tibetan children, where the medium of instruction is Tibetan up to class V and where Tibetan history and culture have a special place in the curriculum, which otherwise follows the official Indian requirements. About half the Tibetan schools are financed and supported by the Indian government. Within the refugee community the pressure to send children to school is very strong. Even reluctant parents do not get away with keeping their children at home. Tsepak Rigzin explains the school system and analyses the problems that have arisen. The question which looms large is: what are the employment opportunities for the young graduates who cannot be absorbed by the administration or in the settlements?

One of the most crucial problems faced by the community was and continues to be the care of orphans whose parents had lost their lives during the flight or in the early days of exile. The Tibetan Children's Villages (TCVs—inspired by the SOS Children's Villages) were set up for just this purpose. Jetsun Pema writes about this important undertaking where currently about 14,000 children (14 per cent of the Tibetan refugees on the South Asian subcontinent) grow up in the children's villages. Meanwhile the leadership of the TCVs train their own teachers and have also developed appropriate teaching materials.

Important for the preservation of culture is, of course, the cultivation of the arts and crafts. Dagmar Bernstorff visited the five Tibetan cultural centres in India, where from high philosophy to music and dance, from *thangka* painting to traditional crafts, all facets of art and literature—the vehicles and symbols of Buddhist thought—are taught and practised. Culture is personified and transmitted by its people, while the libraries—now three of them—preserve the sources of Tibetan Buddhism, literature and history. The cultural institutions aim primarily at helping Tibetans preserve their identity. However they reach out beyond the exiles and the small circle of Tibetologists and integrate Tibetan art and philosophy into world culture.

Certainly Tibetan women have risen to the challenge of exile and accepted responsibilities they did not have before, as Tsering Norzom Thonsur relates. Exile for them has meant hardship but new possibilities as well.

As can be expected, flight and exile have changed the lives of monks and nuns. The monks have succeeded in rebuilding some of the monasteries in India and in Nepal and re-established monastic life. However exposure to a new world has also given some monks second thoughts about a lifelong dedication to the vows. Ven. Sherab Gyatso gives us a realistic insight into monastic life, especially the mental growth of young monks, while arguing that the monasteries remain centres of learning and ongoing shelters of Tibetan culture.

Exile has opened new possibilities for Tibetan nuns, who earlier held a position inferior to the monks, as they remain novices and are not allowed to be fully ordained. As Ven. Karma Lekshe Tsomo tells us, now that young novices are literate, their chances of reaching higher levels of learning have improved. The full ordination of nuns is also something that many believe is important and the struggle to achieve this is on.

Tibetan medicine is perhaps least affected by change. The medical centres in exile and in Tibet still share the same theories and the same drugs. The challenge comes ironically from the growing popularity of systems of alternative medicine. Tibetan drugs find a vast market in China and abroad, which leads to pressure on the flora and mineral resources of the Tibetan mountains. Jürgen Aschoff points to a paradox: while Tibetan medicine is getting ever more popular in the West, the Tibetans themselves increasingly rely on western medicine.

Tibetan refugees in Europe and North America face challenges of a different kind—namely, retaining their identity, surrounded as they are by an entirely different culture. Gyaltsen Gyaltag analyses the different stages of adaptation, acculturation and assimilation which the Tibetan refugees in Switzerland experience. More so than in the diaspora in South Asia, generational conflicts arise here.

Part III looks at the preparedness for the return to Tibet. Eva Herzer clarifies that autonomy can take many forms and there are almost as many models as there are autonomy arrangements.

The path of non-violence does not come naturally, even though Buddhism stresses this very principle. Ven. Samdhong Rinpoche has developed theories and methods of education for non-violence which will soon be integrated into the educational system of the Tibetan diaspora.

The views of the authors are not uniform but often divergent. Tsepak Rigzin is of the opinion that there were hardly any schools in Tibet before 1950, but Ven. Samdhong Rinpoche maintains, that there existed an informal system of education.

The Dalai Lama is committed to a non-violent struggle for the liberation of Tibet and autonomy within China. The Tibetan Youth Congress however does not agree, but demands full independence for Tibet. Even the question of non-assimilation or integration into Indian, Nepali, European or North American societies is a controversial theme among the exiles.

Some authors lament the loss of identity among the youth, who—so they think—are hooked on pop music and popular Indian movies. But the two Swiss Tibetans Gyaltsen Gyaltag and Wangpo Tethong have their own views based on empirical research and point out that finding one's identity is a process lasting many years, which usually leads back to Tibetan culture after adolescence. The Tibetan diaspora has risen to the challenges and adapted to change in many innovative ways.

The editors thank His Holiness the Dalai Lama for generously granting a long interview. The former ministers Tashi Wangdi, T.C. Tethong and Tempa Tsering were most supportive of our enquiry. The leaders of the Tibetan settlements at Bylakuppe allowed us insights into Tibetan social reality at the grass roots level. And the chairpersons of the cultural institutions did not tire of our curiosity.

We especially thank Vidya Rao and Hemlata Shankar at Orient Longman, who edited and saw this book through press with great understanding, professional competence and unruffled by the pressure of time.

DAGMAR BERNSTORFF

New Delhi, September 2003 HUBERTUS VON WELCK

I

Historical and Political Framework

CHAPTER ONE

Tibet, the 'Hidden Country'*

MICHAEL VON BRÜCK

Tibet is a vast, far-reaching, thinly settled plateau, criss-crossed by numerous mountain ranges and waterways. Throughout its history, communication between the various regions was and still remains difficult, even more so than the communication with bordering non-Tibetan regions. In spite of the sparse settlement, or perhaps because of it, there has been an unusually large diversity of cultural traditions and political structures. To establish proof of a uniform or homogeneous political-religious system in Tibet is impossible. Apart from the centralised structures of political power in the cities and main monasteries, there were regional federations of varying degrees of internal loyalties and semi-autonomous administrative units. Almost completely detached from all of that were the nomads, who lived in the extensive plains in a pre-national culture in which the religious significance of higher lamas and especially that of the Dalai Lama was recognised, but was not accorded any political authority.[1]

The History of the Three Early Dharmarajas: Songtsen Gampo, Trisong Detsen, Ralpachen

There is little reliable information about the earliest Tibetan kingdoms. It is believed that the ninth king, Podekungyal, was

*The following observations are based on the detailed analysis of the religion and politics of Tibet in my book: Michael von Brück, *Religion und Politik im Tibetischen Buddhismus*, München 1999.

[1]Dodin, Th. and Räther, H. (ed.), *Mythos Tibet.* Wahrnehmungen, Projektionen, Phantasien, Cologne 1997, p. 338.

a contemporary of the Han-Chinese Emperor, Wu-ti (185–40 BC). Tride Songsten, who went down in history as King Songsten Gampo (*Srong-btsansgam-po*, reigning from AD 629–49) was born in 617. He married, among others, the Nepalese princess Bhrikuti Devi (referred to by the Tibetans as Belsa, the Nepalese Woman), who allegedly brought with her a statue of Buddha, Akshobhya, and the Chinese princess, Wen-ch'eng Kung-chu (called Gyasa, or the Chinese Woman by the Tibetans), who is believed to have arrived in Lhasa in 641 bringing with her a statue of Buddha Shakyamuni, especially revered by the Tibetans. According to legend, Belsa and Gyasa had temples built for their respective statues. First Gyasa built a temple and named it Ramoce Tsuklakhang. For Belsa's statue, a lake was filled with earth and rocks, and a temple called Rasa Trulnang Tsuklakhang, later also referred to as Jokhang, was built upon it. This temple, in the heart of the capital city, Lhasa, remains to this day the holiest of shrines for Tibetans.

The gates of the temples faced the direction of China and Nepal, but for security reasons, the statues were exchanged when it was thought that a Chinese army was about to conquer the city of Lhasa. Exchange, rather than seclusion, was the message of this early political legend.

It is evident that Tibetan politics was already strongly influenced by power struggles in the seventh century, and that Tibet was able to hold its own in the power play between China, the Tartars and Mongols, the Nepalese, and the Hindus in the south.

The development of Tibetan writing, derived from the Sanskrit script of the Gupta period, by the scholar Thonmi Sambhota, was a direct result of the cultural ties Tibet had established with India. It was a key factor in securing Tibet's external political balance. The widespread use of uniform writing promoted political unification and the centralisation of the government by enabling a structured administrative system. Tibet's cultural ties with India and China, as well as the political unification of Tibet, were mostly enabled by the introduction of Buddhism as the national religion.

In the year 640, Tibetan troops conquered parts of northern Burma and regions in Nepal. Contact with southern neighbours intensified, especially because Tibetan settlers were able to gain a foothold in the Himalayan regions. In 645, Songtsen Gampo sent nine emissaries to the Chinese court and asked for permission to build a temple and monastery complex in the mountains of the Shansi province. This political move corresponded with the interests of the T'ang dynasty to establish a political alliance with Tibet through cultural relationships.

According to the Tibetan historian Bu-ston (1290–1364) Songtsen Gampo even travelled to the north of China for the inauguration of the first temple. In any case, the construction laid the groundwork for the great Buddhist architecture on the Wu-ta'i Shan.

Songtsen Gampo died in the year 649. He was later venerated as the incarnation of Bodhisattva Avalokiteshvara. After his death, Tibet was able to extend its influence into the Tarim Basin and from there, far into the Chinese heartland. Until the eighth century, the relationship was characterised by constant wars and conflicts with the Chinese governors of the bordering provinces and the imperial troops.

Like his predecessors, King Trisong Detsen (*Khri-srong lde-btsan*, 755–797) was an advocate of Buddhism despite considerable opposition from the nobility, who were followers of the ancient Bön belief. The conflict in this case was by no means restricted to religion; mainly, it was about the contrast between central and peripheral powers. Ultimately, Trisong Detsen was able to impose himself through the political influence of oracles. Furthermore, Trisong Detsen invited the Indian Pandit Shantirakshita to Tibet in order to spread Buddhism and to fight the influence of Bön. According to reports, although Shantirakshita was successful in his efforts, his teachings—based primarily on the Indian Mahayana philosophy —offered no plausible alternatives to the Tibetan belief in spirits and demons. And so the King invited the famous Indian tantric Padmasambhava to come to Tibet and subjugate the Bön spirits with tantric incantations. Padmasambhava brought the spirits and demons under his control, and made them take an oath to protect (*dharmapala*) the new religion. In other words, the ancient pre-Buddhist Tibetan spirits of the rivers, woods and mountains were 'tamed' and integrated into Buddhism through reinterpretation.

These spirits now appeared in their old forms as aspects of consciousness with terrifying powers that could be countered by soothing and integrating the spirit.

About Padmasambhava himself, we know very little that can be historically verified. Traditional tales about him are wrought with mystery. His hagiography was only concluded in the fourteenth century, and many of the so-called Terma texts, or Treasure texts, which he placed in secret locations to be found later when the time was right, stem from this period. Based on that, it is believed that the Master was born in Uddiyana as the son of King Indrabodhi. It is also believed that he came to Tibet in 747 and remained there for fifty years. There he wrote comments on Bardo Thödol (*bar-do thos-grol*) and Guhyamalagarbha Tantra.

Shantirakshita, on the other hand, has a more clear-cut historical profile. He established the first monastery Samye in the region of Drakmar and modelled it on Otantapuri in India. On the occasion of a legendary gathering (792–94)[2] convened by Trisong Detsen in the Samye Monastery, which had been equipped with an exemplary Sanskrit School by Shantirakshita, it is said, the King decided in favour of the Indian form of Buddhism after listening to a debate between the Chinese scholar Ho shang and Shantirakshita's student, the Indian Kamalasila.[3] This means Tibet primarily took over two aspects of Indian Buddhism:

- the strict hierarchical structure of monastic institutions
- the Buddhist scripts (sutras) and the corresponding expository philosophical literature (shastras).

---

[2]Demiéville, P., *Le Concile de Lhasa*, Paris 1952.

[3]Kamalasila was later murdered, probably a victim of an intrigue of the 'Chinese faction'.

This was the foundation for the form of scholarship that developed according to the Indian model and became rooted in monasteries.

The monarchy assumed responsibility for the material support of the temple monasteries, and Trisong Detsen decreed that future rulers would be obliged to carry on the tradition. In return, the monasteries became powerful arms of the centralised Tibetan state.

Chinese sources, however, have a different interpretation from that of the Tibetans and the Indians of the debate at Samye and its consequences. Namely, that the Chinese method became the dominant one.[4] In any case, the result could also have been influenced by the political interests of the King: around 750 a military alliance between Tibet and Siam was formed against China, and in 763, Trisong Detsen sent a mighty army against central China which vanquished Ch'ang-an, forcing the Chinese Emperor to flee. The Tibetan army installed a tributary emperor and retreated. The religious and cultural contacts with India certainly played a role in this conflict, and the ensuing increase in the dominance of the Indian form of Buddhism may well have been an impact of the political and military situation: there were constant border conflicts between China and Tibet, and the Tibetan wars against various Turkic nations[5] made an alliance with Nepal and India in the south a political necessity.

In 815 King Ralpachen (*Ral-pa-can*, the third dharmaraja [Religious King] after Songtsen Gampo and Trisong Detsen) came to power.[6] His political stance also remained pro-Buddhist;

---

[4]Demiéville, supra, 333ff. Only fragments of Indian testimonies have been maintained. Tucci attributes more credit to the Chinese sources because the Tibetan ones are of a much earlier date and the Indian system had just only gradually begun to assert itself in Tibet.

[5]Between 785 and 805, Tibetan troops advanced in the west against Turkish tribes and Arab-Chinese alliances almost to the Oxus and are believed to have even occupied Samarkand around 800.

[6]Only these three kings and the Dalai Lamas were later revered as incarnations of Avalokiteshvara, the Bodhisattva of Compassion.

in fact, the ties with India strengthened under his rule, and he invited three Indian Buddhist masters (Silendrabodhi, Danasila and Jinamitra), who wrote the first Sanskrit-Tibetan dictionary together with the Tibetan scholars Kawa Paltsek and Chogro Lui Gyaltsen. The dictionary established the standards for translation of Buddhist terminology. While Buddhist scripts had previously been translated from Chinese and Sanskrit, from that time on, Sanskrit alone became the valid source language for Buddhism. Under Ralpachen's rule, the power of the monasteries increased further. As in India, the monasteries were financially supported by the monarchy, they took on political roles, and were exempt from taxation. For this reason, the negotiations involving the Tibetan/Chinese peace treaty of 821–22 (engraved on a column in Lhasa) were conducted on both sides by monks. Ralpachen apparently had high-ranking monks entered on the records as being on the same level as the King, and finally became a monk himself.

Ralpachen's older brother Darma had been passed over as heir to the throne for political and personal reasons, and therefore, had an interest in overthrowing Ralpachen. After an intrigue-laden contest, he finally succeeded in doing so with the help of the anti-Buddhist Bön federation of priests.

The assassination of Ralpachen in 836 unleashed a wave of persecution which almost eradicated Buddhism from Tibet. Monks were forced to marry and convert to the Bön belief, and were conscripted into the army. Those who refused were sentenced to death. At the peak of the persecution, in 842, a monk named Lhalung Palgye Dorje shot the King with a bow and arrow in front of the Jokhang Temple. This episode is commemorated to this day in the 'Black Hat' dance.

The motivation behind the persecution of Buddhism was by no means purely religious, and King Lang Darma was probably not the villain that he is made out to be in later Tibetan historical descriptions. He was more concerned with the increasing economic power of the monasteries which were ruining the monarchy with their privileged exemption from taxation and military service. Inheritances and gifts were donated more and more to the monasteries (not only in the form of land but also in the form of produce for the sustenance of the monks), which resulted in the siphoning of an important source of income from the state. The ever-increasing number of monasteries transferred power from the nobility and landowners to the monasteries and their abbots, which changed the ancient structure of agriculture as more and more people were making a living by farming monastic property or shepherding monastic flocks. One ensuing problem was that these servants were also exempt from military conscription at a time when the military threats from China were increasing and Tibet's central Asian territory was decreasing. Lang Darma's war against Buddhism, which took place almost concurrently with the persecution of Buddhism in China for similar reasons, actually had very logical political reasons.[7]

Lang Darma's death was followed by a schism in the monarchy which lasted until 1247, when Sakya Pandita, Lama of the Sakya Monastery, was given full plenary powers for the entire country by Godan Khan, the grandson of Ghengis Khan. This period was characterised by the struggles of individual regional potentates for power and influence and the general degeneration of the centralised authority of the state.

In the tenth century, Buddhism was revived by the Guge monarchy of west Tibet, a revival known as the Second Propagation of the Teachings. During this time, new schools, or orders, were established: Kadampa, Sakyapa, Kagyüpa, Gelugpa. These schools defined life in Tibet through the centuries and continue to do so to this day. The unique philosophical and psychological methods of spiritual training which characterise Tibetan Buddhism were established in the monastic schools of these orders.

The second propagation was completed when the Tibetan scholar Bu-ston (1290–1364) collected over 4,500 texts that had

---

[7]Tucci, G. and Heissig, W., *Die Religionen Tibets und der Mongolei*, Stuttgart 1970, p. 11.

been translated into Tibetan. These texts were put together in a two-part canon titled *Kangyur* (*bka'-'gyur*, 108 volumes of Vinaya, Sutra and Tantra texts) and *Tengyur* (*bstan- 'gyur*, 225 volumes of expository literature).[8] In 1322 Bu-ston wrote his history of Tibetan Buddhism, which remains a major source of our knowledge of developments up until the fourteenth century.[9]

The Second Propagation of Buddhism is connected with two names: Rinchen Sangpo and Atisha. A monk named Rinchen Sangpo (*Rin-chen bzang-po*, 958–1055) was sent in the seventh decade of the tenth century to Kashmir by King Tsenpo Khore, founder of the Tholing monastery, to study the teachings and writings of Buddhism and to invite Buddhist scholars and artists to Tibet. The King later abdicated and became a monk known by the name of Yeshe Öd (*Ye-shes 'od*). His main concern was to re-establish monastic discipline according to the rules of the vinaya, and in particular, to enforce celibacy for monks and prohibit animal sacrifice. Rinchen Sangpo, who spent a total of seventeen years in India studying monastic discipline and the Mahayana philosophy, is considered one of the most important translators of Buddhist writings. In addition to that, he founded numerous monasteries in the south of Tibet.[10] In 1042, the well-known scholar Atisha (982–1054) arrived in Tibet from Bengal to contribute to the revival and reform of Buddhism. Under his direction, over a hundred Buddhist texts were translated from

---

[8]To begin with, various handwritten volumes of the *Kangyur* and *Tengyur* were prepared; an early *Tengyur* edition was brought to the Zha-lu monastery in south Tibet in 1334 for safe-keeping. The first printing of the *Kangyur* occurred in Beijing in 1410. A Mongolian translation was begun immediately, but was completed only in the eighteenth century.

[9]Edition (in Tibetan): Szerb, J., *Bu-ston's History of Buddhism in Tibet*, Vienna 1990.

[10]A recently published book on the subject: van Ham, P. and Stirn, A., *Vergessene Götter Tibets, Wiederentdeckung Buddhistischer Klosterkunst im Westhimalaya*, Stuttgart/Zürich 1997.

Sanskrit into Tibetan and previously translated ones were revised. Atisha eliminated non- Buddhist practices such as animal sacrifice and magic from the Buddhism he encountered and stressed the importance of monastic discipline and philosophical study. He met Rinchen Sangpo and initiated him and his student Dromtön (*'Brom-ston*, 1008–1064) in various tantras.

The connection between the textual studies of Mahayana philosophy (Madhyamaka and Yogacara) and tantra, the identification with deities through visualisation in order to activate corresponding potential in one's own consciousness, had a profoundly influential effect on the Kadampa school founded by Atisha as well as on Tibetan Buddhism well into the future. Atisha died in 1054 in Tibet. According to Tibetan sources, the introduction of the Kalachakra tantra, the last great tantric system, is associated with his name.

The Mongolian Khans and the Sakyas

Following in the spirit of Atisha's reforms, the Sakya Monastery (*sa-skya*) was founded in 1073. The Kadampa monasteries of Zha lu (1040) and Reting (1057), both politically and religiously influential, were built almost simultaneously. The monasteries of the Kagyüpa (also known as Kagyur) school, in particular Drikung (1167) and Tsurphu (1189), appeared roughly a hundred years later. Each of these monasteries followed the principles of its respective founder and differed from the others in theory and practice. The economic and political importance of these institutions as well as their religious differences, led to rivalries and violent contests for supremacy that did not cease for centuries.[11]

These great religious communities emerged as a symbiosis between spiritual and wordly power after times of restlessness and social disintegration. Thereafter, the history of Tibet was defined by abbots, as in the case of Sakyapa, or by powerful

[11]Tucci and Heissig, supra, p. 41.

landowners who, as patrons and political supporters of the various schools, were founders of monasteries. Since these noble families turned all their attention to their own monasteries, their interests became inextricably entwined with those of a particular monastic community.

The political rise of the Sakya school is closely related to the military domination of the Mongols. In 1207, a Tibetan delegation travelled to the court of Genghis Khan in order to negotiate friendly relations and prevent a military takeover. Tibet committed itself to pay tribute to the Khan, but ceased payments upon his death in 1227. Soon after that, Godan Khan, a grandson of Genghis Khan, advanced his troops as far as the surrounding region of Lhasa. There, in 1244, he delivered a letter to Pandita Sakya, the head lama of the Sakya monastery, bidding the Tibetan lamas to instruct the ignorant Mongolian people—in other words, asking them to initiate a cultural religious mission.[12] The lamas would be richly compensated in return.

This was the beginning of a political system characterised by the special relationship between patron and priest (*yon mch od*) that was to become an influential factor in Tibet's political life for centuries to come, at first, during the rule of the Sakya lamas, and later, since the time of the third Dalai Lama, also for the Gelugpa. It was a pragmatic, political solution to the clash between two utterly different peoples. Though Buddhism had regained some of its former influence after years of persecution, Tibet was a splintered society without a central authority. The Mongols, on the other hand, a conglomerate of nomadic tribes, had swift hordes capable of wrecking instant havoc and devastation, but unable to maintain control of conquered territory for long since they lacked a bureaucracy and a logistically capable administration. The newly empowered Buddhist clergy needed military protection, while the Mongol Khans needed the civilising force offered by the Tibetan monastic community.

---

[12]Shakabpa, W.D., *Tibet: A Political History*, New York 1984, p. 61f.

Following the death of Godan Khan in 1253, first Mongka Khan, then Kublai Khan (1260) came to the throne. Kublai Khan invited the successor of Sakya Pandita, his 19-year old nephew and student, Phagpa, to his court. Phagpa made Kublai Khan promise to prostrate himself in front of his teacher every time they met. Kublai Khan agreed to perform this sign of obeisance, but only in private, so as not to publicly damage his image of authority. Furthermore, Kublai Khan promised to seek Phagpa's advice in all matters pertaining to Tibet. He would make his own decisions only in matters pertaining to Chinese and Mongolian problems. In addition to that, during religious meetings and ceremonies, Kublai would be seated below Phagpa, but would sit on the same level when it came to affairs of the state.[13]

Kublai Khan did not want to tolerate any other school besides Sakyapa, but Phagpa, himself a Sakyapa, had the political wisdom to insist on tolerance and religious freedom for the other Buddhist denominations. This decision brought him the support of the other groups, particularly their monasteries, but it undermined the long-term influence of Sakyapa on the political history of Tibet. It even led to a certain Mongolisation of the Tibetan upper classes, some of whom took to wearing Mongol dress. This drew criticism from the conservative lamas who were mistrustful of any close relationship with the Mongols. Tibetans of the Sakya school who were proselytising the Mongols fell into a classic pattern of cultural assimilation.

When it came to political power, the influential lamas did not remain neutral. When Kublai Khan conquered the whole of China in 1280, Phagpa congratulated him, especially because it meant an effective means for propagating Buddhism. Phagpa was stating the obvious—according to the sources at our disposal, he never actively called for crusades. However, the lamas also exerted

[13]The height of the seating was, and remains, an opportunity in Chinese and Tibetan political etiquette to demonstrate order of rank, because it precisely shows where there is subordination or equality of rank in the hierarchy.

their political influence to hinder a Mongolian attack on Nepal and India, although in this case, the decision was probably influenced by close religious affiliation to those neighbouring countries.

The shift in the political hierarchy between Tibetans and Mongols was an interesting development. While the relationship between Godan Khan and Sakya Pandita was still that of a lord and his underling, Godan gave orders and delivered ultimatums. Kublai Khan and Phagpa developed a special bond that united patronage and religious authority. This model, with some modifications, remained the standard until the end of the Manchu reign in China. However, the influence of the Sakya school in Tibet and on the Mongol court ended with Kublai Khan's death in 1331.

The political power shifted to the Kagyüpa school which had already firmly established the custom of *tulku*, the practice of choosing the reincarnation of a lama as the successor for a religious and political personage, with the second Karmapa, Karma Pakshi (1204–83).

The fact that the Mongols had exclusively patronised the lamas of the Sakya school until the death of Kublai Khan in 1331, gave them a special political and economic status to the detriment of other groups, which in turn led to violent power struggles throughout Tibet in the fourteenth century.

Provincial governors waged wars against each other, and the main monasteries were deeply involved in these conflicts. Intrigues, torture, murder, even among monks, was the order of the day until Changchub Gyaltsen took control in 1358 and initiated a series of reforms that brought peace to the country. Some of his reforms were of an administrative nature, for example, the division of the state into districts called *dzong*. Other reforms were agricultural. He also reformed the penal system which until then had allowed the execution of criminals without trial, but now demanded an orderly process resulting in varying degrees of punishment, including the death sentence. Changchub improved the infrastructure by building bridges, installing ferries on the Tsangpo river and militarily securing the borders with China. He also ensured better education for the lamas,[14] and since then the Sakyapa have been known for their erudition. The library of the Sakya monastery was one of the largest in the land until the occupation of Tibet by the Chinese in 1950. It housed thousands of priceless manuscripts and block prints of all Buddhist traditions, including some that were saved when Muslim invaders destroyed the Nalanda monastery in India in the twelfth century. A small portion of the library could be brought to safety after 1959, during the exodus of Tibetan monks from Sakya to north India.

The Dalai Lamas

At first the Dalai Lamas were acknowledged as higher incarnations (*tulku*) of lamas from the Drepung monastery of the Gelugpa school. The founder of this branch of Buddhism, Tsongkhapa, died in 1419. After the death of the Regent[15] Gongma Drakpa Gyaltsen (1432), whose reign over Tibet brought relative peace and stability, the political system collapsed and a series of small-scale internal Tibetan wars ensued lasting for roughly one hundred years. The main conflict was between the governors of the Tsang and Ü provinces. One, an advocate of the Gelugpa school, the other of the Karmapa school, which meant these conflicts created power struggles between the monasteries as well. Because the custom of patronage ruled, the monks in the mightier monasteries found themselves drawn into the military conflicts. As a result, political lines could be identified by their religious affiliation. While Kagyüpa was supported by the Tsang monarchy, more and more powerful rivals appeared within the Gelugpa group which was linked to

[14]Shakabpa, supra, p. 81f.

[15]During that time, actual political power was in the hands of the Regents, although the degree of their authority varied greatly by region. After the time of the fifth Dalai Lama, on the other hand, the Regents represented the highest political authority in Tibet between the death of a Dalai Lama and the time the next one came of age.

the Phagmo rulers. The wars were often long-lasting, brutal, and persistent, and even led to the reciprocal destruction of monasteries.[16] This pattern is characteristic of Tibet's history: the power struggles between regions, clans, and religious schools, or sects, are so deeply linked that they can hardly be disentangled.

Through these circumstances, a new centre of power, the line of the Dalai Lamas, gradually began to develop. That the Gelugpa school was able to gain political advantage under the direction of the Dalai Lama was the result of two historical constellations:

- the chaotic political situation in the central provinces of Ü and Tsang
- the new Mongol Khan's interest in supporting the Gelugpa school.

In 1560, armed conflicts broke out between the supporters of the Gelugpa and Kagyüpa in Lhasa. When local attempts to quell the violence failed, Sonam Gyatso (1543–88, the Abbot of the Drepung monastery[17]) was called upon to mediate. His intervention was successful. As the Abbot of Drepung, he was a renowned scholar, and on top of that, he had political influence as well, since he had been consulted in 1559 by the Prince of Nedong (Nedong Gongma) who had turned to him for advice. The successful peace mission in Lhasa was probably one of the reasons why Sonam Gyatso came to the attention of Altan Khan, ruler of the Tümed Mongols, and was invited to his court to take on the role of teacher and to revive the old relationship of patron and teacher between Mongols and Tibetans. At first Sonam Gyatso declined, but in 1577 he finally consented after

---

[16]The Gelugpa repeatedly occupied the monasteries of the Kagyüpa and vice versa. Gedun Gyatso, born in 1475 and posthumously declared second Dalai Lama, built the Chokhorgyal monastery in 1509. It was attacked and heavily damaged by forces of the Drikung-Kagyüpa in 1537.

[17]The school of the Drepung monastery was founded in 1416 by Jamyang Dorje, a student of Tsongkhapa. In time, Drepung became the largest monastery of Tibet, with roughly 7,700 monks.

Altan Khan renewed his invitation. With this decision he hoped to gain the military support of the Mongols, a support greatly needed because the power base of the Gelugpa had been shaken by internal conflicts and the decline of their patrons, the Phagmo rulers. Like the Sakya Lamas in the thirteenth century, he too turned to the Mongols for 'external protection against growing inner disintegration'[18] in Tibet. In the summer of 1578, Sonam Gyatso arrived in the foremost Mongolian nomad camp and was welcomed with great festivity by a delegation of the Khan. He instructed the Khan on Buddhism and converted him, and preached to the people as well. Thereupon, Altan Khan exempted the Buddhist monasteries from paying taxes and the monks from military service, and bestowed upon Sonam Gyatso the title of Dalai Lama (*Dalai* meaning ocean in Mongolian) as well as the title of Dorje Chang (Holder of the Diamond Scepter). In return, Sonam Gyatso granted Altan Khan the title of religious King, Brahma of the Gods. The reciprocal dispensing of titles was a common practice in central Asia and at the Chinese court. The predecessors of Sonam Gyatso, Gedün Gyatso (1475–1542) and Gedün Drub (1391–1475) were posthumously awarded the titles of the first and second Dalai Lama.

It was the fifth Dalai Lama, Ngawang Losang Gyatso (1617–82), however, who was first able to centralise and use his political and religious power after a long struggle delineated by a clearly calculated political strategy. This consolidation led to a relatively stable period of cultural and economic growth. Because of the intense rivalry between the various Tibetan factions, the Mongols wanted to have this Dalai Lama raised in Mongolia for security reasons, which shows how dependent the Gelugpa were on the Mongols for their power base in Tibet. Those circles in Tibet that were nationalistic in orientation, such as the Kagyüpa of the Tsang province who had a politically sophisticated advocate in their Regent (*sde srid*, Desi), were opposed to this foreign influence.

---

[18]Barraux, R., *Die Geschichte der Dalai Lamas*, Düsseldorf 1995, p. 97.

Some Tibetan sources report that the fifth Dalai Lama practically forced his way into Shigatse as a conqueror in 1642. A Mongol leader named Gushri Khan had apparently declared him sole ruler of Tibet, and appointed Sonam Chopel (a.k.a. Sonam Rabten) as regent (*sde srid*, Desi). In this way, the fifth Dalai Lama had truly become the spiritual and worldly leader of the entire country. Other sources, however, such as the autobiography of the fifth Dalai Lama himself, whose credibility in this matter is quite high,[19] have a different interpretation which would place the rise of the fifth Dalai Lama to sovereignty over Tibet at a later date.

The fifth Dalai Lama decided to build a new palace for himself, a decision that became a turning point for him, because for the first time he saw himself as the head of all Tibet and not just as high *tulku* of the Drepung monastery. He expressed this vision by building his new residence on the ruins of the Triste Marpo palace that Songsten Gampo had built for his Nepalese princess in the year 636 AD. The foundation for the Potala Palace was laid in 1645. In 1648, the monks of various Karampa monasteries were forced to convert to the Gelugpa sect. In 1654, Gushri Khan died. His successors were weak rulers, something the fifth Dalai Lama knew how to take advantage of. It was only after 1660 that he became the true sovereign of Tibet.[20] Although the Mongol Khans retained the title of 'King of Tibet' until 1720, the title was purely honorary and had no political significance at all.

In the meantime, the Chinese Manchu emperor Shun-chih became aware of the growing powers of the Dalai Lama of Tibet. Between 1649 and 1651, he sent the Dalai Lama various invitations to visit Beijing, which he finally accepted in 1652. The reasons and goals behind this visit have been assessed

---

[19]Yamaguchi, Z., 'The Sovereign Power of the Fifth Dalai Lama: sPrul sku gZims-khang-gong-ma and the Removal of Governor Nor-bu', in *Memoirs of the Research Department of the Tokyo Bunko*, The Oriental Library No. 53, Tokyo, 1995, p. 2ff.

[20]Ibid., p. 9.

differently in the annals of Chinese and Tibetan history. The Tibetan version stresses that the Manchus were closely allied with the Mongols, and therefore also wanted to build relations with Tibet. The Chinese, however, maintain that the Manchu emperor wanted to ask the Dalai Lama to intercede on his behalf and dissuade the Mongols from further attacking and pillaging China.

Either way, it is evident that the Dalai Lama was increasingly called upon not only to mediate conflicts between the various Mongol clans,[21] but also between the Mongol and the Chinese troops which only strengthened his influence. However, when the danger of a revolution arose in China and the emperor K'ang-hsi asked Tibet for support, the Dalai Lama refused. He showed political acumen in other areas as well, for example, by lowering taxes in Kham, a politically sensitive border region, to placate the populace.

The fifth Dalai Lama was a scholar of Sanskrit and wrote important discourses that also revealed his poetical interests. He opened academies for monks and lay people where Sanskrit, Mongolian, astrology, poetry, medicine, riding and archery were taught. He was successful in unifying the country, albeit, as described above, not without the use of force. The Dalai Lama was able to steer an independent path for Tibet between the mighty Mongols and Chinese. His shrewd political strategy brought peace and agricultural reforms, as well as reforms to the criminal system, including more humane punishments and more transparent legal proceedings. On the one hand, he established a power base for the Gelugpa at the expense of the other sects, but on the other hand, he did strive to create a new foundation that would unify the diverse Tibetan traditions and thus avoid destructive friction between the different schools of Tibetan Buddhism. To that end, he took *dharma* instruction not only from Gelugpa scholars but also from the lamas of the Nyingma sect. The political importance of the fifth Dalai Lama is also

[21]Ibid., p. 7.

evident in the fact that his death was kept secret for about fifteen years, so as not to endanger political stability and the ongoing construction of the Potala Palace.[22]

After the death of the fifth Dalai Lama, political power was in the hands of the Regent Sangye Gyatso, and the reign of the sixth Dalai Lama was marked by the rule of the Regent—the Dalai Lama himself had openly opted for a life of sensual pleasures.[23] The succeeding Dalai Lamas were weak rulers, caught between the interest groups of the dominant and influential monasteries, the Tibetan nobility and the increasingly potent interests of the imperial Chinese regime.

Although Tibetan diplomacy succeeded in maintaining Tibet's independence in spite of the tensions between the expansionist policies of the Manchu emperor in China and the Mongol clans, internal conflicts and external pressures forced the Tibetans to compromise and to forge alliances that may have been politically legitimate but nevertheless afforded little stability to the nation. The fact that Tibet was freed from Mongolian occupation with the help of Chinese troops in 1718–20 was to have future political consequences. In 1726, the Chinese emperor was called upon to mediate an internal quarrel that had broken out between the Tibetan ministers, which had pushed the country to the brink of a civil war. The Manchus used the opportunity to once again establish a military base in Lhasa. Following that, two Manchu envoys *(amban)* took up residence in Lhasa. The claims to power in Tibet currently made by China stem from this period.

A minister named Polhanas emerged as the victor from those conflicts; he was undoubtedly a clever politician and a good administrator who supported the monasteries and financed the new editions of *Kangyur* and *Tengyur* (Narthang Edition). His reign over Tibet lasted for a total of nineteen years of relative

---

[22]Barraux, supra, p. 125.

[23]Schulemann, G., *Die Geschichte der Dalai Lamas,* Leipzig 1958, p. 267ff.; Barraux, supra, p. 128ff., a more restrained opinion is found in Shakabpa, supra, p. 128ff.

peace and stability, but at the same time he made sure that the seventh Dalai Lama remained politically powerless. Polhanas died in 1747. He was succeeded by his son, Gyumey Namgyal, who became embroiled in conflict, not only with the Dalai Lama but with the Manchus as well, since he wanted to re-establish Tibetan independence. For this reason, he renewed contact with the Dzungar Mongols. When the envoys heard of this, they tricked Gyumey Namgyal and his entourage with an invitation and had him murdered. The Tibetans, angered by this treacherous move, stormed the residence of the envoys and killed them along with 100 Chinese soldiers. Another 200 Chinese soldiers were forced to flee and seek haven in the Potala, where they were guaranteed the personal protection of the Dalai Lama who asked the populace, in vain, to refrain from violent retaliation. In 1751, a Manchu officer arrived in Lhasa, followed by a Chinese army, to investigate the matter. Seven Tibetan leaders were sentenced to death by dismemberment, six others by beheading, and countless participants in the uprising were imprisoned.

In 1790, war broke out between Tibet and the Gurkhas in Nepal based on territorial disputes and differences in trade policies. At first the Nepalese had the upper hand and the Tibetans were forced to pay tribute, but in 1792 a Chinese-Tibetan force headed by the Chinese general Fu Kiang-an was able to vanquish the King of Nepal. Thanks to the role of the Chinese empire in this affair, the Chinese envoys in Lhasa were able to strengthen their position. The relative sovereignty of Tibet was curtailed when the Emperor declared his envoys as provincial governors in 1792. This cutback of the Tibetan government's and the eighth Dalai Lama's power was legitimised by the Chinese in a reverse, and one-sided, application of the previous 'patron and priest' relationship between the Tibetans and Mongols. In effect, in the new 'Chinese-Tibetan' relationship, all matters of state, including financial, defence and external policies, had to be presented to the envoys for approval. In 1793, China established a new decree governing the selection of religious dignitaries in which the Chinese envoys would be responsible for the search for reincarnations. Because nepotism and abuse had corrupted the old system, from then on the reincarnation would be determined by drawing lots among various candidates under the supervision of the Chinese envoys.

During the time of the ninth Dalai Lama (1806–1815) the influence of the Chinese diminished considerably. The Manchu emperors, who were having their own internal political turmoils, were trying to solidify their power in Tibet by placing Chinese monks in Tibetan monasteries for their own political purposes. In order to prevent a possible British influence in Tibet, Chinese monks were used to spread propaganda against foreigners, especially Europeans, whose presence in the country would have allegedly endangered the old religious system. The abbots were thus able to keep the monasteries isolated from outside influence —even sweets and soap coming from abroad were considered a potential threat to the faith.[24] This policy of isolation was later upheld by the British for their own political purposes. On the one hand, this policy was useful for furthering the interests of foreign powers like China and Britain, who wanted to solidify their power base in Tibet, on the other hand, it also served to strengthen the hold monastic hierarchies had over the monks and over Tibetan society which they did not want to endanger in the least through modernisation. This constellation was the reason why the thirteenth Dalai Lama's attempts at reform failed at the beginning of the twentieth century and also the reason why Tibet, isolated and backward, became the victim of the Chinese invasion of 1950.

As portrayed in this short description, Tibetan internal and external political policies during the eighteenth and nineteenth centuries were marked by a pattern of power struggles between various parties:

1. The government and its rival institutions
2. The three main monasteries of Lhasa
3. The military
4. The Chinese envoys

---

[24]Shakabpa, supra, p. 173.

In addition to that, there were differences between Lhasa, in the Ü province, and the Tsang province, headed by the Panchen Lama in Shigatse, as well as differences between the rulers of Kham and Amdo. These groups all formed various alliances with the Chinese government. De facto, the Dalai Lama was often left out of the picture.

Tibet between the Colonial Powers— The Thirteenth Dalai Lama

The search for the thirteenth Dalai Lama, Thubten Gyatso (1876–1933), was clearly an anti-Chinese political undertaking. The Regent and Kashag decided not to use the Chinese method of drawing lots. Instead, the search was conducted according to the Tibetan custom of testing, in which the young boy must identify, or recognise, articles that belonged to the former Dalai Lama. In 1895, the thirteenth Dalai Lama began his spiritual and secular reign.

Already around 1850, Great Britain had annexed Ladakh in the state of Kashmir, and both the Gurkha territories around Almora and Darjeeling were part of the British empire. Tibet, worried about the security of its borders, refused any contact with the British. The first military confrontation between Tibet and the British took place in 1888 at the Lungthur border post. While the four cabinet ministers of the Kashag wanted to reach an accord with the British, the representatives of the main monasteries used the Tsongdu, the national assembly consisting of members of the government and the monasteries, to hinder negotiations. Whoever was part of the Kashag, or was otherwise pro-British, was persecuted. For example, Kalon Shatra, the former representative of Darjeeling, was accused by the monks of collaborating with the British and imprisoned for over a year. It was said that contact with the British posed a threat to Tibetan lifestyle and religion. The strategy of the main monasteries was to hinder any attempt at modernising society.

Great Britain, however, was determined to prevent the Russians from gaining any influence in Tibet, and wanted to open up the land to trade and commerce. With this purpose in mind, the British sent a military contingent from India to central Tibet in1903 under the leadership of Colonel Francis Younghusband. As the troops were approaching Lhasa in 1904, the Dalai Lama fled into exile at Urga in Mongolia where he obviously intended to seek Russian support.[25] The later attempt by the Chinese Emperor to depose the Dalai Lama was unsuccessful. The Treaty of Lhasa between Great Britain and Tibet was signed on 7 September 1904. Tibet was represented by the Head Abbot of Ganden (Ganden Tripa) who had been designated Regent by the thirteenth Dalai Lama before going into exile. Article 9 of this treaty states that the territory of Tibet was out of bounds and that no foreign power had the right to interfere in the internal affairs of the country. The British, however, were granted the right to open centres of trade which would be protected by small military units. Britain was the only foreign state that was allowed to operate a telegraph station. These privileges were to play a later role in Tibet's relationship with India after her independence. The government in Lhasa at that time was too weak to push for immediate national independence. China was not a signatory of this treaty, and in 1910 sent an army to Lhasa, first annihilating eastern Tibet on the way. All appeals from the Dalai Lama for a peaceful resolution were in vain. The Chinese troops marched into Lhasa during the Monlam Festival, murdering and burning everything in their path. The thirteenth Dalai Lama, who had just returned from exile, tried to prevent the Tibetans from shooting back because he still believed the conflict could be resolved through negotiation.[26] Finally he was forced to flee to British territories in Kalimpong and Darjeeling. He hoped that the British would be able to mediate between Tibet and China.

---

[25]Goldstein, M., *A History of Modern Tibet*, Berkeley 1989, p. 45.

[26]Goldstein, supra, p. 55ff. The envoys had spread the proposition that the Dalai Lama should retain his role as religious leader, but give up political sovereignty. China's military attack destroyed any possibilities of negotiations.

However, after the Chinese revolution of 1912 and the abdication of the Manchu dynasty, the troops in Lhasa could not be reinforced, and so the Tibetans were able to defeat and expel the Chinese in 1912. The Chinese forces retreated through India. The Dalai Lama declared Tibetan independence to the Chinese president, Yüan Shih-kai, and returned to Lhasa in January.[27]

With the help of his ally and minister, Tsarong, the thirteenth Dalai Lama developed a plan to modernise the military and the government. Already in 1915, the Dalai Lama had sent the pro-British minister Tsarong to Sir Charles Bell, the British Representative in Sikkim, to inform him of Tibet's intention to head off Chinese forces at the east Tibetan border—that Tibet could no longer pay the troops—and of their intention to purchase military equipment from Great Britain. There was a general fear that the British, deeply involved in the war in Europe, would neglect central Asia, giving China yet another opportunity to occupy Tibet.[28] The British-Indian government refused any further involvement in Tibet.[29] However, even though Tsarong was not given the amount of machine guns the Tibetan government had asked for to defend Tibet against the Chinese, the 5,000 weapons he was given were enough to push the Chinese further east in 1917 and 1918 and thus allowed him to negotiate a truce with China.[30] In the face of constant Chinese threats, Tsarong was in favour of tripling the size of the Tibetan army to 15,000 soldiers. But that plan was not economically feasible without increasing taxes, a move which would mostly affect the main monasteries and the secular landlords. Tsarong, who was general Chief-of-Staff, Kalon, and at the same time a close advisor to the Dalai Lama, and therefore a politically

[27]The translation of this 'Declaration of independence' is available in Goldstein, supra, p. 60f.

[28]Ibid., p. 80f.

[29]The diplomatic note in response to Bell's request is available in Goldstein, supra, p. 80f.

[30]Goldstein, supra, p. 83.

powerful figure, drew the wrath of the conservative abbots upon him with his plans. While increasing the size of the Tibetan army may have strengthened Tibet against China, internally it would have shifted the balance of power between the monasteries, the government and the Dalai Lama in favour of the government and would bring with it a certain amount of secularisation.[31] Tsarong's intention to modernise Tibet by introducing British social values and cultural patterns[32] was also not accepted, but particularly his idea of conscripting thousands of untrained warrior monks (*dobdo*) from the main monasteries of Drepung, Sera and Ganden into the Tibetan army to fight against China met with heavy resistance, because it would mean a significant loss of influence for the Gelugpa monasteries.

During the Monlam Festival in 1921, with 20,000 monks staying at the main monastery of Lhasa, rumours were circulating that a military clash would soon occur between the monks and the army, and that both Tsarong and Sir Charles Bell's personal physician, R.S. Kennedy, would be murdered. The Dalai Lama was able to secure peace in the capital city, but only by threats of drastic punishments.[33] In the following period, the conservative faction gained more and more influence, and in 1925, Tsarong lost his high command of the army, though he remained a member of the Kashag until 1930. There were heavy disputes regarding taxation with the powerful Panchen Lama of Shigatse.The Tashilhunpo monastery was the largest landowner in Tibet, and the government in Lhasa was demanding that Tashilhunpo pay higher tributes and cover a quarter of the entire costs for the army. The Panchen Lama refused to give in to these demands, and fled in December 1923 to Mongolia, and from there on to China, looking for support against Lhasa. The Dalai

[31]Goldstein, supra, p. 91.

[32]Besides a modern army and a division of administrative powers, such influences included western dress, food, sports, the use of the handshake, etc.

[33]Goldstein, supra, p. 95ff.

Lama's government sent out troops to stop his flight, but they were too late. So the Dalai Lama installed his own administrator, Dzasa Lama, to manage the affairs of the Tashilhunpo monastery and to collect the taxes. The two religious leaders of the Gelugpa school engaged in a lengthy correspondence in which it became clear that both of them had the same motive, namely, to preserve their religion and to find the most authentic way to pass down the spiritual traditions of Buddhism and still apply them to everyday life. The question was how to accomplish this goal: by strict adherence to traditional ways, or by a cautious introduction of religious-political reforms.[34] There were basically two points of conflict between the Dalai Lama and the Panchen Lama: (1) to what extent did the government of Lhasa have authority over the Tsang province, and particularly over the Tashilhunpo monastery, and (2) the new policy of modernisation that the Dalai Lama had set in motion.

Besides supporting military reform, the thirteenth Dalai Lama also advocated a complete social and political reform for the nation. He modernised the penal laws, for example, outlawing amputation as a form of punishment, and opened the first English school in 1924 in Gyantse, which had to be closed three years later because of pressure from the monasteries. The monasteries wanted to maintain their monopoly over the education system, but the Dalai Lama was able to win control over the education of the monks which he wanted to oversee himself. A police force was formed in Lhasa which in turn led to rivalries with the army. A telegraph line was set up between Lhasa and Gyantse with the help of the British, and there were also plans to build a hydroelectric power plant. Other plans included the introduction of motor vehicles and the construction of roads, and the participation of Tibet in international diplomacy and the global postal system.[35]

---

[34]Goldstein, supra, p. 110ff.

[35]Goldstein, supra, p. 121.

After the death of the thirteenth Dalai Lama in 1933 the political climate of Tibet became very unstable. Conflicts that had been simmering for a long time now surfaced.[36] Although the Dalai Lama had introduced numerous reforms, he had not really been able to establish them. His success was blocked by powerful monasteries and the conservative attitude of the influential abbots of Drepung, Ganden and Sera. The constant internal power struggles during his years of leadership, such as the rivalry with the Panchen Lama who more or less directly opposed the Dalai Lama in many inner and external conflicts, left a heavy burden on Tibetan politics.

Reforms and Strategies of Cultural Innovation—The Fourteenth Dalai Lama

The fourteenth Dalai Lama, Tenzin Gyatso, was born in 1935. The details of his life are known and need not be repeated here.[37] It should be noted, however, that his reign began at a time when Tibet was beginning to lose its independence under pressure from the Chinese military.

During the colonial times of the nineteenth century Tibet found itself surrounded by British dominance to the south in India, Russian interests in central Asia, and China in the east. Out of consideration for the Chinese and because of rivalries with the Russians, the British tried to keep Tibet a neutral territory and free from foreign, specifically Russian, influences. But at the same time, especially after the collapse of the Manchu empire in 1912, maintaining a balance with the Chinese played an important role in British foreign policy. After gaining

---

[36]Shakabpa, supra, p. 275.

[37]Dalai Lama, *Das Buch der Freiheit, Autobiographie des Friedensnobelpreisträgers,* Bergisch-Gladbach 1990; Levenson, C.B., *Ein Dalai Lama wird geboren.*, Wiedergeburt und Berufung des 14. Dalai Lama, Freiburg i.B. 1998; v. Brück, M., *Denn wir sind Menschen voller Hoffnung,* München 1988, p. 34–41.

independence in 1947, India continued to uphold the British position when it came to their relationship with Tibet.[38]

The Chinese Occupation

In 1949, Mao Zedong's troops gained control of China and in October of 1950, in spite of assurances given to the Indian ambassador to China, K.M. Panikkar, during the last week of August that China would refrain from using force, Radio Beijing announced the 'liberation' of Tibet, after the People's Liberation Army had invaded the Chamdo region in the east of the country.[39] In view of the threat to the nation, on 17 November 1950, full executive powers were granted to the fifteen-year-old Dalai Lama.[40] At the same time Chinese military forces from Khotan invaded the western section of Tibet, after having marched unnoticed through the Indian territory of Aksai Chin. On 26 October 1950, the Indian Government issued a statement of protest against the use of force by the Chinese against Tibet, and in another statement made on 31 October, reiterated the need to respect Tibet's autonomy. China refused intervention in what it said were its internal affairs. On 7 November, the Government of Tibet appealed to the United Nations to denounce China's military aggression. However, the British envoy to the UN refused to become involved in the affair, stating that the situation was too complicated and Tibet's legal status

---

[38]See chapter 3a.

[39]A short description of the latest chapters in the history of Tibet is available in: Forster-Latsch, H. and Renz, P.L., *Tibet: Land, Religion, Politik*, Frankfurt a.M. 1999, esp. p. 100ff.

[40]The situation in eastern Tibet, especially in Kham, was complicated: After 1945 various tribes and their leaders had tried to gain autonomy from the central Tibetan government in Lhasa and thereby had formed pacts with the Chinese. At any rate, the guerilla warfare against the Chinese occupation of Tibet was fought from here. Compare: Forster-Latsch and Renz, supra, p. 125ff. and p. 118ff.

unclear. The Indian delegation supported the British move to postpone the question of Tibet.[41]

The matter did not appear on the United Nations' agenda for another nine years. On 11 December, 1950, the Tibetan government made a last appeal for help by sending a telegram to the United Nations asking them to send a delegation to Tibet to investigate the matter. There was no reply. Not only Tibet's isolation and lack of political experience, but also the diplomatic weakness of the nations involved and the allowances that were made for China based on the Simla Convention of September 1914 (not ratified by China), were factors which played a role in the Tibetan tragedy. Shortly after taking over his executive duties, the fourteenth Dalai Lama had already taken first steps to implement the reforms that his predecessor had planned for the nation, starting with the exemption of many farmers from compulsory labour and a more democratic restructuring of the administration.[42] However, all independent attempts at reform initiated by Tibet were systematically boycotted by the Chinese.

The Dalai Lama initiated negotiations in Beijing that were later reflected in a contract signed on 23 May 1951, called the

---

[41]Compare with detailed, though somewhat divergent description in chapter 3a, and chapter 17.

[42]The Tibetan agrarian constitution was a type of feudal system in which the government, the monasteries, and a handful of estate owners owned the land and leased part of it to labourers. The land was inherited, and comprised the main source of wealth. The labourers paid part of their taxes through their labour, but for the rest, they could do whatever they wanted with the land except sell it. Some labourers were quite well-to-do. The system is described in: Stein, R.A., *Tibetan Civilization*, London 1962; Epstein, I., *Tibet Transformed*, Beijing 1983; Goldstein, supra, p. 3ff. The Tibetan system of punishment had already been liberalised by the thirteenth Dalai Lama. There was a legal system and, at least in principle, the option to appeal to the Dalai Lama, although this practice was made difficult by the bureaucracy involved. Compare: French, R.R., *The Golden Yoke: The Legal Cosmology of Buddhist Tibet*, Ithaca, Cornell University Press 1995.

17 Point Treaty, in which China guaranteed Tibet's right to relative religious and cultural autonomy under the sovereignty of Chinese troops. Tibet was forced to accept its annexation by China under military pressure. On 9 September 1951, Chinese troops occupied the capital city of Lhasa. The occupation forces became increasingly repressive, so that finally the Dalai Lama himself travelled to Beijing to negotiate a more acceptable situation for his country with Mao Zedong. For many years the Dalai Lama was able to keep the incensed people of Tibet from fighting back against the Chinese, but finally on 10 March 1959, revolt broke out, triggered by an attempt by the Chinese military authorities to get the Dalai Lama to go unaccompanied to a military camp outside the city. The people of Tibet viewed this as an attempt to kidnap their leader and crush their last hope for change. Fighting continued for several days, and Chinese artillery fire destroyed some sections of the city. The palace of the Dalai Lama was specifically targeted with the intention of eliminating him. After much hesitation and upon the insistence of his advisors, the Dalai Lama finally fled to the south on 17 March. He appointed a provisional government in Lhasa and at first wanted to set up camp in South Tibet. Chinese air attacks, however, forced him to embark on a long march across the snow-covered passes of the Himalayas to India—a march in which many of his people lost their lives. On 31 March 1959, the Tibetan fugitive finally reached the border and was granted asylum by Prime Minister Jawaharlal Nehru of India. Since that date, the fourteenth Dalai Lama is a leader in exile of a government that is not recognised internationally. Since March 1963, he has been advocating a democratic constitution for exiled Tibetans living in India which is also intended to be used as a model for an independent Tibet.

The land reforms which were actually implemented in Tibet were based on the Chinese model and were put into effect by the Communist Party of China.[43] They led to conditions of

[43]Forster-Latsch and Renz, supra p. 110ff; Norbu, Dawa, *Tibet: The Road Ahead*, Delhi 1997.

hunger and famine. The population of Tibet was forced to undergo unbelievable repression which continues even today.[44] There were many uprisings, of which the five largest achieved worldwide attention.[45] Because of the oppressive circumstances, the monks and nuns took on a more political role and became supporters of the resistance against Chinese occupation.[46] Led by the fourteenth Dalai Lama, exiled Tibetans attempted to open negotiations with China. At the same time, they succeeded in drawing international attention to Tibet's plight by establishing cultural and especially religious ties with the West. Starting in 1979, the Dalai Lama sent numerous delegations to Beijing and to Tibet to investigate the situation and the chances of negotiating with the Chinese.[47] Since 1987, he has made the following demands of China: (1) Creation of a zone of peace in Tibet, (2) Stopping the resettlement policies which are threatening to extinguish Tibet as a nation, (3) Adherence to the basic human rights, including the right to cultural and religious self-determination, (4) Ending the exploitation of Tibet's natural resources and the stockpiling of atomic weapons, (5) Starting

[44]Documentation on the subject: *Tibet—Dream or Trauma?* (Publ. by the Institute for Threatened Peoples and the Society of Tibetans in Germany), Göttingen/Vienna 1987; Kelly, P., Bastian, G. and Aiello, P., *The Anguish of Tibet*, Berkeley 1991.

[45]Forster-Latsch/Renz, supra p. 109ff

[46]The sociologist and Tibetologist R.D. Schwartz supported a similar thesis ('Buddhism, National Protest, and the State in Tibet', in: Kvaerne, P. (ed.), *Tibetan Studies. Proceedings of the 6th Seminar of the International Association for Tibetan Studies*, Oslo 1994, p. 728ff.), that Buddhist monks became political due to colonial oppression (in Burma and Sri Lanka by the British, in Tibet by the Chinese), thereby creating new venues for reforming religious and political structures. This applies to Tibet as well, though the Tibetan monks already had a political role, but it was mostly in the sense of maintaining the status quo of power between the various monasteries to which they belonged, and in the resistance to modernisation.

[47]Dalai Lama, *Buch der Freiheit*, supra, p. 277ff.

negotiations about the future status of Tibet and its relationship to China.[48]

The Strasbourg Declaration of 1988 (see page 426) in which the Dalai Lama offers China the option to take responsibility for Tibet's defence and external affairs in the future is not a sell-out of Tibet's interests as some opponents of this plan claim, but rather a sensible 'realpolitik'. Based on the pressures of the current political situation and his firm belief that Buddhism basically advocates non-violence, the fourteenth Dalai Lama has rejected the notion of leading Tibet on a path to independence within the foreseeable future.[49] Beijing, however, continues to stall the resolution of this situation and follows its policy of repression in Tibet. On the fortieth anniversary of the People's Uprising in Tibet on 10 March 1999, the Dalai Lama once again invited China to initiate negotiations and stressed that the intention was not to attain independence for Tibet, but rather 'to gain true autonomy for the nation, the preservation and promotion of its unique cultural and religious integrity, and the social and economic development of Tibet.'[50]

This would mean a future division between religion and politics for Tibet, whereby the Dalai Lama would not claim any official political post for himself as soon as an acceptable solution has been reached regarding the status of Tibet.[51] After all, from the historical perspective, although the institution of the Dalai

[48]The Dalai Lama presented the Five Point Peace Plan at a speech on Capitol Hill in Washington on 21 September 1987. Compare: Dalai Lama, *Buch der Freiheit*, supra, p. 303f. Indeed, after the Chinese did not show any signs of willingness to negotiate, in 1991 the Dalai Lama once again carefully raised the question of Tibet's independence, but left the problem of negotiation open. Compare: Erffa, W. von, *Uncompromising Tibet*, Delhi 1996, p. 134f.

[49]The fourteenth Dalai Lama was awarded the Nobel Peace Prize in 1989 for the non-violent fight for freedom and his efforts towards inter-religious understanding.

[50]Press release epd Nr. 11, 18 March 1999, p. 20.

[51]Ibid.

Lama has brought a certain unity and a cultural flowering to the land, the tight coupling of religion and politics within the institution has also led to conflicts of interests and to a dilution of the religious ideals.[52]

In the eyes of the fourteenth Dalai Lama, Tibet must aim for a modern democratic political system. Herein, the goal is a far-reaching separation of the religious and political institutions, albeit a standard model for this does not exist at present, either in Asia, in Europe or the United States of America.

Given the realities of his exile, the fourteenth Dalai Lama has learnt about other political and religious traditions, both through study and his own encounters. It was during this period that he came face to face with the principles of democracy, human rights and pluralism of religions as well as the non-violent political ideal which Mahatma Gandhi had preached in India's political fight for independence. He adopted these ideas, interpreted them within Buddhism, and applied them within Tibetan culture and politics. His plan, to transform Tibetan society and the political institutions in exile into a democracy, was slowly implemented, despite opposition from the old monastic institutions and influential families who were often closely linked to the hierarchy of the main monasteries and who also controlled important positions in exile. But his plan was also implemented against the lack of understanding from the population, who venerated the Dalai Lama as Avalokiteshwara, the Bodhisattva of Compassion and whom they trust to make a wiser judgment than that of a changing parliament. The Dalai Lama does not let himself be misled by this. Judging against the background of Tibetan history, with its power conflicts and intrigues, he knows that Tibetan culture can only survive if it is modernised, and by doing this, accepting the ideals of democracy in order to teach people more responsibility, as well as changing the political

[52]That the tight link between religion and politics led to problems regarding spiritual purity in the institution of the Dalai Lama is a well-grounded thesis by M. Hermann, *Mythen und Mysterien der Tibeter*, Stuttgart 1955, p. 372ff.

decision-making process into a more transparent one. After all, transparency and responsibility are age-old Buddhist virtues. That an ancient culture marked by confident traditions can only cautiously accept these deep changes is obvious. The situation of exile is, on the one hand, about offering possibilities: the deadlocked structures have been softened due to the institution's lack of power, which is a positive sign for reform—recall the reform policy of the thirteenth Dalai Lama which was bogged down. On the other hand, modernising society is more complicated by the problems in exile: the cultural identity of exiled Tibetans is dependent on their religious culture, which in turn can only be kept alive through its institutions—the result is a more or less conservative Tibetan nationalism. The Dalai Lama confronts this with perceptiveness and the ability of critical reappraisal. That the creation of a democratic awareness within the population needs time, education and economic possibilities for development cannot be ignored (see chapter 5b). There is after all the Tibetan Youth Congress (TYC), which has opposed the policy of compromise with China since the 1980s, and although this is an uncomfortable opposition in the Dalai Lama's eyes, he encourages them to promote democracy.

The fourteenth Dalai Lama is a reformer, whether in foreign or domestic policies, who has applied the ideal of non-violence to the political strategies of his own government. This of course is in direct contrast with the past history of Tibet, in which violence was legitimately used to achieve political goals. He is also a religious reformer, proven by the way he measures and tests rituals and customs against the standard of the original principles of Gautama Buddha.

The charismatic Dalai Lama astounds people across the globe with his message of non-violence and universal responsibility of all people and religions. He, who is himself a refugee without power but who still carries the aura of a 'God-King', he who dismisses hate towards the oppressors of his people and practises sober realpolitik, he who believes that people can truly come together and mould politics through knowledge, awareness and the bonding of hearts, has become an icon for millions of people from all walks of life and religions. The winner of the Nobel Peace Prize is for many, a vision of hope. Tibetan Buddhism, or what we think is Tibetan Buddhism, has been increasingly discovered by scientists as well as Christians, who were not satisfied with the belief system in which they grew up. Natural scientists are particularly interested in the Buddhist and tantric patterns of interpretation, because they find similarities in modern scientific discoveries within the prevalent categories of space and time, as well as in those of the continuum of consciousness and material processes.[53]

During its history, Tibet has been involved in a lively open exchange with the Mongolian peoples, with China, but especially with India and Nepal from which it drew its state religion— remaining effective over hundreds of years, its alphabet, which has enabled a common administrative structure, and countless cultural customs. The chosen isolation in the nineteenth and early twentieth century to confront the influences of Western culture and the politically precarious interests of colonial powers such as Great Britain and Russia in central Asia is rather untypical for Tibetan history. This isolation has led to the fact that Tibet never received any, what we would consider today, diplomatic recognition as an independent political entity, during the restructuring of the world into nation-states originating in Europe and the United States of America, which took place at that time.

[53]The Dalai Lama himself is very interested in the relationship between Buddhism and Western science and participates in relevant congresses, even organising some himself, for example, the Congress with Francesco Varela and others in Dharamsala 1996. Varela, F. and Bstan-Dzin-Rgy-Mtsho (Dalai Lama), *Sleeping, Dreaming, Dying. An Exploration*, London 1997.

CHAPTER TWO

Tibet's Position in International Law

GERALD SCHMITZ

Historical Attempts at Fixing Tibet's Status

It was in the seventh century that Tibetan nomadic tribes first came together under the leadership of Songtsen Gampo to form a society that extended beyond the individual clans. Hostilities that ensued between Tibet and China are known to have terminated in at least eight treaties in the eighth and ninth centuries. Of these, the Treaty of 821/823 merits particular attention.[1] The contracting parties designated therein are the 'King of Tibet' (Songtsen Gampo) and the 'King of China' (Hwang Te). Through its content and formulation the treaty at several points assures both parties of mutual respect for their borders. Official ties between Tibet and China snapped following the collapse of the Tang dynasty. Richardson refers to a kind of no-man's land between the two since there was no longer any attempt on the part of even China to exercise its control over the border region.[2] However, Tibet too witnessed a collapse of central authority.

It was only with the Mongol invasion led by Genghis Khan that significant changes followed for Tibet's status—changes that have a bearing even on the current discussion. Following the Mongol invasion of Tibet in 1240, the Tibetan lama Sakya Pandita arrived at the court of the Mongol prince Godan Khan and initiated the conversion of the Mongols there to Tibetan

---

[1]See (van) Walt van Praag, Michael C., *The Status of Tibet*, Boulder, Colorado 1987, p. 1, with the complete text in Appendix, p. 205ff.

[2]Richardson, Hugh E., *Tibet and its History*, Boston, London 1984, p. 32f.

Buddhism. He was made Regent of Tibet by the Mongol prince, a conferment that was merely symbolic in nature since Godan Khan was at this point of time not the ruler of all the Mongols, and the lama on his part could not exercise the authority formally conferred upon him due to the internal fragmentation of Tibet. Nevertheless, this was in keeping with the fundamental relationship between the two concerned persons—a relationship marked by religion and symbolism—that von Walt describes as the beginning of the so-called lama-patron or priest-patron relationship.[3] When Kublai Khan bestowed on Lama Phagpa (1235/39–80) the title of Priest-King of all three Tibetan provinces (Ü-Tsang, Kham and Amdo), this procedure was virtually repeated. However, Kublai Khan was also initially not the ruler of all the Mongols. Even after his complete assumption of power, the lama (honoured with the title of 'Tishri' or 'Spiritual Teacher of the Empire') found it difficult, as did his successors, to exercise central and undisputed leadership within Tibet.[4]

The lama-patron relationship represents the Tibetan version of the Sino-Tibetan connection. In the context of this relationship the pre-eminent Tibetan lama, who was at the same time also the temporal ruler, was treated on par with the Mongol leader and latter-day Chinese Emperor. While the lama was responsible for the religious instruction and spiritual well-being of the ruler of China, the latter in return extended military protection to Tibet.[5] As opposed to this, the Chinese side today underlines that the source of the lama's power over Tibet derived from Chinese rulers, linked with the establishment of a tribute system. It speaks of its relationship with Tibet as one between ruler and vassal.[6]

---

[3]For full details see (van) Walt, supra, p. 5f.

[4]Richardson, supra, p. 34.

[5]For more details see Dalai Lama, *Das Buch der Freiheit*, Bergisch Gladbach 1990, p. 17; Charles Bell, *Tibet einst und jetzt*, Leipzig 1925, p. 125.

[6]Tang Chi'an, 'Commentary on the so-called Patron-Lama Relationship in Shakabpa's A Political History of Tibet' in: *Tibet Studies* (Lhasa) 1/1989, p. 64ff.

Coinciding with these events was the establishment of Mongol rule over China, which was to extend from 1271 to 1367 under the Yuan Dynasty. It is indeed surprising that although the southern part of China had not yet been conquered when the dynasty was established, the supreme responsibility for all spiritual needs had nevertheless been vested in the Tibetan lama years before. The lamaist religion came to enjoy precedence over all other religions in the Empire, at the latest by 1260 when Kublai Khan ascended the throne.[7] Thus what we have here is a parallel process that was in no way linked to the conquest of Chinese territory. Nonetheless, a relationship that was originally Tibeto-Mongolian got carried over to subsequent relations between Tibet and China following the collapse of the Yuan Dynasty. Although the Tibetan side underscored the personal nature of the relationship between the Dalai Lama and the ruling Chinese emperor in each case, at the same time it also assumed willingness, at least tacit, on the part of successive emperors to continue with this relationship.

Thus, with the exception of the Ming period, there was basic agreement between the Chinese and the Tibetans that this formal relationship would be the basis of future Sino-Tibetan relations right into the twentieth century. Indeed in the period that followed, particularly in the eighteenth century, there were innumerable shifts in power involving at times a complete loss of Chinese influence over Tibet. Yet the formal basis of the relationship itself never changed. What did however pose a problem was the erasing of the sharp distinction between the two Empires—a development that began in the thirteenth century—and the imparting of an aura of mystique to a relationship that rested on individuals on

[7]For the overall picture see Gernet, Jacques, *Die chinesische Welt*, Baden-Baden 1985, p. 312,327; Franke Herbert and Trauzettel, Rolf, *Das chinesische Kaiserreich* (Fischer Weltgeschichte), Frankfurt/M 1984, p. 227ff, 232.

the one hand, while at the same time representing the relationship between two people.[8]

It is precisely this lack of distinctive clarity that allowed for a flexible interpretation of the relationship on both sides, depending on prevailing power constellations. It is also the reason for the diametrically opposed stands taken on this issue today.

This conflicting interpretation cannot be completely resolved by historians either, since both Chinese and Tibetan historical accounts of the day were only partly committed to objectivity.[9] Further, the intent expressed by both sides through this relationship was not founded on the present-day understanding of sovereignty and interstate relations, influenced for most part by the West. It is therefore widely believed that present-day categories of international law cannot be applied to traditional Sino-Tibetan relationship.[10]

Likewise, determining the status on the basis of prevailing power relations appears pointless. This subject has already been dealt with in the previous chapter so no further elaboration is necessary here. It need only be pointed out that pre-modern Sino-Tibetan power relations underwent such dramatic and frequent changes, that any attempt at determining the status would only be a fleeting assessment, which would in part hardly hold out for the next two decades.

---

[8]In 1653 (during the time of the Ching Dynasty) this formal relationship was at any rate said to have been renewed before the then Emperor during the visit of the fifth Dalai Lama in Peking Cf. (van) Walt supra, p. 12 on the one hand and Shen Tsung-lien and Lui Shen-chi, *Tibet and the Tibetans*, New York 1993, p. 44 on the other.

[9]Cf on this (van) Walt, supra, p. 11,13, in general: Gernet, J., supra, pp. 293, 423.

[10]See for instance Weggel, Oskar, Zum 40. 'Jahrestag der Befreiung' Tibets: Wie China seine Souveränitätsansprüche über die "Autonome Region" zu rechtfertitigen versucht' in: *China aktuell*, Juni 1991, pp. 361-73; see also *China aktuell*, December, 1991, p. 774; see also Strupp, Michael, *Chinas Grenzen mit Birma und mit der Sowjetunion*, Dissertation Hamburg 1987, pp. 59, 65 for Sino-Burmese relations.

Thus, it is only in the nineteenth century—characterised by the influence of the British colonial power in India and the erosion of Chinese influence over Tibet—that new indicators of a formal nature emerge for determining the status of Tibet. Henceforth, agreements were increasingly entered into to ensure the preservation and expansion of possessions. Listed below is relevant literature providing specific details on the substance of such agreements.[11]

Numerous agreements on Tibet were concluded particularly between China and Great Britain. These included the Chefoo Convention of 1876 which was to permit Britain to send in research missions; the Convention of 1886 relating to Burma and Tibet which regulated trade with Tibet; the Convention of 1890 relating to Sikkim and Tibet that fixed the boundary between the British Protectorate of Sikkim and Tibet; the Agreement of 1906 in which China assumed protective duties towards Tibet vis-a-vis Great Britain; the Trade Agreement of 1908 during the negotiation of which a Tibetan delegate even participated as a member of the Chinese delegation. Further, an Anglo-Russian Agreement on Persia, Afghanistan and Tibet was concluded in 1907 in which the parties agreed that contacts with Tibet would be sought exclusively via China. Alongside these treaties, Great Britain also entered into direct agreements with Tibet without China's involvement. An example of this was the Lhasa Convention of 1904 (cf. Chapter 1, p. 32) which became necessary after the Chinese failed to push through their commitments to Britain with regard to Tibet as per the Agreement of 1886.

These sometimes contradictory agreements primarily served to protect Great Britain's colonial interests in India. Keeping in mind the International Court of Justice's pronouncements on treaties establishing spheres of influence, the above-mentioned

---

[11]For relevant texts see for instance (van) Walt, supra appendix; Richardson, *Tibet and its History*, supra appendix; International Commission of Jurists, *The Question of Tibet and the Rule of Law*, Geneva 1959, Part V(Documents).

Tibet under Communist China since 1949

The year and type of territorial sub-division

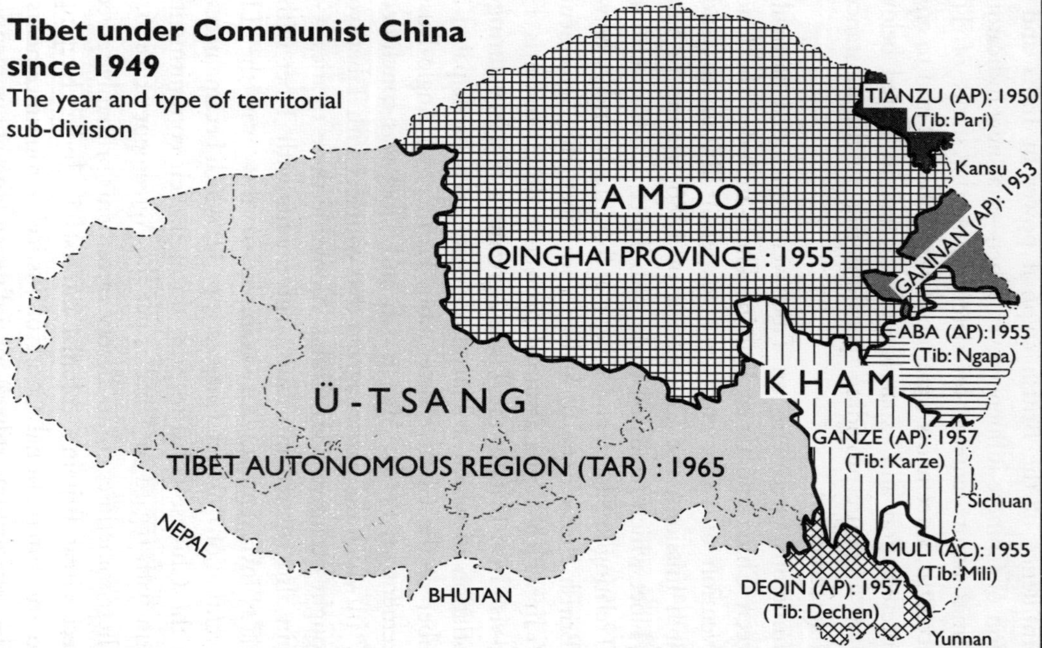

Source: AMI 1998, IO, CTA 1971

Digital Cartography & Design: Planning Council, CTA, Dharamsala 1999.

agreements do not carry any essential significance for appraising Tibet's legal status. Rather, the ICJ has stated in its West Sahara Report that these agreements do not assume the character of status agreements.[12] This is also the case where the territorial sovereignty of one of the parties is explicitly recognised, to the extent that prevailing conditions contradict this recognition.[13] Even treaties concluded independently by Tibet prior to 1912 do not provide an adequate pointer to its status. Thus the International Commission of Jurists points out that Tibet's treaty-making authority could just as well have been its own or derived from China.[14]

Similarly, the term 'suzerainty' used for the most part by Great Britain in the nineteenth century to denote China's control over Tibet is of little help since the term does not exist in international law and is consequently itself open to interpretation.

The advent of British troops in Tibet with the Younghusband Expedition of 1904 may be considered the turning point in Tibet's autonomy status, in terms of actual power held (cf. Chapter 1, p. 32). The withdrawal of the troops saw Tibet militarily overcome and politically weakened. Furthermore, in the years that followed until 1911, China's military victories meant that it also actually exerted greater control. The majority of the authors are of the opinion that Tibet's status resembled that of a Chinese protectorate.[15]

---

[12]Cf. ICJ Reports 1975, 55f.

[13]Cf. the ICJ's judgement on the Anglo-Moroccan Treaty of 1895 on the West Sahara, supra, p. 53f.

[14]International Commission of Jurists 1959 supra, p. 76. For details on original authority see Pochhammer, Wilhelm von, *Die Auseinandersetzung um Tibets Grenzen*, Frankfurt/M, Berlin 1962, p. 20: Tibet's own statehood under Chinese overlordship.

[15]As set down in the International Commission of Jurists' 1959 Report on Tibet, supra, p. 83; Petech, Luciano, *China and Tibet in the early XVIIIth century*, Leiden 1972, pp. 226, 234, 260; Richardson, supra p. 50, but as a qualified statement on p. 76; Tieh-tseng Li speaks of the status of a buffer state, p. 124.

Power equations underwent a further change with the overthrow of the Manchu Dynasty and the abolition of monarchy in China in 1911. The newly-formed republic was not in a position to maintain a military presence in Tibet. Chinese troops were gradually pushed back upto the frontline firmed up more or less at the Eastern boundary of the present day Tibet Autonomous Region in 1918. As early as in 1912, the Dalai Lama had declared Tibet's independence in a telegram to the Chinese President Yüan Shih-kai.[16]

Perhaps the most serious and consolidated attempt at formally fixing Tibet's status occurred at the Simla Conference of 1914. The outcome was the so-called Simla Convention drawn up as a tripartite agreement between Great Britain, Tibet and China. The agreement provided for the division of Tibet into Inner and Outer Tibet. In simplified terms what is—from China's perspective—Outer Tibet extends across what goes by the name of the Autonomous Region today, while Inner Tibet extending beyond encompasses large sections of the present-day provinces of Qinghai (the Tibetan Province of Amdo) and Sichuan (Eastern-Kham). The agreement even went so far as to accept China's 'suzerainty' over the regions of Central and Eastern Tibet (referred to as Outer Tibet in the agreement), though explicitly withholding the right to interfere in the administration. Tibet was even referred to as a part of China in an appendix. However, since the Chinese Parliament did not ratify this treaty, none of these rights can be claimed and asserted as stated in the Anglo-Tibetan Simla Declaration.[17]

---

[16]For the text see (van) Walt, supra, p. 50.

[17]Cf. text in (van) Walt, supra, p. 322 ff. The same conclusion was reached by the International Commission of Jurists in the Tibet Report of 1960, p. 140f; Richardson, supra, p. 114; Rama Rao, T.S., 'The Legal Position of Tibet' in: *IndYBia* 1980 Part II, p. 205–263 (*Studies of the History of the Law of Nations*), p. 230. Since China is expressly denied the right to interfere in the administration of Outer Tibet, Tibet's status as a part of China—which moreover only finds mention in the Appendix as a result of an exchange of notes—must be viewed with reservation.

Tibet's Status before and after the Chinese Invasion of 1950

Taking the last major changes wrought in Sino-Tibetan relations (Tibet's declaration of independence in 1912 and Tibet's annexation in 1951/59) as a point of departure, the construction of a legal base today involves drawing upon these events and examining them together with their implications.

It is not just the Chinese side that challenges the historical existence of an independent Tibetan state. Forming the subject of discussion here alongside the three classical attributes of a state (national territory, state authority, a national group) are formal aspects such as the existence of an official declaration of independence. In effect there are no serious doubts on this account at least for the period after 1913.[18] During this period, Tibet's status is not infrequently described as being one of de facto independence.[19] One inevitably finds that Tibet's isolation from the outside world during this period and the Tibetan state not asserting its will for recognition in foreign policy is interpreted and appraised negatively by many authors, even in the West. Yet there is no justification for this argument, because an active foreign policy is no requirement for independent statehood.[20]

---

[18]For detailed information on the individual attributes of a state and other problems see Schmitz, Gerald, *Tibet und das Selbstbestimmungsrecht der Völker*. Berlin, New York 1998, pp. 123-39.

[19]*Tibet Report of the International Commission of Jurists* 1960, p. 162, but different from its opinion in the 1959 Report, p. 212, where Tibet is regarded as merely being representative of the problem of dealing with autonomous areas.

[20]Cf. for instance Verdross, Alfred & Simma, Bruno, *Universelles Völkerrecht* (*Theorie und Praxis*), Berlin 1984, p. 602, Art. 961; Brownlie, Ian, *Principles of Public International Law*, Oxford 1990, p. 89 f; Vitzthum Graf, Wolfgang (Hrsg), Völkerrecht, Berlin, New York 1997, p. 227, note 148. According to a minority opinion, regimes that are not recognised should be accorded the status of so-called de facto regimes for which the proscription of annexation would equally apply as in the case of states.

The Chinese military intervention in 1950 marks a turning point in Tibet's actual position of independence. This event was followed by the so-called 17-Point Agreement concluded between the Tibetan and Chinese delegates in 1951 for 'the peaceful liberation of Tibet'. The agreement essentially regulates Tibet's re-incorporation into the association of nationalities under the Chinese state. There are several good reasons to presume that the conclusion of this agreement did not affect Tibet's status.[21] Among them were the controversial powers of the Tibetan delegates at the negotiations, China's threat to use force at the conclusion of the agreement and the Dalai Lama's repudiation of the treaty in 1959. However, it is a completely different question as to whether the continuous occupation of Tibet since 1950 and its virtual incorporation into the People's Republic of China proved to be an impediment to the existence of an independent Tibetan state.[22] Whether and under what circumstances a state can get wiped out by annexation— which itself always constitutes a breach of international law—is a point of heated debate in doctrinal thinking. It could no doubt be argued that annexation as such does not lead to the extinction of the concerned state.[23] However, the overwhelming majority realise the need for facts, once created (even those created in contravention of the law) to be accepted by international law at

[21]Cf. on this the *Tibet Report of the International Commission of Jurists* of 1959, pp. 97, 99 and 1960, p. 164f; (van) Walt, supra, p. 155. The most weighty argument may be that the agreement was null and void *ab initio* due to the threat of force against the Tibetan delegates and particularly against the Tibetan state.

[22]This has been refuted by (van) Walt, supra, p. 180f.

[23]The prohibition of the use of force between states is deemed an unwritten law. As a result, territory acquired through illegitimate force is not recognised. In this regard the following resolutions may be underlined as being of particular significanc: Security Council Resolution 242, dated 22.11.1967, Preamble, para 2; General Assembly Resolution 2628 (XXV) dated 4.11.1970 Clause I; General Assembly Resolution 3314 (XXIX) dated 14.12.1974: definition of aggression, Article 5, para 3.

some point of time, rather than their existence merely being rejected or denied. As per this opinion an annexed state will in any event cease to exist when it may no longer be expected to mobilise its strength and re-emerge. The question as to when this is the case can only be cogently answered by considering individual doctrinal questions and examining case studies. This would however be beyond the scope of this contribution.[24] What is of crucial importance is not the one-time act of incorporation but the development subsequent to it, so much so that one may speak of the gradual waning of the annexed state.

In this respect, Tibet, whose incorporation into the People's Republic proceeded in various phases after 1950 represents a particular challenge.

Thus, the old Tibetan system of government continued to exist after the Chinese intervention of 1950 until the flight of the Dalai Lama in 1959. It was only between 1959 and 1965 that a far-reaching policy of assimilation was implemented in the economic and administrative spheres (land reforms, establishment of People's Communes, creation of the Tibet Autonomous Region, etc.). Unrest and uprisings accompanied this policy and continued right up to 1970. A study for consolidating Tibet's annexation cannot ignore the need for securing a certain measure of demonstrably long-lasting peace in the region backed by prospects of stability, alongside economic/administrative integration. However, peace can also be secured through military means since the mere stability of the newly-created situation assumes pre-eminence in this perception. There can be no serious doubts about the Chinese government's exercise of full administrative and economic control in Tibet at least since the 1970s and their reorganisation of the structures

[24]Depending on which attribute carries emphasis (as for instance structural consolidation, secure possessions or the passage of time), the discussion is conducted under different headlines such as consolidation, effectiveness, acquisitive prescription or the statute of limitations. For details on this see the compilation provided by Schmitz, supra, p. 148f.

in these areas to correspond to those of the People's Republic of China.

International law has many of its rules founded in state practice, so the conduct of third parties has considerable influence on the facts of the case under evaluation. Thus, the question of the continued existence of a Tibetan state will naturally also necessitate a look at the practice prevalent elsewhere. However, unlike in the case of the Baltic states, there was no reaction from a third party among the international community that provided any support to Tibet's cause for sovereignty.[25]

Although, there were some condemnations of Tibet's assimilation by China by representatives of states in the UN General Assembly, no resolution was passed by the UN on this occasion and there were no explicit declarations of protest by governments against China. Resolutions on Tibet were passed by the UN General Assembly only in 1959, 1961 and 1965.[26] Tibet's right to self-determination was referred to just once therein, the traditional autonomy enjoyed by Tibet was likewise recalled but once; that apart, China's violation of Tibet's sovereignty went completely uncensored. In fact, the USSR, India, Nepal, Australia and Germany explicitly recognised Chinese sovereignty over Tibet. Isolated instances of resolutions passed by national parliaments on Tibet do nothing to alter this generally negative picture, for it is governments who give concrete shape to foreign policy, not parliaments.

An overall assessment of the situation points to the following conclusion: Tibet as a state has become extinct since it has been totally assimilated both administratively and economically into the Chinese state. This assimilation is so entrenched that a re-emergence of the Tibetan state does not

---

[25]See reference to further literature Schmitz, supra, p. 26f, 153ff.

[26]Resolution 1353 (XIV) dated 21.10.1959; 1723 (XVI), dated 20.12.1961 and 2079 (XX), dated 18.12.1965.

seem possible.[27] Such a prognosis may however be overtaken by history at a later date, as the example of the Baltic states goes to prove. These states finally succeeded in regaining their independence from the Soviet Union. The doctrine of international law admits the possibility that a state that has disappeared because of an entrenched annexation in violation of international law is permitted a retroactive restoration of its sovereign status.[28] In other words, the state can re-establish itself as the legal entity it previously was.

The Right of a People to Self-Determination and the Tibet Question

The foregoing conclusion on the status of Tibet is not easily conveyable to an interested public since they could infer that one had abdicated the legal position. Even the Tibetans' right to self-determination (and consequently to independence) appears to be duly lost. As opposed to the question of the existence and claim to sovereignty of an annexed state, what is at issue in this legal instance is the right of the people and not of the state. This shows that the above conclusion is premature. The right to self-determination is in its essence a right of choice and in its

[27]The very same conclusion is reached by Partsch in McCorquodale, Robert and Orosz, Nicholas (eds.), *Tibet: The Position in International Law, Report of the Conference of International Lawyers on Issues Relating to Self-Determination and Independence for Tibet,* Stuttgart, London 1994, p. 110. Partsch however questions the former independent statehood of Tibet. See also Berman in McCorquodale and Orosz supra p. 93 (arg. ex. p. 90) who takes into account the extinction of a state through a forced treaty of annexation. For a different opinion see (van) Walt, supra, p. 180ff and pp. 185, 181, 183.

[28]See Dahm, Georg and Delbrück, Jost in: Wolfrum, Rüdiger, *Völkerrecht* Vol. I/1, Berlin, New York 1989, p. 144; Fastenrath in: EPIL(10), p. 466; Vitzthum, supra, p. 226, note. 143. Brownlie (p. 84) points out that the practice with occupied countries during and after the Second World War involved a restoration.

objective content aimed at determining the external status of a people.[29] It can be realised through:[30]

- the establishment of a sovereign, independent state
- a voluntary union or merger with a state
- the choice of any other status.

Self-determination cannot therefore be equated with independence as conceived for the state. It could also mean heading in the opposite direction to merge with another state. Since there are no set specifications regarding the extent to which a country can give up its independence both internally and externally, many intermediate forms are possible. It may be pointed out in this respect that the term 'autonomy' is only an oblique reference to forms that differ widely from each other in their specifics. Further, as per a partial understanding, the term does not contain the foreign policy and territorial component intrinsic to the right to self-determination, that is to say, the country's own representation in international organisations and its own territorial rights.[31] In terms of practical implementation, the holding of a plebiscite among the population is a logical, though not the only possible mode of procedure. At times a plebiscite is not always possible. At any rate, in keeping with the Western conception of politics, a decision by democratically legitimated representatives must also be deemed adequate. Whether the choice of a status through representatives is permissible in the case of Tibet whose government and parliament-in-exile at Dharamsala may at best be regarded as morally legitimate, but

[29]Besides this generally recognized, so-called external right to self-determination, other forms are also discussed under the categories of internal and federal right to self-determination. The former can be briefly described as the 'right to democratic participation'. The latter comes fairly close to the right to autonomy, though it is still in the process of being developed.

[30]As set forth in UN Resolution 2625 (XXV), dated 24.10.1970.

[31]Cf. Ermacora in: ArchVR 38/200, 295ff.

not representative of the people in Tibet, is yet another question which cannot be conclusively addressed here.

Often, the approach used in discussions on Tibet to determine the legitimate entity behind the right to self-determination entails identifying a collective body of persons with common ethnic and cultural bonds termed 'a people'. The principal UN documents that dwell on the right to self-determination do not define the term 'a people'. It may however be assumed that this constitutes a so-called technical term, the contents of which cannot be determined simply by drawing on general linguistic usage. Otherwise, there would, for instance, be no distinction in minorities bestowed with other rights in international law.

There has been no dearth of attempts to compile a list of criteria—albeit by no means exhaustive—to identify 'a people' as entitled to the right to self-determination.[32] Among these criteria are common ethnic, cultural, linguistic, religious and historical elements. Numerous other attributes—some highly controversial—have been presented by various authors and at expert meetings. Among these are a distinct historical area of settlement and a special status in the constitution for the concerned segment of the population.[33] If, on the one hand, the determining criteria are controversial per se, what, on the other hand, applies to all the concerned lists is that the criteria should

[32]As undertaken by the International Commission of Jurists in: ICJ Review 8/1972,47; Cristescu, Aureliu, *The Right to Self-determination, Historical and Current Development on the Basis of United Nations Instruments*, New York 1981, p. 42, § 279; Murswiek in: Der Staat 23/1984, 538f; Doehring (Das Sbr) p. 23. A list of relevant attributes was likewise the outcome of a meeting of experts from the UNESCO on the right to self-determination held in February 1990 in Paris. On the problem viewed from a political science perspective, see also Jones Peter, in: HRQ 21/21, 1999, p. 97 ff (corporate right or collective right).

[33]See Crawford, James, *The Creation of States in International Law*, Oxford 1979, p. 100f (distinct settlement area) and Cassese, Antonio in Henkin pp. 95, 109 (special constitutional status).

be met, if not entirely, then at least in adequate measure. This is yet another reason for conflict which may be regarded either as a factor of flexibility or arbitrariness, depending on the position assumed. To date, none of these attempts has resulted in a definition of the term 'people' that is generally accepted in practice and, consequently, by the community of states and the UN in particular.

Any discussion on Tibet inevitably draws an analogy to the decolonisation practice of the UN. It is moreover emphasised that Tibet is treated like a colony by the Chinese, for Tibet's natural resources are exploited and Tibetans discriminated against. The background to this line of argument is that the right of a 'peoples' to self-determination was initially developed as the right of colonised peoples following the Second World War, forming a base to launch these colonies into independence. The Tibetans, it is argued, represent an analogous case, so much so that the right to self-determination becomes valid in Tibet's case too.[34] However, the right to self-determination applied to colonial peoples was a UN practice historically confined to the traditional colonies. That apart, the right to self-determination also evolved into a right for all peoples under alien rule, thereby going beyond the colonial context. This development did not however take place through an expanded application to include analogous cases; rather it is an independent variant.[35] Accordingly, the right to self-determination is granted to all peoples under both colonial and alien domination. What is crucial is to define the criterion of a 'people under alien domination'.

In the absence of a binding or generally accepted definition of the term 'people' the state practice and the cases of application known to carry a consensus in the UN shall serve as a basis of orientation. Thus groups of *case categories* are formed which point to the conferring of the right of self-determination as

[34]As argued for instance by (van) Walt, supra, p. 51.

[35]See also Thürer in: ArchVR 22/2, 1984, p. 120f. On the deliberate distinction in the UN's resolution practice see also Tomuschat in FS Partsch, p. 202f.

virtually constituting the facts of the case. Such groups are not that small in number, though they are of hardly any use for many present-day political conflicts, e.g. the right of self-determination for divided peoples. However, in Tibet's case the following areas of application of the right to self-determination prove of interest:

- As a *claim for restitution* of a sovereign people whose state was wiped out by annexation,
- As a *right to self-defence* of a minority whose existence is threatened by the state.

Alongside the decolonisation process, the *right to self-defence* of the peoples of occupied states constitutes the classic area of application of the right to self-determination.[36] This area, also referred to as the defensive right to self-determination in literature, is not applicable to the Tibetans. As a state Tibet has as said earlier, passed into extinction. However, as an entity possessing the right to self-determination, a people can continue to exist even after the extinction of their state.[37] Arguably, the existence of a collective body of people is subject to laws that differ from those for a political corporation as represented by the entity of a state. To the extent that a distinction is made between

[36]This emerges from numerous passages of a general nature in UN resolutions such as the annual UN resolution on the 'universal realisation of the rights of people to self- determination' as also from case-specific resolutions such as on the Soviet intervention in Hungary in 1956 and in Afghanistan in the 1980s as well as on the Vietnamese intervention in Cambodia.

[37]This may be explained by the fact that the UN's proscription of interventions, while invoking the right to self-determination, was to an extent maintained for years, and the defensive right to self-determination is, dogmatically speaking, not subject to any specific time limit. In the contrary situation, this right would be practically devoid of substance since it corresponds at the beginning with the annexed state's claim to the restoration of its sovereignty, assuming significance in its function as the right of the people when the annexed state can no longer secure its right to sovereignty on its own (Tomuschat also draws attention to this point in FS Partsch, p. 208).

short and long-term annexations, this argument is endorsed in literature relating to international law.[38] In this case the right to self- determination is invoked not merely to ward off foreign aggression but to restore former statehood, which explains the distinction made as a *right to restitution.*[39] Restoration of statehood, as explained above, only represents the maximum claim. A previously sovereign people could adopt the view that a certain status within the state structure is more advantageous, and exercise their choice accordingly.

From the Tibetan point of view, in the event that the right to restitution being granted, the problem may primarily be linked to its geographical implications. Since the right to self-defence and the right to restitution are both linked to the (former) existence of a sovereign state and people, it follows that the geographical application is confined to the population of the former state's territory. The latter could however be smaller than the area settled by this ethnic people which in the case of the Tibetans extends beyond the three Tibetan regions of Ü-Tsang, Kham and Amdo into Nepal and India. However, the Tibetan state of 1912 was actually known to wield authority in one region only, which more or less corresponds to the Tibet Autonomous Region of today.[40] In this case, Tibet's cause can be served by sanctioning a generous measure of mobility to the

---

[38]On the applicability of the right of self-determination in the case of formerly sovereign people see also explicit arguments presented by Murswiek in: Der Staat 23/1984, 538, fn. 42; Gusy in: Arch VR 30/4, 1992, 402f. For similar arguments see also Cristescu, supra, p. 29 § 203 combined with p. 40 § 276, the right of self-determination in Cristescu's perception being threatened only by a linkage developing between two peoples at a later point.

[39]As expounded by Murswiek, in: Der Staat 23/1984, p. 544.

[40]Tibet's independence in 1912/13 proceeded parallel to the withdrawal of Chinese troops and resulted in various ceasefire agreements between Tibet and the Chinese national government as well as the Governors of Sichuan and Qinghai. For details on this see Hoppe in: Mitteilungen des Instituts für Asienkunde, No. 281, 1997, p. 18, 39; Schmitz supra, p. 130ff.

population which would permit Tibetans to settle in the territory entitled to self-determination. At this juncture it must be recognised that the expansion of Tibet constitutes one of the major controversies of the Tibetan issue. The—understandably emotional—call for a union of the three traditional Tibetan regions is however confined by the limits set to the right to self-determination[41] in this form by the doctrine of international law.

The *right to restitution* with a view to restoring a state should be distinguished from the (emergency) right of minorities within a state—a right likewise based on the right to self-determination—to break away from the state to which these minorities and their territory *de jure* belong under threat of survival and virtually as a last resort. At issue here is the right to secede which has not yet been conclusively evolved as a dogma in its many details. The rationale for this right particularly derives from the argument that a group's affiliation to a sovereign people is questionable when the state no longer fulfils the protective duties that fall to it, such as upholding human rights. It also derives from a passage in the UN Declaration 2625.[42]

The relevant passage is cited below:

> Nothing in the foregoing paragraphs shall be construed as authorising or encouraging any action which would dismember or impair, totally or in part, the territorial integrity or political unity of sovereign and independent states

[41]Cf. Tomuschat in *Modern Law of Self-Determination*, p. 9; Murswiek in Tomuschat, supra, p. 26; Kimminich in: Tomuschat, supra, p. 91; Thürer in: Arch VR 22/2, 1984, p. 127; Hanneman in: VJIL 35/2, 1995, 504f (with a reference to Buchanan: *Secession, The Morality of Political Divorce from Sumter to Lithuania and Quebec*, 1991); Crawford, supra, p. 100, 117 (who however at the same time presumes a geographical separation from the rest of the state, p. 101, 116). For the contrary opinion see Gusy in: Arch VR 30/4, 1992, p. 407.

[42]Cf. Tomuschat in FS Partsch, p. 211; Verdross and Simma, supra, p. 318 Art 512; Murswiek in: Der Staat 23/1984, p. 541.

> conducting themselves in compliance with the principle of equal rights and self-determination of peoples as described above and thus possessed of a government representing the whole people belonging to the territory without distinction as to race, creed or colour.

Hence, as per the prevailing opinion, a state's claim to preserve its territorial unity is subject to the proviso of compliance with the ban on discrimination, which in extended terms applies to all groups of the population, with the view to ensuring their protection and survival. Incidentally, the International Commission of Jurists also deliberated on the right to self-determination in its *Tibet Report* of December 1997, speaking out for the cause of the Tibetans therein.[43]

The right of self-determination as the *right of self-defence* backed by the permission to secede, is virtually directed against one's own (unpopular) state from within. With that, the latter's territory and population diminish against its will. Thus this right stands opposed to the historical role of international law which initially created rules for states to interact with each other for the express purpose of ensuring their existence. Accordingly, the conditions under which a minority can invoke the right of self-defence must be placed in an extremely narrow framework. Much of the detail here is still a matter of contentious debate. Generally, however, the state must be blamed for a policy towards the affected segment of the population which threatens the existence of the group per se and for which policy it is accountable. This does not merely have to do with the physical existence of the group but also, for instance, with the preservation of those cultural and religious characteristics that make up the distinctive character of the group. Secession is only permissible as a last resort against certain measures adopted by the state (such as genocide, persecution, etc.) which must

[43]See the 1997 *Tibet Report of the International Commission of Jurists*, p. 337f.

incidentally be especially strongly proscribed by international law.[44] Simply reviewing the measures which could be resorted to this case is in itself a very sensitive matter. At any rate, the process of assimilation with the majority population on the part of the minorities would not constitute a sufficient basis for claiming the right to self-defence.[45]

A close look at the situation in which the Tibetans find themselves inevitably reveals that much that is criticised as being deplorable is related to a problem involving the state system within the People's Republic under which other minorities suffer just as much, as to an extent the Han Chinese themselves. This finding is the result of a comparison of reports of human rights organisations on Tibet with the overall situation in the People's Republic.[46] Here, there are three areas that pose problems: the influx of Han Chinese into Tibet (the so-called Sinification), birth control (or in more palatable terms: family planning) and the violation of the freedom of religion.[47] With regard to the so-called Sinification of Tibet, there is often too little consideration of the way in which the interest of Tibetans, outside the annexed territory, to preserve their distinctiveness in the ethnically Tibetan regions, collides with the right to freedom of movement of the rest of the population. In the area of family

---

[44]In part, this doctrine is confined to 'self-evident cases'. See Doehring (Das Sbr), p. 32. So also Thürer in: Arch VR 22/2, 1984, 127 fn 33. Addressed under the aspect of 'ultima ratio' by Suzuki in: VJIL 16/4, 1975–1976, p. 798; Tomuschat in: *Modern Law of Self-Determination*, p. 10: 'step of last resort'.

[45]At any rate international law does not at present provide any protection for the continued existence of national minorities; Hofmann in ZaöRV 52/1, 1992, p. 9; Verdross and Simma, supra, p. 838, § 1253. However, the International Commission of Jurists is obviously of a different view: *Tibet Report* of 1997, p. 120.

[46]Examples to prove this point are: excessive measures resorted to by the police, arbitrary detentions (the so-called administrative arrests) and curtailment of general civil rights and liberties.

[47]Instead of a detailed presentation see in this regard Schmitz, supra, pp. 248–321.

planning it must necessarily be proved, particularly since family planning is practised all over China, that the Tibetans are far greater victims of this policy, which may perhaps even result in a stagnation or decline in population. However, there is a dearth of reliable statistics here.[48] To my mind, religious suppression in Tibet is at present a particularly valid reason to justify the claim to a position of self-defence. To be sure, freedom of religion is violated even in other parts of China, with other faiths, yet it may be said that for no other ethnic group is religion as an actively pursued creed and group identity so inseparably linked as with the Tibetans, who define themselves more through Tibetan Buddhism than through ethnic characteristics.[49]

A further complex issue concerns the territorial boundaries that would apply while exercising the right to secede, particularly since in this case—unlike with the claim to restitution—the former state boundaries do not automatically come into play. Thus, the territory with which a people secede while exercising their right to self-defence can be larger or smaller than the former national territory. In this regard, the Dalai Lama and the International Commission of Jurists have favoured a plebiscite for the Tibetans.[50] However, this has raised both legal and other practical problems, particularly since, even prior to 1950, the Tibetans did not constitute the majority everywhere, particularly in the periphery of the ethnic or even so-called historical Tibet. Even in this case, it is necessary to examine the situation from

[48]Cf. on this Hoppe, supra, p. 49ff., 83 ff. who speaks of a controlled slowdown of growth.

[49]According to Hool, Catherine, *Die chinesische Tibetpolitik*, Bern et.al. 1989,p. 88, the suppression of religion in Tibet would be tantamount to suppressing the Tibetan national identity. The Austrian delegation of legal experts which visited Tibet in 1992 had the following to say on the importance of religion in its report: 'It is the country, the culture, the art, it is the way of life of the people in town and countryside', p. 5, no. 11; on p. 26, no. 9, the Tibetan religion is described as the factor that carries the idea of nationality.

[50]The 1997 Tibet Report of the International Commission of Jurists, p. 344f, as also the interview with the Dalai Lama in chapter 6.

a different perspective, taking into consideration both the rights of the other minorities (particularly the Mongols and the Hui) as well as the various instruments of international law, and weighing these carefully.[51] Besides it has been pointed out that even outside the Tibet Autonomous Region there are administrative units for traditional Tibetans settlements in the adjacent provinces which can be taken up. This can be combined with the plebiscite.

At this juncture it is necessary to clarify that the argument endorsing the Tibetans' *right to self-defence* does not entail abandoning the basic position of the existence of a former Tibetan state on the basis of which *the right to restitution* is pursued. Rather, this case category of application of the right to self-determination offers itself as an independent option alongside that related to the state. The right to self-defence is subject to other preconditions and has other territorial and people-related dimensions. The two case categories are therefore not mutually exclusive but may be invoked alternately. This means that Tibetans are entitled to the right to self-determination both as a formerly sovereign people and as a minority. However, the right to self-defence is of consequence here only to the extent that many Tibetans live outside the territory of the former state of Tibet.

Outlook for the Future

In his 5-Point Plan of 1987 and the subsequent Strasbourg Declaration the Dalai Lama proposed that Tibet be associated with China and that competencies for internal and external matters be divided. Until such time as Tibet is converted into a zone of peace, it proposed that responsibility for defence rested with Peking. On the other hand, since the mid-1990s, the

[51]On the problem of self-determination and the drawing of boundaries see Shaw, Malcom N., 'Peoples, Territorialism and Boundaries' in: *EJIL* 8/3, 1997,478ff, especially 503ff.

Government-in-Exile in Dharamsala has been demanding that the aim of the political struggle be fixed by conducting a plebiscite among the Tibetans. Full-scale independence was also conceivable here as a demand, however realistic or unrealistic an option it may appear to be. The referendum has meanwhile been deferred. However, even the International Commission of Jurists has endorsed this course of action in its latest report on Tibet dated December 1997. The Dalai Lama on his part points to his Middle Way which is obviously what is represented as the goal in the Strasbourg Declaration.

Even the demand for mere autonomy for Tibet (rather than independence), which would indirectly amount to accepting Tibet as a part of China at least for the future, does not mean that the right to self-determination stands relinquished. The latter merely confers the right of choice which could also result in the choice of a status that provides for extensive self-governance for Tibet within the People's Republic of China, in internal matters such as cultural, economic, and environmental policies. With regard to the right to self-defence it must be stressed that in terms of its objective, this right predominantly anticipates full-scale secession since it is the protection of the people from the policy of the state that constitutes the primary objective. If the people nevertheless confine themselves to autonomy, then it goes without saying that this autonomy must be guaranteed in the constitution (more so than is the case in the Chinese constitution today) and organised on an extensive scale in order to ensure protection.

In devising a stable autonomy arrangement for the future, a fundamental element could lie in staggering Tibet's voluntary association with China over different time phases of enforcement to include a regulated arrangement for the influx of non-Tibetans, thereby allowing the autonomous Tibetan Government to first of all consolidate the social and economic structure to such an extent that the cultural and economic life of the Tibetans is on firm ground and able to meet the challenge posed by Chinese immigrants. For this, the degree of integration enforced at present must first and foremost be relaxed in some areas. However, there are at present no signs that the Chinese government will consider a change of position.

References

Bell, Charles, *Tibet einst und jetzt*, Leipzig 1925.

Bericht der österreichischen Rechtsexpertendelegation über ihren Besuch in China/Tibet 1992 von Ermacora/Benedek, Wien, Graz, September 1992.

Brownlie, Ian, *Principles of Public International Law*, Oxford 1990.

Cassese, Antonio, 'The Self-Determination of Peoples' in: *The International Bill of Rights*, edited by Louis Henkin, New York 1981.

Crawford, James, *The Creation of States in International Law*, Oxford 1979.

—, 'The Criteria for Statehood in International Law' in: *BYIL* 1976–1977, pp. 93–182.

Cristescu, Aureliu, *The Right to Self-Determination, Historical and Current Development on the Basis of United Nations Instruments*, New York 1981, UN-Doc.E/CN.4/Sub.2/404 1978.

Dahm, Georg/Delbrück, Jost/Wolfrum, Rüdiger, *Völkerrecht* Bd. I/1 Berlin/New York 1989.

Dalai Lama, *Das Buch der Freiheit*, Bergisch Gladbach 1990.

Dinstein, Yoram, 'Collective Human Rights of Peoples and Minorities' in: *ICLQ* 25/1976, p. 102 ff.

Doehring, Karl, *Das Selbstbestimmungsrecht der Völker*, Karlsruhe 1974, quoted as Doehring (Das Sbr).

Ermacora, Felix, 'Autonomie als innere Selbstbestimmung' in: *ArchVR* 38/200, pp. 285–97.

Fastenrath, Ulrich, 'States, Extinction' in: *EPIL* (10), p. 465–467 Amsterdam, New York, Oxford, Tokyo 1987.

Franke, Herbert/Trauzettel, Rolf, *Das chinesische Kaiserreich* (Fischer Weltgeschichte), Frankfurt/M. 1984.

Gernet, Jacques, *Die chinesische Welt*, Baden-Baden 1985.

Goldstein, Melvin, *A History of Modern Tibet*, Berkeley, Los Angeles, London 1989.

Gusy, Christoph, 'Selbstbestimmung im Wandel' in: *ArchVR* 30/4, 1992, pp. 385–410.

Hanneman, Andrea J., 'Independence and Group Rights in the Baltics: A Double Minority Problem' in: *VJIL* 35/2, 1995, p. 485–527.

Hofmann, Rainer, 'Minderheitenschutz in Europa' in: *ZaöRV* 52/1, 1992, pp. 1–69.

Hool, Catherine, *Die chinesische Tibetpolitik*, Bern, Frankfurt/M et.al. 1989.

Hoppe, Thomas, *Tibet Heute*, Mitteilungen des Instituts für Asienkunde Nr. 281, Hamburg 1997.

International Commission of Jurists, *The Question of Tibet and the Rule of Law*, Geneva 1959.

—, *Tibet and the Chinese People's Republic*, Geneva 1960.

—, *Tibet: Human Rights and the Rule of Law*, Geneva 1997.

Jones, Peter, 'Human Rights, Group Rights and Peoples' Rights' in: *HRQ* 21/21, 1999, pp. 80–107.

Li, Tieh-tseng, 'The Legal Position of Tibet' in: *AJIL* 50/1956, pp. 394–404.

McCorquodale, Robert/Orosz, Nicholas (eds.), *Tibet: The Position in International Law, Report of the Conference of International Lawyers on Issues relating to Self-Determination and Independence for Tibet*, London 6–10 January 1993, Stuttgart, London 1994, quoted as: (author) in McCorquodale/Orosz.

Murswiek, Dietrich, 'Offensives und defensives Selbstbestimmungsrecht' in: *Der Staat* 23/1984, pp. 523–48.

Oeter, Stefan, 'Selbstbestimmungsrecht im Wandel' in: *ZaöRV* 52/3–4, 1992, pp. 741–76.

Petech, Luciano, *China and Tibet in the early XVIIIth Century*, Leiden 1972.

Pochhammer, Wilhelm von, *Die Auseinandersetzung um Tibets Grenzen*, Frankfurt/M, Berlin 1962.

Richardson, Hugh E., *Tibet and its History*, Boston, London 1984.

Schmitz, Gerald, *Tibet und das Selbstbestimmungsrecht der Völker*, Berlin, New York 1998.

Shaw, Malcolm N., 'Peoples, Territorialism and Boundaries' in: *EJIL* 8/3, 1997, pp. 478–507.

Shen Tsung-lien/Liu Shen-chi, *Tibet and the Tibetans*, New York 1973.

Strupp, Michael, *Chinas Grenzen mit Birma und mit der Sowjetunion*, Hamburg 1987.

Suzuki, Eisuke, 'Self-Determination and World Public Order: Community Response to Territorial Separation' in: *VJIL* 16/4, 1975–1976, pp. 779–862.

Tang Chi'an, 'A Commentary on the So-Called Patron-Lama Relationship in Tsepon Shakabpa's A Political History of Tibet' in: *Tibet Studies* (Lhasa) 1/1989, pp. 62-69.

Thürer, Daniel, 'Das Selbstbestimmungsrecht der Völker' in: *ArchVR* 22/2, 1984, pp. 113–37.

Tomuschat, Christian, 'Das Recht auf die Heimat' in: FS Karl Josef Partsch, pp. 183–212 Berlin 1989.

—, (ed.), *Modern Law of Self-Determination*, Dordrecht, Boston, London 1993 quoted as (author) in Tomuschat (*Modern Law of Self-Determination*).

Verdross, Alfred, *Universelles Völkerrecht* (*Theorie und Praxis*), Berlin 1984^3.

Weggel, Oskar, Zum 40. 'Jahrestag der Befreiung' Tibets. Wie China seine Souveränitätsansprüche über die "Autonome Region" zu rechtfertitigen versucht' in: *China aktuell*, June 1991, pp. 361–373.

—, 'Normalisierung zwischen den beiden größten Entwicklungsländern der Welt-zum Besuch Li Pengs in Indien' in: *China aktuell*, Dezember 1991, pp. 769–75.

Vitzthum Graf, Wolfgang, (Ed.), *Völkerrecht*, Berlin, New York 1997.

(van) Walt van Praag, Michael.C., *The Status of Tibet*, Boulder 1987.

Abbreviations

AJIL	American Journal of International Law
ArchVR	Archiv des Völkerrechts
BYIL	British Yearbook of International Law
EJIL	European Journal of International Law
EPIL	Encyclopedia of Public International Law
FS	Festschrift
HRQ	Human Rights Quarterly
ICJ	International Court of Justice. Reports of Judgements, Advisory Opinions and Orders
ICLQ	International and Comparative Law Quarterly
IndYBia	Indian Yearbook of International Affairs
VJIL	Virginia Journal of International Law
ZaöRV	Zeitschrift für ausländisches öffentliches Recht und Völkerrecht

CHAPTER THREE

Indian Visions

GYANESHWAR CHATURVEDI

Introduction

The Tibetan saga of the past few decades can be best understood in the context of the conflicting discourses of Tibetan ethnicity and Chinese nationalism, camouflaged as anti-imperialism. This relationship between the two has to be viewed specially in terms of the nature of the Indian response. The Indian response is crucial to our understanding because it is more than a mere mirror of the happenings in the neighbourhood. India emerges as an actor, a player, whose intervention determines the direction and nature of the Sino-Tibetan encounter, with grave consequences for all the three parties, but specially for Tibet.

Also crucial to the analysis of the Sino-Tibetan relationship in the 1950s is understanding how, as in so many other countries, in the case of Tibet also, authentic indigenous Tibetan identity was sought to be distorted and destroyed by the superior military might of the People's Republic of China. This was achieved by a deliberate and self-conscious Chinese 'construct' of Tibetan ethnicity draped in Marxist jargon, far removed from the reality of an ancient and esoteric faith on the 'Roof of the World'. The Tibetan self-view was not unaware of the need to modernise a feudal social order, but this was understood by the Tibetans as part of a slow process of evolutionary change, and not something to be suddenly precipitated by a violent and

[1]For an analysis of the relationship between ethnicity and nationalism, see Brass, Paul R., *Ethnicity and Nationalism*, New Delhi 1991.

abrupt break of continuity. Even if we take the view that all identity formation is essentially a construct and that therefore the Tibetan self-view is also a construct, surely it has a greater legitimacy and moral credibility than any alien construct imposed from outside. The Chinese discourse about Tibet first *constructs* the 'Tibetan Other' and then *demonises* it, thus creating a comprehensive ideological rationale for the subsequent multi-pronged assault on the very identity of Tibet. The silence of those who could have prevented the outrage, or made efforts in that direction, is characterised by naivete and ambivalence. Prime Minister Jawaharlal Nehru was to discover, with considerable personal anguish, and with irreparable loss to the state, whose interest he had sworn to safeguard, that freedom is indeed indivisible.

The Indian Response to the Chinese Occupation of Tibet in 1949

This article constitutes an attempt to place the understanding of the triangular relationship—Tibet, China and India over time, firmly in this theoretical framework. It also seeks to analyse the nature of the Indian response to the Sino-Tibetan question, in the larger context of world politics.

It is ironical that whereas the Indian Prime Minister, who was also Foreign Minister, remained a committed defender of freedom all over the world, his attitude towards Tibet displayed signs of a strange ambivalence. His assessment passed through three distinct stages.

1. In the initial years, after Independence, Nehru seemed to accept the status of *Tibet as an independent country.*
2. Thereafter he moved to the view that *Tibet ought to enjoy a degree of internal autonomy under overall suzerainty of China.*
3. Eventually he was reconciled to *Tibet becoming a province of China.*

These changes in the Nehruvian stance have to be seen in the context of the internal and external constraints, real and fancied, in which Indian foreign policy has to operate. Did Nehru have any options? Were there alternatives?

But first the three stages.

The First Stage

In 1947, Nehru welcomed Tibet to the Asian Relations Conference as an independent country along with China.[2] Then just two years after independence, in 1949, Nehru committed, twice in a single speech, that he viewed the status of Tibet at par with China, Nepal, Burma and other independent neighbouring countries. On 22 March 1949 he said 'I would also include Tibet and China, Nepal, Burma, Malaya, Indonesia and Ceylon.'[3] In the same speech he repeated 'Our relations with Afghanistan are exceedingly friendly and our relations with Tibet, Nepal and all the neighbouring countries are also very friendly'.[4]

C.V. Ranganathan and V.C. Khanna, both former members of the Indian Foreign Service, observe: 'It has been argued that, both on moral and strategic grounds, the Nehru government should have moved energetically to ensure international recognition of Tibetan independence even before the communists consolidated their position in China. In the opinion of many international law experts, on 15 August 1947, Tibet was more fully qualified to be treated as an independent state than a great number of countries which are members of the United Nations today.'[5]

Was Indian military intervention in Tibet, to stop the Chinese advance, a realistic option of Indian foreign policy in the 1940s? According to Neville Maxwell:

---

[2]See '*Tibet Since the Asian Relations Conference*', Tibetan Parliamentary and Policy Research Centre, New Delhi 1998

[3]Nehru, Jawaharlal, *India's Foreign Policy*, The Publications Division, Govt. of India, New Delhi 1983, p. 42

[4]Ibid.

[5]Ranganathan, C.V. and Khanna, Vinod C., *India and China: The Way Ahead after 'Mao's India War*, New Delhi 2000, p. 26.

The last British officer in command of India's eastern defence, Lieutenant-General Sir Francis Tuker, had recommended only three years earlier that 'rather than see a Chinese occupation of Tibet, India should be prepared to occupy the plateau herself', the estimate was that India had only to send a brigade of troops to Tibet and China would have held off.[6]

The Second Stage

India's explicit stand favouring an independent status for Tibet was diluted in subsequent years. By 1950, after the Peoples' Liberation Army had captured Lhasa, speaking in the Indian Parliament, Nehru referred to Tibetan autonomy under Chinese suzerainty:

> We further said that we were anxious that Tibet should maintain the autonomy it has had for at least the last forty years. We did not challenge or deny the suzerainty of China over Tibet.[7]

However this change in his stance is not the end of ambivalence. His sympathy for the cause of Tibet still comes through:

> In their replies they [the Chinese] always said that they would very much like to settle the question peacefully, but that they were, in any event, going to liberate Tibet. *From whom were they going to liberate Tibet, is however, not quite clear.*[8]

The Third Stage

While Nehru's semantic jugglery over sovereignty and suzerainty continued unabated, he looked on helplessly as Tibet

---

[6]Shah, A.B. *India's Defence and Foreign Policies*, Bombay 1966, p. 87, quoted in Neville, Maxwell, *India's China War*, Dehradun (Indian Edition) 1977, p. 72.

[7]Nehru, Jawaharlal, *India's Foreign Policy*, supra, p. 302.

[8]Ibid. Italics mine.

metamorphosed first as the de facto and then as the de jure province of the People's Republic of China.

In November 1947, a few months after the Asian Relations Conference, the first Indian position paper stated that India, in order to emerge as 'a potent but benevolent force in world affairs' needs to maintain friendly relations with its neighbours. 'To prejudice her relations with so important a power as China by aggressive support of unqualified Tibetan independence is therefore a policy of few attractions.'[9] In the following years, the Government of India tried consistently not to upset the Chinese and discouraged the Tibetans from taking active diplomatic steps.

India was an important actor in the Tibetan tragedy, but not the only one. The British and the US Governments' attitudes need to be looked at as well. The British Foreign Office discussed in 1943 the withdrawal of the concept of Chinese suzerainty over Tibet, which legally meant nothing.[10] They knew very well, that when they withdrew from India, its northern border would be left undefined and insecure. But the British decision-makers came to the conclusion that it was best to leave things as they were so as not to provoke China—then Nationalist China ruled by the Kuomintang under Chiang Kai-shek—to assert its claim on Tibet. The British stuck to this attitude even after the Chinese civil war was won by the communists and Mao Zedong came to power.

The only country to clearly see the danger of a communist take-over of Tibet and subsequent security risks for South Asia was the USA. In 1942, President Roosevelt wrote a letter to the Dalai Lama,[11] requesting his permission to covertly station two

---

[9]Goldstein, Melvyn, *A History of Modern Tibet 1913–51*, Berkeley, California, 1989, p. 564, quoted in: Smith, Warren Jr., *Tibetan Nation: A History of Tibetan Nationalism and Sino-Tibetan Relations*, New Delhi (Indian edition) 1997.

[10]Smith Jr., Warren W., ibid., p. 246.

[11]Ibid., p. 244ff.

Americans in Lhasa in connection with the transport of war supplies through Tibet. The two Americans did arrive in Lhasa and developed sympathy for the Tibetan cause, even advising the Tibetans on how to obtain international recognition. While they were there, the Dalai Lama—or rather his government—sent a letter to President Roosevelt in 1943,[12] explaining why Tibet considered itself to be an independent country. In 1946, the US Ambassador to India in a report to the State Department described Tibet as a stabilising factor in Asia and a bulwark against communism.[13] However the State Department had its own compulsions, as the then Chinese government under Chiang Kai-shek had been an ally in the war against the Japanese. These considerations were no longer valid after the communist take-over in China. In July 1950 the US State Department approved military assistance to Tibet,[14] contingent on Indian cooperation, but this co-operation was not forthcoming. The State Department then took the position of maintaining a friendly attitude towards Tibet, short of giving China cause for offence.

When Tibet's case was brought before the United Nations by El Salvador in November 1950, both the British and the American delegations were willing to support the resolution, but held that it should be introduced by India as the country most concerned with the issue. However, the Indian delegation did not see fit to do so, guided by the concept of India's global role as a mediator in Cold War conflicts. Hence, both the British and the US delegations decided not to intervene or sponsor the resolution, lest it was interpreted as an 'imperialist conspiracy.'[15] The Tibetan government unfortunately did not have enough diplomatic experience to influence the course of events.

---

[12]Ibid., p. 245.
[13]Ibid., p. 254.
[14]Ibid., p. 260–61.
[15]Ibid., pp. 284–87.

On 29 April 1954, India and China signed their far-reaching 'Agreement on Trade and Intercourse between the Tibet Region of China and India'. Under this, India agreed to relinquish all extra-territorial rights in Tibet inherited from the British and recognised China's sovereignty over Tibet. The preamble of the agreement enunciates the Five Principles of Peaceful Coexistence —Panch Sheel—which were included in most treaties and agreements India entered into with other, mainly non-aligned countries. These principles are: mutual respect of each other's integrity and sovereignty, non-aggression, non-interference in each other's internal affairs, equality and peaceful co-existence.[16] The Agreement carried a note containing 15 points relating to India, including withdrawal of its military escorts stationed at Yatung and Gyantse; the transfer by India of postal services and rest-houses in Tibet at a reasonable price to China and the return of all lands other than the land at its trade agency compound walls at Yatung and some minor matters such as hiring of employees or means of transportation at reasonable price. The Agreement was ratified on 3 June 1954.[17] The British Raj had crafted Tibet as a buffer-zone between China and India, thereby strengthening the security of India against possible hostile Chinese intentions. But one of the earliest actions of the Indian government was to undo the advantages of this British policy

What made Nehru and the Indian Government change their mind about the status of Tibet? This has to be seen in the context of Nehru's world view. He rightly saw the entry of India and other former colonies into international affairs as a major event of the post-war era: 'India's situation was viewed as a part of the larger freedom of all countries and peoples of the world.'[18]

[16]The term echoes the five principles of conduct for Buddhist laypersons and hence carries symbolic value.

[17]Government of India, Ministry of External Affairs: Notes, Memoranda and Letters exchanged and Agreements signed between the Governments of India and China 1954–1959, White Paper, New Delhi 1959, p. 98–101.

[18]Nehru, J., *Speeches*, Vol. I, New Delhi 1958, p. 235–237; Nehru, J., *The Discovery of India*, London 1956[4], p. 547–548.

He considered India and China, representing two major ancient cultures, as destined to lead the emancipation of hitherto dependent Afro-Asian countries. The Prime Minister reasoned before the Lok Sabha:

> Big changes have taken place in the world since the last war. Among them has been the rise of a united China....The fact is that China has become a great power—united and strong... the two great powers striding across the world are the United States of America and the Soviet Union....But if you peep into the future...the obvious fourth country in the world is India.[19]

Nehru's view also has to be seen in the context of the policy of non-alignment, which undoubtedly was Nehru's contribution to the Cold War scenario unfolding in the 1950s. He was himself convinced that India had an important mission to further world peace.[20] Questioned in Parliament about his Tibet policy, particularly the surrender of Indian privileges, he defended himself:

> Regardless of what happened in Tibet or China we could not, in conformity with our own policy, maintain our forces in a foreign country. That was a relic of British imperialism, which we did not wish to continue, even if there had been no change in Tibet. So we withdrew them....The privileges which we surrendered in Tibet were privileges which we do not seek to have in any country in the world, Tibet or any other.[21]

Speaking in the Lok Sabha on 30 September 1954, he said:

> Several Hon. Members have referred to the 'melancholy chapter of Tibet'...where did we come into the picture unless we wanted to assume an aggressive role of interfering with

[19]Nehru, J., *India's Foreign Policy*, supra pp. 304–05.

[20]See Bernstorff, Dagmar Gräfin, *Indiens Rolle in der Weltpolitik, Eine Untersuchung über das außenpolitische Selbstverständnis indischer Führungskräfte*, Baden-Baden 1965.

[21]Nehru, J., *India's Foreign Policy*, supra, p. 313.

> other countries...we don't go like Don Quixote with lance in hand against everything that we dislike.[22]

The larger issue of freedom for all countries did not include Tibet.

However, the question of the validity of the border between the two Asian countries according to the Simla Agreement of 1914 had not been dealt with in the 1954 Agreement, therefore conflict was programmed. According to J.N. Dixit, the former Indian Foreign Secretary:

> Nehru felt that China's and India's adherence to the principles of Panch Sheel would strengthen the forces of non-alignment and establish a bulwark against the negative implications of the Cold War for developing countries. Later trends and events however proved that this optimism was premature and misplaced. There were also indications of China not sharing India's views about Asian consolidation and Asian resurgence in a cooperative framework. Undercurrents of the 'Middle Kingdom Complex' and a sense of Chinese centrality in Asia began manifesting themselves in bilateral interactions between Nehru and Zhou Enlai....China felt that India was a competitor for Asian leadership, which it could not countenance.[23]

One might assume the position that theoretically there were numerous alternatives available to the Indian decision-makers. But these alternatives have to be squarely placed within the parameters of feasibility. No policy decision can be evaluated outside the universe of constraints. Once China had occupied Tibet in October 1950, armed conflict with the northern neighbour was unthinkable for two reasons. Firstly, so soon after Independence, India was ill-equipped to take on the might of the People's Liberation Army. Secondly the international situation was hardly conducive to such a military adventure. The Soviet Union, at that time, was firmly on the side of communist

---

[22]Ibid, p. 304.

[23]Dixit, J.N., *Across Borders*, New Delhi 1998, p. 36

China. The USA would have asked India to pay a price which non-aligned India could never have paid. There was no chance of engaging the Chinese successfully in a rational dialogue over the future of Tibet. As Chester-Bowles commented, Nehru was not unaware of the possibility of a clash between the two giants. But he wanted to obviate that possibility and certainly did not want it just then.[24] Ranganathan and Khanna ably pointed out:

> To Nehru and his advisors, the PLA march into Tibet brought into bold relief a problem to which they might have given little attention earlier, the security of the northern borders. Nehru believed that good relations with China would also help ensure peace on the borders. However, at the same time, Nehru had to apply his mind to the demands of realpolitik in the face of the perceived challenge to Indian security by the arrival of the People's Liberation Army on the other side of the Himalayas.[25]

The Indian government did try to convince the Chinese government of the necessity to give autonomy to the Tibetans and the then Premier Zhou Enlai seems to have promised it to the Indian Prime Minister particularly during their talks in 1954. Nehru trusted the assurances of his Chinese counterpart. But the perceptions of Tibet did not match. While India perceived Tibet as the repository of ancient wisdom, it perceived China as a collaborator in the Great Asian Solidarity. The Chinese saw Tibet as the last refuge of reactionary medieval feudalism, and China perceived India as a competitor for influence in Asia.

The Debate in India

Nehru's China Policy and particularly his lenience regarding Tibet did unleash controversy in India. Criticism came mainly from three sides:

---

[24]Chester Bowles , K., *Promises to Keep: My Years in Public Life*, Delhi 1972 (Indian Edition), p. 490.

[25]Ranganathan C.V. and Khanna Vinod C., supra, p. 28.

1. From supporters of realpolitik; 2. from Gandhians and religious leaders; and 3. from some of the opposition parties.

Neville Maxwell writes:

> The Government's Tibet policy was strongly attacked in Parliament, and Vallabhbhai Patel, Deputy Prime Minister (and Home Minister),...Nehru's great rival, wrote him a long, critical letter in November 1950. Patel implied that Panikkar, the Indian ambassador in Peking, had had the wool pulled over his eyes by the Chinese whom he accused of perfidy and malevolence and described as a potential enemy. He warned that China's move into Tibet 'throws into the melting pot all frontier and commercial settlements with Tibet, on which we have been functioning and acting during the last half a century.[26]

Patel suggested a thorough analysis of the consequences for India's policies, regarding the security of her borders, her trade routes and also possible repercussions in favour of the Indian communists.

The journal of the Gandhi Peace Foundation—*Gandhi Marg*—brought out a special issue on Tibet. Rajeev Vora, the editor, says:

> In the last fifty years...we have betrayed Tibet...under some strategy born of fear, we have sacrificed a whole people, nation and culture, and when the awareness of this blunder dawned on us, some courage was initially shown as an act of repentance, by according 'shelter' to the Government of His Holiness the Dalai Lama and some Tibetans. But this act of repentance was left incomplete because recognition to the Tibetan Government-in-Exile and support for their freedom struggle, was still not forthcoming. But incomplete repentance is no repentance at all.[27]

---

[26]Maxwell, Neville, *India's China War*, Dehradun, 1977, p. 72. The letter is reprinted in *Indian Leaders on Tibet*, supra, pp. 9–11.

[27]Vora, Rajeev, *Bhumika*, in: Rajeev Vora, (ed.) *Tibet: Daman, Mukti-Sadhna Aur Bharat Ka Swadharm*, Gandhi Shanti Pratishthan, New Delhi, 1998, p. 4.

Acharya Rajneesh (Osho), expressed a widely felt opinion:

> Tibet is best left alone as a laboratory of the inner human quest. But not one nation of the world has raised its voice against this contemptible assault. And China has not only attacked but also integrated Tibet in its map. Now Tibet is a part of its territorial area. And we continue to think that this is a civilised world, where innocent people, who harm no one are so easily destroyed. And with them is destroyed something which is precious to humanity. If there was anything civilised left in humankind, then each nation would have stood up against China's attack on Tibet. This is an attack on matter of consciousness. It is an attack of materialism on spiritual heights.[28]

Both B.R. Ambedkar, the leader of the lowest castes, himself a convert to Buddhism and Ram Manohar Lohia, the socialist politician, urged Nehru to stand by Tibet. The battle for the freedom of India, they felt, had to be fought against China in Tibet, on the Sino-Tibetan border and not on the Sino-Indian border. Dr. B.R. Ambedkar stated in his characteristic categorical manner:

> Instead of according recognition to China in 1949, had India accorded this recognition to Tibet, there would have been no Sino-Indian border conflict.[29]

Ram Manohar Lohia in 1963 observed:

> Let me just repeat what I have said before about Tibet. First, language; second, script; third, life-style; fourth, religion; fifth, slope of land; sixth, history; seventh, will of the people. On all these seven counts Tibet cannot be a part of China. It is closer to India than China...Tibet is Tibet; it is independent,

[28]Acharya Rajneesh, *Jyoti aur Tamas* in: Vora, Rajeev (ed.), *Tibet: Daman, Mukti-Sadhna Aur Bharat Ka Swadharm*, supra, pp. 132–135.

[29]Ambedkar, B.R quoted in *Indian Leaders On Tibet*, DIIR, Dharamsala 1998, p. 17.

it has its own style, its people want to live in freedom. This is the greatest truth.[30]

Tibetan Exile in India

In March 1959 the Dalai Lama arrived at India's border and was granted political asylum (see Chapter 1). While India's conceding suzerainty over Tibet to China should have made the Chinese happy, granting asylum to the Dalai Lama sent the contrary signal to the Chinese, who interpreted this action as an indication of New Delhi's intention of encouraging secessionism in Tibet against Chinese authorities.[31]

On the issue of granting sanctuary to the Dalai Lama, Nehru's foreign policy was caught in a dilemma of its own making. Having surrendered Tibet to the Chinese as part of the 1954 Agreement, the least it could do from the viewpoint of both morality and strategy, was to give refuge to the young and venerated Lama from Tibet. Despite Chinese protests and provocations, Indian public opinion left the Government with no option but to give sanctuary to the Tibetans. Moreover Nehru was not devoid of sympathy for the Tibetan cause. Intellectually he was close to Buddhist rationalism; he could empathise with the freedom and dignity of a small and peaceful ethnic community. He was torn between two concepts and ambivalence could be the only outcome. Nehru's ambivalence was the result of this dichotomy between sympathy and constraints.

At the time of the Dalai Lama's arrival in India in 1959 skirmishes along the new Chinese/Indian border had already taken place. They erupted in the Indo-Chinese border war in 1962, when Chinese troops marched into India at different places along the border and suddenly retreated after two weeks of

---

[30]Lohia, Ram Manohar, *Tibet, Cheen aur Hindustan* in: Rajeev Vora (ed.) supra, pp. 120–24.

[31]Dixit, J.N., *Across Borders,* supra. p. 62.

inflicting humiliating defeats on the unprepared Indian troops. This is not the place to elaborate on this war. Suffice it to say that it left deep scars on Indian national pride and self-image of itself as a peacemaker; it shattered the vision of the Grand Asian Alliance. It took more than twenty years for a thaw in the frozen relations between India and China. Only in the late 1980s and 1990s were efforts made to 'normalise' relations.

The reality of the Tibetan Government-in-Exile functioning from Indian soil is an irritant for the Chinese government who misses no opportunity to protest. But the Indian Government has been consistent in its support to the Tibetan refugee community, manifest in the financing of the Tibetan schools, looking after the security of the Dalai Lama, accepting ever new migrants from Tibet, continuing the lease for the settlements etc. aspects which will be dealt with in the following chapters of this book.

In this author's view the time has come to recognise the Tibetan Government-in-Exile. With the growing global concern for Human Rights and for the preservation of ethnic identities, the Indian lead would galvanise world public-opinion, particularly in Europe and in USA. To Tibet it would belatedly offer justice for earlier wrongs and to India itself it may well be the catalyst to usher in the birth of India as 'Prometheus unbound'. The mystical character of Tibetan Buddhism and the unique way of life which it enshrines, carries within it some of the most sacred elements of the ageless wisdom of Indian civilisation itself. Tibet has kept the Indian mystical tradition alive. To now allow the Tibetan way of life to be endangered can only be at the peril of Indian identity itself.

References

Appadorai, A., *Select Documents on India's Foreign Policy and Relations, 1947–72*, Delhi 1982.

Brass, Paul R., *Ethnicity and Nationalism*, New Delhi 1991.

Chaturvedi, Gyaneshwar, *India-China Relations: 1947 to Present Day*, Agra 1991.

Indian Leaders On Tibet, Tibetan Central Administration, Dept of Information and International Relations, Dharamsala, 1998.

Dixit, J. N., *Across Borders*, New Delhi 1998.

Dutta V.P., *India's Foreign Policy*, New Delhi 1984.

Galbraith, J.K., *Ambassador's Journal*, Boston 1969.

Goldstein, Melvyn, *A History of Modern Tibet 1913-1951*, Berkeley, California l989.

Jain, R.K., *China-South Asia Relations 1947-1980*, New Delhi 1981.

Maxwell, N., *India's China War*, Dehradun (Indian edition) 1977.

Nehru, Jawaharlal, *India's Foreign Policy*, The Publications Division, Govt. of India, New Delhi 1983[4].

Ranganathan C.V. and Vinod C. Khanna, *India and China, The Way Ahead After 'Mao's India War'*, New Delhi 2000.

Smith, Warren W.Jr., *Tibetan Nation: A History of Tibetan Nationalism and Sino-Tibetan Relations*, New Delhi (Indian Edition) 1997.

Vora, Rajeev (ed.), *Tibet: Daman, Mukti-Sadhna Aur Bharat-ka-Swadharm*, Gandhi Shanti Pratishthan, New Delhi 1998.

CHAPTER FOUR

Chinese Views

JOACHIM GLAUBITZ

Only as late as in the seventh century AD, was the existence of Tibet reliably documented and the scholar finds a centralised Tibetan state which already has its unified code of law, maintains official contacts with the outside world and is characterised by a distinctive religion and culture. This was also the time when Tibet adopted a script which became the vehicle for the gradual spread of Buddhism. In the middle of the eighth century, Tibet included parts of what later became Chinese Turkestan and today's Kansu Province. The ninth century is characterised by frequent clashes with China which did not always prove superior to its small neighbour. We know that at least in one case the Chinese emperor had to flee his capital and the Tibetans enthroned a new ruler. According to the Tibet expert, Josef Kolmas:

> ...on the whole Tibet during the period of the Tang dynasty (618–907) was in every aspect an independent state with a comparatively strong military potential maintaining intensive diplomatic relations with neighbouring countries. The relations between China and Tibet were still relations between two sovereign states, marked, however, by a strong difference in the organisation of the state and in economic and cultural development.[1]

The break-up of Tibet into small principalities during subsequent centuries and the consequent turmoil and divergent developments within various parts led to a decay of the political

[1]Kolmas, Josef, *China Handbuch*, Düsseldorf 1974, p. 1405.

and cultural life. Only the western part of the country was by and large not effected; it even experienced a remarkable cultural upswing. The lamaist church began to fill the political vacuum; numerous lamaist sects appeared, and monasteries became cultural, economic and political centres.

Tibet, internally unstable and torn apart, had ceased to be a military threat for the Chinese. During the period of the Five Dynasties (907–60) China itself was in turmoil and did not return to political stability until the beginning of the Mongol rule at the end of the thirteenth century. During the Sung dynasty (960–1279) China was threatened by the Khitan and Juchen in the north and finally it was conquered by the Mongols. Kublai Khan, the first Mongolian ruler of his dynasty (Yüan 1279–1367) in China, embraced Buddhism and made Tibet a tributary state. Even before Mongolian rule over China had been established the Lama Phagpa (1235–80) became the 'spiritual mentor' of the Khan who in 1276 enthroned him as high priest and ruler over Tibet. Thus the 'lama-patron' relationship and rule of priests in the capacity of kings was established in Tibet. It also meant the political preference of the Sakya order.

The rule of the Mongols marked a decisive change in the political status of Tibet. Josef Kolmas writes following a Chinese point of view:

> The country which was completely independent until the middle of the thirteenth century slipped with the beginning of the Mongolian Khanate, the later emperors of the Yüan dynasty, increasingly into the sphere of the Mongolian rulership with its centre in Peking. This is the reason why over the next centuries the tradition developed to regard Tibet generally as an administrative part of China. The Chinese Ming Dynasty (1368–1644), which succeeded the Mongolian Yüan Dynasty in China essentially followed the same practice to invite leading Tibetan Lamas to the imperial court in order to renew their appointment and to bestow on them new titles.[2]

[2] *China Handbuch*, supra, p. 1406.

It was characteristic of the Ming court to show some kind of benign neglect concerning Tibet and not to care about the events in this Central Asian state.

In the following Manchu Dynasty (1644–1911) this changed completely. The Manchus on the Chinese throne spread the power of China into the territory between Russia and China and in 1635 brought Inner Mongolia under their control.

Around the end of the seventeenth century, the princes of Outer Mongolia, who were considerably pressured by the bellicose Dsungars, submitted to the outstanding Manchu emperor Kang-hsi. The Dsungar Prince Galdan, who wished to establish a great empire including Eastern Turkestan and Tibet as well as Outer and Inner Mongolia, was regarded as a serious threat by the Chinese government. The Dsungars continued their attacks until the middle of the eighteenth century, although in 1696 Prince Galdan was defeated by the Chinese in the battle of Urga . The Dsungars ransacked the Tibetan capital Lhasa and tried to gain control over the nomination of the Dalai Lama. If they had been successful this would have meant a deep loss of prestige for Peking and waning influence within the realm of the Lamaist-Buddhist culture. In 1720 a Chinese expeditionary army occupied Lhasa and enthroned a new Dalai Lama. Thus China had ensured its supremacy over Tibet. Since 1728 two representatives of the imperial Chinese government, so called *Ambans,* resided in Lhasa; they had to report to Peking about events in Lhasa. When in 1750 during a riot two *Ambans* were killed, China intervened in Tibet with its army. In course of time the *Ambans* interfered in the affairs of the Tibetan government and expanded their authority. When between 1788 and 1792, Tibetan forces and the Gurkhas of Nepal repeatedly clashed militarily, the Chinese central government took over the responsibility for all military, political, economic and administrative affairs of Tibet. According to the opinion of some historians the Himalayan state had at the end of the eighteenth century lost the last remnants of its autonomy.

In the course of the nineteenth century, Great Britain entered the arena and tried to start negotiations with Tibet. These resulted in a convention and a trade agreement concerning Tibet, however both documents had been negotiated between London and Peking without inviting the Tibetan government. In 1903–04, the British-Indian Government undertook a military expedition against Tibet led by Colonel F. Younghusband. The Tibetan army was defeated, British troops pushed forward up to Lhasa and in 1904 an agreement was forced upon Tibet. This remained the first and only international treaty which was negotiated and concluded directly with Tibet without Chinese mediation. However, although China in those days was weak and unable to take care of its interests vis-a-vis Great Britain and Russia (in 1906 and 1907 respectively) the British recognised China's suzerainty in Tibet and agreed to negotiate with Lhasa only through the Chinese government. This recognition consolidated Chinese supremacy over Tibet. Further, China strengthened its position within the border area with Tibet and sent in 1910 a military unit of 2000 men to Lhasa.

However the end of imperial China after the collapse of the Manchu dynasty in 1911 also shattered China's dominant position in Tibet. The thirteenth Dalai Lama, who in 1910 had fled to India, returned to Lhasa in 1913 after the Chinese army had left and announced a Declaration of Independence. But, since all relevant documents and official declarations of the Republic of China under its President Sun Yat-sen concerning international law mention Tibet as well as Outer Mongolia as parts of Chinese territory, tensions between Peking and Lhasa demanding independence were unavoidable. In this situation Great Britain became active again and arranged in October 1913 at Simla (present-day Shimla) in India a British-Chinese-Tibetan conference on problems of Tibet's border and its status according to international law. The Tibetan demand for independence was challenged by the position of the Chinese delegation that Tibet had to be regarded as an integral part of China. However according to the leaders of the delegation China would be willing to abandon plans of turning Tibet into a province of China, but Peking would claim the right to station a Chinese governor in Lhasa with 2600 troops and the unlimited control of Tibet's relations with foreign countries.[3] A compromise draft treaty proposed by the British considered a division of Tibet according to the Mongolian model, i.e. into an Outer and Inner Tibet. Both parts of Tibet would be recognised as territory under Chinese suzerainty, but the administration of Outer Tibet (outer as seen from China) as well as the election and enthronement of the Dalai Lama would exclusively be a Tibetan privilege. China had to promise not to convert Tibet into a province, but Great Britain would be obliged to renounce any annexation, even partially, of Tibet. China would not be allowed to send troops into Outer Tibet but should have the right to keep a high Chinese representative in Lhasa with appropriate military protection. This draft of a treaty negotiated in July 1914 at the conference in Simla had been initialled by the representatives of the three attending states, however, the Chinese government did not recognise the decision of its plenipotentiary and the Chinese parliament did not ratify the treaty.

The British and Tibetan representatives, however, signed the treaty declaring that China must not draw any privileges from the treaty as long as it has not signed it. This treaty, incidentally, demarcated the border between Tibet and India (the so-called McMahon Line) which continues to be a conflict between present day India and China. During the following decades internal chaos hindered the government in Peking to practice the sovereignty over Tibet it had claimed. This gave the thirteenth Dalai Lama the chance to develop a fruitful co-operation with the British government: Tibetan students went to England for studies, the military was trained according to British standards, paper money and stamps were introduced, and in 1936 the Tibetan government permitted the establishment in Lhasa of a 'semi-permanent' British representation which in 1950–52 was changed into an Indian Consulate General. The period of the Republic of China, i.e.

[3]Kindermann, Gottfried Karl, Der Ferne Osten. Dtv-Weltgeschichte des 20. Jahrhunderts, Vol. 6, München 1970, p. 155.

the time between 1911 and 1949, can be regarded as a phase of factual autonomy of the Himalayan state. Tibet could handle its internal affairs with almost complete independence, and in its foreign relations, too, it enjoyed a high degree of autonomy.

This changed after the victory of the communists led by Mao Zedong. Therefore the year 1949 marks a new chapter in the history of Tibet. In October 1950 the Chinese People's Liberation Army (PLA) entered the Himalayan state in order to 'strengthen the national defence at China's Western borders'. In November 1950 Tibet appealed in a telegram to the United Nations and charged China with open aggression.[4]

Tibet had to yield to China's pressure. On 23 May 1951 both sides concluded an 'Agreement on measures concerning the peaceful liberation of Tibet', consisting of 17 articles. This was a de facto endorsement of Chinese sovereignty over Tibet. In the agreement which had been recognised but was later refuted by the fourteenth Dalai Lama, China guarantees not to call in question neither the traditional system of government nor the status of the Dalai Lama, further it promised the Tibetans the unlimited right of religious freedom. However, these guarantees very soon turned out to be empty promises.

After the PLA had entered Lhasa in the summer of 1951 the Chinese government established a military command for the region of Tibet. The effort of the Chinese central government to transform Tibet according to Communist ideology was refused by the Tibetans with persistent opposition. Therefore the Chinese leadership had to postpone the so called democratic reforms until 1962. Nevertheless, the situation remained tense. Throughout 1958, riots occurred which escalated in March 1959 into an uprising in Lhasa. The fourteenth Dalai Lama refused the Chinese demand to use the Tibetan army against Tibetan guerillas. The Chinese threatened to arrest the Dalai Lama, but, he succeeded in fleeing to India.

---

[4]Everding, Karl-Heinz, *Tibet, Lamaistische Klöster, nomadische Lebensformen und bäuerlicher Alltag auf dem Dach der Welt*, Cologne 1999, p. 62.

Now the Chinese dissolved the government in Lhasa, and handed over all governmental functions to a Preparatory Committee. For the time of the Dalai Lama's absence the Chinese authorities introduced the Panchen Lama as acting chairman of the committee. In December 1964 the Dalai Lama, who formally was still the Chairman of the Committee, was discharged and branded as a traitor. In 1965 the Panchen Lama, was also removed from his function. On 9 September 1965 the Chinese leaders formally established the Tibetan Autonomous Region. The region was officially restricted to the Western Tibetan central area, called Ütsang. The eastern Tibetan provinces, i.e. Amdo and Kham, which during the Qing and Manchu dynasties had already been added to the Chinese empire, were put under the authority of the bordering provinces and autonomous regions respectively of Qinghai, Sichuan, Yunnan and Gansu. The establishment of the Tibetan Autonomous Region *de jure* meant the sealing of the division of Tibet.

The suppression of religious freedom and the use of force in order to bring Tibet into line with other provinces culminated during the so called Cultural Revolution from 1966 to 1969. The Red Guards who on the behest of Mao Zedong wandered through the country like vagabonds, also did irreparable harm in Tibet. An expert on Tibet comes to the following conclusion:

> Out of the more than 4000 religious sites and monasteries that were left in Tibet from former times no more than 100 remained untouched. Thereby the holy places often were so completely destroyed that not even the basements can be recognised. Valuable historical material like documents, records, treaties and texts disappeared in Chinese archives where they still are today, unavailable for scholarly research. According to official Chinese statistics at that time 79.6 per cent of the religious sites were destroyed and 93.9 per cent of the monks had to take off their robes.[5]

[5]Ibid., p. 64.

The Chinese side, too, admits that 'during the chaotic Cultural Revolution' religious sites had been destroyed. At the same time, however, the Chinese insist that the Government in Peking has spent millions of yuan over the last decades for the renovation of monasteries and for the revival of religious practice. According to these reports almost 1800 religious sites had been repaired.[6] Experts call this development 'a museum-like restoration of a few Tibetan cultural monuments'.[7]

The events of the last two decades reveal an almost insoluble dilemma. The policy of reforms under Deng Xiaoping since 1980 was accompanied at the beginning by a certain liberalisation of spiritual and religious life. Temples and monasteries of Confucianism, Buddhism and Taoism could again dare to display modest activities. In Tibet, however, the revival of religious life immediately became a seed of national opposition against an ever stronger Chinese presence. This again provoked new measures of suppression by the Chinese and consequently stirred up further protests by the Tibetans.

There are signs that the leadership in Peking (or influential people within it) realised the futility of the policy of destroying the religious identity of the Tibetans by force and suppression. However, there are no signs yet that a new policy is developing. The Chinese cannot have missed the fact that the Dalai Lama in his recent pronouncements is not demanding the independence of Tibet any more but merely far-reaching autonomy. In his declaration on 15 June 1988 in the European Parliament in Strasbourg (see page 426) he signalled his willingness for a far-reaching compromise with China in order to end the spiral of violence. Because of this position the Dalai Lama was severely criticised within his own environment. So far an agreement with Peking could not be reached and in 1991 the proposal was retracted.[8]

---

[6] *Beijing Review*, August 17–23, 1998, p. 20.

[7] Everding, ibid.

[8] Everding, ibid.

Since the Chinese government regards Tibet within the borders of the Autonomous Region of 1965 as an inseparable part of Chinese territory and fiercely denies that there existed between 1911 and 1950 a status of factual independence, the Dalai Lama, too, in the past made remarks that clearly contradicted his announcements not to strive for national independence. One example was the following remark in his speech in 1988 in Strasbourg: 'Every Tibetan hopes and prays for the complete restoration of the independence of our nation.'[9] This, of course, strengthened the position of the hardliners in Peking. Nevertheless, the pronouncements of the spiritual leader of the Tibetans encourage the general impression that he is prepared to recognise China's suzerainty over Tibet, but that he wants to achieve in return full self-determination for Tibet's internal affairs, notably all questions concerning religion and culture.

Since the problem of Tibet is such an import issue of domestic as well as foreign policy, it would be very unnatural if there were no efforts on both sides to think about solutions. Therefore it was no surprise when in June 1998 the President of China remarked that there do exist unofficial channels of communication between the Chinese government and the Dalai Lama. The Tibetan side, too, admitted that unofficial contacts with the Chinese have intensified. At the end of the year 2000 it was revealed that the elder brother of the Dalai Lama, Gyalo Thondup, who had been in the past already engaged in communicating with China, had again travelled to China twice and that in October 2000 he had delivered to the Dalai Lama a private message from the Chinese side. Thereupon the Dalai Lama proposed to send a delegation to Tibet. This led to the conclusion that the informal contacts that had been disrupted two years ago had been restored.[10] However, from remarks made

---

[9]Hoppe, Thomas, Liu Jen-Kai, Schädler, Monika, Sternfeld, Eva, *Das Autonome Gebiet Tibet, Wirtschaft, Geographie, Gesellschaft.* in: China aktuell, May 1997, p. 466, footnote no. 5. See p. 426, and chapter 6.

[10]*The Economist*, 16 December, 2000, p. 71–72.

by the Dalai Lama one could conclude that the Chinese government was not prepared to receive a delegation. The spiritual head of the Tibetans regarded this as proof for a hardened attitude in Peking and a lack of political will to resolve the Tibetan problem.[11]

However in the autumn of 2002 an emissary from the Tibetan Government-in-Exile made an unpublicised trip to Peking at the invitation of China's Ministry of State Security and held talks with a state security vice-minister. These talks, according to a diplomat, focused on the future and put aside 'historical questions'—namely China's insistence that Tibet has always been part of China. Right after this encounter, two senior envoys of the Dalai Lama paid a historic visit to Peking and Tibet. The two envoys, Lodi Gyaltsen Gyari and Kelsang Gyaltsen, were invited by the Communist Party's United Front Work Department. Their trip to Tibet—the first in twenty years—was widely publicised in the Chinese press.[12] Kelsang Gyaltsen later regarded the visit as a foundation for contacts with the Chinese leadership on a regular basis.[13] According to the Tibetan Government-in-Exile, for the first time, the envoys were treated as equals by Chinese officials.

The same envoys visited China a second time from 25 May to 8 June 2003. The purpose of this visit was to establish contact with the new Chinese leadership at two levels: the government and the Chinese Communist Party, and to broaden understanding of the situation in China. As Lodi Gyari said, the reception was very friendly and views were exchanged frankly in a warm atmosphere. The delegation visited areas inhabited by Tibetans in the provinces of Yunan and Zhejian in south-east China and talked to Tibetan officials there. They also visited Buddhist sites and met with the President of the Buddhist Association of China. The mission is seen by the Tibetans as an

---

[11] *International Herald Tribune*, 23 May 2001.

[12] *Far Eastern Economic Review*, 19 September 2002, p. 24.

[13] *Frankfurter Allgemeine Zeitung*, 10 October 2002.

effort to advance the prospect of earnest negotiations to find a mutually acceptable solution for the Tibetan people.[14]

Nevertheless, for the Chinese leaders, who are at present facing increasing social and economic problems with considerable potential for unrest all over the country, it should be very difficult to meet the demands of the Dalai Lama for internal self-determination. Such a concession to the Tibetans, how desirable it may be, would certainly provoke similar demands among the two other large non-Chinese minorities, the Uighurs and the Mongols. There is a high probability that the Chinese leaders are well aware of this danger. Therefore, according to the logic of power politics there seems to remain only the continuation of the suppression combined with the extensive policy of settlements, i.e. the massive sinicisation of the Tibetan population and other ethnic groups. However, it is obvious that in the long run this cannot be regarded as a solution.

The situation regarding sources on China's policy of settlement in Tibet is difficult. According to an official Chinese information of 1993 the Han-Chinese part of the population in Tibet comprises only 2.8 per cent. Other, semi-official sources, speak about 9 per cent, i.e. roughly 210,000 Han-Chinese. This number does not include the military personnel estimated at 250,000 men. On the whole, therefore, we have to consider about 15 per cent of the population in Tibet as Han-Chinese. There is, however, a certain natural protection of this Himalayan region: its average altitude of 4000 metres which makes conditions of life difficult because of the rarified air. Tibetan functionaries report the failure of a project to resettle farmers from central and western China to Tibet in order to cultivate farm land because of the climate and altitude.[15]

Apart from the burden, which Tibet as a source of unrest

---

[14]Statement 11 June 2003.

[15]Weggel, Oskar, 'Immer Ärger mit Tibet', in: *China aktuell*, January 1997, p. 26.

means for China's domestic policy, the religious and political weight of the Dalai Lama as well as his international activities are a permanent challenge to the Chinese leaders.

This has been highlighted in recent years by two extraordinary events: in 1995—the decision on the successor of the tenth Panchen Lama who died in 1989, and the secret flight of the seventeenth Karmapa Lama in January 2000 to India. As successor of the Panchen Lama, the second-ranking lama within the hierarchy of Tibetan Buddhism, people close to the Dalai Lama had discovered and recognised in a Tibetan monastery a child as the reincarnation of the late Panchen Lama. This was publicly confirmed by the Dalai Lama, but not accepted by Peking. The Chinese leaders detained this boy and sanctioned the choice of another six-year old as the reincarnation of the eleventh Panchen lama. This Lama who is officially approved by Peking and has been installed in the Tashi Lunpo Monastery at Shigatse is generously honoured in a demonstrative way and used as an instrument of Chinese policy towards Tibet. Power and influence within the Himalayan state are at stake; he who controls the spiritual leaders and is able to influence them will decide future politics in Lhasa.

The international community reacted to these events. On 20 June 1996 the German Parliament discussed the human rights situation in Tibet. In a resolution the members demanded a stricter adherence to human rights and a more determined support of the Dalai Lama and his efforts for the cultural and religious autonomy of Tibet. This and several other activities concerning the Tibet issue organised by German NGOs made the Chinese side cancel at short notice a visit to China by the then German Foreign Minister Kinkel. Consequently German-Chinese relations worsened for some time.[16]

The second event was extremely embarrassing for Peking. In January 2000 it became known that the seventeenth Karmapa

[16]For details see Weggel, Oskar, 'Deutsche Chinapolitik—Überlegungen im Zeichen der Krise', in: *China aktuell*, June 1996, p. 598–611.

Lama had escaped from Tibet and fled to India. The Karmapa Lama is the third-ranking lama in Tibetan Buddhism after the Dalai Lama and the Panchen Lama. In India, he was received by the Dalai Lama. The flight was especially embarrassing for Chinese leaders because the 14 year-old Karmapa Lama was one of those spiritual leaders who had been groomed by Peking and was therefore regarded as politically reliable. The Dalai Lama, too, recognised him as the legitimate holder of the title.

One and a half years after he had left China, the seventeenth Karmapa Lama spoke for the first time about the motives of his flight. In the monastery Gyu-To not far from Dharamsala he explained to representatives of the international media that it was his own decision to leave his monastery because the Chinese authorities obstructed his spiritual education. He would only return to Tibet in the company of the Dalai Lama whom he recognised as the leader of the Tibetan movement of autonomy.[17]

This background of the Karmapa's flight throws light on the fact that the Chinese even half a century after they conquered Tibet still have considerable difficulties in controlling the religion and culture of the Himalayan state. This will not change soon. The Dalai Lama's efforts to explain the situation of Tibet during his extensive travels all over the world is not without effect. Tibet remains the touchstone for the sincerity of the repeated Chinese promises to improve the practice of human rights. At the same time one must not underestimate the spiritual effect of the Dalai Lama's meetings with Asian Buddhists. These encounters have a political dimension. It is especially obvious in connection with the Dalai Lama's visit to Mongolia. In 2000 this journey could not be made for 'technical reasons'. In fact the Chinese ambassador in Ulan Bator protested against the planned visit to the Mongolian government, and Russia, in close cooperation with China, denied the Dalai Lama the necessary transit visa. In Mongolia the Dalai Lama would have been the

[17] *Neue Zürcher Zeitung*, 30 April 2001.

guest of the most important Buddhist monasteries, and it could be expected that Buddhism in Mongolia would be boosted by the visit.[18]

When the visit eventually took place in November 2002 the Chinese Ministry of Foreign Affairs reacted angrily. It charged the Tibetan leader with scheming to split China.[19] Further, rail traffic between China and Mongolia was suspended for two days apparently in protest against the visit.[20] The question is sensitive with regard to the Mongolian minority in China. The Dalai Lama, who considers himself to be the religious leader of his people, refuses any political engagement; however, because of his deliberate renunciation of politics he enjoys an even stronger political power which cannot be ignored in the process of solving the problem of Tibet. Moreover, within the Chinese political elite there are voices arguing that the Dalai Lama is essential for maintaining stability in the country. This is exactly what the Dalai Lama himself is trying to convey:

> If the Chinese government gives us a high level of autonomy I can persuade those Tibetans who want independence that autonomy is in the best long-term interest of Tibetans. I can help reduce the danger of instability.[21]

It remains to be seen whether the new leader of the Chinese Communist Party, Hu Jintao, who is well aware of the situation in Tibet, will test this message and negotiate.

---

[18] *Far Eastern Economic Review*, 17 May 2001, p. 10.

[19] *Neue Zürcher Zeitung*, 5 November 2002.

[20] *Far Eastern Economic Review*, 21 November 2002.

[21] *The Economist*, 16 December 2000, p. 72.

CHAPTER FIVE

A Tale of Two Chinese Cities

VICTOR CHAN

I knew very little about Tibet when I first met the Dalai Lama twenty-nine years ago in Dharamsala, India. But I knew this much: the Dalai Lama and 80,000 Tibetans had crossed the Himalayas to escape the Chinese. I asked him: 'Do you hate the Chinese people?'

His answer was immediate:

> No. I most definitely do not hate the Chinese. As you may know, the Tibetan people have suffered greatly because of the Chinese invasion. Many, many people have died. Nearly every Tibetan family in Dharamsala has a sad story to tell. Most have lost at least one family member due to Chinese atrocities. However, my quarrel is with the Chinese Communist Party. Let me make one thing clear: I still consider the ordinary Chinese my brothers and sisters. No. I don't hate them.

In April 2001, in a small bunker-like room within the bowels of Taipei's Linkou Stadium, I again asked the Dalai Lama the same question. As an ethnic Chinese with strong sympathies to the Tibetans, I am obsessed by how Tibetans feel, deep down, about the descendents of the Yellow Emperors.

This time the Dalai Lama stared at me balefully. His answer was curt:

> No. None whatsoever. And in Taiwan, there is no sign at all from the Chinese people that they consider me anti- Chinese.

Having known him for so long, I could recognise the telltale signs—he was annoyed by the question. He had been asked this before. The Dalai Lama has made reaching out to the Chinese one of his life's most important missions. And he believes that his actions speak for themselves. Visiting Taiwan for the second time, he tried hard to connect with the Taiwanese. He was succeeding brilliantly; there was no mistaking the extraordinary chemistry between him and the Chinese people of Taiwan. Seventeen thousand tickets to initiation rites presided over by him were snapped up in days. He filled the entire Linkou Stadium when he gave a talk about ethics in the new millennium.

Lee Teng-hui, the former President of Taiwan, is one of his ardent admirers. In my meeting with him in his office, he told me in his accented English:

> The Dalai Lama is a great person. So deeply religious. He said he is not a god. But I'm a Christian, so I understand his deep compassion. He is the best man I have ever met in the world. He is my brother—my spiritual brother.

Annette Lu, the out-spoken Vice President, declared in her welcome speech to the Dalai Lama:

> This is a sacred, solemn and wonderful moment. We are attending a banquet of the mind and I hope the Dalai Lama can become a stabilising force when we experience economic slowdown and political uncertainty.

Lu is spearheading a 'Send Taiwan's love to Tibet' campaign to raise US$ 150,000 to build a school for the disabled in Dharamsala.

Yes, no doubt about it. There was certainly a love-fest under way between the ethnic Chinese of Taiwan and the Dalai Lama.

After giving teachings to tens of thousands of Taiwanese Buddhists for four hours in the Linkou Stadium, the Dalai Lama was digging into his midday meal with gusto. This was his last meal of the day. On a tiny table in front of him was a bowl of noodles, a large plate of Chinese Buddhist vegetables, a small plate of greens and what looked suspiciously like french onion soup. There was also a pot of hot water, his preferred beverage at all hours of the day. He held a bowl of rice in his left hand and ate slowly with chopsticks.

I wanted to know the implications of his visit to Taiwan. 'By coming to Taiwan you are jeopardising any tenuous opening you might have with Beijing.'

The Dalai Lama replied:

> What is important for me is contact with ordinary Chinese people. It is impossible for me to go to China. One of the best ways to connect with the Chinese, to increase awareness of the Tibet situation, is through Taiwan. After my 1997 visit here, I met a group of Chinese scholars in New York. They unanimously told me that my Taiwan trip was extremely useful. Large numbers of Chinese in the PRC, especially those living in the coastal areas, saw me on Taiwan TV.

A year before the Taiwan visit, I spent a few days in Hong Kong. Although I now live in Canada, I was born and raised in the former British colony. I decided to call on an old friend, Henry Kan (not his real name). He is the scion of one of the most prominent families in Hong Kong, a family that has achieved a near-Kennedyesque stature, because of their substantial civic contributions, in the last few decades. However, the Kans have suffered a series of debilitating financial setbacks some ten years ago and have only now got back on their feet. I knew the family well when I worked in Hong Kong in the early 1980s—I went to the Shatin horse races with the patriarch and socialised with Henry and his brother.

I got Henry on his cell phone. He was delighted to hear from me and wanted to know what I was up to—we had not seen each other for more than ten years. I told him about my two little girls and how fatherhood had curtailed my nomadic instincts. Then I told him about the project I was working on, a book about the Dalai Lama, Tibet and China.

There was a long silence at the other end; I thought the connection was cut off.

'Henry, are you still there?'

'Yes, Victor. I'm still here. I think it best we stop this

conversation right now. I can't talk to you anymore. I'd be in deep trouble if word got out that I've been talking to you.'

I was stunned. 'Henry, you're not making sense. What the hell are you talking about?'

> Victor, you're playing with fire. My God, a book on the Dalai Lama! I've a great deal of business dealings with China. I'm on some of the most high-level advisory boards with the Chinese. Let me as an old friend give you some advice. Drop the book—right now. In the meantime, be extremely careful whom you talk to. I'm not joking. Don't try to call me again. I will not return your call. From now on, you don't exist.

Click.

It came as a shock to me to be dumped so unceremoniously over this matter of Tibet. For the next couple of days, I was out of sorts. I could not bring myself to call up old friends. Like a displaced person with no roots, I walked around the giant bazaars of Hong Kong and stared with fascination at the inexhaustible supply of cell phones and cameras.

In retrospect, I shouldn't have been too surprised by Henry's reaction. After all, I have lived in Hong Kong for the first twenty years of my life. I know something about the mindset of its inhabitants.

The Hong Kong Chinese are one of the most pragmatic peoples of the world. They are like weathervanes, forever blowing with the prevailing wind. Their true north is self-preservation; their religion is money. Everything else is secondary and expendable. This trait accounts for their phenomenal success in the business world.

The Hong Kong Chinese have this incredible one-pointed focus in their genetic makeup. Nothing is allowed to distract them or get in the way of this single-minded pursuit of wealth and stability. Not family, not touchy-feely ethical principles. And certainly not Tibet, one of the most sensitive and explosive issues confronting China. Any self-respecting Hong Kong Chinese will do whatever it takes to give Tibet a wide berth. The last thing they want is to be embroiled in the controversy. There was nothing unusual in Henry's action. It was pure self-preservation. And self-preservation is a finely honed talent of the Hong Kong Chinese.

For what it is worth, I'll tell you what a Hong Kong Chinese like me thinks about Tibet. Bear in mind, however, that I'm not your typical Hong Kong Chinese. For one thing, I'm thoroughly westernised, the product of British schools and Canadian and US universities. I have spent most of my life outside Hong Kong. I am an incurable traveller who has lived in North America, Europe, and the Himalayas. Concepts of fair play have become part of my mental makeup. Yet I believe I retain a strong sense of Chinese identity. This is because I was exposed to the essentials of Chinese culture at an early age. My mother made sure, over my kicking and screaming, that I had a no-nonsense grounding in Chinese philosophy, calligraphy and Tai Chi. For another, I've been intimately involved with Tibetan culture for the last three decades.

For me, without the shadow of a doubt, Tibet is the biggest blot on recent Chinese history. There is only one word that could adequately describe China's misguided adventure in Tibet. That word is shame. It is shameful for the most populous country in the world to brutally crush a tiny nation of a few millions. What the Chinese have done in Tibet will go down in history books alongside the atrocities of the Nazis and the Khmer Rouge.

It is shameful the way the Chinese have tried to snuff out Tibetan civilisation and culture. They have done this effectively and relentlessly by simply allowing large numbers of opportunistic Chinese to immigrate to the Tibetan plateau. The indigenous cultures of Manchuria and Mongolia have virtually disappeared under the same modus operandus. How much longer the Tibetan and the Uigher cultures have left is anybody's guess.

What the Chinese have done in Tibet is nothing short of barbaric. I have no doubt Confucius, Zhuang Zi and Lu Xun and other great Chinese thinkers would turn over in their graves in shame. Centuries from now, the government of the People's Republic of China will be remembered for its stupendous economic turnaround—for the first time in its history, over a billion of its citizens have adequate food and clothing. But the PRC will also be remembered for being the world's most unscrupulous coloniser, the destroyer of one of the world's most unique, most spiritual civilisations.

The Dalai Lama's views of the plight of Tibet are characteristically idiosyncratic. He believes that if we only focus narrowly on Tibet, the situation there looks hopeless. But if we expand our vision, taking into account the seismic shifts in the consciousness of the Chinese people in recent years, then there is cause for optimism.

He told me:

> I recently received an email from a Chinese man from the Mainland. He said he had never met me before. Everything he knew about me he got from Chinese propaganda. Then he dreamt that he had an audience with me and had gotten some blessings from me. Since then he developed a strong faith in Tibetan Buddhism. He wanted to know how he could become my disciple when he had never met me. I wrote back to him and said, 'I have never met the Buddha. But I still consider myself to be his disciple. So, if you want to be my disciple, this is something entirely up to you, I have no say in this. Buddha never accepted me as his follower. Even though it is now 2,500 years after his death, as soon as I devoted myself to him, I became his disciple.'

His private secretary added that though the number of Mainland Chinese seeking him out is miniscule, it is increasing.

Yes, this is a good sign. And it is gratifying to see with my own eyes the outpouring of affection for the Dalai Lama among the ethnic Chinese in Taiwan. But sad to say, I don't expect too many of my Hong Kong compatriots to follow suit any time soon. Within the multifarious communities of Greater China, they are the least likely to express solidarity with the Tibetan people. They have a lot to lose and they will not rock the boat. They will, as usual, take the easy way out: they will simply pretend Tibet does not exist.

CHAPTER SIX

An Interview with Tenzin Gyatso, the Fourteenth Dalai Lama

DAGMAR BERNSTORFF AND HUBERTUS VON WELCK

DB/HvW: Your Holiness, in 1959, after your arrival in India, what steps did you take for the preservation of Tibetan culture?

DALAI LAMA: (sighs) Firstly, our language and the study of Tibetan history is very important. Therefore, we impressed upon the Indian government that we need special Tibetan schools. Pandit Nehru[1] graciously supported that. Tibetan culture is very much related to Dharma, Buddhist culture. Therefore we study Buddha Dharma as our past tradition which came from Nalanda [in India] and has been alive in Tibet for several centuries, so that must be preserved.

Secondly, the Tibetan refugees should not be scattered all over India but they should have one place where they can live together. Pandit Nehru agreed and he asked the Indian chief ministers whether there was a possibility of resettlement of Tibetan communities in their states. So today there are settlements in many Indian states.

DB/HvW: You had a very clear vision of what had to be done and you also said Tibetans had to modernise. In your opinion what are the areas of modernisation of Tibetan society and culture? And what would the institutional consequences be?

DALAI LAMA: Perhaps the structure our government has taken is an aspect of modernisation. Right from the beginning we

---

[1]Jawaharlal Nehru, Indian Prime Minister 1947–64.

made a lot of effort for democratisation and equality, male and female; in the religious field, I think, equality is basically there among nuns, monks and lamas and lama tulkus. But regarding studies, I think, at least in the last few centuries, education was completely neglected in Tibet, especially education in the nunneries.

DB/HvW: Isn't there a move to modernise the nunneries and to give Buddhist nuns a more equal status and access to higher examinations?

DALAI LAMA We pay special attention to make them equal. Officials, monks, laypersons, we want them completely equal. In the field of studies, monks and nuns should be able to study all the texts. Although traditionally the principle is there, but we have neglected it. So we must make special efforts to give the nuns equality. That also is part of modernisation.

DB/HvW: But is it not true that nuns are not fully ordained and remain novices?

DALAI LAMA: That is the difficulty; that is beyond my control. Some people would like the Dalai Lama to decide. But our Vinaya rules say that all decisions must be made by the Sangha, the assembly of monks, and not by a single person. The Dalai Lama is not above the Sangha. I am one of those who really make every effort to introduce the Bikshunis,[2] but then the Bikshuni tradition is now available only in the Chinese tradition and not in other traditions, like in Thailand, Burma, Sri Lanka or in the Tibetan tradition. Although in the past there are some records of Tibetan lamas giving ordination to Bikshunis in Tibet, but according to our Vinaya text that is not helpful. The only possibility is that learned Tibetans understand. On several occasions we held meetings with monks, lamas, abbots and discussed this point, but then the majority still held the view that it will not be possible. The only way out is a Sangha of international Buddhist monks, who will have a thorough discussion and look at the present situation in the world and

[2]Fully ordained nuns.

raise their voice. Nowadays in the political and in many other fields there is complete equality. The feminist movement is very helpful for opening this discussion. Therefore, according to the present reality, we need the restoration of the Bikshunis.

I said to Taiwanese monks if we Tibetans as an exiled government send invitations to Thailand or Burma they will ignore it. So the appropriate step is that some Taiwanese organisation or the Mahabodhi Society[3] makes a proposal for this Sangha and invites [people]. It is very essential to prepare texts and literature about the Chinese Bikshuni's lineage. For the last fifteen years we have been doing this work. We have already done all the translations from the original Chinese texts into Tibetan. The English translation of course is not yet done. So first we should get all this literature translated and then circulate it among the leaders of the Sangha in Thailand, Burma or in Sri Lanka. If this gathering happens I will be there from the Tibetan side. For me there is not much difficulty but we in Tibet cannot do it unilaterally. You see, in the past, in Theravada Buddhist countries, they considered Tibetan Buddhism as not true Buddhism, but as lamaism. We already face some kind of prejudice, because we practice Tantrayana, because of Tantrayana we Tibetans are already discriminated. I think that is not nice. The Chinese Bhikshuni tradition, their authenticity should be made clear at the conference and after frank discussion with all the important representatives the Sangha will accept that it is necessary to give full rights to the nuns now. This is OK, this is good.

We have already introduced the study of philosophical texts in the nunneries for more than twenty years. They now study through dialectical discussions. On one occasion all the nuns who had studied these texts got together at Dharamsala and debated in Tibetan in an excellent way, in a very good way. There is progress. In 1961 we opened teacher training institutes. Then there were two nuns; at that time my hope was that more

[3]An Indian Buddhist Association.

nuns should work as teachers in various schools. But at present there is not a single nun as teacher.

DB/HvW: You have introduced the teaching of science subjects in the monasteries, what other changes would you like to see in the monasteries?

DALAI LAMA: [long pause] I personally prefer fewer monasteries, fewer in numbers, but good ones. In India and Nepal there are more than 300 monasteries. I heard that in Nepal some huge monasteries have been constructed, but there are only few monks inside. And some of those few ride a motorcycle with a girl on the pillion! I was told, refugees from Tibet feel very happy when they reach Nepal, they are happy to be in a free country. But when they make a pilgrimage to a monastery and they see those stupid monks there, it is a great disappointment for them. And that in a free country, which is supposed to preserve our tradition!

DB/HvW: Let us turn to lay persons. How has life in exile changed the status of Tibetan women?

DALAI LAMA: As far as the administration is concerned, we emphasised that there should be more women. During our public meetings, whenever I go to the Tibetan settlements, I appeal to women that they should make more effort to be equal in various fields.

DB/HvW: Young Tibetans—do they, in your opinion, accept the Buddhist values of tolerance and non-violence and the Tibetan way of life, exposed as they are to contemporary life styles?

DALAI LAMA: Generally I think so. There is now a new development for more than twenty years, that a few hundred Tibetans come from Tibet every year. Some remain here and some return. I think more than 20,000 young Tibetans, including some children, who escaped from Tibet, have joined our monasteries and our schools. The young Tibetans who have recently come from Tibet are more aggressive. In the last twenty years a few cases of murder have happened by those Tibetans. They easily lose their temper and then they use knives, etc. Tibetan boys who are born here, I think, they are very lazy. But those who come from Tibet, specially those monks, are hard working. There is a difference between Tibetans who come from Tibet and Tibetans who are born in India. Tibetans who are born in India are perhaps a little more peaceful.

Another aspect is that in the late 1960s and early 1970s, many Tibetan youths seemed to be less interested in Tibetan Buddhism. Although everybody says Tibetan culture, Tibetan culture, yet the interest in Buddhism decreased. But this trend has been reversed now. In the 1960s some dedicated monk teachers really explained Buddha Dharma and they also looked after the students very sincerely. In these schools there was no discrimination between monks and nuns, also not between monks and lay person or boys and girls. The monks and nuns taught dialectical discussion, but now, that has been discontinued. Generally the students of the younger generation are less interested in Buddhist Dharma and some western educated students even openly criticised it. They blame it for Tibet's loss of its own country. I think that is a generalisation. Because of too much of devotion in the name of religion there was some negligence in some secular areas and that became the cause of our suffering. That is clear. I am frankly telling the Tibetans that the Chinese call us barbarians and backwards and say the Chinese themselves are more advanced. This not because of their brain, the Tibetan brain and the Chinese brain are equal, the potential is equal. The Chinese and the Tibetan civilisations, I think, are more or less equal, Chinese Confucianism and our own civilisation. Perhaps the Tibetan script is more advanced. We have an alphabet but the Chinese have no alphabet. Then spiritualism, Tibetan Buddhism is, if not more advanced than Chinese Buddhism, at least not backward. The field where the Chinese have reason to consider the Tibetans as backward is modern education. This is a question of attitude. A few generations of Chinese have had a modern education since Sun Yat-sen's[4] revolution in China and the beginning of the

[4]Sun Yat-sen (1866–1925), Chinese President and political reformer, who overthrew the last emperor of the Ch'ing dynasty and founded the Republic.

democratic movement. But we in Tibet were completely isolated, completely ignorant.

In the late 1970s, 1980s and 1990s and now, in the twenty-first century I think more and more Tibetan youths are showing a genuine interest in Tibetan Buddhism and that is, I think, because more and more westerners are showing interest in Tibetan Buddhism. Therefore, these young Tibetans, who really look to the West and are so much advanced and so much developed show their interest in Buddhism. I think that has some impact.

DB/HvW: It is like Gandhi's teachings coming back to India via *Small is Beautiful*, Schumacher's book famous in the 1970s.

DALAI LAMA: Some young Tibetans are seriously thinking about a kind of organisation for the study of Buddhism. It is really important and worthwhile to organise the study of Buddhism, not by joining a monastery and studying for fifteen to twenty years. That is too long, too difficult. But at the same time more and more young people show their interest in studying Buddhism say, for a period of three to four years. Some young Tibetans are thinking of joining a monastery not to become monks, but as lay persons. But so far we don't have lay people in monasteries.

DB/HvW: In Thailand and Burma young men join a monastery for three to six months and then go back to secular life.

DALAI LAMA: A few years ago at an abbots' meeting, I suggested, that the Thais have this practice. In the Vinaya it says that as long as you can be a good monk you remain in the monastery. If you find it difficult then you have the liberty to leave voluntarily, not in disgrace. Then I pointed out that Buddha himself had made that clear. Some abbots were concerned that the number of monks might dwindle. As I mentioned earlier, I prefer a smaller number of monks and monasteries, but good quality. But at that time I was not successful (laughs).

DB/HVW: Some young Tibetans graduate here and then migrate to Europe or North America. Will they be able to maintain their Tibetan identity or will they just merge into another culture?

DALAI LAMA: According to our experience Tibetans who are in Switzerland for the last thirty years, almost forty years, now in the second or even third generation, generally speaking, they kept the Tibetan identity quite well. Also in America and in Canada, for almost thirty years they kept the Tibetan identity. Some disappeared or were absorbed.

DB/HvW: People who have migrated often become much more aware of their own culture.

DALAI LAMA: True, since it is important to keep one's own tradition, maintain one's identity including the language. It is worthwhile to make efforts for that. In Switzerland and now in America, some Tibetan children have started studying Tibetan language at weekends. I have been complaining that many Tibetans, including some old people, are too excited to go to America. The centre of the Tibetan community will be India. Here we must build our society economically, educationally, a healthy society in various fields. First is our own country—Tibet, second in exile our main home is India. Then follow the Tibetan communities in Europe, America, Japan, Australia and in a few Arab countries. The small settlements outside will all link with the Tibetan community in this country.

I was told that some Tibetans are very eager to go to America even by cheating. I heard some Tibetans in Nepal, not monks but laypersons, go to the American Embassy putting on a monk's robe. But then for a short break they will go outside and smoke—that is very sad! But in a way if they are more in number in America and eager to organise some learning centres for Tibetan studies and other activities it becomes easier. There is a negative side and a positive side as well.

DB/HvW: Your Holiness, you stand for genuine autonomy for Tibet. Which degree of genuine Tibetan autonomy do you think will be practicable and acceptable to all concerned? What do you mean by the 'middle path'?

DALAI LAMA: I think, when the real dialogue starts then the details are a matter of discussion. But in principle, as I mentioned earlier, the Chinese central government will look after defence and foreign affairs. Then naturally in education and spiritual matters and also in the economy, I think, the basic plan should be drawn by the Tibetans themselves. Engineering or some other works of course should be carried out by Chinese because we need experts, we have no experts. But technicians and experts should come on the invitation sent by the Tibetans. At present they brought lots of Chinese in the name of help to Tibet, this is not right. In a few words: in those areas where Tibetans can manage, can work, all authority should be in Tibetan hands, but in those fields, where we cannot manage Chinese experts must come and help. Although we already have some very detailed proposals like our own parliament and judiciary within the autonomous status, I think, up to what level the Tibetan autonomous institutions have the authority and the power will have to be decided. Perhaps some rules will be set by the Central authority. But if those because of the difference of circumstances do not suit the Tibetans, then I think the Tibetans should have the right to reject such rules.

DB/HvW: The Chinese don't seem to trust your middle path approach. They seem to think that there is some hidden agenda. Is there a hidden agenda?

DALAI LAMA: When I was in Taiwan I was asked whether I have a mission or will join with the Taiwanese independence movement. I wish someone from China should come to Taiwan and look and watch me day and night, what I am saying, what I am doing. Then I told a press conference, please, the reporters and media people may watch me. Yes, international people and the international community please check us, including yourself, the Friedrich Naumann Foundation (laughs).

The reason why I asked for autonomy and not independence is that Tibet is materially backward, there is no doubt. In modern education we are very backward, because we have completely neglected this field. We Tibetans remain at the bottom of development, we never looked around. If somebody hits us, we still remain like that. I often tell Tibetans, earlier especially the monks, the clergy, considered westerners or western education as enemies of Buddha Dharma. They thought the study of English is very harmful for our culture. That was the kind of attitude then and it was a great mistake, great mistake. Take China under Sun Yat-sen. They learnt French, Japanese or English and through foreign languages they studied modern concepts. We Tibetans completely neglected that. One example is: the thirteenth Dalai Lama sent four or five students to England to study English around 1912 or 1914. Originally he wanted to send students continuously. Then he opened an English school in Gyangtse, but that was eventually closed. Within my lifetime, when I was ten or eleven, an English school opened in Lhasa. The Tibetan government invited an English teacher, who came there but a few months later the government stopped it all mainly due to opposition from the monasteries.

The Chinese look at us as backward, so we must catch up. In the name of religion, in the name of Buddhism we neglected modern education. We need a lot of technology, a lot of investment and a lot of machines and therefore we have to remain in the People's Republic of China, provided the Chinese side respects our culture and gives us the freedom to preserve our own cultural heritage. That is why there is no reason to have a hidden agenda. I make it clear that the future of Tibet is entirely up to the Tibetan people. It is up to the Chinese to truly respect our culture and help us sincerely, then the Tibetans will react accordingly.

DB/HvW: Your Holiness, linked to the autonomy question, you have talked about an area of ahimsa [non-violence] in Tibet. What is your vision of such a zone of ahimsa? How will ahimsa work between states, between the state and the citizens and between citizens?

DALAI LAMA: Ahimsa—non-violence. Tibet's natural environment is peaceful and needs special care because it is delicate. So although it is very important to use nature's resources and we also need some development of industries, we have to take special care not to damage the environment. Then there is the sense of contentment, inner peace. If there is an aspect of profit, money, regardless of the environment, then this means absence of inner peace.

My dream is that people should become more compassionate and peaceful by education, through Buddhist influence. We Tibetans already have non-violence in our tradition, basically. But Buddhist education and aspects of modern education, like environment issues, human rights, equality of the sexes—I feel non-violence will give deep results. I often mention inner disarmament and external disarmament, meaning inner demilitarisation. Whenever we confront some problems, then we should not think how to counter them by violence, but through dialogue and finding some mutually acceptable solutions. That is the ethos of non-violence. We need inner disarmament, less hatred, less ill feeling and respect for the other side and their interest. That is very important. We as a country, at least in the autonomous region, will have no military forces, no factories that produce weapons. The environment in Tibet is very delicate and we have to plan everything accordingly. Through education, the society should become more compassionate. Some crime is always there, so a police force is needed and there will be small weapons. If Tibet creates a zone of peace, demilitarised, the threat to the whole of northern India will be much less. Then the Indian government will happily reduce forces. That is the best way to develop mutual trust and friendship between India and China—on the basis of trust.

Defence should be the responsibility of the Chinese central government because of the long border between India and China. If there is a problem along this border then we Tibetans, as Buddhist students of India, cannot open fire on Indians, let the Chinese do that!

DB/HvW: After the return to Tibet: how will the Tibetans in exile integrate with their brothers and sisters in Tibet itself? And how will they co-exist with the Chinese living in Tibet?

DALAI LAMA: I don't think there will be much of a problem between Tibetans who come from India, who are born in India and educated in this country and our countrymen inside Tibet. The attitude of the Taiwanese towards me, towards Tibetans, is very friendly, very warm. They are the same Chinese. Even though they also maintain that Tibet is part of China, their attitude is very friendly. The communists spoilt all this, I feel.

DB/HvW: Is autonomy an attractive model for Tibetans who live in Tibet? They only know and experience the so-called autonomy of the 'autonomous region'. Do you foresee that the Tibetans will accept your concept?

DALAI LAMA: My impression of the opinion of Tibetan people inside Tibet is that they are political minded. They see that my proposal is the best way. Some say Tibet should get full independence, as they have completely lost their faith in the Chinese and are very sceptical. But those political minded ones are more sensible and not very emotional. They will agree to my proposal.

DB/HvW: Which region should in your opinion comprise autonomous Tibet, Ü-Tsang or Kham and Amdo as well?

DALAI LAMA: Since my main goal is the preservation of Tibetan culture and not political independence, or separation from China, I don't see anything wrong in demanding the same autonomy pattern for the whole area of Tibetan culture, for people of the same ethnic group and language. The Chinese constitution itself allows autonomous districts in some areas like Sechuan, Yunan. So if instead of many small autonomous bodies there is one organisation that is much easier.

DB/HvW: You have always stood for peaceful means to liberate Tibet. Would a non-violent campaign similar to the one Mahatama Gandhi led, be feasible in Tibet?

DALAI LAMA: I believe non-violence is the best way because violence is essentially against human nature. I feel human nature is more generous. The existence of human beings is based on human affection, which is at the beginning of our very life. After birth we cannot survive without human affection. Anger, hatred, fighting are also part of human nature but not the dominant one, I feel. Anger is a negative factor but compassion, a warm heart are positive factors for good health and a happy life. For any social animal, human affection, a sense of community is essential. Therefore war, violence is basically harmful for humanity. Since human beings are social animals, conflicts among them must be solved by peaceful means. Violence is one way to solve a problem, but at the same time it also creates new problems. The violent method is powerful, but it has very strong side effects. In the twentieth century many problems were solved by force, but with great harm to the losers. Look at the First World War, the Second World War, the Korean War, the Vietnam War, because of the military involvement there is deep harm. And even in the Kashmir War, after fifty years the problem is still there. With peaceful means and closer understanding there would not be any problem, that is my feeling. Now, specially in Tibet's case, whether we like it or not, we Tibetans and Chinese have to live side by side. So in order to live happily, friendly, peacefully in good spirit of neighbourhood, we carry on this struggle but it must be by non-violent means. Finally, there must be understanding between Tibetans and the Chinese. Even though the governments are different but we are the same people, the Chinese and the Tibetans. We must find closer understanding, mutual respect. For that the support and awareness of Tibet on the Chinese side, I feel, is very very necessary. Clearly the Tibetan struggle is a just struggle and the Tibetans have every right to fight. If that is understood we shall gain sympathy and justice. But if the Tibetans use violence, with Chinese bloodshed, then it will become very emotional and difficult. We want support from the Chinese community, from Chinese intellectuals and for that our non-violent struggle is very very essential. On the practical side: many years ago I talked to some militant youths. For the sake of discussion I told them, let us think of violence. A few guns are nothing, we need a substantial number of guns and sufficient ammunition. And the first question is, from where to get the funds. From the Indian government—impossible! From America ? That is also difficult. After Kissinger's visit to China everything has changed. Supposing we do get some support or funds, where could we buy these guns? And how to send these weapons to Tibet? Difficult! By land? Very difficult. Therefore, it is easy to say 'jihad', holy war, but practising it is not easy. If a few hundred or few thousand guns reach Tibet and a few hundred Tibetans take these arms and several thousand Tibetans fight with China and some hundred Chinese soldiers are killed, for China hundred soldiers are nothing, hundred thousand, two hundred thousand, nothing. But a hundred soldiers killed in Tibet that means something for us. Then what happens if thousand or ten thousand Tibetans are killed? Some of our militant youths understood. In the long term interest, I think, the non-violent way is the best. It may take some time, but once we succeed that will be a real achievement and there will be no side effects.

DB/HvW: It is true that people who practice non-violence need a lot of courage and training.

DALAI LAMA: I often argue with Indian friends who always shout Gandhiji, Gandhiji. But I respond, although the British imperialists were bad enough, when the Britishers were here, there was an independent judiciary, there was freedom of press, freedom of speech. In China, in a totalitarian regime, there is no independent judiciary, no possibility to appeal. So it is very difficult. Then look at India's case: the country of the colonisers, Great Britain, was a small island but India is a huge country. That is the power of India. In the case of Tibet it is the opposite. China is so powerful and Tibet is very very small, it can easily be wiped out. Another aspect is that at the time of India's freedom struggle the world was different from the world of today. Today there is much more support for human rights, for self-determination and the right of preservation of culture. These principles are now universally accepted, that is our advantage. The Chinese themselves, I think, don't believe in their own system, in their own ideology. They hold power by force.

DB/HvW: Surprisingly a large number of people in the West have turned to Buddhism. Whether they have become true Buddhists is a different matter, but Buddhism apparently has a great appeal. What surprises us is, in a world centred on material well being, on the concept of the fun society, how can people accept the Buddhist truth, that life is suffering, that the phenomena are transitory and that you have to liberate yourself from it? Do you have an explanation why Buddhism has become so attractive in the West?

DALAI LAMA: Firstly, people specially in the West are very fond of change, something new, something new.

DB/HvW: New clothes, new car, new religion...

DALAI LAMA: and hairstyle. Somebody told me, my spectacles were old fashioned, I need new ones (laughs).

The religion has served many generations and now they say it is old and they want something new. Maybe that is one factor. Then there are more serious people, who want to study ancient Indian thought and specially Buddhist philosophy, that is a very vast field. So they are attracted towards Buddhist philosophy not as Buddhists but they have an interest in the philosophy. Some people who believe in superstition and miracles are attracted towards Tibetan tantric practices. On the Tibetan side they also sometimes exaggerate like, if you receive this initiation you will live long and your health will increase. But the Tibetans themselves will have to demonstrate that they have long lives; sometimes our lamas have to be treated in a hospital in America or Europe—including myself—so our prayers, our miracle powers failed (laughs). Some Westerners have an attraction for rituals, that is unrealistic. Regarding peace of mind as a result of Buddhist practice, Buddhist philosophy, I think there is some benefit. That is through analytical meditation, study, think, think, think, not through miracles. So we do want to see philosophical study. Whether you become a Buddhist or not—I prefer not, remain a follower of your own religion—in the meantime adopt some Buddhist concepts about reality, all the suffering, suffering nature. Too much desire or too much greed and too much self-centredness lead to more trouble and more worries. There should be limits. Some people always want more and more. I have expressed my view that in things which are limited, like money, or material facilities etc. we should have contentment. If you have to face scarcity, because of your practice of contentment there will not be any great shock. But in other aspects like mental quality, altruism, infinite altruism, or knowledge—there is no limit. Therefore in such areas discontent is very good then you will further improve and further develop. I think we are usually the opposite: in the spiritual field we are content with small things, a little daily prayer, but in material matters there is discontent, always want want want, isn't it? (laughs).

DB/HvW: Your Holiness, how do you see your own future role?

DALAI LAMA: To me the most important thing is not just to think of my own country, but the most important thing to me is the usefulness of my existence. Some benefit for some people, that is my main concern. For that freedom is very important, freedom of speech and of movement. If that does not materialise in Tibet in my lifetime then I may die in this country peacefully, gracefully.

II
Tibetan Society in Exile

CHAPTER SEVEN

Government in Exile

TSEWANG PHUNTSO

Government and Administration

Today, after more than four decades in exile, the Tibetan refugee community has managed to rebuild their lives in a completely alien environment with about 130,000 refugees worldwide achieving almost total economic self-reliance.[1] The majority of the refugees in South Asia are settled in 46 settlements, comprising of 24 agricultural, 16 agro-industrial and 10 handicraft units.[2] Almost all the settlements are provided with primary and secondary schools, primary health care centres, and cooperative societies. In addition, most settlements have clinics to provide traditional Tibetan holistic health care services. There are also monasteries, nunneries and temples to fulfill the spiritual needs of the people.

For the organisation of the refugee community, and more importantly to guide the Tibetan struggle for national self-rule, the Tibetan Government-in-Exile with the Central Tibetan Administration (CTA) have set up their headquarters in Dharamsala, 500 kilometres north-west of New Delhi in the Indian state of Himachal Pradesh. The government and CTA have over the years served as a rallying point around which the suffering

[1]The editors are grateful to Mr. Masood Butt, Department of Information and International Relations, CTA, for updating this chapter.

[2]India 29, Nepal 10, and Bhutan 7 settlements; the figures overlap, as many settlements are engaged in agriculture and/or handicraft and agro-industries. Figures: Department of Home. CTA, March 2002.

but determined refugees can rebuild their lives and future. The Tibetans, both inside and outside Tibet, recognise the CTA as their sole and legitimate government. It is also increasingly recognised as the legitimate government and true representative of the Tibetan people by parliaments around the world.

The success of the Tibetan refugee community is attributed to its hard work, spirit of independence and adaptability. This has enabled the Tibetan refugees to make the best use of humanitarian assistance received from the government and people of India as well as from international aid organisations. Since institutional development is a key to the success of every organisation and society, it is not unfair to say that a part of the Tibetan success story should be attributed to the presence and effective functioning of the CTA. Their work is based on the guiding principles laid down right at the beginning by H.H. the Dalai Lama to preserve Tibetan culture, but at the same time modernise and democratise Tibetan society.

The Dalai Lama is and has always been the head of state and all executive power is vested in him. However he is probably the only ruler in the world, who has voluntarily given up political power step by step, on his own initiative and without pressure from below. In 1991 a constitution—the *Charter of the Tibetans in Exile*—was adopted by the Assembly of Tibetan People's Deputies (ATPD, the Parliament in Exile) and it has been amended eleven times. The most far-reaching amendments concern the election of the *kashag*, the cabinet, consisting of a maximum of seven ministers, called *kalon* with the *kalon tripa*, the prime minister, as chairman. Earlier the Dalai Lama used to appoint the *kalon tripa* as well as the members of the *kashag*. An amendment in the year 2000 however stipulates, that the Dalai Lama suggests three names for each post of *kalon* and the Assembly elects one each and the kashag in turn elects the kalon tripa from their midst. This amendment was soon followed by another in 2001 which introduced a very fundamental change: at the suggestion of H.H. the Dalai Lama, the ATPD decided that the *kalon tripa* must be elected directly by the people. The elections were held in the autumn of 2001 and Samdhong

Rinpoche was elected with 80 per cent of the votes. The new, directly elected *kalon tripa*, with the approval of the ATPD, appointed a small cabinet (*kashag*) of only three more *kalon*[3] (the maximum would be seven members of the kashag) The *kashag* executes the policy decisions of the Assembly and supervises the Central Tibetan Administration (CTA) which has seven departments.

Given below is an excerpt from an interview with the *kalon tripa* Samdhong Rinpoche:

Kalon Tripa Samdhong Rinpoche on the role of the Dalai Lama in political decision-making (Interviewed by Dagmar Bernstorff on 29 March 2003)

D.B.: Samdhong Rinpoche, the Tibetan Government-in-exile is based on the Charter of the Tibetans-in-Exile and gradually a democratic process has been introduced. You are the first directly elected *kalon tripa*. The Charter says comparatively little about the role of his Holiness the Dalai Lama in the political process. He is of course the Head of State apart from being the spiritual leader. Rinpoche, you have a long experience of working with the Dalai Lama, what is the role of His Holiness in the political decision making?

SAMDHONG RINPOCHE: The Charter did not change anything concerning the role of His Holiness. The Charter says, His Holiness is the head of the government, as well as the head of state. So whatever the government decides, the decision is made and implemented in the name of His Holiness. The Charter did not specify much detail in this respect. But His Holiness has the final authority to make any executive decision and that still exists here. If we propose anything as advice to His Holiness, the convention, the tradition is that the advice of the *kashag* is not binding on His Holiness. He has his free will to take any decision and that would be binding on the *kashag*. His Holiness plays a very important, effective role in keeping with

[3]See second photograph in the photo section.

the Charter. But he has several times announced his withdrawal. That is his wish. However to implement his wish as the first step the Charter has to be to amended. But now already His Holiness delegates his power more and more to the *kashag* and therefore he doesn't like us to report to him and take his approval on each and every decision. We understand that and we try to reduce the paperwork as far as possible.

D.B.: How often does the *kashag* meet with His Holiness?

SAMDHONG RINPOCHE: There was a tradition a long time ago that the *kashag* meets His Holiness every week when he is in Dharamsala. But that had already been reduced. So now in the last three months the *kashag* met His Holiness only once. And that was very brief. I met His Holiness twice on behalf of the *kashag*. So that makes it three, on average once a month.

D.B.: He has to give his consent to laws though.

SAMDHONG RINPOCHE: Yes and he could send them back.

D.B.: Do you have the impression that the Tibetan people are getting more familiar with democracy?

SAMDHONG RINPOCHE: Better. But His Holiness is impatient. We also feel some kind of impatience. The people are not picking up this kind of spirit. But it is understable, to change people's attitude needs some time. We had hoped that the second generation Tibetans-in-exile would be completely changed. But that didn't happen. Now the third generation might be better.

Kalon Tripa Samdhong Rinpoche on non-violence and governance. (Interviewed by Dagmar Bernstorff on 29 March 2003)

D.B.: Samdhong Rinpoche, you are now heading the government for over one and a half years, have you been able to introduce non-violence into the functioning of your government?

SAMDHONG RINPOCHE: We are in exile. We have no country to rule and therefore we are able to govern with quite a high degree of non-violence. For policy decisions, we have three basic criteria: Firstly, is the decision based on facts, secondly, is it based on truth; and thirdly, is it non-violent? If we are satisfied, yes, it will be non-violent and based on truth, then we take the decision by democratic procedures.

But there are many projects, which are already in progress and which are not non-violent. Yet we are not able to stop at random. For example, the government owns a number of hotels; we are privatising them. But it takes time and during this period we have to kill a lot of principles. In the hotels we have to serve non-vegetarian meals. This kind of direct violence is linked to the government and we can't say: you stop it right now. That is the big dilemma.

This is one example, there are many others. Personally I can go freely anywhere and oppose any kind of violence. I argue against violence and war with full force. But now I am leading an organisation, and there are limitations. Of course I need not convert everybody to non-violence, but I can't oppose them as forcefully as I used to oppose them.

Within two or three years we will be able to privatise all the business ventures. Then the government will not be directly dealing with any kind of violence as far as the economy is concerned. But in the administration some kind of discipline has to be imposed. Any person can commit illegalities or irregularities. Then we have to punish them and we are hurting people. But by and large we do not encourage or allow direct violence, structural violence or indirect violence. That is our effort. I think we made a good beginning.

D.B.: Have you tried to make changes in the Tibetan schools, to introduce non-violence in education?

SAMDHONG RINPOCHE: Yes we have tried and I am still trying. We are thinking of setting up experimental schools for non-violent education. Our new education policies are being drafted.

D.B.: What are the highlights of the new education policies?

SAMDHONG RINPOCHE: The highlights of the new education policy would be: first and foremost our emphasis is not on indoctrinating or conditioning the minds of the children but to help them to open their own intelligence. My basic idea of education is derived from Jiddu Krishnamurti. He says 'flowering of goodness and awakening of human intelligence is the purpose of education.' So we would like to help children to awaken themselves. That is one thing. Secondly education must aim at making the person self-supporting. Not seeking employment somewhere else, but to generate livelihood by themselves. The present education system is uprooting the younger generation from the settlements because of the search for employment. Therefore our community gets destroyed. We want to settle young people back in the Tibetan settlements and they should be self-supporting.

And the third principle is to make educated people non-violent, or at least less violent. That is the basic thrust of our education. I want people to change from competition to co-operation.

The Central Tibetan Administration

The Department of Religion and Culture seeks to preserve and promote Tibet's spiritual and cultural heritage, which is on the verge of extinction in its own homeland. The department gives back-up support and services to 223 monasteries and 15 nunneries,[4] with 11,067 monks and 1,230 nuns.[5] In addition, the Department supervises the work of several cultural institutes, such as the Central Institute for Higher Tibetan Studies at Sarnath in Varanasi, the Library of Tibetan Works and Archives in Dharamsala, the Norbulingka Institute at Sidhpur near Dharamsala, the Tibetan Institute of Performing Arts in Dharamsala, and Tibet House in New Delhi.[6]

[4]Figures from the Department of Religion and Culture, CTA, March 2002. The Bön Monasteries are included.

[5]Planning Council, Central Tibetan Administration, Tibetan Demographic Survey 1998, Vol. 1, Dharamsala 2000, 215. cf. chapters 15, 18.

[6]See chapter 15.

The Department of Home is responsible for all rehabilitation schemes. The department's activities and roles are broadly categorised into four divisions: administration, agriculture, planning and development, and welfare. The agricultural division supervises the agricultural works in the settlements, including animal husbandry, whereas the planning and development division engages in the overall planning of development works in the settlements, which includes conceiving, designing and formulating proposals for non-agricultural development projects. The Department of Home also maintains contact with various international aid agencies and organisations, involved in the rehabilitation of Tibetan refugees.

The Department of Finance formulates the annual budget of the CTA. Its income generation has recently been changed drastically. The Department used to run 25 business enterprises like hotels, restaurants, transport services, etc. A policy decision was taken by the new *kashag* headed by Samdhong Rinpoche. The *kalon tripa* considers entrepreneurial activity by the government in competition with private business to be violence. Moreover many of these firms were running at a loss. Therefore the *kashag* decided to privatise most of these businesses within three years and many of them have been disinvested by now. The department is responsible for collecting the annual voluntary contribution of Indian Rupees 36 per year (from the age group 6 to 18) and Rs 46 per year (from above 18 years) from all the Tibetans living in the Indian subcontinent and US$ 36 per year (from the age group 6 to 18) and US$ 46 per year (from above 18 years) from Tibetans living abroad. The department administers the functions of His Holiness the Dalai Lama's Charitable Trust, the Tibetan Administration's Welfare Society, and the Social and Resource Development Fund—all registered non-profit organisations for the development of the Tibetan community in exile.[7]

The Department of Education is entrusted with the

[7]Figures from Department of Finance, March 2002.

responsibility for the education of Tibetan refugee children and to work out a system that combines the best of modern education with Tibet's traditional culture so that the children retain their traditional values, and at the same time develop a modern, cosmopolitan outlook on life. The aim is to instill in them pride in their country and culture and equip them with technical and professional skills required for earning their living in an increasingly competitive world.[8] The department currently administers 82 schools of these 64 are in India, 14 in Nepal and 4 in Bhutan. The Sambhota Tibetan School Administration under the Department of Education looks after 16 of these schools. Twenty-eight Tibetan schools in India are functioning within the Central Tibetan School Administration under the Ministry of Human Resource Development, Government of India. The remaining 38 schools are run by autonomous bodies, such as the Tibetan Children's Village (18), the Tibetan Homes Foundation (2), the Snowlion Foundation, Nepal (14), and other bodies (4). As of March 2002, 27,879 Tibetan children are enrolled in the Tibetan schools in exile with a teacher-student ratio of 1:21.[9] The Department of Education also provides (97) scholarships for college and university education.

The Department of Security ensures the security of His Holiness the Dalai Lama and also monitors the developments in occupied Tibet and China. Besides, the Department runs Reception Centres in Kathmandu, New Delhi and Dharamsala to cater to the needs of new refugees arriving from Tibet; the Department helps the new refugees in finding employment and gaining admission into schools and monasteries; it provides a little capital for those who wish to start business enterprises in exile.

The Department of Health caters to the basic health needs of

---

[8]Central Tibetan Administration, *Tibet 84: 25 Years of Struggle and Reconstruction*, Dharamsala, 1984.

[9]Figures from Department of Education, March 2002. See also chapter 13.

the Tibetan refugees, running 61 primary health care centres and seven referral hospitals. It also looks after the *Men-Tsee-Khang* the Institute for Tibetan Medicine and Astrology with its branches.

The Department of Information and International Relations (DIIR) educates Tibetan and international public opinion on the political, human rights and environmental conditions in Tibet via print media, radio and Internet. The DIIR serves as a protocol office of the CTA and liaises with the international media and Tibet Support Groups throughout the world. It also supervises the work of the Offices of Tibet in 13 countries. These offices function as the embassies of the CTA and are based in New Delhi, Geneva, New York, Tokyo, London, Kathmandu, Budapest, Moscow, Paris, Canberra, Pretoria, Taipei, and Brussels.

The CTA has also three independent bodies: the Election Commission, the Public Service Commission and the Audit Office. The Election Commission conducts and oversees the elections for the ATPD, the *kashag* and local People's Assemblies in the settlements. The Public Service Commission is looking after recruitment, training, and appointment of the civil servants of the CTA. The Audit Office is responsible for auditing the accounts of all the CTA departments and its subsidiaries.

The Beginning of Tibetan Society in Exile

Government and administration were set up in a relatively short time. Soon after the arrival of the Dalai Lama in India on 31 March 1959, there was a steady flow of Tibetan refugees, which ultimately turned into a mass exodus. By the end of June 1959 almost 20,000 Tibetans had fled their homeland, the number eventually reached 85,000. While some refugees managed to bring their families, many had to flee alone, leaving their families behind. Similarly, while some managed to survive the ordeal of the difficult journey over the Himalayas, many, particularly old and young people, lost their lives on the way. When they arrived in India, most of the refugees were starving or wounded, ill from the low altitude, and stunned by the profound cultural shock of descending on an alien world. In such a desperate situation, the refugees naturally looked to the Dalai Lama for leadership and assistance. Therefore, the Dalai Lama's immediate concern was the survival problem of refugees, particularly the fate and future of young children. 'During the summer of 1959, my immediate task was to somehow save the refugees,' said the Dalai Lama.[10] 'It is even harder for children than for adults to be uprooted and taken suddenly to an entirely different environment, and many of them died in the early days from the change of food and climate. We had to do something drastic to preserve their health—and their education was also a matter of great importance.'[11]

On 25 April 1959, the Dalai Lama called an emergency meeting of the few senior Tibetan officials who had accompanied him from Tibet, and those who had arrived earlier in India, to discuss the situation and plan for the reconstruction in exile. The meeting was held in Mussoorie, a beautiful hill station in northern India, which served as the Dalai Lama's initial headquarters. The discussion at the meeting was also greatly influenced by the advice of the Indian Prime Minister, Pandit Jawaharlal Nehru, who had called on the Dalai Lama at Mussoorie the day before. His advice to the Dalai Lama was to 'rest and consider things well without being hasty'.[12] The meeting identified a few areas of concentration: rehabilitation of the Tibetan refugees, education of Tibetan children, preservation of Tibetan culture and identity, gathering and disseminating information regarding Tibetans both inside and outside Tibet, pursuing the Tibetan question at the United Nations, and preserving and promoting unity among the Tibetan refugee community.

---

[10]John F. Avedon, *In Exile from the Land of Snow*, New York 1984, p. 72.

[11]Dalai Lama, *My Land and My People*, New York 1962, p. 226.

[12]J.F. Avedon, supra, p. 70.

Soon after the meeting, the Dalai Lama re-established the Tibetan Government-in-Exile, to meet both the immediate and long-term needs of the Tibetan people. The Central Tibetan Administration of His Holiness the Dalai Lama is the continuation of the Government of independent Tibet. The Dalai Lama said: 'In 1959, when I escaped with a few cabinet ministers, the Tibetan government, which has a history of three hundred years, also came into exile. The exiled Tibetan government is not a new creation. Wherever the Dalai Lama resides, the Tibetan people consider that as the seat of the Tibetan government.'[13] The reestablished administration included the *kashag* Office and the other key departments (see above).

Rehabilitation of the Refugees

In the beginning, two large transit camps were set up in consultation with the Government of India: one at Missamari, located ten miles from Tezpur in the Indian state of Arunachal Pradesh; the other at Buxa Duar, a former British prisoner-of-war camp situated near the Bhutanese border in West Bengal. Within a few weeks after the setting up of the camps, 6,000 refugees arrived at Missamari and 1,000 at Buxa Duar. As the camps could accommodate not more than 9,000 persons between them, simultaneous efforts were made to occupy the refugees with road building works in the cooler regions of North India to prevent fatalities due to intense heat, overcrowding, and an epidemic of amoebic dysentery. The first batch of 3,394 people was sent for roadwork in Sikkim in September 1959 in several groups; and another batch of 400 to

[13]His Holiness the Dalai Lama's keynote speech to the Second International Conference of Tibet Support Groups, Bonn (Germany), 14 June 1996, text in: Tibetan Parliamentary and Policy Research Centre, The Political Philosophy of His Holiness the XIVth Dalai Lama, New Delhi 1998, p. 118ff.

Kalimpong, Darjeeling, and Shillong in North India and Bhutan. Later, in early 1960, more people were sent for roadwork in the North Indian States of Himachal Pradesh, Arunachal Pradesh and Jammu and Kashmir.

Agriculture-based Settlements

The Dalai Lama's vision of an exile society took shape in his new headquarters, an abandoned British hill station called Dharamsala. On 29 April 1960 the Dalai Lama moved to his new headquarters. In Dharamsala, the Dalai Lama revitalised his small administration-in-exile and called a special meeting of the deputies and staff members on 2 September 1960 to formulate new rules and regulations and reallocate portfolios of the *kalon*. Besides, he established a bureau[14] in New Delhi to serve as the Tibetan link with the Indian Government and with international relief agencies that were coming to the refugees' aid. Similarly, The Office of Tibet in New York was set up to raise the issue of Tibet at the United Nations and to disseminate information on Tibetans inside and outside Tibet.

Rehabilitation, however, was the immediate task at hand. Although the roadwork had provided the much-needed temporary employment for the refugees, it turned out to be hard and dangerous. Since most of the roadwork was carried out in mountain areas, which were almost perpendicular with sheer drops of many thousand metres into the valley below, the refugees, with no practical training of rock-climbing, had to risk their lives climbing up the cliffs to explode the blasts. Many died or were injured. The migratory and unsettled nature of the roadwork proved to be extremely hard, particularly for children and old people. Apart from the above difficulties, many roadworkers contracted tuberculosis and other communicable diseases due to lack of nutrition and sanitation.

In addition, right from the beginning, the Dalai Lama took

[14]Bureau of His Holiness the Dalai Lama, New Delhi.

into consideration that the Tibetan struggle might take generations and therefore, he was determined to make solid preparations. The Dalai Lama said: 'Some Tibetans at that time, however, put forward the idea of temporarily settling all the Tibetan refugees along the border areas of the Himalaya so that we would be ready to return to Tibet at the first opportunity. But we decided to give priority to more permanent rehabilitation with facilities to enable all the Tibetans to live in homogenous communities and provide the young with good education, modern as well as our own traditional education, so even if the struggle takes generations, new generations could replace the older ones and take on the responsibility.'[15]

With these thoughts in mind, the Dalai Lama approached Prime Minister Nehru for assistance in the permanent rehabilitation of the refugees. Nehru, on his part, canvassed the state governments for vacant land. Mysore state (later renamed Karnataka) immediately responded, offering initially 1,500 hectares of an uninhabited stretch of jungle in gently rolling hills at Bylakuppe, 80 kilometres west of Mysore city, situated at the altitude of 900 m above sea level.[16] The state government agreed to accept initially 3,000 Tibetan refugees and provided a grant of Indian Rs 3,784,800 for the rehabilitation project.

Soon after, the first Tibetan agricultural settlement was set up in December 1960 at Bylakuppe, accommodating a total of 3,217 Tibetan refugees by the end of 1965. For administrative reasons, the settlement was divided into six camps, each with 250–300 hectares of land. In the first few years, the settlers engaged in clearing jungle, digging wells, and constructing houses, during which they were paid daily wages and given regular rations. The settlers were divided into artificial families of five people, relatives or not, and each family was given two

[15]His Holiness the Dalai Lama's keynote address to the Second International Conference of Tibet Support Groups, Bonn (Germany), 14 June 1996, supra.

[16]The Office of H.H. the Dalai Lama, *Tibetans in Exile: 1959–1969*, A Report on Ten Years of Rehabilitation in India, Dharamsala 1969, p. 4.

and a half hectares of land. They were accommodated in one-room brick-walled, tile-roofed single story houses, built on a 50 sq.m, part of which also served as kitchen garden.

A co-operative society was set up in 1961 and later formally registered. The cooperatives procure and advance seeds, fertilisers, and pesticides; market agricultural produce collectively; and provide common services such as tractors, trucks and warehousing. Besides, the co-operatives play a crucial role in managing carpet weaving centres, flour mills, poultry farms and other ventures such as retail outlets in the settlements. In the same year, a school was opened in the settlements, which was later managed by the Tibetan Schools Society, an autonomous body under the Ministry of Education (later Human Resource Development) of the Government of India. When the Bylakuppe settlement first started, a small dispensary was set up in a tent to care for emergency medical needs of the refugees. Later in 1964, a special complex of concrete houses was built with assistance from foreign aid organisations, to accommodate a dispensary with in-patient facilities.

For the first five years, the settlers cultivated cotton, tobacco, rice, millet, paddy, lentils and oilseeds, all of which failed miserably. Farming in South India was so different from Tibet's unique high-altitude agronomy that many settlers became totally discouraged and helpless. However, the agony of the repeated crop-failure was solved in 1965, when a Swiss technical advisor, in consultation with the Agriculture University of Bangalore, conducted soil tests and also tested the yields of bullock-ploughed and tractor-ploughed fields. This test resulted in the cultivation of maize crop instead of cotton, tobacco and other crops and also the replacement of bullock ploughs by tractor ploughs. The new crop and methods proved so successful that, by the end of 1966, the settlement became self-supporting.

The Bylakuppe settlement had served as a model for planning other agriculture-based settlements later. In 1962, the second settlement was set up at Chaglang in the North Indian state of Arunachal Pradesh, accommodating 1,503 refugees by March 1963 on 1,900 acres of densely forested land. In February 1962, the third settlement was opened at Tezu in the Lohit district of Arunachal Pradesh, accommodating 864 Tibetan refugees. The fourth settlement, established at Mainpat in Chattisgarh (formerly part of the Indian State of Madhya Pradesh) in March 1963, accommodated 1,726 Tibetans on 750 hectares of land. In May 1963, the fifth settlement was set up at Chandragiri in the State of Orissa, accommodating 3,000 refugees. In April 1965, the sixth settlement was founded at Mundgod, nearly 495 km north of Bylakuppe, accommodating 4,000 refugees on 2000 hectares of land. By 1969, 21 agricultural settlements for over 20,000 refugees were operating in India, Nepal and Bhutan. Later, eight more agriculture-based settlements were set up at Hunsur and Kollegal in Karnataka State, Bhandara in Maharashtra State, Bomdila in Arunachal Pradesh, Changtang and Leh in Ladakh, Herbertpur in Uttaranchal (earlier part of Uttar Pradesh), see map on page...

Agro-Industrial Settlements

It was not viable to rehabilitate all the refugees in agriculture-based settlements. Not only was it hard to find relatively large tracts of land, it was also not practical to rehabilitate all the refugees in farming. Many refugees were traditionally nomads and traders and had no idea of farming. With this in view and also to expedite the process of rehabilitation, it was found necessary to seek other avenues of resettlement.

Thus, a plan was made to rehabilitate many of the refugees in small-scale industries. To facilitate this, the Tibetan Industrial Rehabilitation Society (TIRS) was established in October 1965, with its headquarters in New Delhi. It was registered as a charitable society under the Indian Societies Registration Act of 1860. For the next three years, the TIRS launched several small industrial projects. These included a wool mill at Bir , tea estates at Bir and Chauntra, Tibetan crafts at Bajnath, all in the Kangra Valley (Himachal Pradesh), a limestone quarry at Kumrao, a hydrated lime plant at Sataun, a fibre glass factory at Paonta

Sahib, and a handicraft centre in Puruwala (in the Sirmour District of Himachal Pradesh). More than 4,000 refugees were ultimately settled in these projects. They were meant not only to provide adequate employment opportunities for the residents, but also skills in different crafts. In each industrial centre school and health care facilities were provided by the TIRS with funds raised from foreign agencies. Besides, the TIRS established a Himalayan Marketing Society, based in New Delhi, to market the products of these settlements. However, many of these efforts failed due to lack of technical and managerial skills. The majority of the industrial settlements gradually began to depend more on traditional carpet weaving and roadwork in summer and woollen garment trade in Indian towns and cities in winter.

Handicraft-based Settlements

Over the centuries, Tibet had shared an intimate cultural and trade relationships with its neighbouring countries. These interactions resulted in the development of many traditional crafts in Tibet. These included metal work, woodcraft, clay modelling, appliqué work, *thangka* painting, handmade paper, leather work, weaving of woollen cloth and carpets etc. Although in the traditional society there were no institutions to promote these crafts, they were practiced in homes and the products were sold locally, or through traders to different parts of Tibet. These traditional crafts became extremely popular in some parts of Tibet: e.g. Gyangtse was known for quality carpets and Lokha for woollen cloth.

In the early 1960s, some Tibetan craftsmen established themselves in Kalimpong, the traditional Tibetan trading post in North India, and others settled temporarily in Darjeeling and Nepal. Thus, hoping to preserve and promote the traditional Tibetan crafts as well as to provide employment options for the refugees, the CTA, in consultation with the Government of India, set up several handicraft-based settlements as a part of the rehabilitation scheme. 'Our performing arts, our literature, science and religion as well as those crafts from which we could earn a livelihood—painting, metalcraft, architecture, woodworking and carpetmaking—these, we took special pains to safeguard. To achieve this we employed modern methods although they were altogether new to us and posed many difficulties,' said the Dalai Lama.[17]

The first handicraft-based settlement was founded on a two-hectare estate in Darjeeling in October 1959. The thirteenth Dalai Lama, during his exile from Tibet in 1910–11, had used this site as his temporary residence and therefore it has a special sentimental value for the Tibetans. The settlement or centre provides shelter and employment for 450 people. Education and medical needs of the refugees were also taken care of. Besides, the centre runs an old people's home and a crèche for small children. The centre's products, such as carpets, woollen sweaters, Tibetan women's aprons, wood carved decoration items, wooden toys, leather goods, etc. are being marketed locally as well as abroad with the help of aid agencies. Encouraged by the success of the first handicraft-based settlement, other centres were set up in the following years. These included the handicraft centres in Dalhousie, Dharamsala, Kalimpong, Shimla, Clement Town, Rajpur, and Dehradun—all in India. Similar settlements were also set up in Nepal. In these handicraft-based settlements, cooperatives were established to procure raw materials and market the products. While the cooperatives marketed the settlement's produce both in India and abroad, the settlers engaged also in individual trade of sweaters—knitted initially by themselves, but later bought from the factories in Ludhiana (Punjab)—to supplement their income. Each winter they set up makeshift bamboo-walled and plastic-topped stalls on the sidewalks of bazaars and marketplaces all over India. By the latter half of the 1960s, sweater-selling became the supplementary trade of the majority of Tibetan refugees.

In March 2002, 85,382 Tibetan refugees were rehabilitated

---

[17] J. Avedon, supra, p. 92.

in the Indian sub-continent in 29 settlements in India with a population of 78,791, ten settlements in Nepal with 4,952, and 7 in Bhutan with 1,639 settlers. There are still 25,344 Tibetans outside organised units working in private enterprise or service industries under 10 Tibetan Welfare Offices and one Chief Representative's Office in India.[18]

New Challenges

The death of Chairman Mao Zedong in 1976 and the end of the Cultural Revolution in China and Tibet resulted in the opening of China to the outside world. This dramatic change also led to the opening of Tibet and the first-post 1959 contact between Beijing and Dharamsala in March 1979. Many Tibetans, both inside and outside Tibet, seized the opportunity to undertake the arduous cross-Himalayan journey and visit their family members and relatives. Many families met for the first time after two decades of separation. But with the passage of time, a steady stream of new refugees from Tibet came to settle in India and Nepal.

From 1987–1994 Tibet was rocked by a series of demonstrations for independence. The Chinese reacted by escalating the machinery of repression, especially against those involved in demonstrations. This made life in Tibet all the more difficult, resulting in a mammoth increase in the flow of refugees. Between 1986–1996 some 18,700 refugees arrived in India and Nepal.[19] The situation became still worse after 1994 when the Chinese government introduced harsher policies to deal with Tibetan nationalism. More than 44 per cent of the new refugees are teenagers and young adults (age 14–25); 33 per cent adults (age 26–59); more than 17 per cent young children (age 0–13); and only 5 per cent are over the age of 60.[20]

---

[18]Figures: Department of Home, March 2002.

[19]Planning Council, *Integrated Development Plan—II (1995–2000)*, Central Tibetan Administration, Dharamsala 1994, p. 42.

[20]Ibid, p. 43.

In order to look after the needs of these new refugees, the CTA opened a Reception Centre in Dharamsala in 1990. Later, its branches were opened in Kathmandu and Delhi. While the Kathmandu Reception Centre is supported jointly by the UNHCR and CTA, the centres in Dharamsala and Delhi are funded by the CTA with support from the United States Government. When the refugees reach Nepal, the Reception Centre in Kathmandu provides them with shelter, food, and financial assistance to meet their travel expenses from Kathmandu to Delhi and then to Dharamsala. Once they reach Dharamsala, the Reception Centre arranges an audience for them with the Dalai Lama and then seeks their admission in various institutions.

The rehabilitation of the children below the age of 18 and monks and nuns is comparatively easier as the children can be sent to the existing boarding schools—either at the Tibetan Children's Villages or Tibetan Homes Foundation in Mussorie—and the monks and nuns to the monasteries and nunneries in India. The rehabilitation of adult refugees is problematic. Though a few adult refugees were rehabilitated in the existing handicraft-based settlements in the past, many could not be integrated properly. There are several problems associated with this. Many of the adult refugees are unskilled and most of the existing settlements are overcrowded. The Government of India cannot provide additional land to rehabilitate more refugees. Hence the CTA gives a lump sum grant ranging from Rs. 1,500 to 3,000 for those who wish to start a small business. For others, the administration has opened, since 1993, an Adult Education Centre (AEC), renamed Sherab Gatsel Lobling in Dharamsala, where the refugees receive five years of full-time education in English, Tibetan and rudimentary mathematics as well as in arts and crafts. Recently, with the help of the Danish International Aid Agency (DANIDA), the CTA has initiated a project to build a permanent vocational school complex in Dehradun.[21]

[21] *The Social and Resource Development Fund (SARD): Annual Report 1998/1999.*

Apart from this, the Department of Health is taking care of the health needs of the new refugees. Since many of the new refugees are torture victims, the Department of Health has started a special programme to provide psychological counseling and medical care to them. The Department of Religion and Culture provides stipends to the new refugees admitted in monasteries and nunneries; it also meets the cost of additional teachers required to teach the new refugees. The Department of Security interviews every new refugee on the situation in Tibet and documents their account.

Redesigning the Rehabilitation Scheme

Over the years, the rehabilitation scene had changed considerably. The landholdings in the settlements have shrunk with the natural growth of the population and a new generation of educated and skilled Tibetans has thrown up new opportunities and challenges. This requires a new in-depth appraisal of the on-going rehabilitation work in order to chart a new course for the future. A senior Indian official said that the problem of Tibetan refugees was basically a problem of three generations: the generation who came as refugees, the generation born in India and the generation that was still young. This posed peculiar problems of rehabilitation and reconstruction. He said, 'While the problems are known, sometimes the answers are difficult to find. Or even if we know the answers, sometimes implementation is difficult.'[22]

In view of this situation, a high-level workshop was organised in New Delhi in October 1986 to review the situation and restructure the scheme. At the conference, the then Indian Home Minister, Mr. Buta Singh, emphasised the need for more diversification to target the needs of the second generation and timely execution of the rehabilitation programmes both by the

[22]B.J. Heerji, Additional Secretary of the Ministry of Home Affairs (Rehabilitation Division), Government of India, 20 October 1986.

respective state governments and the Tibetans.[23] An Indian expert on small-scale industries said, 'The present generation of Tibetan refugees, aware that their traditional vocations are not going to help them in the long run, must realise that small-scale industries is an area of great potential which is yet to be introduced to this group of beneficiaries.'[24]

The workshop, which was attended by officials of the concerned Ministries of the Government of India and state governments, as well as by Tibetan officials, discussed in detail various issues ranging from water supply and roads in the settlements to working capital for the cooperative societies, rehabilitation of additional refugees, education of children, acquisition of immovable property by Tibetan refugees, etc. The Chief of the World Bank Mission at the workshop emphasised the importance of maintaining cohesiveness with physical approximity as this, he said, would help the Tibetan refugees to preserve their culture and identity in exile. The UNHCR Representative assured that his agency would continue to provide 'legal protection' to the Tibetan refugees, though 'material assistance' ended in 1975 as the Government of India and UNCHR considered the Tibetan refugees in India as economically self-sufficient.

In view of this, efforts have been made over the years to redesign and diversify the rehabilitation scheme. The Planning Council was instituted in 1988 to improve the use of the CTA's human, physical and financial resources in the development of the refugee community. The council was instrumental in establishing the Handicraft Development Board and the Tibetan Computer Resource Centre, and introducing the concept of micro-enterprise and micro-credit in the community. The

---

[23]Council for Home Affairs of His Holiness the Dalai Lama, *Conference-cum-Workshop on Tibetan Refugees in India: A report*, Dharamsala, 1986.

[24]S.B. Shrivastava, Deputy Director, Industrial Management & Training, Department of Small Scale Industries of the Government of India.

Council also initiated the five-year integrated development plan (1995–2000) for the CTA and efforts were made to improve communication and coordination among various sectors of the CTA, both in Dharamsala and the peripheral settlements. Recently, the Planning Council has conducted a detailed demographic survey[25] of the Tibetan refugee community and a random sampling survey of the socio-economic status of the community. These studies will definitely be of great use for the proper planning of the development initiatives in the community.

In addition, the Department of Home has also taken a more aggressive approach recently in this direction and has launched the 'second phase of the rehabilitation and reconstruction work' by mechanising agricultural production and diversifying the products and also introducing micro-enterprises in the settlements. 'We propose the second phase of development as a means of achieving greater self-reliance, self-sufficiency and sustainability,' said Mr. Tempa Tsering, then Minister of Home.[26]

Financing the Administration

The central and state governments of India have played a key role in financing the rehabilitation work of Tibetan refugees. The Indian government finances the Tibetan schools under the scheme Central Tibetan Schools Administration (CTSA). The US Congress supports the health services. In addition, many international aid agencies, private organisations and individuals have played a significant role.[27] Further resources for the rehabilitation work and more importantly to run the Central

---

[25]Planning Council, Central Tibetan Administration, Tibetan Demographic Survey, 2 vol., Dharamsala 2000.

[26]Department of Home, *CTRC Update 2000*, Central Tibetan Administration, p. 1.

[27]The Department of Home in its CTRC Update 2000 lists 64 international donor organisations and 29 individual donors (editor's note).

Tibetan Administration, comes from the Dalai Lama's personal funds. In 1950, when the Chinese invasion of eastern Tibet forced the Dalai Lama to move his headquarters temporarily from Lhasa to Dromo, he brought with him some gold dust, silver bars and other treasures on the advice of his ministers, to use in future emergencies.[28] Although the Dalai Lama soon returned to Lhasa, his treasures were sent straight to Sikkim, where they remained hidden for nine years in the King of Sikkim's abandoned stables located on the hillside below the palace in Gangtok. This treasure was later converted into currency, materialising nearly one million US$.[29] With this money, the Charitable Trust of His Holiness the Dalai Lama was established in January 1964. The investment of the trust's fund was made primarily on two projects: a 10–ton unit paper mill in Madhya Pradesh and a 30,000–ton cast iron spun pipe plant in Bihar. Although the income from the investment in company shares and bank deposits was not very satisfactory, the trust served as primary source of seed money for every exile project at the initial stage.

Towards the end of 1978, the trust disinvested its funds from company shares and bank deposits and began to invest directly in various income-generating projects. These included: Tibetan Woollen Yarn Centre in Panipat in Haryana State, Charitrust Tibetan Handicraft Exports in New Delhi, Gurupura Village Hand-Spinning and Weaving Centre in Hunsur (South India), Centre for Tibetan Arts and Crafts in Dharamsala, and other training projects. These projects not only provide employment opportunities to many Tibetan youths, but the income from these ventures also contributes to running of the CTA. Between 1964 and 1989, the trust contributed Rs 6,140,000 (approximately US$ 136,400) towards social, health, cultural, and educational activities.[30]

---

[28]Dalai Lama, *My Land and My People*, supra, p. 85.

[29]J. Avedon, supra, p. 91.

[30]*H.H. the Dalai Lama's Charitable Trust: 1964–1989*—A souvenir brochure, p. 11.

His Holiness the Dalai Lama's Charitable Trust is currently administered by the Department of Finance along with two other non-profit organisations: Tibetan Administration's Welfare Society (TAWS) and The Social and Resource Development Fund (SARD).

Voluntary Contribution from the Tibetan Public

In 1972, a section of the Tibetan refugees initiated a campaign to make voluntary, annual contribution of Rs 12 (now Rs 46) from every Tibetan refugee, plus two per cent of the salary, and 10 percent of the net profit from institutions to cover part of the recurring costs of the CTA. This campaign received massive support from the Tibetan refugees and soon chapters of the Tibetan Freedom Movement, which took the responsibility of collecting the voluntary contribution from the refugees, sprung up in all the Tibetan refugee settlements. Apart from this, some Tibetan sweater-sellers also initiated a movement to collect annual contributions from all the sweater-sellers. Thus, over the years, a substantial amount of money was contributed voluntarily by the Tibetan refugees towards the maintenance of the CTA. This voluntary contribution from the refugees amounted to approximately 46 million Indian rupees for the financial year 2001–2002, about 1 million US dollars.

The Central Tibetan Administration is linked closely with the Tibetan people in the settlements. As nearly half of the migrants live in the Indian state of Karnataka the CTA posted a Chief Representative there to liaise both with the settlements and the State Government and facilitate the development programmes, and above all 'To maintain and strengthen the spiritual and political linkages between Tibetans in South India'.[31] At the same time, the CTA connects with the international community through their representatives in thirteen countries.

---

[31]See leaflet: Office of the Chief Representative cum South Zone Development Coordinator, Bangalore, March 2000.

CTA Organisational Structure

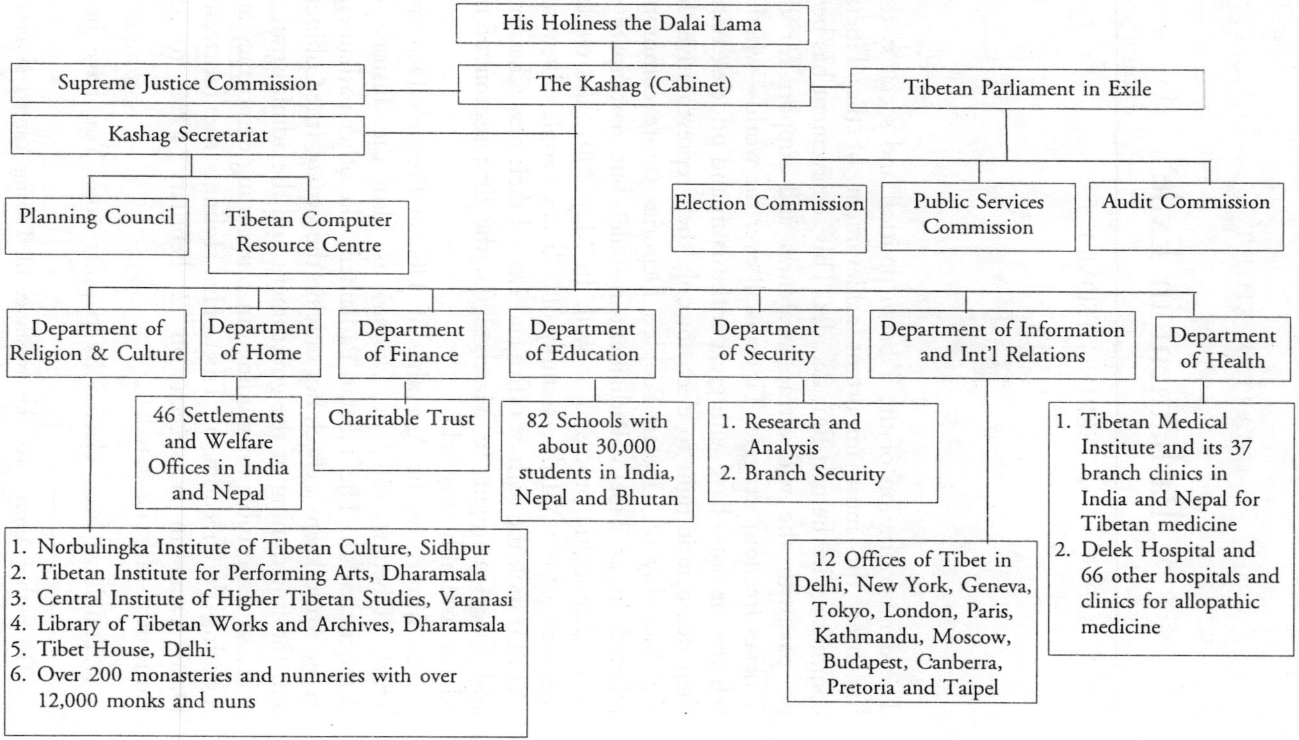

CHAPTER EIGHT

Parliament in Exile*

TSERING TSOMO

The democratisation of the Tibetan political and social system has been the most important achievement of the Tibetan community in the past four decades. This achievement has been on par with the widespread awareness and support for the Tibetan freedom struggle. Tibetans all over the world—whether refugees or not—have with great enthusiasm and pride exercised their democratic right to elect not only their representatives for the Assembly of Tibetan People's Deputies (more commonly referred to as Tibet's Parliament-in-Exile) but participate in other democratic processes as well. In May 2001, the elected members of the XIIIth Assembly of Tibetan People's Deputies (ATPD) took the oath of office and elected their new Chairman and Vice Chairman. In March 2003, the fifth session of the XIIIth Assembly was held.

The history of the Assembly of Tibetan People's Deputies, which Tibetans call the *chithue,* is also the history of democratisation. The Tibetan Parliament like other parliaments in the world keeps a check not only on the *kashag,* (the Cabinet), and the functioning of the government and the administration, it is also responsible for guiding our burgeoning democracy and restoring the freedom of Tibet. His Holiness the fourteenth Dalai Lama in a speech on 2 February 1996 to the Parliament-in-Exile stated:

...You have been elected by popular vote. You have been

*The author appreciates the assistance of Tsering Yangki la in the preparation of this article.

> elected by the Tibetans living in exile. We do not have our country. We are living in exile as refugees at the moment. Under such exiled conditions, the purpose of doggedly establishing a Parliament, a cabinet and a government-in-exile is not only for the sake of the over 100,000 Tibetans in exile....But our chief objective is to restore the freedom of our lost country, and before that our immediate responsibility is to urgently solve the deteriorating conditions inside Tibet.[1]

Experience with the Parliamentary Form of Democracy

During a period of great turmoil in the world and confusion amongst the newly-exiled Tibetan community, Tibetans embraced the global democratic revolution under the guidance and initiatives of the Dalai Lama. In 1960, at Bodh Gaya, the place of Lord Buddha's enlightenment, the religious and temporal leader of Tibetans laid the foundations of democratic rule—a Tibetan democracy-in-exile, which would be rooted in non-violence and peace, and where religion and polity would coexist harmoniously, a system which would be endowed with the characteristics of liberal democracies yet possess the values and traits of Tibetan culture and tradition.

The fourteenth Dalai Lama has often outlined the reasons for his promotion of democracy in Tibetan exiled society. Years before Tibet lost its independence, he had taken initiatives to create a more democratic society through the appointment of a Reforms Committee. However the Chinese annexation of Tibet brought this effort to a halt. In his Foreword to the *Constitution for Tibet* promulgated in 1963, His Holiness the Dalai Lama stated:

---

[1]Speech at the Assembly of Tibetan People's Deputies, 2 February 1996, in: A.A. Shiromany, ed., *The Political Philosophy of His Holiness the XIV Dalai Lama-Selected Speeches and Writings,* Tibetan Parliamentary and Policy Research Centre, New Delhi 1998, p. 321.

> Even prior to my departure from Tibet in March 1959, I had come to the conclusion that in the changing circumstances of the modern world, the system of governance in Tibet must be modified and amended so as to allow the elected representatives of the people to play a more effective role in guiding and shaping the social and economic policies of the State. I also firmly believed that this could be done through democratic institutions based on social and economic justice.[2]

Our leader perceives democracy as very important for Tibet's future polity and society. He further explained the reasons for his promotion of democracy:

> If Tibet is to survive as an equal of the modern international community, it should reflect the collective potential of all citizens, and not rely on one individual. This means the people must be actively involved in charting their own political and social destiny.[3]

His Holiness also argued that the strengthening of democratic norms followed in exile will not only have a strong impact on democratisation in Tibet but also effectively counter Chinese propaganda. The Chinese government continues to assert that the Tibetan national struggle aims at reviving the old society. However, as the Dalai Lama in his speeches clearly affirms again and again, no Tibetan whether in exile or in Tibet has any desire to restore Tibet's past social order.

His Holiness the Dalai Lama envisions a future Tibet, which will have a multiparty system with separation of powers between what we commonly refer to as the three pillars of democracy: the legislature, the executive and the judiciary. Today His Holiness' firm commitment to a 'secular education of his people and to the establishment of representative, democratic

[2] *Tibet's Parliament in Exile*, Tibetan Parliamentary and Policy Research Centre, New Delhi 1999, p. 11.

[3] Introduction to the Guidelines on Future Tibet's Constitution, in: A.A. Shiromany, ed., supra, p. 277.

institutions' has been gradually implemented in an exiled setting.[4]

The Origins

The history of Tibetan democracy in exile began with the Tibetans' surprise at the initiatives of the Dalai Lama and their adamant refusal to accept anything that would erode our leader's power over the polity. As mentioned earlier, it was in Bodh Gaya in 1960, that the Dalai Lama stressed the urgency for the Tibetan Government-in-Exile to break with the past and move towards a democratic society. The spiritual and temporal leader advised the Tibetans in exile to elect from amongst themselves people who were not only knowledgeable but also competent and patriotic. He asserted the need for collective action and individual responsibility towards an evolving and vibrant democratic polity.

One could divide the evolution of the Tibetan Parliament into two periods. The first period from 1960 to 1990, followed by the second period from 1990 to the present. The comparative analyses of the two periods are based upon aspects of changes in the membership, tenure, and the increase in the role and power of the Parliament.

1960–90

The first Tibetan representative body known as the Commission of Tibetan People's Deputies was elected on the basis of the three provincial regions of Tibet (*Cholkha*): Ü Tsang, Dotoe and Domey (the latter two provinces better known as Kham and Amdo respectively), and a representative each from the four religious sects, the Nyingma, Kagyu, Gelug and Sakya and the traditional Bön religion.[5] The first Deputies were sworn in on

[4] *Tibet's Parliament In Exile*, supra, p. 5.

[5] The exiled community is spread all over India and the world making the electoral process complicated. However this arrangement is maintained in order to retain a sense of identity linking us to Tibet.

2 September 1960; this day is still observed as Democracy Day by the Tibetans in exile.

A major change of the election procedure followed the drafting of a democratic Constitution. The process began in 1961, and the Draft Constitution was promulgated on March 10, 1963. The Provisional Constitution implemented in exile not only democratised the Tibetan polity but also included international human rights instruments, particularly the Universal Declaration of Human Rights and the Fundamental Principles of the Law of the Land. However the ultimate decision as to whether to amend, adopt or reject the Constitution was to be decided when Tibetans living in exile and in Tibet were united in a free Tibet.

During the infancy of the Tibetan Parliament, often due to inexperience, the Deputies left the supervision of the administration in the hands of the Cabinet Ministers and Department Heads. Moreover the role of the Deputies was nominal, their power was limited and the Commission of Tibetan People's Deputies did not have a Secretariat to back up their work. However through the years changes occurred, and in 1963 the Assembly was entrusted with the authority to end the traditional practice of appointing monks and lay officials (*Tsedrung and Shodrung*) to each office as well as to abolish the hereditary titles and prerogatives. In 1966 the Deputies' powers were further enhanced with the authority to oversee the working of the Departments of the Government-in-Exile although the ministers (*kalon*) continued to remain beyond Parliament's scrutiny. The Third CTPD took up their new responsibility by initially attaching Deputies to various offices, and later introduced annual meetings of the heads of the settlements and monastic institutions in order to review their activities. With the increase in responsibility, a separate Assembly House with a Secretariat was set up. After the sixth session in 1979 the Parliament was renamed the Assembly of Tibetan Peoples' Deputies (ATPD).

The membership of the Assembly increased from thirteen members in the first Assembly to seventeen in the second with three additional seats reserved for women from each of the three regions and one eminent person nominated by the Dalai Lama. In 1991 the membership was increased to 44–46, including two reserved seats for women from each of the three provinces. The tenure of the Deputies initially was three years. However in 1985, during the VIIIth ATPD, it was extended to five years.

The 1990s: A Decade of Reforms

The 1990s witnessed a radical change for Tibetan democracy in exile. This change must be attributed to the vision and leadership of the Dalai Lama. Since the process of democratisation began, he has emphasised the need for Tibetans to elect their own government, gradually relinquishing his own powers. When the synopsis of the draft Constitution for a future free Tibet was publicised, Tibetans called for a change in the clause that gave Parliament the power to even impeach the Dalai Lama! The Tibetans would not hear of any clause that however subtly implied the effacement of His Holiness' authority. By the late 1980s however, His Holiness the Dalai Lama made his position known that once Tibet became free he would not assume any political power.

In 1989 at the Sixteenth General Body Meeting of Government officials, representatives of settlements and monastic institutions as well as representatives of non-governmental organisations, the Dalai Lama called for further reforms. However it was on 11 May 1990 that he relinquished his power to appoint the *kalon*, the cabinet ministers. In his address he announced:

> From now on the people's decision will be final. I feel that the Dalai Lama should have no role here. The future Assembly will be entrusted with the power of appointing the *kalon*.[6]

His Holiness however reserved the right to nominate not less than double the number of candidates for the office of *kalon*, for the Assembly to choose from. The tenth Assembly was thereafter

[6] *Tibet's Parliament in Exile*, supra, p. 16.

dissolved and the *kalon* chosen by the Dalai Lama resigned, leading to an interim period from 12 May 1990 to 28 May 1991 when more major changes were introduced.

Since 1991, the ATPD has matured into a responsible representative body, guarding the rights of the community in exile, and for a future Tibet by directing the executive through open parliamentary procedures. The process of self-government was accelerated in 1991 with the increase in the number and the rights of the members.

The Charter of Tibetans-in-Exile

A decisive step towards genuine democracy was the adoption of the 'Charter of Tibetans in Exile' in 1991. As early as 1961 the 'Constitution for Future Tibet' was promulgated after the Dalai Lama's declaration in favour of a democratic system of governance. The Constitution documents democratic reforms, which would serve as a guideline and a basis for future Tibet's policy and development. However, the Constitution was drafted for an independent country, and could not be faithfully implemented in an exiled setting.

The 'Charter for Tibetans-in-exile' is a document prepared for the interim period in exile. The Constitution Redrafting Committee, instituted by the Dalai Lama, drafted it in 1990. The Charter was after careful deliberations unanimously passed by the XIth Assembly on 14 July 1991, the Dalai Lama had approved the Charter on 28 June 1991.

The Charter is the supreme law governing the Central Tibetan Administration and is binding on all Tibetans under the jurisdiction of the Government-in-Exile. The document takes into account the realities of our exiled situation. It also complies with International Law and more importantly with the laws of India.

The Charter lays down the rights and duties of the exiled community. While serving as a guideline in exile it does not ignore the homeland. Article 15—the Directive Principles clearly states the achievement of Free Tibet as 'the legitimate goal of the Tibetan people.'[7] It therefore also serves as a model for the future and for a free Tibet.

The Charter has 11 chapters, with 115 articles. So far there have been 11 amendments. The latest amendment was made in March 2001 and concerns the direct election of the Chief *kalon* or *kalon tripa*, his/her tenure, elections of the Ministers (*kalon)*, duties and tenure of the *kashag* and its dissolution.

Structure of the Assembly of Tibetan People's Deputies

The Tibetan Parliament in exile is a unicameral legislature—it has just one house. And it is, of course, a legislative body without political parties. In the present XIIIth Assembly there are 46 seats. Ten Deputies have been elected from each of the three Tibetan *cholkhas* (provincial regions), two nominated by each of the four sects of Tibetan Buddhism and two from the Bön religion (these do not necessarily have to be monks). Two Deputies come from the Tibetan settlements in Europe and one from North America, while between one to three members are nominated by the Dalai Lama from amongst Tibetans who are outstanding philosophers, literary persons, scientists and social workers.

The Chairman and the Vice Chairman are either unanimously selected or elected by secret ballot by the members of the Assembly. The present Chairman and Vice-Chairperson are Mr. Pema Jugney and Ms. Dolma Gyari respectively. The two have the authority to represent the Assembly in dealing with organisations and individuals. They preside over the meetings of the Standing Committee and other parliamentary committees and are responsible for the administration of the Parliament. The Parliamentary Secretariat, which co-ordinates the parliamentary procedures and recordings of the sessions, assist them. The News Bulletin on the session proceedings produced by the ATPD is

[7] *Charter of the Tibetans in Exile,* (in Tibetan), Assembly of Tibetan Peoples Deputies, 2nd Edition, Dharamsala 1998, p. 6.

distributed to the Tibetan settlements and other offices through the diaspora community.

The Assembly of forty-six members is a large body and not all members stay in Dharamsala, the seat of the Tibetan Government-in-Exile. The Standing Committee looks after the day-to-day responsibilities of the ATPD. Except for legislative and financial matters, the Standing Committee in its power and functions is equivalent to the full Parliament. The Standing Committee consists of:

- Two members from the representatives of each province,
- One member from the representatives of each religious lineage,
- One member from the nominees of His Holiness the Dalai Lama.[8]

Whenever necessary the members of the Assembly are divided into various committees to facilitate a more efficient and coordinated working of the House.

The Assembly meets twice a year, in March and in September for about two weeks. The issues of discussion range from local matters to international affairs. The schedule of the House while in session is delineated as following:

- Question hour
- Statements of the *kalon* or individual members
- Passing of legislation
- Voting of Grant-in Aid and control of public finances
- Zero hour
- Processing of miscellaneous budgets
- Debate on motions or statements.[9]

Role, Powers and Responsibilities of the ATPD

His Holiness the Dalai Lama has in his numerous speeches to the members often emphasised the need to invest more powers

---

[8]Tibet's Parliament in Exile, supra, p. 5.

[9]Ibid.

in Parliament since they are the elected representatives of the Tibetan people in exile. Simultaneously he has called upon the representatives to be accountable and responsible to the Tibetan people in exile and in Tibet. He has stressed upon the responsibility of every voter to be unbiased of gender, provincial and individual animosities while electing their representatives and to elect persons who possess quality and aptitude.

The main powers and responsibilities of the ATPD include election of members of the Cabinet, examining the decisions of the *kashag* and its administration in the light of the policies and programmes adopted by the Assembly, enacting laws and frame rules and regulations, issuing policy decisions, as well as controlling and overseeing the finances, including the expenditure of the government-in-exile. The Assembly also oversees the functioning of the local Assemblies, the work of the Tibetan Freedom Movement subcommittees (*Bhod Rawang Dhenpai Legul*). It hears public grievances and petitions of Tibetans in exile, and monitors the aspirations and problems of the Tibetan people, inside and outside Tibet.[10]

The Assembly also approves the appointment of the Supreme Justice Commission, the highest judiciary body.

Today the Parliament is not only a law-making body. It has become more and more a multi-functional institution, performing a variety of roles—many of these are interrelated.

Recent Reforms in the Election of the Chairman of the Cabinet

Since the XIth ATPD, the Parliament had the power to elect the Cabinet (*kashag*) members.. The most recent changes in the Charter concern the election of the Chairman (*kalon tripa*) of the Cabinet (*kashag*). These recent reforms aim at giving the people a direct role in the election of their leaders.

In September 1998, the Dalai Lama wrote to the Assembly calling upon the members to consider a change in the election

---

[10]Ibid.

process of the Tibetan Government. After major discussions and deliberations, in September 2000, the ATPD amended the articles in the Charter that pertained to the election of the *kalon* (ministers). It was then decided that instead of the Dalai Lama nominating candidates for the Cabinet, he would only nominate three candidates for the Chairman of the Cabinet (*kalon tripa*). The Assembly would then elect one of the candidates as *kalon tripa,* who in turn would have the freedom and authority to choose and present his/her team of cabinet members to the Tibetan Parliament, which has the power to approve.

However, during the last session of the XIIth ATPD (March 2001) another fundamental change in the election of the Chairman of the Cabinet was introduced.. At the suggestion of the Dalai Lama, the rules of the election of the *kalon tripa* were further changed and the Tibetan people in exile were given the right to elect the Chairman of the Cabinet directly. In his address to Parliament on March 16, 2001, the Dalai Lama stated that the previous practice by which he proposed the names of the candidates for the chief *kalon* to be voted on by the ATPD left him entirely unsatisfied and unconvinced and was also inconvenient to him. A direct election of a chief *kalon* by the public would certainly have the mandate and popular backing of the people.

The Spiritual and Temporal Leader Gives up His Privilege, to Nominate the Cabinet and its Chairman

It was to be a two-stage process—primary elections followed by the main elections. The primary elections for the office of chief *kalon* were held on 12 May 2001 and the Ven. Samdhong Rinpoche, Chairman of XIth and XIIth ATPD received over 80 per cent of the preliminary votes. The final elections were held on 29 July 2001 and by 28 August 2001, Ven. Samdhong Rinpoche was declared elected as the *kalon tripa*. The Parliament session of September 2001 saw the members unanimously electing the three candidates chosen by the chief *kalon* to be his colleagues.

One of the most significant developments in the process of democratization was the direct election of the chairman of the cabinet, kalon tripa, by Tibetans all over the world except inside Tibet in one day in 2001.

This new procedure brought forth a change of guard at the helm of affairs. Ven. Prof. Samdhong Rinpoche was elected with an overwhelming majority and took over as kalon tripa, chairman of the cabinet. He decided to nominate only a small cabinet of three other colleagues, (the maximum being seven), firmly entrenched in the adage 'small hearth, big fire'. With his clarity of vision on political, administrative, social, educational and economic matters, Samdhong Rinpoche introduced a number of initiatives as the kalon tripa, the chairman of the cabinet. The Assembly response was equally enthusiastic.

In his first cabinet statement Samdhong Rinpoche outlined a number of broad policy matters: creating a conducive atmosphere for the consistently stated policy of negotiated settlement with the Government of China; privatization and disinvestment of government-run businesses; to introduce natural and organic farming methods; strengthening and revitalising co-operative societies for a self-sustaining refugee community; to Tibetanize the syllabus in Tibetan schools up to higher secondary level; presentation of the synopsis of a 'Tibetan Non-violent Grand Strategy' were some of the highlights. The members vigorously discussed these matters and approved all the policies of the new kashag.

The kalon tripa sought to bring transparency into the functioning of the executive and the financial position of the Government. For effective governance, many committees were set up to look into matters which need urgent remedial measures. For the first time, the Finance Minister brought out a report on the status of the financial condition of the department. These are steps initiated with a view to making Tibetan democracy based on truth and non-violence.

Despite many earlier efforts, financial accountability of the Executive to the Legislature remained one of the most contentious issues between the cabinet and the Assembly. This too has been resolved following the cabinet decision to seek sanction by the Assembly of all the funds, including project based funds, which used to be administered by the departments without transparency.

Over the years the members of the ATPD, given their accumulated experience and knowledge, have matured to a great extent. The quality of debate has improved but still needs much more to be desired. Due to the peculiar and distinct features of the Tibetan Government-in-exile, for instance, the kalon, the members of the cabinet, are not Members of the Assembly and in the absence of political parties, the Members have to play the role of both Government and opposition depending on the issues. An effective scrutiny of the functioning of the Government has been established and the Members do provide a bridge between the Government and the people. A little more effort on the part of the Deputies is desirable. But very positive signs of a vibrant democratic set up are manifest which could be emulated in future Tibet.

PENPA TSERING

The Challenges Ahead

Tibetan democracy in exile has come a long way. This is evident in the functioning of the Assembly of Tibetan People's Deputies, the highest legislative institution. Tibetans have become more enthusiastic, mature, and relatively more responsible in the exercise of their democratic rights. Political participation has increased and the recent Assembly elections in the spring of 2001 not only witnessed active campaigning but also a wide participation of women candidates. However it would be presumptuous to say that the Tibetan experience with democracy has been smooth and successful. Like all flourishing and established democracies, Tibetan democracy in exile is evolving, rooting itself in reality and the values of Tibetan society.

The challenges that Tibetans and the Tibetan parliamentary form of democracy face are manifold. There is truth in the arguments among Tibetans that democracy is an integral part of our struggle. Indeed a more democratic polity and society in exile would not only counter Chinese propaganda but would also create a more creative and empowered struggle in exile.[11]

[11]Pema Thinlay, 'Democracy is an Integral Part of the Tibetan Freedom Struggle', in: *Tibetan Bulletin* May-June 1996, p. 13.

However, like any other parliamentary democracy, Tibetan democracy is an uphill task, where contradictory elements of democracy, political ignorance, parochial interests and many other issues are to be confronted.

1. As Chairman, in his concluding speech at the end of the XIIth Assembly, Ven. Samdhong Rinpoche, emphasised the challenges facing Tibetan democracy in a parliamentary form of governance. In his speech titled, 'Apology' he dwelled on the past ten years of his service as the Chairman of the Tibetan Parliament, his trials and tribulations, his expectations and his disillusionments. The Ven. Samdhong Rinpoche elaborated on the importance of the Charter for Tibetans-in-exile as a guideline for the Tibetan administration as well as the importance of establishing the Rule of Law. He reminisced how at the beginning of the XIth ATPD, he had proudly declared the birth of a Tibetan political system from 'the rule of man to the rule of law'. He believed that a Charter only relevant on paper would have no value. However, the Rinpoche felt that many officials saw the Charter as hindering and constraining their work. Most of the rules became tools of individuals who either quoted it to attack someone or ignored it to support a friend.[12]

2. How representative is the Tibetan Parliament? Presently Tibetans living in India, Nepal and Bhutan vote for their candidates on the basis of their provincial and religious affinities. It must be understood that this tie up and link between Tibetans and the democratic process in exile is important and crucial. However the pattern of selection of candidates through this arrangement leads to many contentious issues in an exiled situation. Although the exile population of Tibetans belonging to the three provinces is extremely uneven, each province is entitled to ten seats. Similarly the four schools of Tibetan Buddhism and the traditional Tibetan religion Bön are each allotted two seats, even though their respective exile populations

[12]Prof. Samdhong Rinpoche, unpublished speech, delivered at the closing ceremony of the XIIth ATPD, 26 March 2001.

are also quite uneven. It has been pointed out that monks have in fact two votes, one as the representative of their sect and one as the Member of their region.

On the other hand, Tibetans living in North America and Europe do not elect their representatives on the basis of provincial or religious affinity. They elect their representative from among themselves. In recent years, the Tibetan population in North America has increased considerably. According to figures published by the Planning Council in 1999, USA and Canada together had a population of approximately 7,000 Tibetans, but with only one seat in the Assembly.[13] In contrast, Europe with a population of about 2,324 Tibetans has two seats in the Assembly. Likewise, Tibetans living in Australia/New Zealand and Taiwan/Japan number roughly over 1,000, but they do not participate in the elections of the Parliament although according to a statement from the Election Commission's office, Tibetans living in Taiwan did take part in the election of the Chief *kalon* in May, 2001.

3. This leads us to the third challenge. How accountable are the members of the Assembly to the electorate? Although the elected executive has political and financial accountability to the legislature, the legislature in turn must also have political and financial accountability to the electorate. In fact, the Deputies are the chief communicators and links between the executive and the people. The issue of accountability is debated in every liberal democracy, but the issue is further complicated in the Tibetan case. The election of forty seats of the Assembly takes place not on the basis of constituency but on the basis of provincial (*cholkha*) and sectarian affiliations. The incumbent may be from a place far from the voter's. The Tibetans in exile live in the forty-six settlements spread across India and other countries in South Asia. This spatial gap does lead to the lack of accountability of the Deputies, as there is no fixed spatial constituency.

4. The Dalai Lama and the Cabinet (*kashag*) have frequently

---

[13]All data on population taken from Planning Council, Central Tibetan Administration: *Tibetan Demographic Survey 1998*,, Dharamsala 2000.

stressed the crucial need for the people to elect members who are 'learned, dedicated and able to represent the aspirations of the Tibetan people and provide leadership in our struggle for freedom.'[14] He has often reiterated this in his speeches to the people as well as to members, urging them to rise above sectarian and provincial interests and work for the common national interest of Tibet and its people. To the representatives of the people he asserted their accountability to the electorate, '...once one becomes a Member of the Assembly, it is very important that one acts as a common representative of all the people, whatever may be the origins.'[15] The urgent needs of the people and the Tibetan struggle must override provincial and sectarian interests. The success of Tibetan democracy will depend upon the people and the leaders they elect. The Parliament has to rise above individual, provincial and communal interest and strengthen collective action and individual responsibility.

5. The next major challenge for Tibetan parliamentary democracy is the need to strengthen democratic responsibility among the general Tibetan population. The lack of political awareness, and voters' apathy are critical for the successful functioning of a democracy. History shows that democracy is rarely established without widespread struggle and mobilisation, sometimes over long periods of time and at considerable national and personal cost. For the majority of nation-states, their rulers did not easily concede democracy. Fortunately for Tibetans in exile, the democratic process has not been the outcome of pressure from the people, but rather was planned and pursued from the start by the Head of State.

Although the Tibetan government along with several non-governmental organisations initiated political education, there is a need for more political will, action and responsibility among the Tibetan people. Rights and duties go hand in hand. After

---

[14]Statement of the kashag on the Fortieth Anniversary of Tibetan Democracy Day, *Tibetan Bulletin*, September-December, 2000, p. 27–28.

[15]Speech at the Assembly of Tibetan Peoples Deputies, 28 July 1993 in: A.A. Shiromany, ed., supra, p. 293.

the elections to the XIIIth Assembly, the results for four of the forty-three seats could not be announced.[16] Voting for the two seats of the Kagyu religious sect could not take place, and the Ü-Tsang province could only elect nine Deputies. Similarly, Tibetans in North America could not elect their Member for the single seat allotted to them. In order to be declared elected, a candidate must get at least 33 percent of the total valid votes. One of the reasons for the failure to elect the tenth Deputy from Ü-Tsang and the Member for North America could be the large number of candidates. This may be true especially in the case of North America where there were five candidates for one seat. However, low voter turnout might also have been a factor that resulted in many candidates not getting the required 33 percent of valid votes. One cannot ignore the fact that re-polling is an additional burden on the already scarce resources of the Tibetan government. But by-elections have taken place since.

6. Although the Tibetan community has a political party, the National Democratic Party of Tibet, it does not function as one. Political parties are important especially in a democratic set up. Unfortunately, as Samdhong Rinpoche stated in his concluding speech, rather than having a multi-party system, the one party that we have in the community has also not been accepted as a political party.

With the continued leadership of His Holiness the Dalai Lama and an active, responsible society, Tibetan democracy can be sustained. However, to achieve greater success, we must make sure that each and every individual shares the responsibility and makes a contribution to the common cause.

We must aim at implementing the vision of our leader whereby Tibetans are collectively involved in changing our own political and social destiny. And towards this end the Assembly of Tibetan People's Deputies, the supreme legislative institution of the Tibetan community, has a major responsibility in generating new ideas and directives that will help us create a successful democratic order.

---

[16]Exile Parliament Election Results, *Tibetan Review*, Vol. XXXVI, No. 6., June 2001, p. 14.

CHAPTER NINE

Virtual Tibet: The Media

THUBTEN SAMPHEL

The Effect of Media and the Internet on Tibetan Attitudes

Tibetans in exile are embracing the internet just as they did Buddhism more than 1,300 years ago. Like a new revelation, the power of the internet to create virtual communities has fascinated Tibetans in exile. This fascination is intensified by the fact that the ability to create a cohesive community, across international borders, has been denied to Tibetans in Tibet by an internet-shy China. And Tibetan exiles, scattered as they are across the globe, are converting this fascination into a rash of cyberspace activities that, because of their power to transmit information instantaneously, are profoundly changing the world of the Tibetan diaspora and beyond. In the process, Tibetan exiles have created a virtual Tibet that is almost unassailable, free, revelling in its freedom, and growing.

'The Tibetan exiles harnessing the power of the internet has enabled them to make information on Tibet instant and reliable,' said Jigme Tsering, manager of the Tibetan Computing Resource Centre, the organisation that services the needs of information technology in Dharamsala. According to Jigme Tsering, who also manages the website, *www.tibet.net*, there are about 250 Tibet-related websites, in English, Hindi, Chinese, Tibetan, French, Japanese, Korean and other languages. Numerous Tibetan Buddhist centres and Tibet support groups maintain websites. 'Even the smallest news is disseminated throughout the world within five minutes. The recent hacking by some Chinese organisations of our own www.tibet.net became news, covered even by CNN,' Jigme Tsering said.

The Tibetans' use of the internet has a significant impact on the content and quality of the debate among both intellectuals and others in China on the issue of Tibet. Within a week of the launch of the Chinese language website in August 2000 by the Department of Information and International Relations of the Central Tibetan Administration, more than 10,000 visitors hit the site, the majority being from China. Later, the department was bombarded by both enthusiastic and outraged messages, reported Dawa Tsering, head of the department's China desk. One enthusiastic letter from China likened the Chinese language website to a 'torch being shone in the darkness'. An angry letter sent on 18 November 2002 says,

> I have been to Tibet. Our government's policy towards the Tibetans is most lenient. Don't continue to shut your eyes and talk like a fool....What the Dalai Lama preaches is not practical in developed societies and your vain efforts will be wasted.

A sympathetic letter mailed on 28 December 2002 says,

> I'm Chinese. When I was a student I was taught that the Dalai Lama was a reactionary rebel. Ever since I visited your website and read the various statements of the Dalai Lama, I am left with great shame at the way our government treats the Tibetans and the disdain shown by ordinary Chinese to them. I recognise the fact that the six million Tibetan people have the right to attain their freedom as soon as possible. As said by the Dalai Lama 'I strongly believe that whether the Tibetans and Chinese live as members of one family or as neighbours we need to live peacefully and with mutual respect.'

The ability of the Chinese to speak freely on the once-taboo topic of Tibet, although anonymously, is an indication of the fundamental societal changes sweeping China, the courage and genuine concern of individual Chinese and the power of information technology to overcome the restrictions imposed by a one-party state. And this has spurred exiled Tibetans and their supporters to girdle the globe with Tibet websites.

Traditional Attitudes to News

However, the traditional Tibetan attitude to news and information has not always been this enthusiastic. It was deferential, and because of this deference, information and knowledge were enshrined on the altar and became remote, inaccessible, the object of unquestioning faith. The pace of information dissemination was slow. For example, in old Tibet when a Tibetan author wrote a masterpiece, his instinct was not to rush to the printers. He buried his work, in the hope that centuries later some smart reporter would discover his work, its antiquity giving it a halo of wisdom, sacredness and a special spiritual significance, a Tibetan version of the gospel truth. Those who discovered such works of lasting value were called *terton*, discoverers of buried treasures. This was precisely what happened to the classic *The Tibetan Book of the Dead.* C.G. Jung, rival in fame to Sigmund Freud, described *The Tibetan Book of the Dead* as belonging to

> that class of writings which are not only of interest to specialists in Mahayana Buddhism, but which also, because of their deep humanity and their still deeper insight into the secrets of the human psyche, make an especial appeal to the layman who is seeking to broaden his knowledge of life.[1]

But Tibet had to wait for several centuries before this work, the definitive Tibetan contribution to our understanding of human psychology, was made available to the lamas. If an enterprising *terton*, old Tibet's version of a nosey reporter, had not dug up the book from one of the mountains, the world would have lost a real treasure.

---

[1] *The Tibetan Book of the Dead,* W.E. Evens-Wentz (ed.), London 1957[3], p. XXXVI.

The Tibetan exiles' brush with the outside world has changed all this. Now Tibetans consider information and knowledge as a tool to be used for the improvement of their community rather than as an object of worship. The secularisation of the Tibetan attitude to knowledge and information is nowhere better seen than in the Tibetan refugees' successful effort at creating a lively and vocal press. The creation of a free press in the world of the Tibetan diaspora is contributing to the building of a Tibetan civil society, strengthening the right to free speech and the roots of the exiles' nascent democracy. It has given the Tibetans a powerful voice in their non-violent freedom struggle. Above all, the exiles' free press has managed to persuade an increasing number of Chinese, both in and outside China, to look at the issue of Tibet through Tibetan eyes.

Historical Origins of Pre-exile Media

However, the origins of the Tibetan media, especially the print media, paradoxically started not in Tibet but in India, a result of Tibetan isolationism. Two Germans were largely responsible for introducing Tibetans to the contemporary concept of news, news-gathering and dissemination. Heinrich August Jaeschke, 'perhaps the most brilliant of a series of Moravian linguists to work in the Himalayan region,'[2] published his path-breaking *Tibetan-English Dictionary* in 1881. This dictionary became one of the foundation stones of Tibetology and was particularly useful for missionaries in their attempts to spread the gospel among the Tibetan people. The first modern Tibetan language newspaper was *Ladakh Kyi Akbar* or *Ladakh News*. August Hermann Francke, another German and Moravian missionary and the author of *A History of Western Tibet*, brought out the *Ladakh News* in 1904 in an attempt to spread the light

[2]Bray, John, 'The Contribution of the Moravian Mission to Tibetan Language and Literature', published in the journal *Lungta*, 1998, Amnye Machen Institute, Dharamsala, India.

of the gospel in Ladakh and among the Tibetan-speaking world. He

> employed a style of language which, while conforming to traditional Tibetan grammatical and spelling rules, was nevertheless close to the colloquial. He hoped that once people had become accustomed to the newspaper they might prove more receptive to the Moravian Mission's more specifically Christian publications.[3]

In 1904, the story of the year was the British invasion of Tibet. This was given extensive coverage in the *Ladakh News*. However, the readers questioned the accuracy of the news reports. Francke remarked that his readers particularly doubted the authenticity of the story that the Tibetan troops who were equipped with protective amulets proved vulnerable to British bullets.

For the first edition of *Ladakh News* 150 copies were printed. Soon the number of copies was scaled down to a more realistic figure of 60. Twenty were sent to Darjeeling for distribution.

The Christian missionary agenda of the paper was clearly reflected in such aphorisms as 'If the Lama himself is not perfect, how can he guide the dying to a better re-birth?' The paper went on to explain that the only true great lama was Jesus Christ himself.

Ladakh News did not meet with much success and closed shop in 1908. Another paper, along similar lines, was started in Lahaul and Spiti in 1927. It was called *Keylong Kyi Akhbar* or *Keylong News*.

However, in the 1990 issue of *Tibet Studies*, a scholarly journal published from Tibet, a three-page article by Bai Runsheng claims that Tibet's first newspaper, *Vernacular Paper*, was started by the Manchu *amban*, Lian Yu, and his deputy, Zhang Yintang in April 1909. The newspaper was bilingual, in Tibetan and Chinese. The article does not mention where in

[3]Bray, John, 'A.H. Francke's La Dvags Kyi Akhbar: the First Tibetan Newspaper', Seminar paper presented at the Conference on Ladakh, School of Oriental and African Studies, London University, December 1987, printed in: *Tibet Journal*, vol. 13, no. 3, 1988.

Tibet *Vernacular Paper* was printed, its content, frequency and circulation.

But the true origins of Tibet's print media lies in the birth of *Tibet Mirror*, a monthly Tibetan-language newspaper, started by Gergan Tharchin, or Tharchin Babu, as he is fondly remembered by the Tibetan emigré community of Kalimpong and Darjeeling.

> The Rev. G. Tharchin was a pioneer in several fields: the first Tibetan journalist in the entire Tibetan-speaking world, a towering modern man of letters in a field traditionally dominated by lamas, a lone moderniser in a tradition-bound society, and above all the most articulate spokesman for Tibet's freedom.[4]

Tharchin Babu was a Christian but, unlike *Ladakh News*, there was no attempt to proselytise in the pages of *Tibet Mirror*. He published the first enduring Tibetan-language newspaper in Kalimpong, the border town in West Bengal, which acted as a flourishing entre-port for the wool trade between Tibet and India.

'In the first issue of October 1925, I printed 50 copies and sent most of them to my friends in Lhasa, including one to His Holiness the thirteenth Dalai Lama,' Tharchin Babu later recounted. 'He sent me a letter with some gifts congratulating me and encouraging me to carry on publishing the newspaper.'[5]

In fact, the thirteenth Dalai Lama wrote, 'If you continue to send me your monthly newspaper containing news about countries like China, Britain, etc., it would greatly help my understanding of the various situations.'[6]

---

[4]Writes Dawa Norbu in his introduction to the two-volume biography of Tharchin Babu, *Called from Obscurity: The Life and Times of a True Son of Tibet—Gergan Dorje Tharchin* by H. Louis Fader, Tibet Mirror Press, Kalimpong, 2002.

[5]'G. Tharchin: Pioneer and Patriot', an interview with Tharchin Babu in: *Tibetan Review*, December 1975.

[6]'All the News—Tibetan Style' by Topden Tsering, in: *Tibetan Bulletin*, January–February 1999.

Despite its miniscule circulation, the impact of *Tibet Mirror*, though confined to a small circle of Tibetan aristocrats and an even smaller circle of Tibetan reformists, impatient for drastic changes in Tibet, was enormous. It brought news of the world to an isolated Tibet.

> It was the only medium in the world through which the Tibetans at least in Lhasa, learnt something of the fast-changing world outside—revolution in China, World War II, India's independence, etc. And the impact was considerable,

recalled Tharchin Babu.[7]

> The Mirror published articles on world events and especially reported what was taking place in India, Tibet and in the region of Kalimpong. It was a rich source of information on the world of high Asia of the time.[8]

Tibetan nationalists, scholars and dissidents held regular conclaves at Babu Tharchin's place to discuss how Tibet could best avoid the gathering political storm. For example, in 1946, two visitors from Tibet landed at Tharchin Babu's doorstep: Baba Phuntsog Wangyal and his friend. They said they had come across a copy of *Tibet Mirror*. Earlier the two had visited Lhasa to warn the Tibetan government that unless it brought about changes in Tibet, the country would succumb to an imminent Chinese communist invasion after the Chinese civil war. They predicted that the communists would win the civil war and were preparing for the 'liberation' of Tibet. They warned Lhasa that the only way out was to obtain British military aid. The two said Lhasa had ignored them. They were 'nobody', had no names, no titles. So they came to Kalimpong in the hope of directly approaching the British government in India. Tharchin Babu travelled with them to Gangtok and

[7]'G. Tharchin: Pioneer and Patriot', supra.

[8]Tashi Tsering, *The Life of Rev. G. Tharchin: Missionary and Pioneer*, Amnye Machen, Dharamsala 1998.

introduced them to Sir Basil Gould, the British Political Officer, who looked after the interests of the British Raj in Tibet and Bhutan. The 12-page memorandum, which Baba Phuntsog Wangyal wrote, was transmitted to London through the office of the Political Officer. A copy was sent to Lhasa. Realising Britain would ignore his pleas for help, Baba Phuntsog Wangyal made a trip to Calcutta and met with Jyoti Basu for Indian communist help in securing arms.[9] But his promises of help then were vague and in the end not forthcoming.

After submitting the memorandum, Baba Phuntsog Wangyal jokingly told Tharchin Babu, 'If the Tibetan government does not listen, I shall bring the Chinese army to Tibet. Then I shall write to you.' In early 1951 Tharchin Babu received a telegram, which said, 'Safely arrived in Lhasa—Phuntsog Wangyal.'[10]

Baba Phuntsog Wangyal, who became one of the first Tibetan communists, brought and guided China's People's Liberation Army to Lhasa. He later served as the interpreter between Mao and the Dalai Lama when the Tibetan leader visited Beijing in 1954. Subsequently Phuntsog Wangyal was arrested and jailed for advocating what the Chinese communists termed as 'local nationalism' or greater rights for the minority nationalities and attempting to establish a re-united autonomous Tibet. He spent 18 years in solitary confinement in Beijing's notorious Number One Prison. Phuntsog still lives in Beijing and in the mid-1990's made it to the cover of the *Far Eastern Economic Review* which carried an extensive story on the theory he developed in prison that there is water on the moon.

Apart from being curious about what would have happened if Lhasa had listened to Baba Phuntsog Wangyal's dire warnings, Tibet's isolationist policy enhanced the impact of a single newspaper on the thinking of nationalist Tibetans. This leaves

---

[9]Jyoti Basu later became independent India's longest-serving chief minister (of West-Bengal).

[10]Tashi Tsering, supra.

one with the question: would a full-grown, modern media, free and unshackled, have saved Tibet from its present tragic fate? Or was it the classic case of too little, too late?

Whatever conclusion one arrives at, the *Tibet Mirror's* advocacy of Tibetan independence received attention not only from Tibetan nationalists but also from the Chinese communists. Tharchin Babu told the *Tibetan Review*,

> But the Chinese communists were very clever. In the 50's they had a trade consulate in Kalimpong and they used to try to woo me. Once a Tibetan aristocrat came to see me here with presents. He said in the usual roundabout aristocratic way that I should not publish more anti-Chinese articles. Instead I should concentrate on the 'progress' made by China in Tibet. If I agreed the Chinese would order 500 copies of every issue of *Tibet Mirror* and they would also make sure that I don't run at a loss. I refused.[11]

Tibet Mirror ceased publication in 1962 when the Tibetan refugees brought out their own newspaper called *Tibetan Freedom* from neighbouring Darjeeling. However, for nearly four decades of its existence *Tibet Mirror* chronicled some of the most important events in the history of modern Tibet. It encapsulated an entire era during which Tibetan nationalist and reformist stirrings collided with the weight of tradition and conservatism. Naturally, Tharchin Babu and the office of *Tibet Mirror* became the meeting-point of intellectuals and reformists who wanted to modernise Tibet so that it would effectively counter the challenges posed by a resurgent China.

The First Exile Newspapers

In 1962, Gyalo Thondup, the elder brother of the Dalai Lama, started *Tibetan Freedom* called *Rawang* in Tibetan. The irony that Tibet had to lose its independence before the Tibetans

[11]Ibid.

realised the worth of a modern newspaper did not escape Tharchin Babu who wrote in the farewell issue of *Tibet Mirror*,[12]

> When there was rawang,
>   There was no *rawang*.
> When there is no rawang,
>   There is *rawang*.

Several years later Gyalo Thondup handed over *Tibetan Freedom* to the Government at Dharamsala. This was a historic first step. It was the first time in Tibet's entire recorded history of more than two thousand years, that official Tibet had ever published and managed a newspaper. With Dharamsala publishing *Tibetan Freedom*, the realisation grew among the officials and young educated Tibetans in exile of the value of information. The print media came to be perceived as an important weapon in the war of words with China. These Tibetans wanted a voice and a platform to discuss what was happening to Tibet in the context of the larger events that were shaping the world.

With this in mind, a group of Tibetans started *Sheja*, a monthly newsmagazine, in October 1968. 'We first started producing *Sheja* from a three-room building in McLeod Ganj with financial help of Rs 10,000 from His Holiness the Dalai Lama. It was a private undertaking then,' said Kasur Sonam Topgyal, a former chairman of the Tibetan Kashag and a founding member of *Sheja*.[13]

'We intended to educate the Tibetan refugees on the political developments sweeping across the world,' said Kasur Sonam Topgyal who remained the editor of *Sheja* for more than ten years. 'If the Tibetans were to struggle for their country's freedom, it was imperative that they be informed about what was going on,' Kasur Sonam Topgyal remarked.[14]

---

[12]Topden Tsering , 'All the News—Tibetan Style', in: *Tibetan Bulletin*, January–February 1999.

[13]Ibid.

[14]Ibid. Sonam Topyal was Chief Kalon from 1996–2001.

For the Tibetan refugee community *Sheja* came as a breath of fresh air. It was written in colloquial Tibetan, touched upon all the trouble spots in the world, and devoted a regular section to news trickling from Tibet and from behind the 'bamboo curtain'.

Another 'great leap forward' in the creation of the Tibetan press in exile was the establishment of *Voice of Tibet,* started by Lodi Gyari, presently the Special Envoy of His Holiness the Dalai Lama to Washington, D.C. Lodi Gyari remained the editor till the magazine changed its name to *Tibetan Review* in 1968. The magazine, the first Tibet-in-exile magazine in English, was mimeographed and printed and published from Darjeeling.[15]

However, lack of money forced both *Sheja* and *Tibetan Review* to turn to Dharamsala in 1971. The Government responded by setting up a whole new department to house the two publications. It was called the Information Office, the predecessor of the Department of Information and International Relations. As recalled by Kasur Sonam Topgyal, 'When we approached the cabinet for help, they entrusted us with one whole new department....We moved in and that's how the magazines became official.'[16]

The Tibetan Review and the Tibetan Review Generation of Tibetans

Under the editorship of Professor Dawa Norbu, who now teaches at the School of International Studies at New Delhi's Jawaharlal Nehru University, the *Tibetan Review* moved to New Delhi. Before taking over as editor, he secured a guarantee from the Information Office that it would give him full editorial independence. With this guarantee, Dawa Norbu and his successor, Tsering Wangyal, who served as the editor of the

[15]Ibid.

[16]Ibid.

Tibetan Review for more than twenty years, turned the magazine into a venerated institution of the exiled Tibetan world. They created a whole new generation of Tibetans: the *Tibetan Review* generation, born in Tibet, educated in exile and using the forum provided by the *Review* to discuss how to redeem their lost inheritance.[17] The most important role of the *Tibetan Review* was that of galvanising the young exiles with fresh ideas and perspectives that went beyond the confines of their refugee community.

The impact of the *Tibetan Review* was planetary. It became a forum for Tibetans from all four corners of the world and their friends to throw up new ideas and inspirations to strengthen the worldwide Tibet movement. It contributed to creating a global Tibetan émigré community. The *Tibetan Review* became one of the few exile publications that managed to turn around international opinion in favour of the Tibetan people. As Tibetans say, China has its People's Liberation Army, but Tibetan exiles have their *Tibetan Review*. Since the Tibetans refused to take up arms, the PLA was quite useless in Tibet and very, very expensive. Because of this, in the war of words between Beijing and Dharamsala, the *Tibetan Review* became an increasingly credible tool in persuading an ill-informed international community to see the appalling situation in Tibet from the Tibetan-exile perspective.

Independent Media Dent Official Monopoly

Since the three Tibetan publications, *Tibetan Freedom*, *Sheja* and *Tibetan Review*, all started by private initiative, came under the control of Dharamsala, all the firepower of exile reporting was directed against the Chinese communist rule of Tibet. But the Tibetan administration's dominance and monopoly of news and information was gradually reversed as fresh, young blood from

[17] 'Editor-la passes away', an obituary on Tsering Wangyal by Thubten Samphel, in: *Tibetan Bulletin* January–February 2001.

Tibet, with a sparkling flair for writing in the exhilarating freedom of India, started to bring out private journals and magazines in the early 1990s. Such talent and enthusiasm of the new refugees from Tibet, especially from Amdo, was responsible for the growth of a whole range of journals and literary magazines that culminated in the establishment of *Mang-tso*,[18] a Tibetan language newspaper brought out by a group of young Tibetans from Amdo. *Mang-tso*, which led a brief but boisterous life, was succeeded by *Tibet Times*. Launched in September 1996, *Tibet Times*, a private initiative, adopted a racy style. It is still going strong and is attractively designed and presented. The paper has a circulation of more than 4,000 and comes out once in ten days. Since then occasional newsmagazines and journals have mushroomed in exile and the Department of Information and International Relations in 1999 saw fit to produce *Media Tibet: A Directory*.

Tibetan Exile Airtime and Impact

The ability of the exile print media to inform and inspire the Tibetan refugee community received a boost with the launch of the Tibetan language service of the *Voice of America* in the early 1990s. The launch of the Tibetan service of the VOA gave the Tibetan exiles the ability to reach out to Tibetans in Tibet, an awesome new power that significantly dented the Chinese propaganda hold on the minds of the Tibetan people. The VOA Tibetan service was followed a few years later by the launch of *Radio Free Asia*. Its transmission time was longer and its editorial content was not restrained by the compulsions of the US State Department. In the second half of the 1990s the trinity was complete: *Voice of Tibet*, a Norwegian NGO-funded Tibetan language service, was launched. Though its service is only half an hour every day, it complemented the two American services, with much of its news focussed on events and people

---

[18]*Mang-tso* means democracy in Tibetan.

in Dharamsala, the capital of the exile Tibetan world. Listeners in Tibet consider these radio services as 'medicine for a sick person'.

Response from Tibetans beyond the Himalayas was enthusiastic and touching. There is one moving e-mail message from a Tibetan student in China. The letter was sent to *Voice of Tibet.* It reads,

> Hi! I'm a Tibetan student who is studying in China. I'm really grateful for your station because you are all working for the independence of our country. It's been a long time that I wanted to contact with outside Tibetan friends, but it's really difficult in China, you know. Maybe you outside Tibetans think that we who are educated in Chinese style have lost Tibetan personality. No, of course not, we love our country—Tibet and we want to fight for freedom of Tibet. However, we are surrounded by Chinese, we can't talk even. And we are young, our parents and relatives can't understand us, they even know nothing about outside country's information. I'm sorry about my country and my fellow Tibetans outside. My deepest respect to our spiritual leader His Holiness the Dalai Lama—a Tibetan student in China.[19]

Tibetan Exile Media and their Impact on China

The Tibetan exiles launching into airtime and their energetic involvement with the print media and particularly the internet is significant. On the one hand, the exiles have fundamentally changed international public opinion in their favour and have halted the advance of the Chinese propaganda juggernaut on the world stage. On the other hand, the exiles have succeeded in undermining the ability of the Chinese authorities to influence and shape the thinking of the people in Tibet. Finally, the

[19]The letter is with the VOT, Narthang Building, Gangchen Kyishong, Dharamsala. VOT's email is voti@online.no; typos and spelling errors corrected to hide the identity of the writer.

creation of a virtual Tibet has enabled the refugees to penetrate Chinese borders and minds. This ability has vastly contributed to an ongoing debate among mainland Chinese thinkers and writers of the merits of China's current hard-line policies in Tibet and the need for a reasonable solution to the festering problem, which has given China such a bad press.

For example Wang Lixiong, who is based in Beijing and the author of the bestsellers *Yellow Peril* and *The Sky Burial: The Fate of Tibet*, notes:

> The Dalai Lama is 65 years old. Considering the life expectancy and health care facilities of today, it will not be difficult for him to live another 10 or 20 years. During this long time, political changes in China are almost inevitable. It is the attitude of the Dalai Lama that will wholly determine the direction of the Tibetan issue. His wish is the Tibetan people's command....Whoever underestimates his influence is making a big mistake, and will pay dearly for it.[20]

Wang Lixiong's is not the only voice. Wei Jingsheng, who is considered the father of Chinese democracy, while in jail, wrote an open letter addressed to Deng Xiaoping to settle the issue of Tibet peacefully. Wei Jingsheng's outrage, so evident in the open letter, was provoked by the release of the white paper on Tibet called 'Tibet—Its Ownership and Human Rights' by the State Council of the People's Republic of China in 1992. Wei Jingsheng wrote,

> In order to improve the situation and solve the Tibet question, the first thing to do is to understand what the problems are. Only to listen to soothing lies will not help you to understand the reality and find out the problem, and certainly will not solve it....Therefore, I venture to write this letter to you and hope that you would create an academic

[20] *The Dalai Lama is the key to Tibet issue* by Wang Lixiong, an article written in Lhasa and Beijing between May and July 2000. The author lives in Beijing.

> atmosphere of free expression, so that people of knowledge could put forward more insight with regard to this issue and find out the problems. Only by doing so, could we avoid losing the last opportunity of settling the issue and avoid repeating the situation of the former Soviet Union and Yugoslavia.[21]

This change in the attitude of a number of Chinese to Tibet is exasperating for China considering its dominance of the international news outlets on the vexed issue in the 1950's.

> Earlier, when the PLA invaded the plateau in 1949, China was considered the new beacon of the socialist camp—especially for countries which suffered western colonial domination. Because of Tibet's isolation and its absence from influential global forums, international media coverage of the invasion became almost an afterthought and was ill-informed.
>
> At the same time communist China's propaganda machinery worked overtime to successfully put a spin on the event, depicting the invasion as a 'liberation' of long-suffering 'serfs' and 'slaves'. China was also, to some extent, successful in portraying those who opposed the invasion as 'running dogs of the capitalists' bent on wrecking the socialist camp. Tibet was projected as a Cold War issue, which succeeded in silencing the socialist camp....China could tell the world what it wanted the world to believe, without any effective Tibetan response.[22]

The extent of ground that China has lost in the propaganda war alarms Chinese authorities. At a meeting held on 12 June 2000 in Beijing to strategise on improving the effectiveness of China's external propaganda on Tibet, Zhao Qizheng, Minister

---

[21]Wei Jingsheng, 'The Special Status of Tibet', reprinted in: *Tibetan Bulletin*, January–February 1994.

[22]*China's Current Policy on Tibet: Life-and Death Struggle to Crush an Ancient Civilization*, published by Department of Information and International Relations, Dharamsala, 29 September 2000.

of Information on the State Council of the People's Republic of China, said,

> Westerners are waging a protracted and overall war on us on the issue of Tibet. This is a well-planned public opinion and psychological war....The external propaganda on the Tibet issue is a very complicated matter. The Dalai clique and hostile western forces have a history of several decades of anti-China activities and propaganda. As well as having complete experience and expertise, they command an army of specialists in this field....In this overall struggle for public opinion on the Tibet issue, Tibetology institutes should become an effective army...we should use our departments of foreign affairs, information, security, law, nationality, religion, culture, etc.[23]

The vocabulary the minister uses to describe the various campaigns to counter the exiles' dominance of the international media is military. Notice the phrases 'psychological war', 'protracted and overall war', and 'army'. All these are freshly minted battle cries for a new war. But the method the propaganda chief endorses is the Tibetan exiles' strategy of how to make friends and win foes—is of non-violence. China's clear compliment to the Tibetan exiles' international strategy by taking a leaf from their non-violent struggle is surprising since it is China that has given the world *The Art of War*, the classic textbook on deception to conquer the barbarian world. The Chinese propaganda chief encourages the cadres and specialists to use every strand of Tibetan culture—Buddhism, art, media, architecture, literature, history, medicine, dance and music and folklore—to present the Chinese case for Tibet.

---

[23] *Tibet-related external propaganda and Tibetology work in the new era* by Zhao Qizheng, Minister of Information, State Council of PRC, on 12 June 2000 in Beijing, published in: Department of Information and International Relations, CTA, *Beijing's How to Win Friends and Influence People*, Dharamsala 2000.

Media, Civil Society and Democracy

However, the most enduring impact of the exile Tibetan media is on the domestic front. As late as a decade ago, the exile media was a barely audible voice in Tibetan exile affairs. Now the interlocking network of websites, newspapers, magazines, and radio services has emerged as a Fourth Estate with the clout to influence Tibetan thinking on issues such as candidates for the post of the *kalon tripa*, the newly-revamped office of the de facto exile prime minister, to advocating partisan politics in an increasingly pluralistic system. In chat-rooms hosted by Tibetan-exile websites, young Tibetans are talking to each other from across the globe about what is happening in Tibet to looking for suitable dates for the weekend.

The growth of the Tibetan exile media has a significant impact on the development of a democratic community. As a pillar of the exile body politik, the Tibetan media have access to the proceedings of the exile parliament. This transparency of the decisions and deliberations of the exile legislature through the exile media has enabled the refugee community to watch, gauge and understand the actions of their elected representatives and reserve their right to reward or punish the concerned deputies in the next elections.

Most important of all in the building of a civil society is the fact that the mushrooming of the exile media has spawned a growing number of NGOs, mostly based in Dharamsala, the capital of the world of the Tibetan diaspora. These NGOs, all with their newsletters and journals, are adding their own distinct voice and concerns to the deliberations within the exile community and shaping their opinions.

The taking of firm roots of a free, boisterous press in the Tibetan refugee community has facilitated the Dalai Lama's own efforts at the democratisation of the exile Tibetan polity. It has introduced a great deal of transparency in the workings of the Tibetan exile administration. And it has given the Tibetan refugees a strong and decisive voice in their political participation, strengthening the cohesiveness and vibrancy of the community.

List of Websites

www.asienhaus.org//tibn1.htm	(Asienhaus, Hamburg)
www.phayul.com	(New Delhi)
www.tibet.net	(CTA, Dharamsala)
www.tibet.com	(CTA, Dharamsala)
www.tibet.ca	(Canada Tibet Committee)
www.tibetlink.com	(Canada)
www.tibetsearch.com	(USA)
www.tibet-society.org.uk/facts.html	(Tibet Society, London)
http//coombs.anu.edu.au/ wwwvl-Tibetan Studies.html	(Australian National University, Canberra
www.ttibet.com	(Gesellschaft Schweizerisch-Tibetische Freundschaft)
www.manymedia.com	(USA)

CHAPTER TEN

The Settlements: Participation and Integration*

DAWA NORBU

The Sakya Tibetan Society, popularly known as Puruwala Zhichag (settlement), is in one of the most beautiful locations in Northern India. It lies at the foothills of the wooded Shamila ranges, not far from the Giri River in the south, which flows full during the monsoons. In the early 1970s, when the settlement was being built, it was a problem to cross the river during the rainy season, but now the Himachal Pradesh government has constructed a long permanent bridge. The settlement with 130 houses, built in a rectangular shape, spreads amidst fields, where rice, wheat and mangoes are grown. In the middle of this settlement is the *mani lhakhang* or prayer hall, built by the settlers themselves, with prayer wheels all around this structure, which literally means the place, where '*om mani padme hung*' the most popular Tibetan prayer is recited. This folk temple, which is found in most Tibetan settlements, is distinct from the *magon*, the root or main monastery belonging to the Sakya sect, built by His Holiness the Sakya Trizin whose *phodrang* (palace)has been constructed by the settlers on a hillock a little above the monastery.

Every year in late February or early March the whole

*This paper is dedicated to the people and Government of India, who lived up to their ancient humanistic heritage, (despite their own economic and space problems) by providing sanctuary and help to refugees from various parts of Asia since 1947. The refugees from Tibet are one such case in point.

settlement comes alive with the sights and sounds of Tibet. It is the time, when *losar*, the Tibetan New Year, is celebrated. Luckily it coincides with the end of the sweater-selling season, when settlers return home.

The Losar festival begins with a prayer-cum-puja presided over by His Holiness the Sakya Trizin at the Sakya Thubten Monastery, attended by settlers and their office bearers. After this initiation the people go back to their homes and begin week-long festivities, singing, dancing and bursting firecrackers. I have been attending Losar almost every year—because it is a throw-back to my childhood days in Tibet, seeing familiar people, hearing familiar songs and watching the familiar dances that I remember so vividly. Most of my relatives and childhood friends are also settled in Puruwala, and it is a great opportunity to see them once a year.

The Sakya Tibetan Society at Puruwala was originally conceived and planned by the Sakya Trizin and built by his followers with financial assistance from the Tibetan Industrial Rehabilitation Society, New Delhi, in the late 1960s and early 1970s. However by the early 1990s the settlement underwent a basic change in its administration. In 1989, His Holiness the Dalai Lama was awarded the Nobel Peace Prize, and the Sakya Trizin in the Tibetan tradition offered the settlement to the spiritual and temporal leader. Since then the Tibetan Government-in-Exile has been in charge of the administration of the settlement.

As it stands now, the settlement is, like the ones in South India, quite rich and virtually self-sufficient and self- contained in most respects. The settlers speak Tibetan and maintain their culture and way of life. A crèche is attached to the carpet-weaving centre, which employs over fifty weavers, mainly women. There is also a primary school up to class V, where the medium of instruction is Tibetan.

Besides this settlement with which I am most familiar, I visited in January 2000 the oldest Tibetan settlement in Bylakuppe, South India, much larger and more complex than the one at Puruwala. Therefore in what follows, I attempt a

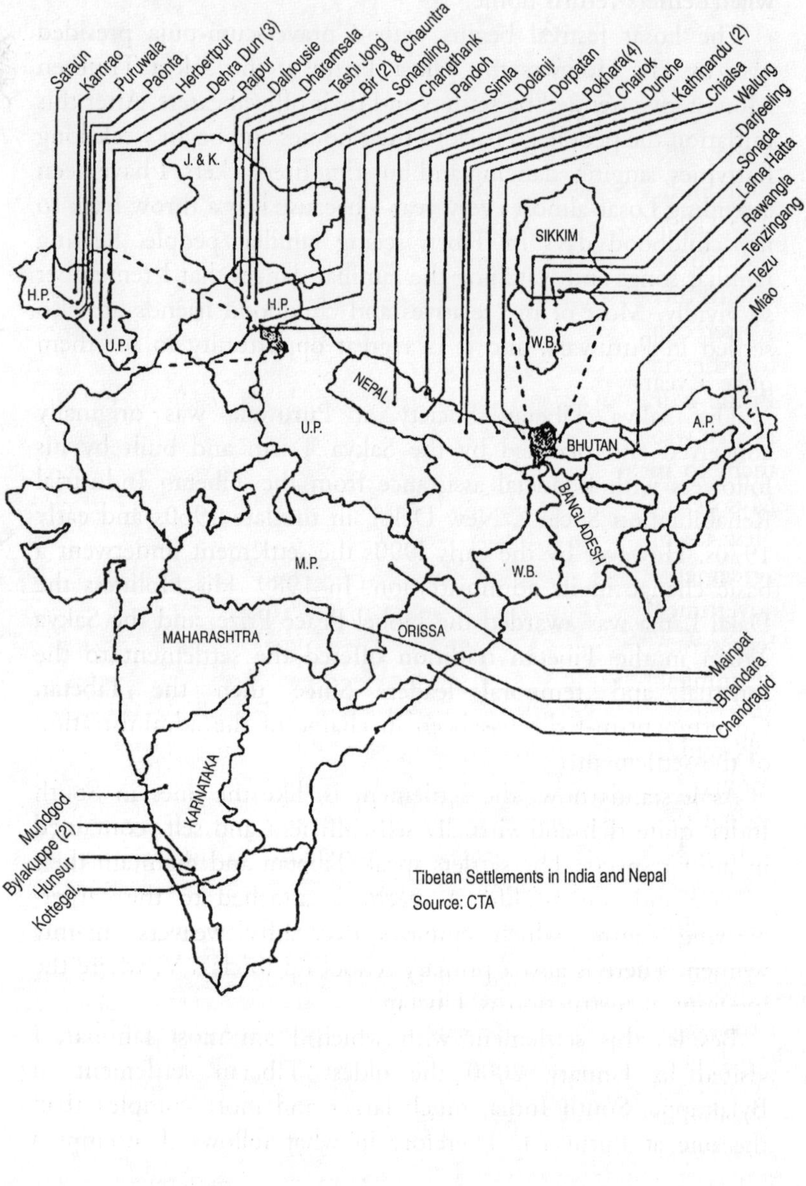

Tibetan Settlements in India and Nepal
Source: CTA

background history and general picture of the settlements in Bylakuppe and Mundgod, both in Karnataka, which will give the reader some general ideas and information about Tibetan settlements in India.

Historical Background

Today there are 46 Tibetan settlements in India, Nepal and Bhutan, home to most of the 100,451 Tibetan refugees in South Asia (1998 figures).[1] It has been said in previous chapters, that the Tibetan leadership, anxious that the Tibetan refugees should retain their culture and identity, did not want them to be scattered all over the subcontinent, but wanted them to live together in settlements. As early as 1959, the Dalai Lama and Prime Minister Jawaharlal Nehru agreed on this principle and Nehru wrote to the governments of the Indian states, requesting them to make land available. The Government of the State of Mysore (now Karnataka) was the first to send a positive reply to New Delhi's request for land on which to settle the refugees. An agreement was reached between the state and central governments (in consultation with the Dalai Lama's representatives) to settle 3,000 refugees on a 1,500-hectare tract of uninhabited jungle land on lease at Bylakuppe, 80 kilometres west of the town of Mysore in Karnataka. Other Indian states followed. In June 1962 the Government of Bhutan also granted enough land to settle about 3,000 refugees with funds from the Indian Government in two separate settlements.

In the beginning it was not easy. The jungle had to be cleared, infrastructure laid and houses built. Adaptation to lower altitudes and a different climate caused health problems for the Tibetans.

---

[1]Planning Council, Central Tibetan Administration, Tibetan Demographic Survey, 2 vols., Dharamsala 2000. There is a floating population of about 6 per cent which could not be counted. The Planning Council reckons that the population increases by 2.2 per cent per year due to natural growth and influx of more refugees. The total Tibetan refugee population in South Asia and abroad is around 130,000.

Moreover, a large number of refugees were nomads, unfamiliar with settled agriculture. Thanks to the combined efforts of the Government of Mysore, the Indian central government, the UNHCR and, of course the Tibetans themselves, villages were established in a comparatively short time. Groups of five persons were alloted two and a half hectares of land (considered a viable unit in South India) and a one-room tenement. Soon international NGOs committed themselves to the rehabilitation work, the Swiss Agency for Development and Cooperation (SDC) arrived first.

Within a span of a few years, the refugees from Tibet became self- supporting and emerged as 'one of the most successful' refugee communities in the world.[2] This self-estimate is corroborated by social scientists who have studied the Tibetan refugees since 1966.

Melvyn Goldstein, the American anthropologist, arrived at Bylakuppe in January 1966 to do fieldwork among the refugees in South India. Within five years of starting the settlement from scratch in 1960, the refugees at Bylakuppe had 'become a tremendous economic success.'[3] He observed 'very little manifestation of the dysfunctional behaviour commonly associated with the 'refugee' syndrome. There was little incidence of mental and emotional disorders and no incidence of alcoholism.'[4] Girija Saklaini, an Indian sociologist, did extensive fieldwork and research on Tibetan refugees living in Dharamsala, Delhi and Dehradun (northern India) and her findings are similarly positive. She wrote that Tibetans have, on the whole, 'successfully emerged from a self-sufficient barter economy into a competitive economy, and have adjusted to the new situation

---

[2]The Dalai Lama, 'Inaugural Speech' in *Conference-cum- Workshop on Tibetan Refugees in India: A Report,* Council for Home Affairs, Central Tibetan Secretariat, Dharamsala 1986.

[3]Goldstein, Melvyn C., Ethnogenesis and Resource Competition among Tibetan Refugees in South India: A New Face to the Indo-Tibetan Interface, in: James Fisher (ed.), *Himalayan Anthropology,* The Hague 1978, p. 399.

[4]Ibid., p. 403.

which is a tribute to the Tibetan community in exile.'[5] She gives three reasons for the Tibetan success in India. First, the Tibetans are hard-working people. Second, their womenfolk also work as hard as men, if not more. And third, the Tibetans have a natural instinct for trading.[6]

The Tibetan refugee achievement is not confined to relative economic success in a country where forty per cent of the host population lives below the poverty level. Tanka Subba, a Nepali anthropologist, studied the Tibetan refugees settled in Sikkim, Darjeeling and Kalimpong (West Bengal) in the mid-1970s. He attributes the smooth transition to the fact that the Tibetans could transfer parts of their society, including women, religious teachers and above all their head of state as a symbol of their identity.[7] Among other things, he found out that 90.9 per cent of the Tibetan refugees in that area spoke Nepali, 84.5 per cent spoke Hindi and 44.8 per cent spoke English. Finally, the refugees' preservation of their cultural identity and religious institutions has been so successful that a well-known European anthropologist, Christoph von Fürer-Heimendorf, has termed it the 'renaissance of Tibetan civilisation' in exile.[8] After surveying the cultural scene among the Tibetan refugees in India and Nepal, he concluded:

> The ability of homeless and impoverished groups of refugees to build and fund in foreign lands numerous monasteries of a remarkably high architectural standard and their success in developing viable monastic communities similar to those of Tibet is one of the miracles of the twentieth century.[9]

---

[5]Girija Saklaini, *The Uprooted Tibetans in India: A Sociological Study of Continuity and Change*, New Delhi 1984, p. 216.

[6]Ibid., p. 219.

[7]Tanka B. Subba, *Flight and Adaptation: Tibetan Refugees in the Darjeeling-Sikkim Himalaya*, Dharamsala 1990, p. X.

[8]Christoph von Fürer-Heimendorf, *The Renaissance of Tibetan Civilization*, Bombay 1990, p. 2.

[9]Ibid.

Right from the beginning in 1959, Jawaharlal Nehru showed keen personal interest in the Tibetan refugee problem. One of the main reasons was that his China policy was severely criticised in India throughout the 1950s, and his critics took the Tibetan crisis as proof of his policy failure. Moreover, in India there was widespread sympathy for the Tibetan cause, because of India's cultural affinities with Buddhist Tibet. It was probably to compensate for his political inability to do anything for Tibet at the international level[10] that Nehru sought to put the Tibetan refugee problem high on India's domestic agenda in the 1960s.

On 31 March 1959, the Government of India granted asylum to the Dalai Lama. On April 4, 1959 Nehru stated in public that India's policy was governed by three factors: the preservation of the security and integrity of India; India's desire to maintain friendly relations with the People's Republic of China; and India's deep sympathy for the people of Tibet.[11] India's deep sympathy for the people of Tibet was translated into its concrete concern for the refugees. Though it was the last component of India's foreign policy, the fact that the Tibetan people figured in that official policy statement meant that the question of Tibetan refugees was high on India's agenda. It made a tremendous difference to the Tibetans. In this way, Nehru's political guilt was compensated by his deep personal concern for the refugees from Tibet.

When the refugees first began to arrive in India in 1959, the responsibility for them was placed not with the Home Ministry but with the powerful Ministry of External Affairs where Nehru himself was also Foreign Minister. In June 1962, at Calcutta, the Prime Minister of Bhutan, the Indian Political Officer of Sikkim and representatives of the Government of India and the Dalai Lama met and agreed that about 3,000 refugees should be settled

[10]See chapter 3.

[11]L.W. Holborn, *Refugees: A Problem of Our Time, The Work of the United Nations High Commission for Refugees*, 1951–1972, Scarecrow, N.J. 1975, p. 719.

on land given by the Government of Bhutan.[12] All these incidents demonstrate that in order for a refugee community to be successfully resettled, the highest echelons of the host government's political decision-making, involvement and interest are necessary.

Indigenous Leadership and Organisation in Tibetan Refugee Society: Organised Participation

Although co-ordination and co-operation among NGOs may not be unique to the Tibetan case; it was, however, more striking and persistent throughout the rehabilitation period, which undoubtedly contributed to the overall success of the Tibetan settlements. But by far the most fundamental features of the Tibetan success lay in the indigenous leadership and organisation that emerged out of the traditional social and political structures. Such leadership and organisation, especially during the initial and critical years, were instrumental in the successful implementation of various projects. They ensured that the NGO funds went beyond mere relief operations to the building of an infrastructure.

When the Dalai Lama escaped to India in 1959, a number of aristocrats and monk-officials (*rtse-grun*) who ran the Tibetan government at Lhasa, came along with him. It was the nucleus of such ex-officials, and some new recruits who, under the aegis of the Dalai Lama, re-established the Tibetan government (*bod-gzhun*) in Dharamsala. The legal fact that no state in the world (including India) recognises this 'Tibetan Government-in-Exile' headed by the Dalai Lama, does not alter the social fact that it provided legitimate leadership to the refugee community as a whole. Its social function, and not so much its international legal standing, is relevant to refugee studies. The fact is, this *bod-gzhun* has all the basic features of a complex political organisation.

As far as refugees from Tibet are concerned, the Dalai Lama's

---

[12]Ibid., p. 723.

complex organisation in Dharamsala has performed three vital and integrative functions. It has assumed a virtual monopoly to represent and act on behalf of the refugees in negotiation with the Government of India and the NGOs concerning relief, rehabilitation and settlement of Tibetan refugees in India and to a lesser extent in Nepal and Bhutan. At the same time it organised the scattered refugees into several settlements and established its direct control over them.

From the beginning the Dalai Lama and his officials interacted with the Government of India on behalf of the refugees. They immediately set themselves up as the sole spokesmen for the refugees and even maintained offices in the transit camps. The Government of India tacitly accepted the Dalai Lama's assumption of leadership over the refugees from Tibet partly as a mark of respect for the institution of Dalai Lama and partly as a concession for India's inability or unwillingness to recognise the 'Tibetan Government-in-Exile', despite persistent pleas and considerable Indian public support for such a recognition, especially after 1962. In any case it was more convenient and effective for the Government of India to recognise the moral authority of the Dalai Lama and the leadership role of his organisation within the Tibetan refugee community. Such a policy resulted, as far as Dharamsala was concerned, in the Indian affirmation of the Dalai Lama and his organisation's right to exercise administrative control over the refugee settlements in India. Moreover, this policy was in line with India's desire that settlements should be designed in such a 'non-assimilative' way as to enable the Tibetan refugees to preserve their cultural identity and religious institution while in exile.

Before we demonstrate the live links between Dharamsala and the various Tibetan settlements, we shall briefly show how the Dalai Lama's organisation interacts with the NGOs and aggregates funds for infrastructural work. Most of the NGOs tend to recognise the Dalai Lama as the legitimate leader of the refugees from Tibet and accordingly include his representatives in their discussions on rehabilitation projects. I can remember only two instances where Dharamsala's right to make decisions on behalf of the refugees was indirectly questioned. The Swiss Red Cross and the Canadian immigration authorities sent their own officials to India to select Tibetan refugees to migrate to their countries, without going through the Dharamsala administration. Otherwise, most refugee matters were conducted on a tripartite basis: Indian, NGO and Tibetan representatives. And in most cases this worked well.

The settlements are not completely identical in their organisation, but they follow a pattern, the terms for the functionaries and the levels may differ. In principle there are three layers of decision-making. At the head is the settlement officer, who belongs to the Tibetan Central Administration. The settlements—nowadays comprising between 1,000 to 8,000 people—are divided into camps, also called villages. The inhabitants elect a camp leader called *chimie*. These are assisted by four spokespersons called *chupon,* representing approximately 250 inhabitants. Originally the *chupon* represented ten households, but as the population has increased, this number is nowadays not strictly adhered to. This echoes the traditional Tibetan decimal organisation, hence the refugees had no problem accepting this system. Every settlement has a cooperative society.

In Bylakuppe, where about half the Tibetan refugees in South India live, there are two settlements: Lugsung Samdupling, founded in 1961, therefore also called the 'old settlement'. It has a population of 7,631 according to the 1998 Tibetan Census. The second, Dekyi Larsoe, founded in 1969, with 3,096 people, is the 'new settlement'. In addition there are about 7,000 inhabitants of the monasteries: monks, novices and staff . The four sects in Tibetan Buddhism have rebuilt their famous monasteries, namely Sera, Tashilhunpo, Kargye and Namdrolling next to the settlements. These monasteries and their monk population follow their own organisation and have to find their own funding; they are not part of the settlement administration. There is a liaison officer though. Only at election times do electoral officers carry out their duties inside the monasteries. Monks perform religious ceremonies in the settlements, play a major role in festivals and the settlers participate in some of the events in the temples.

The structure of the two Bylakuppe settlements mirrors the three-layered hierarchy with the *chupon* or 'head of ten' at the base. This is a traditional Tibetan form of organisation, but nowadays there is flexibility regarding the number of households. The *chupon's* duty is to organise labour for community projects, call for meetings, organise festivals, hear grievances. Such deputies, numbering four in each camp, are annually elected. The most important functionary is the *chimie* or 'general leader' nowadays called camp leader. He/she is the link between the administration and the settlers.[13] Camp leaders are elected for one year and receive meagre salaries from Dharamsala. Camps comprise about 1,000 people, thus the Lugsung Samdupling Settlement has six camps, but given the size two camp leaders—*chimie*—per camp.

Above these democratically elected positions, are the appointees of Dharamsala, and chief among them is the Settlement Officer, *sku-tsab* or *dbu-'zin*. He heads a fully staffed office and is accountable to the Department of Home of the Central Tibetan Administration (CTA). Bylakuppe having such a large population, one of the settlement officers is a 'Representative' of the CTA.

The settlement officers and their staff plan the policies for the settlement as a whole with respect not only to economic matters but also to socio-cultural ones. Such policies and projects are implemented through the useful offices of the *chupon* after consultation with the *chimie.* Internally, the settlement officer seeks to integrate diverse subcultural units by articulating pan-Tibetan identity and ideology. The settlement officer also uses the prestige of his office to mediate disputes, but only if efforts at the lower levels fail. Externally, he often acts on behalf of his settlers in their dealings with Indian legal and political officials.

---

[13]In a meeting the editors attended of nearly all the camp leaders of the two settlements there was only one female camp leader.

The two settlements are well provided with schools: there is a CTSA school, going up to class 12 and five elementary schools up to class 5. The SOS Children's Village also has a secondary school for their 1,160 children, and the Sera Monastery runs its own high school for the novices.[14] (For other facilities see insert on page 206.)

The Tibetan refugee organisation at the Mundgod settlement that Palakshappa describes, seems slightly different. However, we cannot fail to observe the centrality of the Dharamsala-appointed settlement officer and the organising principle of the social organisation. They are characteristically Tibetan.

The economic and political nerve-centre of the Mundgod Tibetan settlement—as in other settlements—is the Tibetan Cooperative Society whose membership is open to all the male heads of all the households in the camp. At the head of the cooperative society is the Secretary, a representative of the CTA. The Secretary and his staff, who operate the settlement's secretariat, are directly paid by Dharamsala. The Secretary acts as an administrative link between the Dharamsala administration and the Mundgod settlement. He is also the proper channel between the settlement and the respective Indian governments, both at the state and centre levels. Moreover, all the foreign charitable organisations operate only through the cooperative society and its secretary. Palakshappa notes[15] that 'due to the pivotal role he has within the Mundgod settlement, the Secretary, though a paid official, commands authority and in many respects is considered as the king of the settlement.'

The Mundgod settlement consists of nine villages, and each village elects a leader called *gambo* meaning 'the elder' (corresponding to the *chimie* at Bylakuppe). The village leader acts as a link between the village and the co-operative society's Secretary. The Secretary delegates authority to the

---

[14]This is an entirely new development thanks to the efforts of an Italian monk. Information Karma Lekshe Tsomo.

[15]T.C. Palakshappa, *Tibetans in India: A Case Study of Mundgod Tibetans*, New Delhi 1978, p. 43.

village leader and the latter transmits messages and policies from the co-operative society; he tries to solve his villagers' problems such as getting loans from the bank, mediating in civil disputes, getting fertiliser from the co-operative; and above all he gets tasks and projects ordered by the Secretary done by the villagers.

Here too the village leader is assisted by group leaders (*chupon*). The group leaders are subordinate to the village leader and are in constant touch with him. They report to the village leader about the needs and problems of families whom they represent and who have elected them. Communication and command flows through hierarchy: from the Secretary to the village leaders, from village leaders to group leaders and from group leaders to individual households.

The Mundgod settlement has an executive committee consisting of all *gambo,* the village leaders, and headed by the co-operative society's Secretary. (In Bylakuppe board members of the cooperative are elected). The committee is an apex policy and planning board for the entire settlement. Palakshappa argues that these village leaders serve in effect as a check on any possible attempts at autocratic rule by the Secretary.

Although Mundgod and Bylakuppe settlements share certain essential common characteristics, there are some differences too. The Bylakuppe settlement reflects the vision of a traditional Tibetan government official as its head; at Mundgod, the settlement officer located his 'office' in the centre of economic activity, namely the Tibetan Co-operative Society. Although the ultimate power was retained by the Secretary, he attempted to encourage democratic participation in the decision-making process by inclusion of village representatives. There is also more pluralism in the terms and conditions of *gambo* and *chupon*; either through election or rotation. More such flexibility and modification are evident in Bylakuppe in recent years, where in the early years the decimally-based Tibetan social organisation was rather rigorously applied.

We have tried to demonstrate in some detail the role of indigenous leadership and organisation in the process of Tibetan refugee rehabilitation and settlement not only because their role has been critical in Tibetan success but also because the general question of leadership and organisation within refugee communities should be a crucial part of the subject-matter of refugee studies. The encouragement of the formation of indigenous leadership and social organisation out of the chaos and confusion that prevails among refugees is critically important if the NGO's efforts is to go beyond the initial stage of feeding and relief operations towards some long-term practical solutions.

Demography of the Tibetan Population in Exile: An Introduction

Background

The demography of the Tibetan population in exile is packed with landmarks and vital contradictions. Low fertility despite low mortality, high literacy against higher unemployment rates, intense mobility vs. necessities of community living are the facts and figures of the Tibetan Demographic Survey 1998[16] (TDS 98) that challenges policy-makers, planners and citizens alike. In the following description an attempt has been made to present the above findings with probable causes.

It is important to recognise that the people must be central in any development endeavour. It is equally important that the population must have a healthy demographic structure upon which the whole edifice of socio-economic progress will be based. From time immemorial, the Tibetan population has undergone various natural demographic transitions without losing its vigour and strength. But this no longer remained the same, after the People's Republic of China invaded Tibet in 1951, which forced tens of thousands of Tibetans to flee into exile and brought in hundreds and thousands of Chinese impacting the demographics of the Tibetan population unprecedentedly. Like in Tibet, the Tibetan population in exile too has undergone a fundamental demographic change over the last four decades of diaspora.

According to the 1998 Survey the Tibetans in exile may well belong

[16]Planning Council, Central Tibetan Administration, Tibetan Demographic Survey 1998, 2 Vols., Dharamsala 2000.

to one of the most mobile nations in the world. Scattered over 93 different points in India, Nepal and Bhutan, about 65 per cent of Tibetans and almost 80 per cent of the young population are seasonally on the move from one region to another covering relatively huge distances annually. Ever since 1991, international migration has intensified when a thousand individuals were granted immigration passages to USA. In South Asia most earn their living by engaging in informal activities, which mainly consists of seasonal retailing services. The general standard of living can be comparable to the surrounding native rural communities, in some areas a little more affluent. After having successfully overcome the initial rehabilitation stage (1959–80), the community is now on the threshold of a development stage, where changing aspirations of intervening generations impact on the developmental activities.

Issues like low fertility rates and declining enrolment in schools, lack of employment opportunities, declining quality education and a wide range of nutrition and health problems threatens the very survival and sustenance of the Tibetan population.

Demographic Attributes—Distribution

According to the TDS 98, the exile Tibetan population had reached 122,078 on 12 June 1998 from the initial estimated population of 80,000 in 1959, out of which 85,147 live in India and 13,720 in Nepal (cf. note 1). The next largest group of exile Tibetans in Asia lives in Bhutan followed by the Russian Federation and Japan together. The continent of America, mainly the USA and Canada, has the largest share of Tibetans in the western world followed by Europe where 68.6 per cent are settled in Switzerland alone. There are only 217 persons in Oceania. And the staff of the Office of Tibet in Pretoria constitutes the Tibetan exile population in Africa.

Age and Sex Structure

The age and sex structure is constructed on a population of both sexes in chosen age groups, depending upon the selective proportion of cohorts (i.e. similar age-groups). The age and sex structure is popularly depicted by an age pyramid with different shapes reflecting the pattern of interrelationships between different age groups by dependency ratio, gender, migration and fertility (see TDS 98 report). The sex ratio establishes exactly the number of males per thousand females which according to the 1998 census stands at 1,262 males per 1,000 females. This mild deficiency in its ratio is partly caused by male dominated migration and partly an indication of a patriarchal leaning of the community.

Literacy

The survey revealed that there is marked improvement in the education of the Tibetan population as compared to Tibetans under Chinese rule, thanks to the early special educational programme initiated by the Central Tibetan Administration and the support given by the Government of India. The effective literacy rate of the Tibetan exile population stood at 74.5 per cent in 1998 while the general literacy rate was 69.3 per cent. But only 2.6 per cent of the total population achieved higher studies with professional careers. This may become the core area of intervention for future educational policies. As in the past, monasteries in exile still play a key role in education.

Fertility

One of the most critical factors is in the area of fertility. The survey indicates an increasing decline of the fertility rate. If this trend continues, it may not sustain and regenerate itself in the near future. With a Crude Birth Rate of 8/1000, the General Fertility Rate (GFR) comes to 34/1000 in the reproductive age group and General Marital Fertility Rate (GMFR) to 70/1000 giving a Total Fertility Rate (TFR) of 1.22, which is considered 'very low'. What could be the reason? According to the TDS 98, 44.05 per cent of women in the 25–29 age group are unmarried and furthermore, if we examine the age group from 25–34, the age group that accounted for 80 per cent of all births during 1998, nearly half remained unmarried. In other words the situation of high non-marriage and conscious delay in marriages may have been caused by high literacy and rising aspirations of the female population coupled with anxieties due to lack of professional opportunities.

Occupational Structure

The high proportion of non-workers (74.1 per cent) to workers indicates either that the population is exceptionally young with a high proportion of youth population, or high unemployment rates. Observation shows it is the latter that may have been the factor since most of the Tibetans find themselves in a transition with no regular income from occupational professions. In fact most of the Tibetans are engaged in wide- ranging activities dominated by the informal services sector business, which is seasonal.

From the regular professions, 22.5 per cent of the total main workers earned their livelihood still from agriculture with low proportion in household industry i.e. 2.7 per cent. Other workers include the professions with specialised services and skills—mainly sweater-selling (16.85 per cent) followed by staff, schoolteachers, etc. About 8 per cent of the total main workers earn their livelihood through traditional skills such as thangka painting, handicrafts, metal casting and woodcarving.

Non-workers consist of unemployed population, students, minor and dependant old age groups. The unemployment amongst the youths who are educated in general studies is as high as 75 per cent. In the Tibetan community in exile 1,250 students graduate every year, 800 at high school level and 450 students obtain college degrees. The chances that these youths are getting regular employment within our community is very low as the total absorption capacity is just 5 per cent annually.

Migration: Perennial and Seasonal

Migration is a form of spatial mobility of a person involving a change of usual residence between clearly defined geographical and administrative boundaries. Migration is the most important basic factor affecting change in the population of the Tibetan exile community. I am referring mainly to internal migration i.e. seasonal movement within the subcontinent. But there is also movement across the national boundaries.

Migration involves physical and psychological detachment from the organised regular settlements—46 till date[17]*—and their programmes. Over the years almost the same numbers of semi and permanent residences have come up which disintegrates those regular settlements affecting their very purpose. Moreover it involves huge financial and management investments. The direction of internal migration i.e. from rural to urban areas makes up over 80 per cent of the total migrants within the community. Education and seeking better earning opportunities are the two main causes of the migration, which remains*

[17]Earlier there were 52 settlements, some of the smaller ones have been merged, hence there are now 46 settlements.

only partially successful due to poor social and economic bases for Tibetans in urban areas. The all time migration outside India became a trend ever since the early 1990s when a first batch of Tibetans were allowed immigration in the USA. And it will remain so unless the economic opportunities improve drastically.

Changing Social Mosiac: Joint to Nuclear Family

Out of 17,935 households in India and Nepal, about 60 per cent can be called nuclear families. (Similar changes can be observed in Tibet under China's policy regarding polygamy). The household pattern shows that the traditional joint family system is gradually being replaced by a nuclear family structure with medium family sizes. This is another major transition that could be observed which can have far reaching impact upon the upbringing of children (education, health etc.) and the over all capacity of a family to cope with rising demands of the times. Only specialised research could provide more insights into its various implications.

Conclusion

The Tibetan population in exile finds itself in a unique diaspora situation in which the dichotomy of rehabilitation on the one hand and development pursuits on the other blur the perspectives of the individual and the community alike. The demographic irregularities of the Tibetan population are nothing but immediate responses to the sluggish progress in finding an amicable solution to the political situation of Tibet. Hence it would be wrong to compare or generalise the population pattern and structure with any other nation having a normal socio-economic and political situation. Moreover the conclusions drawn here are based on one time data collection, which may need further extrapolation with time series information. However meanwhile the enormous number of data collected during the 1998 Census provides a formidable basis for research, planning and development of the Tibetan community. The analysis and findings presented here do throw some light on the magnitude and nature of problems and issues faced by the Tibetan population. Tibetan society in exile is indeed undergoing a phase of intensive change after living over four decades in uprooted conditions. The type of programmes that were initiated since the early 60s and lack of progress in resolving the political issue of Tibet have immensely impacted the intervening generations born in exile having no direct linkages to their ancestral home. Intense migration and low fertility are the two vital demographic factors that led to a phase with a series of abnormalities. This phase may well be seen as a transitional phase. It is well acknowledged that the switching between rehabilitation and development costs both human and financial resources dearly. While political pursuit continues, the action must be taken to redress the socio-economic front. This has been well taken and reflected in current reforms and action programmes of the CTA. A sharing of perspectives and planning at the grass roots level will expedite the process of normalcy further. But even when exile bits are done, the abnormalities in the demography of the Tibetan population may still persist as long as the political issue of Tibet remains unresolved.

KUNCHOK TSUNDUE

The Impact of Refugees on the Host Population

Tibetan refugee settlements in India were deliberately designed in such a way as to recreate Tibetan society with its core values intact. Such a re-creation of pockets of Tibetan culture and society in India was not only the popular desire and determination of refugees from Tibet; it was to a large extent, endorsed and even encouraged by the Government of India as a matter of policy. Two critical aspects of India's policy towards the Tibetan refugees are—(1) the liberal 'non-assimilative' framework as reflected in the separate settlements, and (2) the broad 'delegated' authority of the Tibetan leadership headed by the Dalai Lama over the Tibetan settlements in India.[18] Such a benevolent policy ensures Tibetan cultural identity and social autonomy in a sea of host population. This seemed understandable in the 1960s but it is now coming under increasing criticism. This criticism centres around the argument that Tibetans in India should no longer maintain their social and cultural boundaries from the host society; it implies that

[18]Goldstein, supra, p. 398.

Tibetans should 'integrate' with the Indians. Some Tibetan critics on the other hand maintain that the Hindu caste hierarchy permits the maintenance of caste communities and their identity within each caste. Hence the Tibetans might socially and culturally constitute a *jati* and be permitted to maintain their cultural identity and religious institutions.

As we stated before, one of the motives behind the forced migration from their homeland was the Tibetan apprehension that their cultural identity and religious institutions were in danger of disappearing under Chinese rule. Most Indians sympathised with this concern. The creation of separate settlements for Tibetans meant in effect maintaining social and cultural boundaries vis-á-vis the host society. This in turn means that the interaction between the refugees and the host population is limited to economic transactions in the market.

It may be surprising but true as observed by Palakshappa, Goldstein and several other authors that Tibetan refugees have provided considerable job opportunities for the host population. In agricultural settlements most Tibetans employ rural Indian labourers to till the soil, sow the seeds, and so on. An Indian anthropologist notes that such job opportunities have

> smoothed the relations between the Tibetans and the Indians. Although local Indians might resent that their land had been given to some outsiders, they 'feel satisfied' that they (Indians) have benefited by the establishment of the Tibetan settlement. At least, it provides the Indians with jobs continuously throughout the year, which many of them did not have before.[19]

It deserves mention that the monasteries also employ Indian labour.

Many members of the host population are engaged by Tibetan refugees in other spheres too. In Nepal numerous local Nepalis are employed in Tibetan carpet factories, which are the largest foreign exchange earner next to tourism. Moreover, an

---

[19]Palakshappa, supra, p. 99.

increasing number of Tibetan refugees are entering secondary occupations such as selling sweaters in winter, running restaurants and hotels, etc. in which local workers are being employed as can be seen in Delhi, Dharamsala, Darjeeling, Kathmandu and other places.

The other beneficial type of refugee impact on the host society is the extension of Tibetan facilities to the host population. Most of the Tibetan settlements are located in remote parts of India, which had not received much attention from New Delhi in terms of developmental funds and projects. With the establishment of Tibetan settlements in such areas, the surrounding Indian or Nepali villages began to receive side benefits. Tibetan schools and hospitals are open to the host population as well. While digging tube wells or making irrigation canals for the Tibetan refugees, foreign voluntary organisations have sponsored similar schemes for the surrounding local villages as well. To such remote and poor villagers in India or Nepal, the establishment of a Tibetan colony in their locality means new jobs, more business opportunities and new modern facilities. In fact most settlements have linkages with international donors, i.e. with NGOs as well as with individual sponsors, who support children in the SOS Tibetan Children's Villages or individual monks in the monasteries. Indirectly the local people too profit from this inflow of foreign exchange.

Observations at Bylakuppe*

The Wangyals[20] were among the pioneers when in 1960 the settlement no. 1—Lugsung Samdupling—was founded. In those days they were a family of five: mother, father and three children. They were alloted 2½ hectares of land, a one-room hut, which served as kitchen, living room and bedroom and a small garden for growing vegetables.

Today the Wangyals are grandparents and head a family of fifteen, including five grandchildren. The worries and hardships of the early

*The editors visited Bylakuppe in June 2001.

[20]Names changed.

years in exile show on their faces. The family still has only $2\frac{1}{2}$ hectares of land, not enough to feed the growing family. Two of their four sons successfully run a shop in Goa, the third son serves in the Indian Army. One daughter teaches at the local Children's Village, the other got married in another settlement. The youngest son stays with the parents and looks after the farming. More rooms and a courtyard have been attached to the small hut. Two motorcycles are parked there and a pile of fashionable children's sneakers are neatly piled up in a corner. The daughters-in-law and the grandchildren all live here.

In the winter, when the sons and their wives are away selling sweaters, it is not easy for the old couple to look after five small children. 'But I am lucky', says Mr. Wangyal, 'my sons have work and sustain the family'.

Outside on a central square, clusters of young men chat and share jokes, others demonstrate the power of their motorcycles. Mr. Tsering, a man in his middle thirties, is the camp leader, he has served in the Indian Army for ten years. What is he doing now? Four months each year he works as a sweater seller. His 'village' goes to Hyderabad, where they rent rooms for the season and obtain a 'Hawker's Permit'. Forty to fifty per cent of the camp population engages in selling sweaters. We ask wether they ever had to face conflicts with the local population. No, they have been selling in the same locality of Hyderabad for many years and have become friendly with the locals.

The dominant topic is unemployment among the young Tibetans. But it seems the high-school graduates show entrepreneurial spirit: they open internet cafés, restaurants, workshops as electricians, plumbers, TV mechanics. The cooperative makes space available for these tiny industries.

A Community Centre offers an assembly hall, a temple and a kitchen to cater for festivals. Recently a water-tank has been built with the support of a Danish NGO and the windmill to provide energy for a pump was donated by a Dutch NGO. Now water is available for one hour a day—earlier the settlers could draw water only for 10–15 minutes daily. The tank and the windmill are placed next to a stupa, surrounded by large prayer wheels.

The Cooperative is the engine of the settlement. The Secretary is the most important man next to the Settlement Officer and is paid by the CTA. The 1945 members elect the eight delegates on the board.The Cooperative distributes seeds, fertilizer, gives loans and stores the agricultural products, to be able to sell them at a favourable moment. In principle the settlers are free to grow on their plot whatever they like, but in practice they choose maize, which is sold to cornflake factories or made into chicken feed. Tsampa, the traditional Tibetan dish, can also be made from maize flour and is still the favourite diet of the older generation.

The soil at Bylakuppe is fertile, but so far yields only one harvest per year. Recently a small barrage has been built and now there is hope for a second annual harvest. As agriculture cannot feed the growing population the Cooperative started a carpet weaving workshop and a small factory for incense sticks. A tractor station serves the members and the Indian public as well and a first-aid dispensary offers Tibetan and Western medicine.

Dharamsala may be far, but it is very much present in the person of Mr. D. Dorjee, the Representative of the Central Tibetan Administration and Settlement Officer for Lugsung Samdupling. He is also the President of the Cooperative and of the Bylakuppe Election Commission, Vicechairman of the local Advisory Committee for the Tibetan School and member of the Board of Directors of the local Children's Village (TCV). Mr. Dorjee's task is to coordinate, to implement the directives from Dharamsala, to maintain the structure of the settlement and to mediate in conflicts among settlers, if and when they arise.

The 'new' settlement 'Dekyi Larsoe' has an Assembly of 28 elected members. They meet twice a year and—as they put it—'check' the work of the Cooperative. Mr. Dorjee thinks participation makes his job easier, as the settlers get more involved with the efficient implementation of projects.

The relations with the local Indians are good. The Tibetans have purchasing power and boost the market and the construction business. They even create employment for Indians, particularly for seasonal agricultural labourers. Sometimes eyebrows are raised when the local people notice how Tibetan boys and girls interact easily and freely with each other. Conflicts—if at all—erupt at the time of Tibetan festivals, when the men drink 'chang'[21] in quantities they were used to in the cold climate of the 'roof of the world'.

DAGMAR BERNSTORFF

[21] A drink made of fermented barley.

Economic Integration

The Tibetan refugee settlements in India were built in the 1960s and early 1970s with a specific purpose in mind. They were designed as self-contained cultural units sustained by self-sufficient agro and handicraft economies for a limited rather than an unlimited period of time. This plan proved to be more than sufficient for the first generation of refugees. In fact they, during their life-time in exile, creatively deviated from the planned agricultural economy to the sweater-selling business which they find more lucrative, and less time consuming, though more intensive. As it stands now, the new generation of exiles born and brought up in India or Nepal appears to face a dilemma in both their education and economy. They have reached the limits of educational levels and economic choices offered in the settlements. Where to go from here?

The Tibetan exile population in India and Nepal is 100,490 according to the 1998 census.[22] Of this, literacy defined as those literate up to the primary level in India and Nepal is 69 per cent. But the generation between 19–25 years is 97 per cent literate. And by the late 1990s there were 2,628 higher secondary graduates, a number likely to increase year by year. Where can they find employment? Because the Tibetan establishment in Dharamsala or the settlements in rural India are already saturated, will they be contented with the sweater-selling business, which their non-literate parents pioneered?

The core of the Tibetan exile economy is by all accounts its informal sector, namely the sweater-selling business which official publications never acknowledge or mention. This business takes place in the winter season roughly between October and February. It started with the sale of hand-knitted, colourful sweaters of the type which can still be seen in handicraft centres in India and Nepal or in so-called One-World shops in the West. The fact that people from the cold peaks of

[22]See note 1.

the Himalayas marketed those sweaters lent them great credibility. Soon the demand for these hand knitted woollens outgrew the supply. So Tibetans started buying machine-made sweaters in bulk from factories at Ludhiana (Punjab) and spread all over India, targeting especially small towns and industrial cities. The relations between the producers and the Tibetans are said to be most cordial and based on mutual trust, they get their ware on very easy terms. It is essentially this business, which has made the former Tibetan peasants and nomads better off than the average Indian peasants are today.[23] Tibetans are culturally and economically free to engage in diverse economic activities. Hence the entire able-bodied population of the settlements engage in winter, as stated before, in the sweater selling business all over India. A number of these salesmen and women continue to trade in additional Tibetan items meant for tourists and pilgrims not only during the winter season but throughout the year, especially in hill stations and temple towns. However the majority, after completion of the sweater selling season, resume their settlement routine such as agricultural work and various handicrafts.

While transacting and participating in the larger, though lower levels of the Indian economy, Tibetan commoners have learned the value and utility of elementary lessons of democratic functioning in their business relations with local Indian municipalities and panchayats. The sweater sellers organised themselves almost spontaneously using their age-old tradition of decimal based organisations called *chu-shog* or *rgya-shog*. Having thus organised themselves in groups, then they directly elect their leaders or members to act on their behalf in dealing with the local Indian authorities and to maintain discipline among the sweater sellers themselves. This daily necessity of functioning

[23]The establishment in Dharamsala is apprehensive about this pavement trade. It is feared that the Tibetans mix with the rougher and tougher segments of Indian society and might come to harm (editor's note).

outside the settlement environment might have taught the average Tibetan in exile more practice of democracy at the grass-root level in terms of popular participation than from the formalised and stylised democracy that is coming from Dharamsala.

During my visits to Bylakuppe (January 2000) and Puruwala (February 2001) I saw a whole new generation of Tibetans who are literate yet engaged in the same sweater business that their non-literate parents pioneered. This new generation is increasingly likely to face serious problems of employment and economic activities suited to their education and skills unless they integrate their economy and employment with the larger economic systems beyond the settlements.

In Bylakuppe I have seen a couple of families engaged in coffee cultivation which finds a larger outside market. Similarly in Mundgod some Tibetan families, I am told, are growing tobacco.. But such enterprising families are few; the majority of Tibetan settlers are seasonal sweater sellers in winter, who now and increasingly in the near future face a serious dilemma. Their dilemma might be eased by economic integration with larger economic systems or a satisfactory solution to the Tibetan question. For the settlements were built with a limited purpose in mind, and the emerging new generation cannot possibly go on indefinitely with the same economic activities inherited from their illiterate parents because of their newly acquired education and skills.

Rationality is a cold calculation which makes the Tibetan diasporic future look very gloomy. However, in real life human ingenuity and civilisational competence have played a significant role. The sweater business was not part of the settlement plan; it was an ingenious discovery by non-literate Tibetan peasants and nomads in response to the larger Indian market situation. Perhaps, the new generation of Tibetans in exile might have retained some of the old Tibetan virtues in coping with new problems and challenges which their parents faced in their life time with industry, ingenuity and dignity.

References

Alam, Jayanti, *Tibetan Society in Exile*, Delhi 2000.

Bureau of H.H. the Dalai Lama, *Tibetans in Exile*, 1959–1969, New Delhi 1969.

Conway, John S., 'Canadian Contribution to Rehabilitation of Tibetan Refugees', in: *Tibetan Review*, vol. 13, no. 4. 1978.

Dalai Lama, 'Inaugural Speech' in: Conference-cum- Workshop on Tibetan Refugees in India: A Report, Council for Home Affairs, Central Tibetan Secretariat, Dharamsala 1986.

Fürer-Heimendorf, Christoph von, *The Renaissance of Tibetan Civilisation*, Bombay 1990.

Goldstein, Melvyn C., *Ethnògenesis and Resource Competition among Tibetan Refugees in South India: A New Face to the Indo-Tibetan Interface*, in: James Fisher (ed.), Himalayan Anthropology, The Hague 1978.

Holborn, L.W., *Refugees: A Problem of Our Time, The Work of the United Nations High Commission for Refugees, 1951–1972*, Scarecrow, N.J. 1975.

Palakshappa, T.C., *Tibetans in India: A Case Study of Mundgod Tibetans*, New Delhi 1978.

Planning Council, Central Tibetan Administration, Tibetan Demographic Survey, Vol. 1–2, Dharamsala 2000.

Saklaini, Girija, *The Uprooted Tibetans in India: A Sociological Study of Continuity and Change*, New Delhi 1984.

Subba, Tanka B., *Flight and Adaptation: Tibetan Refugees in the Darjeeling-Sikkim Himalaya*, Library of Tibetan Works and Archives, Dharamsala 1990.

CHAPTER ELEVEN

Of Monks and Monasteries

SHERAB GYATSO

> Once lofty motives and ideals, which, with burgeoning power—growing wealth and political influence—progressively became sullied by worldly concerns. This power then gradually eroded, until finally the modest numbers of individuals still involved were forced to return to their spiritual roots, eking out a living on the fringes of society.

Surely this is how many would characterise the history of monasteries and monasticism in the West. And what of their Tibetan counterparts? The plot was more or less followed up until the latter half of the twentieth century. And many might have anticipated that events then (the Chinese communist invasion and eventual annexation of Tibet, ethnic and religious persecution, the Cultural Revolution and so forth) would complete the cycle, bringing about their decline and marginalisation. In the exiled community at least though, despite the undoubted decrease in wealth and political influence, the monastic visage—whilst perhaps battered and bruised— remains both recognisable and supremely visible. Re-invention and reform are definitely not the order of the day here. Rather, it is in very familiar (and perhaps predictable) guises that the Tibetan monk and the monastery have re-established positions for themselves at the very heart of the new society.

---

[1]Planning Council, Central Tibetan Administration, Tibetan Demographic Survey 1998, Vol. 1, Dharamsala 2000, pp. 106, 215. Monks and nuns combined are 12,297, i.e. 12 per cent of the refugee population.

The Monk Population

According to the latest census figures[1] which exclude *native* monk populations in places such as Ladakh, Spiti, Sikkim, Nepal and so forth, where they have existed for centuries—the combined Tibetan monk population of India and Nepal is 11,067. The number of Buddhist monasteries of the same group is 218[2] (and all this for a population totalling just 98,967[3]). Males make up slightly more than half of the exiled community, this means that one-fifth of them is in robes, roughly 11 per cent of the exile population! A 1958 Chinese census for the Tibetan Autonomous Region informs us that only 9.5 per cent of the population were monks and nuns. Now as escaping Communist oppression was one of the reasons cited for leaving their homeland in the first place, we should perhaps not be surprised to find large numbers of religious practitioners in exile. But the ratio itself is a stunning one. Tibetans still have one of highest monastic populations of any ethnic group. In purely numerical terms then, this would not seem to indicate a tradition in terminal decline (although of course decline may be a many-faceted thing).

Although *novice* monks are only supposed to be ordained from about the age of 6 or 7 onwards, there are some who, even prior to reaching their fourth year, are 'recognised' as having been spiritual masters in their former existence (and as such are included within the count). And as remaining a monk until the end of ones' days is still considered the ideal, the age range stretches, at the other end, to those in their 1970s and 1980s.

Formerly, in Tibet, so highly esteemed was the institution of monasticism that it was generally deemed desirable to have at least one male child from the family enter a monastery. This is a tradition that has more or less fallen by the wayside within the refugee community. And correspondingly, families of those brought up in exile tend to contribute fewer members to the monk population. The figures remain high however, due to the

---

[2]According to the Department of Religion, CTA, see chapter 7, p.130.

[3]Tibetan Demographic Survey 1998, supra.

continual stream of new arrivals from Tibet; large proportions of whom come into exile as monks or seeking ordination.

In the immediate wake of the Chinese invasion many monks managed to find their way into exile, congregating at a place called Buxa Duar in West Bengal. But soon after this (prior to and during the decade or so of the Cultural Revolution of 1966–76) Tibet's borders were completely sealed. During this latter period, with significant assistance from the Indian government, Tibetans set about transforming their lives; creating for themselves their own society in exile. In the diaspora, the lay community and the monks were thrown together. As time progressed, the monks gradually extricated themselves once more, with the surviving members of many of the former (now destroyed or closed) monasteries in Tibet re-establishing their old centres. So by the late 1970s and early 1980s, as restrictions began to relax in Tibet (and many once more sought to escape Chinese occupation and domination), those inclined towards religious practice where able to enter the re-established monastic centres in exile. From then, up until the present day, there has been a steady swelling of the monk population due to the influx of such individuals.

However, not all monks reside in monasteries. Some groups and individuals are to be found living in the seclusion of meditational retreat. Others stay closer to the world, working as officials, teachers and so forth. And Tibetans also see no contradiction in a monk living privately or with his relations, in the midst of society. Indeed that is where one would expect to find those who in their twilight years (particularly after the death of a spouse) adopt monastic garb as a form of declaration that they are going to dedicate what remains of their lives to religious devotion (*Rgan chos byed pa*).

Ordination

There are a considerable number of people within Tibetan society who wear robes but are not monastics (i.e. they have not been through a monastic ordination ceremony, involving the formal adoption of a number of vows). But properly speaking there are two levels of ordination and hence two forms of monkhood. The first of these has commonly been translated as the 'novice' (Sanskrit: *Shramanera*/Tibetan: *dge tshul*). Someone seeking to become a novice makes his application to a senior monk, who is an authority of the Vinaya (the original corpus of teachings setting forth all matters monastic). During a formal ceremony, conducted by a group of seniors the individual is given a new name, begins to wear monastic robes, undergoes a ceremonial 'head-shave', promises to abide by thirty-six vows and hopefully adopts a completely new outlook on life.[4] These vows are shared by all of the Buddhist schools in Tibet, there having existed only one Vinaya tradition. Ordination as a novice can, theoretically, be sought at any age after about six or seven, and is a necessary prerequisite to gaining the higher ordination. Higher, or 'full' ordination (*Bhikshu* /*dge slong*) may not be sought prior to the age of twenty. Again, the aspirant undergoes a formal ceremony, this time adopting two hundred and fifty three vows. Despite the large numerical gulf existing between the vows of the novice and the fully-ordained monk, they do not represent two completely separate codes. The 'full' vows are basically refinements of the novice ones, variations on a limited number of themes. Whilst the individual vows are not secret, it is generally considered inappropriate to discuss them with those whose interest is purely academic (i.e. those who are not actually intending to adopt the vows themselves). This cultural and monastic proscription is one that I feel bound to observe.

A youngster may also don the robes and enter into a monastic community as a precursor to formal novice ordination. Whilst outwardly he may look every bit a monk, without formal ordination, he is not officially recognised as such. He is known as a *bar ma rab byung*—one who is in the process of making a 'transition'; changing from being a holder of lay vows to one with the lower set of monastic vows.

[4]The 36 vows are listed in footnote 6 of chapter 18.

Difficult as it is for foreigners to grasp, ordination is not linked to any 'training'. No basic level of study or understanding is required before one can become a novice and there is no scrutinising of progress, judging one's worthiness for the move into full ordination. In this sense the word 'novice' is a somewhat misleading one. Age is one factor (i.e. it is more or less expected that someone who has been in robes for some time, or who is a bit more advanced in years will eventually get fully ordained). But there is no general rush as soon as one becomes twenty to do so. More important than age is just the desire of the individual. If they act upon a choice to take the lower and then the higher ordination, it will almost certainly come to pass; there are no bars. Ideally the movement to the fully-ordained state should be accompanied with a corresponding tightening-up of one's discipline. It has to be said though that on the day-to-day level, the Tibetan public does not discriminate between the different levels of ordination, and assume that all of those who sport cropped hair and wear the robes at least half decently are 'monks'. Ordination in the Tibetan tradition is generally subordinate to other considerations. Respect is more likely to be commanded, for example, by a learned novice than a fully-ordained, but less well-educated monk. And a monk who is a *tulku* (someone recognised as a spiritual master, reborn) will tend to out-do everyone else in the esteem-stakes.

Some of the weird and (not so) wonderful sights that greet one in and around the Tibetan monasteries have led some foreign observers to conclude that the Tibetan monastic system represents a corruption of the authentic Buddhist one. Misinterpretations, such as that there exist 'lay monks' are rife. This latter for example comes about from failing to distinguish the various glosses of the term *lama* (Tibetan *bla ma* and its cognates). In Tibetan and Tibetic language speaking areas the term is applied variously to those of Tibetan stock, lay Buddhist ritualists, monks in general (and even lay practitioners who wear robes), a spiritual guide (who won't necessarily be a monk), then finally, within the orthodox Gelug establishment (Gelug being the dominant Tibetan Buddhist tradition), the term is synonymous with *tulku*, a reincarnate *lama*. Despite such confusion on the part of outsiders, within the tradition itself, criteria for what constitutes a monk and a monastery are clearly understood. And the monastic vows, codes and practices contained in the Vinaya are still widely studied, and as ideals, at least, still almost universally respected.

The 'Real' Division

Cutting across distinctions of age, origin, number of vows and so forth though is a far more significant division. This is what 'type' of monk the individual defines himself as (there existing no one, single, paragon-like model). Some monks are definitely 'study' monks; their time devoted to a vigorous pursuit of scriptural understanding. Others are 'ritualists', who perform ceremonies (both within and outside the confines of the monastery), as a means of preserving their own monastic traditions or at the invitation of and dedicated to lay devotees. A smaller group see themselves purely as 'practitioners', those who tend to shun worldly pursuits and crave solitude. Lastly there are those who have no clearly defined role or pursuits, tolerated because of society's positive view of monkhood as an 'ideal' (something that is allowed to soar above the occasional 'corruption' of its particular instances.)

Individual choice may determine which of these categories monks find themselves occupying. But 'accidental' factors can also play their part. For an individual is often 'expected' to join a particular monastery because of family or regional traditions: and in that case, they just have to follow whatever programme of activities (or lack of one) that is presented to them.

The Monasteries

The term 'Buddhist monastery' has become a cliché in the West, fodder for bland conversation. Evoked when someone expresses a half-hearted yearning to 'get away from it all', the trite image is of a haven of peace and tranquillity, somewhere where one can sever links with matters mundane and devote oneself to a simple, contemplative existence. It is hard to imagine a ruder challenge to such romantic notions than the large Tibetan monasteries. The atmosphere is likely to be noisy, boisterous and very much that of centres of (rather than retreats from) activity. Being confronted with such an environment invariably demands a radical re-evaluation of notions of (Buddhist) religious expression, perhaps forcing one to the conclusion that in the same way that tranquillity does not guarantee spiritual activity, organised chaos does not preclude it.

Following the divisions of the 'type' of monks alluded to above, we may also distinguish the monasteries, chiefly by way of their main activities (although there exists a degree of crossover). So we find those which are more or less centres of:

- *education*
- *ritual*
- *meditational retreat*
- *an 'undefined' fourth*

With the last of these not only would it be difficult to pinpoint some clearly defined social role, the monks themselves would generally be unable to articulate what it was they were trying to achieve. The lack of some true role does not specifically invalidate their existence (for the unquestioning acceptance of the monasteries' centrality within society means that they are not called upon to justify their continued presence). Clearly though when it comes to such things as the formulation of appeals for donations and the like, each monastery feels the need to suggest some reason why it should be entitled to get help, and on those occasions at least discovers for itself an existential purpose.

The majority of monasteries in the exiled community are 're-established' ones, bearing the name of their former incarnations in Tibet. Indeed in many cases there are now two 'versions' of them; the one re-established in exile and its counterpart in Tibet from whence it derived its name.

Monasteries may also be divided into those that are

institution-based and those that are personality-based. The majority of the monasteries in the above first three categories are older institutions that have been re-established in exile, with clear goals and agendas. The hierarchies within them (invariably including a single, recognisable leader) exist ostensibly to support smooth running whilst working towards the achievement of those goals. Within them, something approaching a democratic system may be invoked to appoint people to higher monastic posts. Lesser ones are generally occupied by rotation. But single figures do not generally (for any length of time) totally dominate or control such monasteries.

In those based around personalities though there will usually be one lama or tulku who has something approaching total control. As each tulku is recognised as having been a spiritual master in his previous existence, from childhood, he has a ready-made ward of former students and local devotees. He may also inherit property, including a monastery (once he attains his majority). Much of the monastery income may come either from offerings given directly to this person or as a result of teaching tours that he undertakes (usually abroad). Whilst the veneer of monastic respectability will be attached to these monasteries in the form of traditional names, in the popular consciousness they will be associated with the individual personage and in common parlance the place will be referred to as 'such-and-such Rinpoche's monastery' (Rinpoche being the polite address for a tulku). With so much power in the hands of one individual, whim often seems to triumph over tradition, and general standards may suffer accordingly. The first type of monastery is of course far closer to the original monastic vision. Some of the mechanisms it employs for election and decision-making have elements of authentic democracy (amongst a constituency of senior monks at least). Whilst the abbots (or heads) of such monasteries may have a lot of power, they must work within clearly defined parameters and have limited terms of office. This situation is in stark contrast with that of the lama-personality monasteries where all the in-charge has to do is stay at least reasonably popular with the members of his ward.

Of the four major Tibetan Buddhist schools it is the Gelug who have the largest monasteries. The 'three seats' of Ganden, Sera and Drepung (re-established in Karnataka State, South India) boast monk populations of 2,510, 4,477 and 4,681 respectively[5] (although there are significant numbers of non-exiled monks included here, such as those from Indian regions bordering Tibet and even from countries like Mongolia or Kalmykya). But the Sakya, Nyingma and Kagyu are also well represented, with populations in some monasteries running, if not into thousands, at least hundreds. On the higher end of the scale then, the monasteries in the Tibetan communities rank amongst the most populous in the world. At the opposite end, there may be a mere handful of monks inhabiting a particular institution.

In terms of their traditions and populations almost all of the re-established monasteries basically follow a single school. Some of the newer ones, such as the Institute of Buddhist Dialectics in Dharamsala, are, in terms of their monk residents (if not so much their educational programmes) meeting grounds for the different traditions. The only university recognised by the Indian government that the exiled community has, the Central Institute of Higher Tibetan Studies at Sarnath, Varanasi, also has a significant monk population[6] with representatives from all the major schools. The fact that monasteries are divided along the lines of tradition and that there is little formal dialogue or joint initiatives between the schools is not generally indicative of bad relations. It is simply a return to the traditional organisational model. Relations are, on the whole cordial, and recent history tells us that any disputes that there might be are as likely to occur between monasteries of the same tradition as those of divergent ones. And whilst common religious educational backgrounds and teachers means that close ties between various respected Buddhist figures are more likely to exist within the same school,

---

[5]Figures from the Department of Religion, Central Tibetan Administration.

[6]Thirty per cent per cent of the faculty and twenty per cent of the students are monks. See chapter 15.

many are cross-tradition. Whether historical differences re-assert themselves in the future remains to be seen. But being partners in a common tragedy probably has, perforce, over recent decades brought members of different traditions closer together.

Of Monks and Motives

In an ideal (Buddhist) world, the monasteries would be teeming with men and boys who, having been moved by the insights and message of the Buddha, and having seriously weighed up all the options, relinquish worldly concerns and opt for the life of the renunciate, striving for spiritual realisation. In the far from ideal world that we occupy though, the situation is a good deal more complicated. And buried somewhere within a mass of shaven heads and maroon-clad forms is a complex tangle of motives and concerns, some more noble, some less so. For some brought up in exile, entering a monastery represents the exercising of a personal choice. However on the slightly less savoury side, there are a few who are there due to pressure exerted by their families; others still, because they are orphans, or offspring of single parents, who could not cope.

Many foreigners are surprised that there is no 'vetting' process. There is absolutely nothing that amounts to a training that a monk 'prospect' would have to undergo. Basically, anyone who shows the slightest inclination to become ordained (as novice) is permitted to do so. Even the directions contained within the Vinaya—the very foundation of all Buddhist teachings—as to who may or may not be ordained are routinely disregarded. Tibetans pay scant regard to the quality of the raw material. Such is the high regard for monk-hood itself that there is no question of limiting admission, indeed the general maxim seems to be, 'the more the merrier'.[7]

Amongst those who come from Tibet to join the monasteries,

---

[7]In contrast the Dalai Lama would prefer 'fewer but better monks', see interview in chapter 6. Editor's note.

mixed in with educational and spiritual concerns there may be more prosaic, economic considerations. Whilst those from the established exile community will have had a primary and secondary school education (although college graduates are rare amongst the monks), there is no guarantee of even basic education amongst those from Tibet. Young, relatively uneducated men in Tibet, living in rural areas have little in the way of educational or employment prospects. Travelling to India to receive a religious education presents them with an opportunity. Many of the most distinguished figures in the society in exile got where they are on the basis of their religious education. There is then a chance in exile for newcomers to make something of themselves. The dearth of prospects that the Chinese Communists have been able to provide has, by a supreme irony, actually boosted the monk population. This was hardly their intention. Generally, exile and monk-hood also offer an opportunity to reassert a cultural and ethnic identity that is being stifled in their homeland. In this sense, there is a rebellious dimension to their actions. For others it was simply the prospect of seeing H.H. Dalai Lama that originally brought them so far from home.

Aside from the educational and religious opportunities that are on offer, on purely practical grounds as well, life in a monastery may present the only financially viable option; for most new arrivals have little or no money. The monasteries will not turn any of them away, and will at least provide them with the basics. In this sense the monasteries provide (perhaps unwittingly) something like halfway houses for some newcomers who are torn between religious devotion and the allure of the modern world. They provide many of them (who will eventually drift out of monk-hood) with stability and a gentle easing into life outside their homeland. The general contribution of newcomers from Tibet though should not be underestimated. It is due mainly to their unswerving faith and energy that the monasteries are presently in such a healthy state.

Financial considerations generally feature less in the decisions of members of the established exile community as to whether to get ordained. Relatively speaking, younger people have more educational and employment options. Added to that, they are at an advantage; having family networks and relatives prepared to help support them, even if they have not yet secured employment.

It would be misleading though to view the aforementioned motives and concerns in isolation. For it is the underlying respect for the institution of monk-hood that is the fertile soil from which they all sprout. It goes beyond a mere 'positive' view of the institution, and perhaps even beyond religious belief. A millennia of acquaintance has rendered it an 'unquestioned' and 'unquestionable' given, a cultural practice that has entered a realm of its own, divorced from everyday concerns of validity and pertinence. Becoming a monk is always an option, not a decision that requires a great deal of agonising over. For Tibetans at least, the institution itself is never called upon to justify its existence. Its continued relevance is not so much an issue that has been settled; it is just not an issue.

Notwithstanding all that I have said about the melange of circumstances that may bring someone into a monastery, in my experience, none of them negate the possibility of someone becoming a good monk (for good monks are not that from the start). Rather, it is a case of eventually growing, or maturing into the role. Monasteries are not there to provide places for those who have a 'calling' so much as to provide an environment for those seeking to develop.

Education and the Daily Routine

Let us look at how, in Gomang College of Drepung Monastery (Mundgod, South India)—one of the chief centres of education —a monk spends his time. For the vast majority of monks involved in study, the day begins early, between 5 to 5.30 a.m. with the morning-prayer meeting. This lasts until 7.30 or 8.00 when breakfast is served. Hourly philosophy classes commence as soon as the prayer meeting is over. Not everyone has class simultaneously though. Those not attending class at any particular time engage in sessions of text memorisation. Between 9 to 11 is a debate session, interspersed with group prayers in the debate courtyard. Dialectical debate takes two forms. In the first of these, individuals pair off and explore the material they have been introduced to in class themselves (under the supervision and occasional intervention of the disciplinarian). The other is when two individuals are set the task of answering quick-fire questions from all of the other members of their class, related to their current studies. Prior to starting debate, monks will have memorised various 'root' texts, then they start receiving daily teachings related to scriptural exposition and interpretation. The debate they engage in is a verbal and intellectual joust. The responder's role is that of defender, fending off attacks to various philosophical and doctrinal positions that he has chosen or been forced to adopt. The questioner's task is to act as an assailant, subjecting his opponent to sustained attack. With a barrage of questions and challenges he continuously endeavours to catch the responder out and expose contradictions in his position. There is no formal referee for the debates, just two parties, continuously trying to get the better of each other; like two sides in a legal case without judge or jury, playing sometimes to whatever audience happens along, but more often than not, to an imagined one. In the larger Gelug monasteries in particular debate forms the very core of the monks' daily activities. It is a highly ritualised activity, both in terms of the way that the debates are formulated and the physical gestures that accompany them. The responder is seated, whilst the questioner stands. Each of the latter's points are delivered in conjunction with intimidating clapping, shouting and foot-stamping. The visual and auditory effect is striking. Someone witnessing proceedings for the first time (until they start to see the order within the chaos) might wonder whether they are witnessing some sort of riot.

Lunch is distributed from the monastery kitchen straight after the debate session. After lunch, a little rest. But classes start again almost immediately, and for those without a class, there is private study. This continues until 5.30 p.m. when there is the evening meal. Then again there is a debate (and prayer) session. Students are not permitted to leave this until the disciplinarian makes his departure (around 10.30–11.00 at night). Many go on debating though for a few more hours, and those who don't, go back to their memorising. The majority of students go to bed around 12.30–1.00 at night.

This is the routine for between ten to fifteen years for those who pursue the *geshe* degree (the awarding of which marks the formal end to their studies in the monastery). During this time there is one holiday a week (Monday), when there is no debate or class (but still, morning prayers). There are some annual periods of up to a couple of weeks without debate, when the monks are supposed to devote themselves more to textual study. Exams (both written and oral) are held annually. Those who wish to engage in other studies (such as Tibetan grammar, poetry and English classes) must find someone in the monastery to teach them in their spare time (as these subjects are not on the curriculum).

It is compulsory for those below sixteen to attend the monastery school (where the curriculum is a bit more varied) until they begin their philosophical studies in earnest. In the early years of exile monks were regularly called upon to do manual work between their studies (such as in the fields[8] or assisting with construction), but this is increasingly less the case. Discipline is strict, with physical punishment sometimes resorted to, and shirking is not tolerated. The majority of the monks are totally devoted to their studies, and they are probably the hardest working and most dedicated individuals that I have personally ever seen. The popular image of Buddhist monks is individuals devoted to an abstinent and contemplative life—contact with Tibetan monks again calls for re-examination of such images. Quiet prayer and contemplation play but minor roles. Here aggressive (verging sometimes on brutal) pursuit of philosophical

[8]This was unthinkable in pre-1950 Tibet (editor's note).

and textual understanding is the raison d'etre. But what individuals go through in this pursuit involves no less sacrifice and surrender, no less dedication. Theirs' is a supreme effort.

In the main three Gelug monasteries (and a number of others) monks pursue the same general academic syllabus, involving five major areas of study, as well as a number of subsidiary subjects. A detailed listing of these is beyond the scope of this work. But they cover, among other things, a mapping-out of the Buddhist path and its practices, logic, monastic discipline, conventional and ultimate views of reality and comparative studies of different philosophical schools. Successful completion of the programme culminates in the awarding of the title '*geshe*' (of higher or lower rank). Even within the same tradition though we find other degrees, such as the *Kachen* and *Rabjam*. In some of the non-Gelug traditions we find institutions that are more or less totally devoted to study or those where there is a mixed academic and non-academic programme. Some of the latter have a separate campus area (*bshad grwa*) for their philosophical study programme. A variety of academic degrees (e.g. *Khenpo*) exist in these other schools. Irrespective of school though, a formal philosophical study programme could be expected to take a decade to complete.

Contrary to common Western expectation neither training in meditation nor group meditation sessions form an integral part of a Tibetan monastic programme. The philosophical subjects covered in the course of a standard monastic education are literally laden with potential themes for meditation. But they are presented academically, not in conjunction with practical meditational techniques or method. Such meditation instruction that there is tends to go on more informally, on a private basis. This is usually within the context of a meditational retreat, where either during that activity itself or in preparation for it, an individual or a small group of monks is given advice about how to perform the practice. However it is a minority of monks who engage in such activities.

Now let us briefly switch to the other end of the scale; for it would be disingenuous of me to give the impression that all monks work as hard as those who belong to such institutions as Gomang. There is a certain monastery in Nepal (which shall remain nameless). It is one of the older, more well-established institutions there, which is best classed as a 'ritual' monastery. Generally speaking it still performs its main task (i.e. prayers and ceremonies undertaken by the monks in the name of lay sponsors, dedicated to their well-being and success, with much of the money going back into the running of the monastery). But there is currently a failure to provide enough for the individual monks to do. There are no classes and the only daily group activity is the morning prayer-meeting. Young monks with little or nothing to do, with no ambitions or organised activities are of little credit to their institutions or communities. Whilst a combination of unhappy circumstances may have been responsible for the plight of the monastery in question, unfortunately it is not an isolated case. In Nepal particularly there are many such places and the 'Nepalese' (Tibetan) monks are subsequently held in lower regard than their 'Indian' (Tibetan) counterparts. Part of the problem within the Gelug school at least, is the dominance of the larger monasteries, which inadvertently does something of a disservice to the smaller ones. Those who are 'serious' about their studies are inclined to migrate to the larger monasteries, sucking out the younger potential talent from the smaller places, making it not worth their while organising study programmes of their own.

Even those monasteries of the 'undefined' group, if nothing else, will have some form of daily group prayer meeting. And as all of those prayers must be committed to memory, the younger monks will necessarily have memorisation sessions and be tested by the elder monks on what they have learnt. The ability to recite from memory though is (in other than the educational centres) an end in itself. Comprehension of what is being recited is not considered essential.

Varying degrees of activity lie between the two extremes. All of the monks in the ritual monasteries will spend some time learning skills relevant to their general activities (such as playing ceremonial horns and drums, sculpting offerings, drawing decorative religious symbols etc.). These are all pretty much essential within any monastery, but in those places other than centres of ritual, it will only be a few monks who learn and practise such skills. The learning of ritual arts and philosophy then are relatively widespread. Aside from these though, it is quite common to find monks involved in other 'traditional' areas (Tibetan medicine, religious [*thangka*] painting, calligraphy and so forth). The literary arts also fall very much within the monastic domain. Monks are not only responsible for penning a large portion of the new literature (both of a religious and secular nature), they also form perhaps the most avid reading audience.

Even if there are no other educational activities monasteries will often have some classes teaching how to read and write Tibetan and Basic English. All monasteries have a degree of office work and it is also common for them to be involved in the recording and publishing of religious texts. Thus computer skills are becoming increasingly common. For some, working with technology in this way represents a happy medium—the chance to indulge their fascination for all things 'modern' whilst simultaneously performing important services.

Organisation and Administration

There is no one over-arching organisation or body that either owns, dictates to, or exercises overall control over the monasteries. And whilst the Department of Religion and Culture of the Central Tibetan Administration has some input, monasteries are, on the whole, self-governing and self-supporting institutions.Even those belonging to the same tradition share no single governing authority. Each is free to create its own regulations (working more or less within the general framework of the Vinaya and social norms), determine its own daily schedule and—for those who offer some form of education formulate their own curriculum.

The traditional posts and division of labour have been re-established in most monasteries. Hence one can expect to find all or most of the following—abbot or principal, disciplinarian, chant-master, storekeeper, secretary, shrine-keeper, librarian and accountant. Of these, the abbot and the disciplinarian are the most important, carrying with them not just responsibility, but real power and prestige. In the larger monasteries it is only the more senior and learned *geshes* who can aspire to these posts. Both are elected for terms numbering in years. The abbot is the symbolic head of the monastery or college. His is usually a more stationary role. Ensconced in his quarters, it is up to others to make their representations and petitions to him. He works within the confines of the monastery constitution (*bca yig*) but wields considerable executive, decision-making powers in both the day-to-day running of the monastery, as well as its longer-term projects and general direction. With the disciplinarian, on the other hand, the broader scheme of things is not the concern. Nor is he there in a consultative role, solving various moral or legal conundrums. Rather, stated simply, he observes, inspects, enforces and (when needs be) punishes. He endeavours to ensure that standards are maintained and that breaches of discipline are kept to a minimum.

In the larger monasteries, both practicality and tradition demand that large, unwieldy monk populations must be broken into smaller units. The wider monastery therefore acts as an umbrella for various monastic 'colleges', which are educational institutions, basically independent of each other. Thus Sera, Ganden and Drepung each now comprise of two colleges (although in Tibet there were many more). On the one hand these places are educational institutions in the sense that they are the venue for academic pursuits of all those who are able to participate. However they also provide domiciles 'for life' (i.e. even beyond the point where the monks have formally 'graduated'). Two smaller units exist with the colleges. These are the 'houses' (*khang tshan*) and the regional groupings (*mi tshan*). The latter contain groups of monks who all come from the same area in Tibet or some other region that traditionally feeds the monasteries. These groupings are housed within the *khang tshan*, which are separate buildings or complexes within the monastery. Thus those from the same *khang tshan*, whilst not necessarily from a single area will come from a limited number of areas (usually geographically close to one another). Should someone desire to enter the monastery, they do so via these units, firstly searching for someone who is either related to them or from the same district as they. They must link up with an elder from their regional group who is prepared to take financial responsibility for them (in these larger monasteries the monks do not pay for their education or upkeep). He will make the practical living arrangements, finding some living and sleeping space for them.[9]

Regional ties are important to Tibetans. They represent more than geographical affinities. Cultural, linguistic, ethnic (and perhaps kinship) ties are all at play here, binding individuals together. The organisational system of the larger monasteries utilises these to create a strong sense of belonging, with loyalty between members of the smallest unit comparable almost to that between members of the same family. Apart from the more obvious practical advantages of such a system, it acts as a powerful force encouraging rectitude. It matters to an individual what other members of his tight-knit regional group think of him. Also those he has left behind in his home district will invariably hear about his progress, and there is a sometimes desperate wish to do them proud, either by distinguishing himself academically or at least not 'blackening' the name of their area by conducting himself inappropriately. Underlying this seems to be the assumption (these days increasingly unreasonable) that their journey, however long, will eventually lead them back home, where they will be answerable to family and neighbours.

On the down side, there is no doubt that misplaced local loyalty often leads monks unquestioningly to throw their weight behind someone in a dispute just because he is from their locality, disregarding the right or wrong of the situation.

---

[9]As they gain in seniority the monks can expect to share a room with fewer and fewer companions. But initially they often have to live in crowded quarters.

Certain aspects of life in the monasteries, such as common academic and ritual pursuits, transcend regional differences, while others depend upon them; they are the glue providing cohesion to each of the smaller constituent parts.

Financial viability has been a perennial problem for Buddhist monasteries through the centuries. In one sense though the matter has been simplified for Tibetans-in-exile. Escaping from their homeland with little but a cause that engendered considerable sympathy, the die was cast at an early date. If monasteries were to survive, they were going to require donors to help them. And so it has proved. Donors come in the form of Buddhist devotees (some Tibetan, but the more significant contributions come from Taiwan, Japan etc.), various official foreign bodies, cultural institutions and individual Western well-wishers. Tibetans have become skilled at formulating financial appeals and interacting with those they see as potential donors (for building and other projects). Some monasteries also take it upon themselves to search for individual sponsors for each of their monks.

Aside from the appeals, various lamas undertake teaching tours, and groups from monasteries now regularly travel to foreign countries putting on cultural and religious performances in order to garner financial support. A number of teachers resident abroad also make large contributions to their former monasteries. All this has meant that the financial situation for the larger monasteries in particular has improved significantly of late. In the past, the small amount of land that was allotted by the Indian government to the first wave of refugees acted as an important source of income for the monasteries. They would farm the land, with the monks regularly enlisted to do the manual work. In the last five or six years though growing wealth has meant that many can afford to dispense with the farming, preferring instead to use the land for building.

Success brings with it new problems. On the one hand, some feel that there is too much of a donor-dependent culture (though given the restrictions imposed by certain cultural taboos and monastic regulations this is perhaps more forgivable in the case

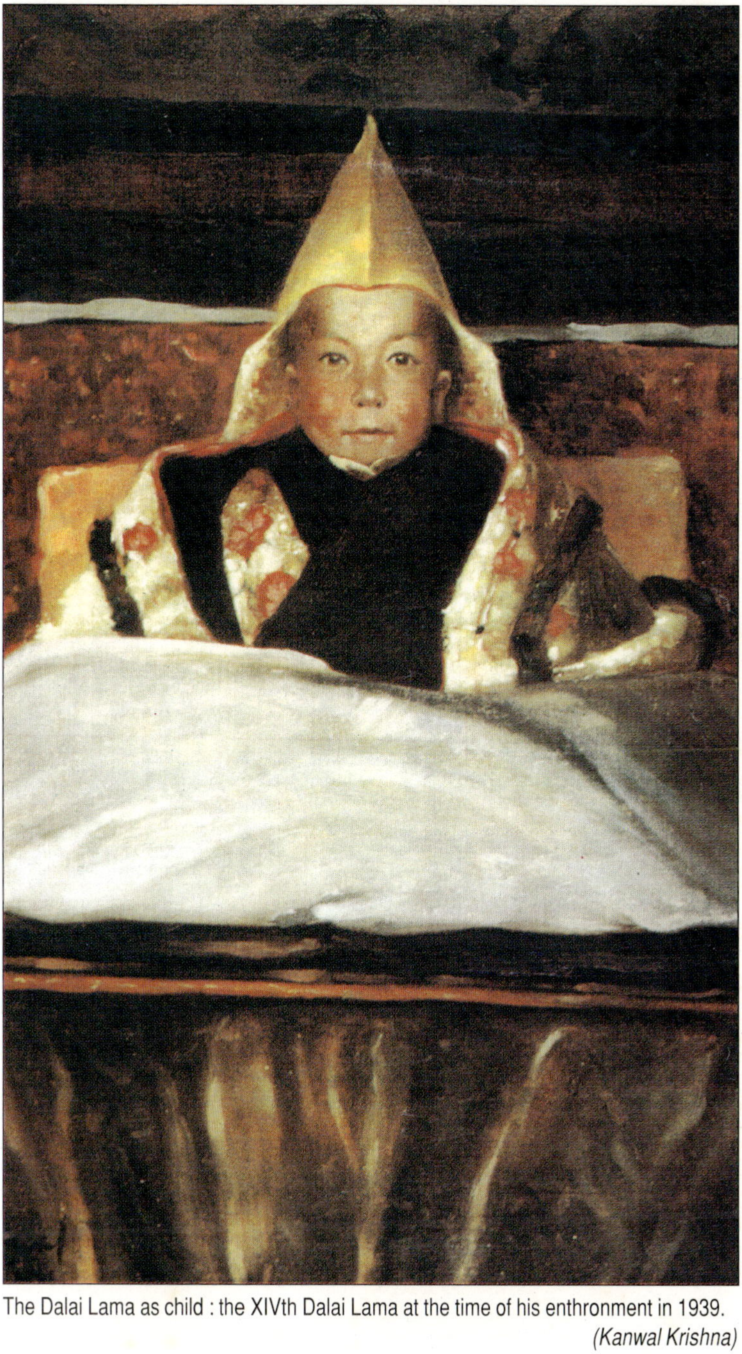

The Dalai Lama as child : the XIVth Dalai Lama at the time of his enthronment in 1939.

(Kanwal Krishna)

The Kashag, elected in 2001: (l - r) Lobsang Nyandak, Minister of Finance and Health; Thupten Lungrig, Minister of Education and Religion; Chief Kalon Ven. Samdhong Rinpoche; Lobsang Nyima, Home Minister. *(Photo: Lobsang Wangyal)*

The Tibetan Parliament-in-Exile : Kalon Thupten Lungrig at question time. Deputy Speaker Dolma Gyari is in the chair. *(Photo: Lobsang Wangyal)*

Tibetan children in India are taught by caring and committed teachers. *(Photo: Lobsang Wangyal)*

A nun receives treatment in the Men-Tsee Khang, the Tibetan Medical Centre at Dharamsala. *(Photo: Lobsang Wangyal)*

The art of *thangka* painting is taught at the Norbulingka Institute. (Photo: Lobsang Wangyal)

A monk reads a 'book' in traditional blockprint. Thousands of such ancient texts are being preserved in the Library of Tibetan works at Dharamsala.

(Photo: Lobsang Wangyal)

The Black Hat Dance remembers the murder of King Lang Darma (836–42) who persecuted the Buddhists. It takes great skill to sew the costumes for the ritual dances, an art that is still alive. *(Photo: Tibet House)*

of the monasteries). Others are of the opinion that too much wealth breeds complacency and arrogance. And whilst the monasteries do provide some employment for local people (mainly menial cleaning jobs and construction work) there is considerable envy and not a little resentment amongst the natives over their perceived affluence.

Attitudes to Monkhood

The greatest social opprobrium was reserved in Tibet for those who gave up their ordination (although some differences existed here, depending on which of the traditions was involved). The greatest crime of all (and if reports are to be believed, on a par with murder) was when a monk and a nun disrobed (in both the more ceremonial and prosaic sense) together. Popular tradition has it that such individuals would be sewn up together in a leather sack and tossed into the nearest river! Well-attested cases do exist where monks would basically be cast into the wilderness, without possession or provision if they were found to have transgressed their root vows. Such unfortunate individuals would end up not only as outcastes from the monastic community, but from society at large as well.

The most obvious attitudinal change that has occurred in exile is with regard to those who voluntarily give up their ordination and return to lay life. It is increasingly the case that monk-hood is viewed as something in the nature of a career (i.e. in which failure or lack of suitability become possible and the prospect of a 'career change' may be contemplated). The ties that bound serious 'study' or 'practice' monks to their ordination—in the form of the expectation of peers, relations and the wider community that they would set an example—originally remained strong in exile. However even this edifice is being chipped away now. And for those without any education, or who are seen as having failed in their attempts to gain one, the option of leaving monastic life is increasingly acceptable. Censure still awaits those for whom hopes had been particularly high, or who obviously transgress their basic discipline—there are four root vows, infraction of any of which would lead to people saying that the individual was no longer a monk; however (in common perception at least) it is usually breaking of the vow regarding sexual abstinence that marks the bitter end. But the weight of expectations seems to have become increasingly light.

A number of social factors contribute to this. On the one hand there is the influence of foreign cultures (i.e. those of India and Nepal), where monk-hood is not such a part of the social fabric. Secondly, there is the encounter with Western culture and modernity that has lead to new notions about individualism and personal choice seeping into the public consciousness. Finally, and perhaps most crucially, there is the 'opt-out'. For the Tibetan communities are societies existing within societies (e.g. India). All traditional institutions (from marriage to monk-hood) have experienced some weakening. And if someone chooses to break with traditional practices, there are few weapons left in the armoury of those who see themselves as cultural guardians. No one (right up to the 'government'-in-exile) is able, very effectively, to project power and enforce their will. Official displeasure cannot express itself in ways as harsh as it once could. No longer does the threat of banishment, social ostracism or stigmatisation menace. And there is generally little recourse to forms of legislative control, for here is a stateless state, and all are equally subject to the laws of another. Furthermore, individuals who do choose to challenge social norms can (and sometimes do) just pack their bags and move outside the Tibetan community. As individuals now have the choice of opting-out of both its institutions and even being a member of the community itself, Tibetan society has had to learn to be more 'forgiving'.

However the general public acceptance of monks disrobing does not necessarily represent a rejection of traditional values. Someone who has recently disrobed will couch his justification in the language of personal inadequacy. It will not be the institution that will be called into question (unlike, for instance the case of the celibate priesthood in the West, each time a new sex scandal surfaces).

The attitude that monks have to the observation of their rules is very informative. Tibetans are more adept than most at 'excusing' the gulf between the ideal and the reality. Thus, in a number of cases the vows are treated more as ideals. This puts them at odds, for example, with those following the Theravadan monastic tradition (in such countries as Thailand and Sri Lanka), where they represent more hard-and-fast rules. Indeed there are many monks who have only the vaguest idea of exactly what their vows are, for aspiration reigns supreme in the Tibetan tradition. Observation of monastic rules is generally subordinate to other concerns in the monastic setting. For example nowhere can count as a Buddhist monastery without the bi-monthly convening of the confession ceremony (*poshadha / gso sbyong*). And while the ceremony is held in many monasteries, attendance is not compulsory (unlike the other activities—be they prayer-meetings, debate or whatever). On a day-to-day basis, it is the rules of the individual monasteries that assert more influence upon a monk, and of which he has to be more wary. Aside from the major vows he will generally not be pulled up for infractions unless in his actions he has also transgressed the monastery rules (those rules and the vows only covering some of the same ground). If, however, he breaks the monastery rules (e.g., showing disrespect to an official, fighting or failing to attend a compulsory activity), he can expect to be punished.

Consternation would greet any suggestion that there should be a serious change or 'up-dating' of the monastic rules. The possibility of making such changes is (in theory) sanctioned within the rules themselves. But, (it would be argued) the type of congregation and level of agreement required to implement such changes render them impractical. But more importantly, there is no historical precedent for such modifications in Tibet, and Tibetans abhor the idea of religious 'innovation': the concepts of religion and preservation go hand in hand.

Standards in discipline are perceived to have slipped. But this is perceived to be indicative of a more general 'natural' process of corruption. Hence if not necessarily forgivable, it is at least understandable and something that (it is felt) must be endured. Vows seem to have moved, to a large extent, into the private domain, largely matters of conscience. There is a popular saying, 'Laws and vows are for personal maintenance' which, on the surface seems merely common sense. And whilst it may be my imagination, it seems to be intoned not infrequently these-days as a way of warding others off, saying, 'keep your nose out of my affairs'.

Monk-hood in the refugee community is, to a large extent, a continuation of what came before in Tibet. Monks of various traditions, monasteries, colleges and affiliated with various teachers are generally linked together by their dress, and by a general faith in the 'Three Jewels',[10] but perhaps not much else. There is little sense of a single brother-hood. The monasteries (even within a single tradition) represent little more than a loose federation. There are fierce undercurrents of independence based upon regional and factional loyalties, which often seem ready to assert themselves when sensing encroachment upon their 'private' domains. Indeed some of the more recent problems in the exile communities are, at root it seems to me, manifestations of this.

Adaptation sans Change

When looking into how the monastic institutions approach the issues of adaptation and reform it is necessary to demarcate two separate spheres. The first is the practical sphere, in which basic livelihood concerns are paramount. Here Tibetan monks, like other Tibetans, have learnt to manage things with a level-headed practicality. And whilst some religious communities and institutions in this world seem hopelessly inhibited and encumbered by observance and prohibition, such that dealing

[10] I take refuge in Buddha, refuge in Dharma, refuge in the Sangha (editor's note).

with technology and modern living are a constant struggle, the same can not be said of the Tibetan monks in exile. Theirs is a remarkably pragmatic approach, such that whenever a clash between (at least minor) religious observation and some practical imperative occurs, the latter prevails. This has allowed many monks to use computer and communication media, become proficient in foreign languages, and become drivers of vehicles, builders of houses etc. In the practical sphere, conservative notions are in abeyance. And any objections and concerns that smack of such notions are summarily dismissed. This really marks one of the most radical breaks from the past. In the latter part of the nineteenth and early twentieth century it was the monastic institutions that stood in the vanguard of the opposition to foreign influence in Tibet. And whilst this opposition was initially positively characterised as nationalistic in spirit, it later came to be judged as a selfish orthodoxy, that strangled the nascent desire to embrace some of the more useful aspects of the modern world. And thus it was that the Tibetans were condemned to technological and organisational backwardness, leaving them totally unable to mount serious resistance to the Chinese invasion.

The second sphere is that of the monastic institutions' traditional core activities. And here we get a very different picture—certainly not one of enthusiasm for change. All of the external adaptation is not some facade; but it must essentially be seen as having come about to protect the core activities, such as study and ritual. The principal task that monks set themselves is self-perpetuation of their traditions and the institutions that safeguard them. More monks means more people to take pride in and pass on the traditions. Everything is geared towards this almost genetic urge for self-preservation and replication. Within this framework (and perhaps due to a less egocentrically-based culture) the majority remain seemingly content to see themselves as something like relatively insignificant cogs within the giant, lumbering machinery of tradition. And what to some foreigners seems (particularly given the huge religious literature and rich array of practice techniques that Tibetan Buddhism possesses) like a baffling partiality in the monasteries toward book-learning and ritual at the expense of 'practice', makes perfect sense to a Tibetan.

With a complete rejection of anything advertising itself as innovation or reinterpretation in the religious context, anything approaching this must, by the employment of some sleight of hand, be transformed (or at least presented) as an extension of preservation. This, incidentally, is how Tibetans have dealt with philosophical development over the centuries.

H.H. Dalai Lama, on one level, undoubtedly represents a major force pushing for positive change, but however great his stature and influence his power to affect change is limited. Let us look for example at the sphere of contemporary education. The Dalai Lama is particularly keen to encourage monks to broaden their educational horizons with regard to science and Western philosophy.[11] But we find no monasteries that have been prepared to make such subjects part of their regular curriculum (though it is true that a number of the more august institutions, such as the Institute of Buddhist Dialectics, have, at times, hosted extra-curricula classes, teaching them). And on the periphery at least, the Dalai Lama has also successfully initiated a scheme whereby five monks from each of the six major monastic colleges in the Gelug tradition are selected to study science for one month a year, at various venues.

His Holiness also continues to organise a series of conferences where eminent Western scientists have the opportunity to engage in dialogue with himself and other Tibetan religious scholars. Such is the Dalai Lama's standing that notice has to be taken of such events. But whilst such proceedings may be greeted with a hushed reverence, as soon as they are over the hubbub returns and there is an almost palpable sense of, 'right, let's get back to the real business' namely, traditional study and ritual practice. It is not vapid religious orthodoxy that is offering resistance here. It is more like the re-emergence of a traditional division of roles.

---

[11]See chapter 6.

Some things fall into the domain of core monastic activity; and contemporary subjects (along with many other even traditional Tibetan activities) just don't and as such can expect to get short shrift.

In another area, that of candidates for ordination, H.H. Dalai Lama also regularly suggests that the emphasis should be upon monastic quality rather than quantity. But this has not translated into practical measures such as control over new admissions. And there has to be the suspicion that H.H. Dalai Lama has made the choice not to press the point too much (running as it does, counter to entrenched Tibetan notions of monasticism). Besides that, what monk would want to be yoked with the historical responsibility for having initiated a general trend away from ordination?

All things considered, genuine dialogue towards reform and reinterpretation seems as far away as ever.

Roles Outside the Monasteries

Let us contrast two roles that the monks play within the wider exile society, one official and the other unofficial. Ten of the forty-six seats in the Parliament-in-exile are reserved for representatives of the main religious traditions.[12] Monks make up the voter constituency here, but they are not obliged to nominate or vote for other monks, and indeed three of the ten at present are lay religious figures. The incumbent elected head of government (Ven. Samdhong Rinpoche) is also a monk, and monks also feature in both the government executive and the various departments. Whilst the members of the assembly occupying the religious seats are there on behalf of the religious constituencies, they are not to be understood as, specifically representing the monastic communities, acting as a counterbalance to lay influence. So thoroughly are the monks and the idea of monk-hood integrated into the wider society that they are not

[12]See chapter 8.

seen as a separate block, constantly vying with the lay authorities. The camps are thoroughly commingled and no significant tensions exist between them. The larger Gelug monasteries particularly though, are still social forces that need to be reckoned with. This is not so much out of fear that their populations might descend en masse and subvert or hold to ransom the government (as they might have done prior to 1959), but so much as what they continue to represent. Each society has its own large, mobile bodies of men who probably exert an inordinate influence over the course of events merely by token of their being 'organised masses'. In some countries it is the armed forces, in others unions. In the absence of other conspicuous groups within Tibetan society it has been monastics who have occupied this position. The large monastic population is not currently perceived as some ominous threat, lurking in the background and requiring mollification. Still, in some quarters there is an awareness of their potential, if mobilised, to be used for good or ill, and hence the impression that they need to be treated with respect.

Of far more consequence to the everyday life of Tibetans though is the unofficial role of the (mainly maroon) spiritual figures within the community. The Tibetan public retains its reverence not only for the 'mystical' office of the *tulku*, but also for those who hold formal religious posts (such as the abbots of monasteries). Tibetans expect there to be one dominant religious figure—one main lama—in each monastery and that there are a number of important but informal public duties that attach themselves to this post. Offering wise council on matters spiritual and mundane is the most fundamental of these. But beyond that, ideally, the lama should be someone who can perform divinations, and is ready to utilise this ability to advise on some (it has to be said) very worldly affairs, such as business prospects and the likely outcome of various courses of action. They are also called upon to perform various religious ceremonies, offer blessings and so forth, giving a spiritual 'seal of approval' to the otherwise mundane. And for those suffering the pain of bereavement, they provide solace both in the form of rituals dedicated to the deceased, and words of comfort to family and loved ones. These figures, with their twin moral and mystical functions are, quite simply, the single most important figureheads within Tibetan society. There is perhaps greater credence given to their judgements and pronouncements than is given to the Buddhist tradition of which they are the products. The intricacies of philosophy and long drawn-out practices to help develop the mind are of little interest to the supplicant. What he needs is someone that he can believe 'transcends' the world, and, by virtue of his doing so, is in a position to guide the way through its knots and snarls. Furthermore this figure should be someone who is prepared to offer direction only 'upon request'. The last thing that the ordinary Tibetan is seeking is someone who is going to complicate his life with genuine religious curb and prescription.

Conclusion

Exile, statelessness and a rude encounter with modernity have presented Tibetan society with a whole new raft of challenges. As far as the monastic institutions go, simply carving out a slot for themselves within the new terrain was inevitably going to demand some change. As far as a diminishing of influence goes, in the new society they certainly have less sway in the realm of governance. Neither do they wield power through being major land-owners or by engaging in activities such as money-lending. Notwithstanding all this, they remain firmly fixed at the centre of Tibetan society. But whilst the institutions' centrality has been restored, the individual's relation to those institutions has undergone change. Monk-hood is now a more transient state. And whilst the ideals surrounding that state are largely left in place, there are perhaps increasingly fewer individuals who are able to live up to these ideals for long periods of time (i.e. a lifetime). The monk population remains large, but is also more fluid, the faces change more rapidly than in centuries (or even decades) past. Less charitable commentators would surely interpret this as a portent of imminent decline. But not I, not yet at least. Should more of the elder monks (the proverbial 'steady hand on the wheel') start to succumb to the world, should people not remain ordained long enough for there to be a stable community of role models for younger aspirants, then crisis will loom large.

The exile population includes a high ratio of monks and provides an environment where individuals can practice religion in freedom and with dignity. But paradoxically it is from exile that those more liberal ideas regarding the duration of monk-hood (which may eventually be seen as having undermined the institution) spread. And far from being rejected by those coming from Tibet, these ideas are generally being accepted and even embraced.

But in our analysis, let us not exaggerate the challenges faced by the institutions or allow ourselves to be overly influenced by Buddhist 'purist' opinion. Some foreign commentators are all too ready to bandy charges of traditions that are 'tainted' or 'corrupt' when they fail to find what they expect in the monasteries. In the monastic institutions' own terms, in terms of the popular interest they inspire (both inside and outside their community), in terms of their large intake and populations, the achievement of academic or other stated goals, their primacy within society and even their present healthy financial situation they are 'successful'. Uncompromising, perhaps, imperfect, certainly, but undeniably thriving. And that is no mean achievement given recent history. I incline towards the view that too much discussion towards reform, reinterpretation and adjustment to the modern world would, at the present time, expose the institutions to considerable risk. The last thing that they need now is some self-induced identity crisis. And there is the perception that it is their unyielding stance that has got them where they are today. Anyway, the fact of the matter is that serious reformation is not on anybody's agenda, and rehabilitation is not necessary when, in Tibetan eyes, the institutions have never been discredited.

Survival of these religious institutions has become inextricably linked with the survival of Tibetan culture in general. Monks are still seen as the foremost promoters of Tibetan culture. This is obviously true in terms of religious tradition. But so many of the arts in Tibet are religious or semi-religious in nature and the maroon involvement in them is pervasive. In terms of literature they are not only the primary consumers and composers of traditional material, they (and their fraternity of erstwhile members) are in the forefront of the modern Tibetan literary movement. People now see cultural preservation as the monks' 'business'. And monks can also be found working in all sorts of secular fields within the exiled communities. They are teachers, administrators, writers, politicians, doctors, almost anything. The unique Tibetan interpretation of the monastic role means that few bars are placed in their way. Even on the family level—not generally seen as their domain—with so many counting at least one of their number as a monk and because even after ordination close family ties are maintained, their presence is felt. From birth until death, it is their chanting and the thud of their drums that remains the soundtrack to life in the Tibetan community.

The Tibetan monastic world defies both idealistic and cynical expectation: neither do we have here a world of pure spirituality nor of Machiavellian intrigue. It exists not on the community's periphery, but very much in the thick of it. It is alive and vibrant. And more than any other recognisable group, it is still the monks who are perceived as carrying on the hopes for the survival of both a religious tradition and a cultural identity.

CHAPTER TWELVE

Exiled Tibetans in Europe and North America

GYALTSEN GYALTAG

The problem of the Tibetan diaspora is not only a matter of material integration, but also of spiritual and cultural rehabilitation.

Introduction

In 1959, undaunted by the uncertainty of the future, thousands of Tibetans followed their religious and political leader, the fourteenth Dalai Lama, into exile. Suffering from frostbite, hunger and exhaustion, about 85,000 Tibetan refugees from all regions and social backgrounds eventually arrived in India, Nepal and Bhutan. Today the number of Tibetan refugees has reached about 130,000 worldwide.

Affluence did not greet the Tibetans in their first countries of asylum. India, Nepal and Bhutan, poor countries by definition, could not provide them with a secure existence. At that time, there was a lack of everything: food, clothing, shelter, medical care, opportunities for education and work, but especially security.

At a time of suffering and misery the Tibetans looked to the Dalai Lama for hope and assurance. He encouraged his desolate countrymen and prepared them for their new life in exile. In 1959, he established the Tibetan Government-in-Exile at Mussoorie, North India. The following tasks had priority: caring for Tibetan refugees, providing education and training for Tibetan children, preserving Tibetan culture, religion and language as well as maintaining the cultural and national identity in exile. In 1960, the Dalai Lama moved the seat of the Tibetan

Government-in-Exile to Dharamsala. From here the Dalai Lama appealed to the Western countries for help. Numerous governments as well as private persons reacted to his appeal with concrete assistance.

The history of the Tibetan exodus in 1959, the accounts of the later flight of individual Tibetans, as well as the survival of the refugees under the wise and far-sighted guidance of the Dalai Lama, provide the common threads that tie the Tibetan communities in Asia, Europe and North America together. In the beginning, everyone believed in a speedy return to their homeland. But since then, over forty years of life in exile have passed. And, a third generation of Tibetan refugees is growing up in exile. There are reasons for a critical review.

Tibetans in Switzerland

Switzerland was among the first few countries that provided an extraordinary amount of help to the Tibetan refugees. When the Swiss heard about the tragic political turn of events on the roof of the world and about the poverty and suffering of the Tibetans in the refugee camps in India and Nepal, they reacted with compassion and humanitarian help that has not been equalled even by bigger states. India, of course, is the exception; it had to carry and still carries the main burden of the Tibetan refugee problem.

Immigration to Switzerland

Thanks to the private initiative of numerous Swiss citizens, a total of 1,806 Tibetans received immigrant status in Switzerland between 1960 and 1996. It is the biggest Tibetan exile community in Europe and is made up as following:[1]

[1]Figures according to information from Statistischer Dienst des Bundesamt für Ausländerfragen (Statistical Service of the Federal Office for Foreigners) dated 31.08.96. The Tibetan Demographic Survey 1998, Dharamsala 2000 mentions 1,538 Tibetans in Switzerland and (*contd.*)

Total	*Female*	*Male*	*Born in Switzerland*	*Under 16 years old*	*Refugee-status*	*Swiss citizenship*
1,806	899	907	602	347	1,279	527
100%	49.8%	50.2%	33.3%	19.2%	70.8%	29.2%

The first group of Tibetans, twenty refugee children and five Tibetan educators, arrived at the Children's Village 'Pestalozzi' at Trogen in the autumn of 1960. Since then the Children's Village has sheltered a total of 96 Tibetan children.[2]

Between 1961 and 1964, 160 Tibetan refugee children were taken into Swiss families thanks to the effort of a private initiative. In 1960, the organisation 'Verein Tibeter Heimstätten' (Society of Tibetan Homes) was founded. This organisation, in co-operation with the Swiss Red Cross, persuaded the Swiss Government to allow 1,000 Tibetan refugees to settle in Switzerland[3] from 1961 to 1981. Nearly all these Tibetans, with a few exceptions, live and work in the German-speaking part of Switzerland.

With the admission of Tibetan refugees, Switzerland set a new precedence in its refugee policy. They welcomed refugees from a completely different cultural background and offered them a second home in Switzerland. Opening its doors to refugees from a different culture such as the Tibetans, is not without problems, but it was the only way of saving the refugees from death or disintegration of their personalities.

The Older Generation

The immigration to Switzerland was not at all easy for the Tibetan refugees. Coming from a different social and cultural

(*contd.*) 12,153 (including Bhutan) worldwide, according to informtation given by the Tibet Offices 1999.

[2]84 Tibetan children from India and 12 from Switzerland (2nd generation).

[3]See Schweizerisches Rotes Kreuz, Sektor Hilfsaktion, Ansiedlung tibetischer Flüchtlinge in der Schweiz, Bern 1976; Tschanz, E., Wie die Tibeter zu uns kamen, in: Schweizerisches Rotes Kreuz, Nr. 5, 1981.

background of a farming and nomad's society with feudal and theocratic features made for a difficult transition at the beginning. With the ten-hour flight to Switzerland, the Tibetans did not just cover thousands of kilometres; the flight propelled them from a religiously-oriented, pre-industrial society into a secular, industrial, achievement-oriented society. Suddenly, the Tibetans were faced with different economic and social structures, in which their own former positions, roles and functions had little value. Cash replaced the familiar barter trade. Old age and family values did not have the same importance as in Tibet. And it was not possible for the Tibetan refugees to be integrated into familiar professions. Then and now, most of them had to earn their living as unskilled workers in factories. For the first time in their lives, they were confronted with the world of technology and mass production. Knowing that they could be replaced like spare parts at any time, reduced their self-esteem. Even their family structure and rhythm of life had to undergo radical changes: Previously their daily routine was dictated by nature; now the clock took over this function. The traditional, self-sufficient, extended family that had formed a functioning socio-economic unit, began to disintegrate in modern, industrial society. And the separation of family life from work life became a daily reality for the Tibetans.

Even today, the older Tibetans speak relatively little German, since they did not receive adequate language instruction.[4] Because of the resulting difficulties in communication, they generally prefer social contacts among themselves. This leads to a certain isolation which has pros and cons.[5] On the one hand it minimises social interactions with the Swiss people and does not allow far-reaching integration which presupposes the absorption of Swiss cultural values. But on the other hand, it gives the Tibetans who are suffering from culture-shock a certain kind of protection.

---

[4]See Ott-Marti, E., *Probleme der Integration von Tibetern in der Schweiz*, Rikon 1980.

[5]See Rose, A. M., *Migrants in Europe: Problems of Acceptance and Adjustment*, Minneapolis 1969.

The Younger Generation

According to their educational environment the younger generation of Tibetans in Switzerland can be divided into three groups:

The first group is made up of 92 Tibetan refugee children who have been admitted to the Children's Village 'Pestalozzi' at Trogen. In this international Children's Village, the principle of a twofold cultural education is applied. In addition to a Western-oriented education, the children receive instruction in their mother tongue and also learn their original culture and religion. However these Tibetan children became exposed to the Swiss way of life only after leaving the Children's Village. This change of milieu often caused insecurities which had to be overcome in a new social environment. Today, 77 of them have finished their job training and are self-employed workers in Switzerland.

The second group consists of 160 Tibetan foster children who were raised in the Protestant or Catholic tradition in middle-class Swiss families. Those children came to Switzerland when they were six or seven years old. On the surface they integrated well and quickly into their new environment. All of them speak fluent Swiss German. But the majority has lost the ability to communicate in their mother language. They received a good, but one-sided Western education. With few exceptions they have finished their professional training and have joined the work force. In the beginning, those children had little or no contact with other Tibetans in Switzerland. It is only when they grew older, after their adolescence, that they became conscious of their Tibetan origin. The process of discovering their own identity made them turn towards their own people and hence to their own culture. This trend became apparent when this group of young people joined the 'Verein Tibeter Jugend in Europa'[6] (Tibetan Youth in Europe) and started to actively participate in this organisation.

The third group is made up of Tibetan children and youth

---

[6]See: Gyaltsen, K.U. and Gyaltag, G., *Jugend im Exil, Hrsg. Verein Tibeter Jugend in Europa* (Festschrift), Zürich 1980.

who were born in Switzerland or immigrated with their parents. For those children the primary care-givers and social focus remained constant. The settlement of Tibetan families was mostly done in groups, hence the friends and playmates, the so called peer-groups, of these children stayed more or less ethnically homogenous. Most of their fathers and a few mothers earn their living as unskilled workers in factories.

The majority of these children, as well as those from the previous two groups, know Tibet only from second-hand information. Those who were born here, as well as many others converse nearly exclusively in Swiss German. They speak Tibetan only with their parents and other Tibetan adults. Within the programme of the Tibetan schools, they receive instruction in Tibetan language, culture and religion. But the few weekend lessons are inadequate to provide an in-depth grounding in Tibetan language and culture. The limited command of their mother tongue and lack of knowledge of their own culture create communication difficulties between the parents and their children. The younger generation is much more familiar with the Swiss environment than the parents. For that reason, they often play the role of mediator between their parents and the Swiss authorities and civil society.

There are considerable cultural differences between the Swiss environment and their home. This leads to parenting and psycho-social problems: causing difficulties in identity development as well as in their education and training.

Problems and Conflicts

The following examples are used to explain some of the issues.[7]

Parenting Problems

The problems of many Tibetan parents are related to the loss of

[7]See: Gyaltag, G., *Die tibetische Familie im Wandel und Spannungsfeld zweier Kulturen*, Rikon/Zürich, 1990. p. 165ff.

their parental authority. There are many reasons for this. First, there are difficulties in orientation and the resulting insecurity of the parents that come with the exposure to an unfamiliar economic, social, cultural and political environment. Another reason is the relatively poor education of the parents compared to the children. Because most of the older generation have nearly no grasp of the German language, their lack of education is very noticeable, especially when they have to deal with the outside world, like the authorities, teachers, with post office, bank and taxes. In these cases, they are dependant on their children. This position of dependency leads to a loss of respect in the eyes of their not-yet-mature children. The last but not least reason is the degradation of the parent as role model. Because of these reasons, the parents have difficulties in fulfilling their parental duties.

Communication Problems and the Generational Conflict

As is to be expected, the Tibetan parents of the older generation have strong roots in their traditional culture. They can identify with the vastly different socio-cultural values in Switzerland only to a limited degree. Their children, who grew up there, are more or less estranged from their own cultural heritage and cannot generate much understanding for it. Instead they turn to the Swiss and Western way of thinking and living with which they are familiar because of the dominance of their socialisation outside the home.

Added to the tension-ridden socio-cultural environment are additional problems resulting from the minority status of the Tibetans. This leads to generational conflicts between parents and children. The causes can be found in the differences in life style, expectations and value systems which are formed on the one hand through social relations and orientations within their circle of friends, colleagues and peers independent from their family. On the other hand the youths model their lifestyle and expectations on popular images from film, TV and magazines.

These have very little or nothing in common with the values of their parents.

Many Tibetan youth feel misunderstood or inadequately understood by their parents. And the children themselves understand their parents even less and less. Frequently these conflicts lead to the withdrawal of youths from their families. Instead they increasingly look towards their peer groups for orientation and support. Very often, controversial issues are not discussed at home and this leads eventually to latent conflict situations. In particular, the behaviour and value system of the youth, formed at school, come into conflict with those of the parents. For instance, respect for the elders or the surrender of the interest of the individual for the benefit of the group or the family. If a Tibetan child wants to go to a summer camp, but the family does not agree, there could be tension. If the father wants to pray and perform religious ceremonies in front of the altar in the sitting room during the weekend, but cannot concentrate because of the loud pop music coming from his children's room, another conflict situation arises.

Generational conflicts and communication problems between parents and children are heightened by the different language competency of the parents as well as the children. The bilingual burden is a central problem for both generations: Tibetan as mother-tongue and German as a foreign language. For Tibetans there are two foreign languages to be mastered: German as the school- and official language and Swiss German as the colloquial medium. This fact makes communication between parents and children more difficult, especially if there are demanding conversations between the two generations. Very often the children are unable to communicate with their parents in Tibetan because they do not possess the necessary vocabulary. The parents on the other hand only have a rudimentary knowledge of German; they cannot communicate with their children in that language. Mediation and 'cultural translation' between parents and child by a third party is often necessary to facilitate an understanding on both sides.

Problems of Identification

The pathways of identification in a highly specialised work and life environment are different from those in the agricultural, nomadic and handicraft-oriented society of Tibet. In this context, Mitscherlich says:

> The natural 'identity crisis' in the passage from childhood to adulthood seems to bring about a stronger upheaval of the personality than in the more traditional, inward-oriented societies.

The social change that destabilised and brought major changes to the Tibetan family had the most profound impact on the process of self-determination in the growing children and youth as partly shown in the previous notes.[8] For a Tibetan youth growing up in Switzerland, it is not easy to find his identity. Because of the dissolution of the time-spatial unit of work and family life, he cannot experience his parents in a world of common activities. The youth going through puberty and identity crisis feels abandoned and helpless, because he cannot find his identity in the roles that his parents live. He has to orient himself somewhere else and make a decision in a work place that is so different, that he and his parents have difficulties gaining an overview. The feeling of loneliness and abandonment give him the impression that his parents are weak and helpless and he cannot count on their support. This socially conditioned weakness of his parents prevents him from identifying with them. This is also the reason why his emotional relations with them are often disturbed.

The Tibetan adolescent can neither withdraw from his Tibetan origin nor from his Swiss social environment. Especially during puberty, when he is overwhelmed by an ambivalence of feelings and emotions, he is torn between contradictory feelings for his parents and for his own origin and the demands of the

[8]Cf.: Brauen, M. and Kantowsky, D. (Hrsg.), *Junge Tibeter in der Schweiz. Studien zur kulturellen Identifikation*, Diessenhofen 1982.

foreign cultural reality of life. Generally the search for identity is done by internalising socio-cultural values and norms. The absorption of those values and norms, whether they come from his own culture or the foreign culture, can only be successful, if they can be applied in concrete situations.[9]

Tibetan parents are generally not able to pass on the relevance of their own values and norms in daily life. First of all, it is not possible to lead a traditional life in Switzerland. Secondly, their culture is marginalised in a dominant foreign environment. Without the demonstration of the applied values, the Tibetan youths have considerable difficulties in directing their own attitudes and behaviour. To succeed, every single youth needs conditions

> that give his behaviour and expectations security, so that his behaviour can meet his expectations and vice versa. Without decisions for specific value orientations the possibility to form an identity is thwarted.[10]

The Tibetan youth loses his original identity as a result of compulsory and necessary adaptation to local conditions. At the same time he cannot simply adopt the identity of the Swiss people. This creates a vacuum that the youth has to attempt to fill by going through an often painful and conflict-laden process of finding himself within the framework of two different cultures.

Integration and its Limitation

Over forty years ago, the first group of Tibetan refugees arrived

---

[9]Süssmuth, R., 'Familiale Kompetenz—Eine vernachlässigte Dimension der Familienerziehung', in: *Vierteljahresschrift für wissenschaftliche Pädagogik*, 54, 1978, p. 236.

[10]Süssmuth, R.: 'Familiale Kompetenz—Eine vernachlässigte Dimension der Familienerziehung', supra., p. 236. See also Claissens, D., *Familie und Wertsystem. Eine Studie zur 'zweiten sozio-kulturellen Geburt' des Menschen und der Belastbarkeit der 'Kernfamilie'*, Berlin 1972 and Erikson, E.H., *Identität und Lebenszyklus*, Frankfurt a.M. 1976.

in Switzerland. Since then, the second generation of Tibetans has already reached adulthood and a third generation is growing up. Today many Tibetans of the first generation are recipients of an old age pension. The question of the Tibetan experience with integration becomes relevant. In the overall picture, Tibetan difficulties with integration are not that different from what other refugees or immigrants of foreign origin experience. But because of the enormous differences in culture and their consequences, the problems are more complex. We can differentiate three stages of integration:[11]

Adaptation, the first stage means adapting their external behavior to the customs of the host country. Immediately after their arrival in Switzerland, the Tibetans had to submit to the legal, social and economic order of Switzerland and had to orient themselves in the new social environment. The segregation of residence and workplace, performing industrial factory work, taxation and health insurance required the first major adaptation. Most Tibetans had to adapt to different clothing and eating habits as well.

Acculturation, the second stage follows after the superficial adaptation. In this phase, first the younger and then the older Tibetans accept and internalise specific Swiss behaviour patterns and cultural values, like punctuality, personal hygiene, a sense of order, the Sunday stroll or keeping their money in a bank account. They saw this process as an enriching experience. At the same time they kept the Tibetan consciousness and solidarity with their own people alive. While going through this stage, most Tibetans lack the distance for a critical reflection of the Western way of life and thinking. This can result in good-natured admiration and imitation.

Assimilation is the third and last stage. It is understood to be the gradual assimilation into the culture of the host country by adapting to the lifestyle, customs and habits, values and way of

---

[11]See: Ott-Marti, E., *Probleme der Integration von Tibetern in der Schweiz*, Rikon 1980.

thinking. In contrast to acculturation, assimilation means the loss of the solidarity with one's own ethnic group and one's own cultural identity.

Obviously, the Tibetans in exile do not strive for integration in the sense of a complete and unconditional assimilation. It is also not possible. Their Asian appearance marks them as strangers in their Swiss environment.[12] The differences between the Central-Asian, Buddhist culture of the Tibetans and the middle-European, Christian culture of the Swiss people are so extreme, that a complete assimilation of Swiss values would pose the danger of a total loss of cultural roots and therefore the loss of their national identity. As it is well known, no peoples, not even a single person, can renounce himself and his origin completely.

Tibetans in Europe

From 1960 until today, Tibetans have gained admission into the following European countries:[13]

Country	*Number*	*Country*	*Number*
Belgium	5	Liechtenstein	17
Denmark	35	Norway	46
Germany	146	Austria	15
France	150	Sweden	31
Greece	20	Spain	2
Holland	21	Hungary	4
Italy	75	United Kingdom	137

[12]See: Brauen, M. and Kantowsky, D. (Hrsg.): *Junge Tibeter in der Schweiz. Studien zum Prozess kultureller Identifikation*, Diessenhofen 1982.

[13]Figures : Planning Council, Central Tibetan Administration, Tibetan Demographic Survey 1998, Dharamsala 2000, p. 38.

Tibetans in Canada[14]

Settlement

After Switzerland, Canada was the second Western country that welcomed Tibetan refugees in large numbers. Since 1959, many Canadians worked together with European charitable organisations to help with the settlement of Tibetan refugees in India. In 1963, the late George Woodcock founded, in Vancouver, the Canadian charitable organisation Tibetan Refugee Aid Society'.

Within the Canadian programme for Tibetan refugees, the first 277 Tibetan refugees arrived between 1970 and 1972. Strangely enough, they were settled in different regions of Canada according to their ties to the different traditions in Tibetan Buddhism. Over the years the number of Tibetan refugees in Canada grew to around 700. Between 1998-2001 there was a new wave of immigration; over 1,000 Tibetans came via the United States to Canada. As a result there are now about 1,700 Tibetans living in Canada. Of those, 1,300 reside in Ontario. The rest live in Alberta, British Columbia, Manitoba and Quebec.

Integration

The Tibetan refugees adapted quickly to the new ways of life. Soon they were able to earn their own livelihood. In all regions they founded organisations that focused on matters like the preservation of their language or the political struggle for the freedom of Tibet. For the children, Tibetan language lessons are available on Sundays. The parents make an effort to pass on a part of the Tibetan heritage to their children. The loss of the

[14]Information on the Tibetan Refugees in Canada is taken from the website of the Canada Tibet Committee. Dr. Brian Given authored the article on the website. Nima Dorjee, a Tibetan living in Canada, kindly provided information to the author on the situation of the Tibetans in Canada.

mother tongue by the youngest generation is the greatest concern for Tibetans in Canada.

Economically most of the Tibetans are doing well. According to Nima Dorjee, ninety per cent of the first 700 Tibetans have their own houses. Among the second generation who grew up in Canada, a relatively large number are university graduates; among them is a Rhodes scholar.

The Tibetan community in Canada is working through the 'Canada Tibet Committee' for their countrymen in India, Nepal and Tibet. Since 1992, this committee runs the Internet based news service 'Canada Tibet News Network' in an effort to connect all Tibetans and Tibet support groups in Canada. This internet service was soon used and valued by many Tibetans and friends of Tibet outside Canada. Therefore the name was changed to 'World Tibet Network' (WTN). Today it serves Tibetans and friends of Tibet worldwide with news about Tibet and the Tibetans in exile.

Tibetans in the United States of America

The First Immigrants

Tibet and the United States have a long common history. But the presence of Tibetans in this country became visible only during the last few years. The earliest immigration into the United States took place in the 1950s, since then until the 1990s, only a handful of Tibetans immigrated to the United States. The number is so small that in publications about the immigration of Asians in the United States, the Tibetans do not even merit a mention.

In a short history of the immigration of Tibetans to the United States, Rinchen Dharlo elaborates on the different stages and their backgrounds.[15] The first Tibetans to step on American soil in 1947 were members of a trade delegation led by

[15]See also: Rinchen Dharlo. 'A brief history of Tibetans in North America', in: *Tibetan Review*, October 1994 p. 12ff.

W.D. Shakabpa, the minister of finance in the Tibetan Government. This delegation was met by the foreign minister of the United States, George Marshall.[16]

The first Tibetans who settled in the United States were Telopa Rinpoche who had been invited by the Johns Hopkins University in 1948 and Prof. Thubten Jigme Norbu, the elder brother of the Dalai Lama, and his friend Dhondup Gyaltsen, who came to the United States in 1952.

The next Tibetan visitors to the United States were groups of young Tibetans from Kham (East Tibet) and Amdo (North Tibet). In the 1950s and the beginning of the 1960s they were brought to Colorado by the American government and trained by the American secret service (CIA). Most of them fought in the guerilla war against the Chinese oppression in Tibet.[17]

In 1964, when the 'Office of Tibet' was founded in New York, there were only about twenty Tibetans living in the United States. The introduction of Tibetan Buddhism to the West meant that more Tibetan lamas visited North America. Some of them settled in the United States with their translators and family members.

The Second Wave of Immigration

In 1967, the Great Northern Paper Company in the state of Maine invited six young Tibetans to Portage and employed them as woodcutters. Because the company was satisfied with their work, they sent for 21 more young Tibetans to be trained and employed as woodcutters. Despite their best efforts the Tibetans could not keep up with their taller and stronger American and Canadian colleagues. They earned relatively little and led a frugal life. Later these Tibetans moved to other states within the USA.[18]

---

[16]See: Shakabpa, W.D., *Tibet—A Political History*. New York 1984, p. 294ff.

[17]Dalai Lama, *Das Buch der Freiheit*, supra, p. 238ff.

[18]Rinchen Dharlo, *A brief history of Tibetans in North America*, supra p. 12f.

During the following years more Tibetans came to the United States. In 1985, 524 Tibetans were living in the United States according to the Office of Tibet.[19] In the 1980s a few well-known Tibetan-American organisations were founded, the US Tibet Committee, the Friends of Tibet and the International Campaign for Tibet. During that time, there was talk of emulating the Swiss model in the United States and settling a 1,000 Tibetans there.[20]

The Third Wave of Immigration

Edward Bednar and Tenzin N. Tethong, the former president of the International Campaign for Tibet, discussed this idea. Soon a debate about the pros and cons of this settlement project spread among American friends and Tibetans, including the Tibetan Government-in-Exile. Most of the American friends opposed this project; they argued that the Tibetans would lose their Tibetan identity in the melting pot of American culture. On the other hand, there was the example of the Chinese, Korean, Japanese or Indian immigrants, who fully participated in the American way of life without losing their cultural identity. After many rounds of discussion the arguments[21] for the settlement gained the upper hand and the Dalai Lama as well as the Tibetan Government-in-Exile agreed to go ahead with the project in 1989.

According to Rinchen Dharlo the main goal of this project was:

> Our goal by settling 1,000 Tibetans in the United States is not the preservation and promotion of the Tibetan culture in

[19]Ibid. p. 14.

[20]Edward Bednar and Member of Congress Frank Barney have discussed for some time the idea of settling 1,000 Tibetans in the United States.

[21]The USA as 'a country of unlimited possibilities' would offer the Tibetan a higher standard of living and better education facilities. The better-off Tibetans could even support their less affluent family members in India and Nepal.

> this country, but the endeavour to save Tibet from death. If the efforts of the 1,000 Tibetans help to save the national identity of six million Tibetans in Tibet, as well as advance our high goal of independence for Tibet, then the risk of 1,000 Tibetans losing part of their identity in this country, is well worth it.[22]

Because of the positive experiences with the settlement of Tibetan families in groups in Switzerland, the 1,000 Tibetans in the United States were also to be settled in groups in contrast to former immigrants. To make this project a reality, a commission called the Tibetan US Resettlement Project was founded. It had to fulfill the following three difficult tasks:

- The introduction and acceptance of a corresponding resolution in the Congress of the United States;
- The selection of 1,000 Tibetans among the 100,000 Tibetans in exile in India and Nepal;
- The organisation of the immigration process and finding accommodation and jobs for the 1,000 Tibetans.

On 27 October 1990, the American Congress passed a resolution that allowed 1,000 Tibetans to immigrate to the United States of America.[23]

A few months later, the Office of Consular Affairs of the American Foreign Ministry announced the procedure of settlement. In co-operation with the Tibetan Government-in-Exile, a complex method of selection was worked out and implemented.[24]

On 16 April 1992, the first group of Tibetans arrived in the USA. Another 21 groups followed at regular intervals and were settled with host families in 18 states. Thanks to the policy of family reunification, the number of Tibetans in the United

[22]Rinchen Dharlo, *A Brief History of Tibetans in North America*, supra, p. 14f.

[23]Ibid., p. 15.

[24]Ibid.

States climbed dramatically in the second half of the 1990s. So today, over 7,000 Tibetans live in the USA.

Some Problems During the Adaptation Stage[25]

Most Tibetans had never travelled that far, especially to a strange, far-away country. At first they all suffered from jetlag. At their arrival at JFK airport in New York, some of them thought they had landed on another planet.

The food and eating habits of the American families posed more problems. For example, the Tibetans were used to drinking a lot of tea in the morning. But most American host families ate biscuits and only drank fruit juice for breakfast.

Another difficulty arose, especially at the beginning because of unrealistically high expectations from both sides. According to the naive notions of most Tibetans, the United States was a place where milk and honey flowed in abundance, where good money was to be made without hard work. The stereotypical picture the American host families had of the Tibetans was that of gentle, religious people. The Americans liked to talk. In the beginning, the Tibetans told them all about their lives in Tibet, India and/or Nepal. But later the material for conversation ran out and the Tibetans talked less and less. The host families thought that the Tibetans did not like them any more. Since many of the immigrants spoke very little English, there were difficulties in communication as well.

One of the biggest problems the thousand Tibetans were confronted with during the first years was separation from their families. With the policy of family reunification this problem was solved to a great extent.

Integration

Over the years, some of the Tibetans who immigrated before 1990 became citizens of the United States. Besides the fact that the American passport made it easier for them to travel to India,

[25]See part "The older generation", supra .

Nepal or even Tibet, most of them had little interest in the implications of citizenship. They did not see themselves as Tibetan Americans. They did not join any organisations of Asian Americans and did not take part in their activities.

In Bhuchung Tsering's[26] opinion it is necessary that the Tibetans in the United States see themselves as 'Tibetan Americans'. This does not mean that they can no longer be active in the Tibetan struggle for freedom. On the contrary, they can do a lot for Tibet if they use the opportunities provided by American civil rights. They can, for instance, press their members of the US Congress to actively support Tibet.[27]

In the first generation of immigrants, the community of Tibetans in the United States is still compact. But the second generation will be faced with the same dilemma as other immigrants: Is it more important to grow up as Tibetan Americans or as Americans? The Tibetans in the United States bear the additional responsibility of working for the preservation of Tibetan identity. No Tibetan can afford to ignore this responsibility and stop thinking about the survival of Tibetan culture.

The first generation of Tibetans who immigrated since 1992 faces one of the biggest challenges. Most of them are working seven days a week and in shifts to realise their American dream. They want to earn enough money to buy a car and/or a house. Or they send money to their relatives in India or Nepal. For that dream, the parents sacrifice other responsibilities, for instance, the bringing-up of their children. As a result the children are left to fend for themselves. Hence there is a danger that the children will grow up mono-lingual, preferring English to Tibetan. Tibetan parents need to rise to this challenge and set their priorities straight.

Today's society in the United States is comparably more tolerant towards ethnic communities. Immigrants from Asia like Chinese, Koreans, Japanese or Indians have generally been able

---

[26]Bhuchung Tsering, 'Enter the Tibetan Americans', *Newsletter of Tibet Foundation*, 1999.

[27]Ibid.

to find a balance between the preservation of their cultural inheritance and the acceptance of an American identity. Perhaps the Tibetans can learn from them.

The Purpose of Exile

At the beginning of exile, there was confusion, poverty and suffering. Homesickness for the lost homeland made acclimatisation in a new country difficult. The life of the Tibetan refugees in exile still does not present an ideal solution, since they lost their homeland due to a political crisis and were subjected to a changed existence in a strange world. Thanks to their ability to adapt, to their drive to survive and work, but also thanks to the support of the Swiss population, the exiled-Tibetans in Switzerland have succeeded in integrating into a foreign cultural environment. In this process they have generally kept their cultural identity, their Buddhist beliefs and their social and political cohesion because of their ceaseless efforts and the wise and far-sighted guidance of the Dalai Lama. Materially, they have achieved a higher standard of living compared to their countrymen in India and Nepal. Furthermore, in their interaction with the citizens of their host country they generally have positive experiences; they enjoy high regard because of their peaceful, tolerant and calm conduct.

The reception of refugees from a foreign culture and their integration into an unfamiliar society is a long-term task. After the basic existential needs are satisfied, problems of personal relations, but also the longing to preserve and foster one's own culture and identity gain more and more importance.

In the long run, the survival of the Tibetan people is only possible because of their unique culture and their Buddhist beliefs. The problem of the Tibetan exile community is therefore not only a question of their material integration, but also of their spiritual-cultural rehabilitation. The Tibetans in exile carry the responsibility of saving their threatened Tibetan Buddhist culture from extinction. The preservation and care for the culture is not enough, because it cannot be a rigid conservation and an uncritical adoption of traditional cultural values in the way a museum preserves a specimen. Buddhist beliefs interwoven with the spiritual and creative expressions of life have to be critically examined. They have to be open to development and renewal. Such an understanding of culture is very important because in today's world a socio-cultural existence without influences from outside, such as the Tibetans experienced before 1959 in their self-imposed isolation, is no longer possible.

In this time of critical reflection and new orientation, traditional norms and values receive new interpretations. And the Tibetans are constantly searching for the essence of their culture and their way of life. It is vitally important for the Tibetans in exile to foster a strong, intact community that can provide support for their members and nurture their self-confidence and self-esteem. Within this community, the Tibetans in exile, especially the young generation, can unfold and master their past, their present and their future together.

In exile, the basic conditions for a life in the traditional culture are absent. That is why the older generation has to adapt to the new conditions without giving up allegiance to their own culture. They have to keep their culture, identity and beliefs alive parallel to their integration into a foreign life.

For the younger generation this often means a painful process of finding themselves. This process not only includes the internalisation and preservation of their original identity but also an attempt to create a meaningful synthesis between the two identities. A critical evaluation of the social and cultural norms and values of both the original as well as the host culture is necessary to find a meaningful synthesis between the two identities. This would allow them to succesfully live in exile and at the same time do justice to their own cultural inheritance.

References

Aeschimann, C., *Aufnahme von Tibeter-Kindern durch schweizer Familien*, Montreux 1978.

Bhuchung, Tsering, 'Enter the Tibetan Americans. *Newsletter of the Tibet Foundation*, 1999.

Brauen, M. & Kantowsky, D. (Hrsg.), *Junge Tibeter in der Schweiz. Studien zur kulturellen Identifikation*, Diessenhofen 1982.

Claissens, D., *Familie und Wertsystem. Eine Studie zur zweiten sozio-kulturellen Geburt des Menschen und der Belastbarkeit der 'Kernfamilie'*, Berlin 1972.

Dalai Lama, *Das Buch der Freiheit*, München 1990.

Dharlo, Rinchen, 'A Brief History of Tibetans in North America', in: *Tibetan Review*, October 1994.

Erikson, E.H., *Identität und Lebenszyklus*, Frankfurt a.M. 1976.

Gyaltag. G., 'Tibet heute—Leben zwischen Anpassung und Selbstbehauptung', in: C. Müller and W. Raunig (Hrsg.), *Der Weg zum Dach der Welt*, Innsbruck 1982.

Gyaltag, G., *Die Tibetische Familie im Wandel und Spannungsfeld zweier Kulturen*, Rikon/Zürich 1990.

Gyaltsen, K. and Gyaltag, G., *Jugend im Exil, Hrsg. Verein Tibeter Jugend in Europa* (Festschrift), Zürich 1980.

Information Office of H.H. the Dalai Lama, *Tibetans in Exile 1959–1980*, Dharamsala 1981.

Mitscherlich, A., *Auf dem Weg zur vaterlosen Gesellschaft, Ideen zur Sozialphilosophie*, München 1963.

Müller, C. and Raunig, W. (Hrsg.), *Der Weg zum Dach der Welt*, Innsbruck 1982.

Ott-Marti, E., *Probleme der Integration von Tibetern in der Schweiz*, Rikon 1980.

Planning Council, Central Tibetan Administration, *Tibetan Demographic Survey 1998*, Dharamsala 2000.

Rose, A.M., *Migrants in Europe: Problems of Acceptance and Adjustment*, Minneapolis 1969.

Schweizerisches Rotes Kreuz, Sektor Hilfsaktion, *Ansiedlung tibetischer Flüchtlinge in der Schweiz*, Bern 1976.

Shakabpa, Tsepön W.D., *Tibet—A Political History*, New York 1984.

Süssmuth, R., 'Familiale Kompetenz - Eine vernachlässigte Dimension der Familienerziehung', in: *Vierteljahresschrift für wissenschaftliche Pädagogik*, 54, 1978.

Tschanz, E.: 'Wie die Tibeter zu uns kamen', in: *Schweizerisches Rotes Kreuz*, Nr. 5, 1981.

CHAPTER THIRTEEN

The Tibetan Schools in the Diaspora*

TSEPAK RIGZIN

Introduction

It can safely be said that before 1959, there were very few schools in Tibet for the common people. The few that did exist were rudimentary, and for the privileged few. The monasteries were centres of cultural and religious life, and philosophical discourse, but this learning was the prerogative of the monks. An estimated twenty per cent of the male population chose monkhood, and thus received education in the monasteries. However schools for the lay citizen were few and far between, located only in towns; schools for girls did not exist at all, and the upper and upper middle classes engaged tutors to teach their children at home.

Attempts were made during the reign of the thirteenth Dalai Lama (1879–1933) to establish schools to import and impart modern education. However the apprehensions of the monastic community combined with the ignorance of the laity prevented their growth.[1] Ironically, it was only after the flight into exile in 1959 that sincere and rigorous attempts were made to develop schools as envisaged by His Holiness the Dalai Lama, with the generous and unstinting assistance of the Government of India.

---

*This article is mainly based on the current functioning of the CTSA Schools, and the opinion and views intermittently expressed therein are purely personal and unofficial. Hence, the content does not necessarily reflect the complete picture of all Tibetan Schools in India, Nepal and Bhutan.

[1]See chapter 1; chapter 6.

The centuries-old cultural and religious ties between India and Tibet certainly prepared the ground for the opening of schools to provide modern education to Tibetan children. In this regard, the role of India remains historic.

The first Tibetan School in India was established at Mussoorie on 3 March 1960 with a batch of 50 selected adolescent students and four Tibetan teachers. Witnesses recall that on the day of inauguration, the fourteenth Dalai Lama opened the door of the Aron building embellished with five coloured silk scarves. After a few moments of deep and vibrating meditation, people rushed into the hall with full force. In the near stampede that ensued, an elderly VIP fell down. Seeing this, the Dalai Lama remarked with a smile, 'Oh, it is a good sign. There will be a great rush of Tibetan children to receive education.'

So began the story of the Tibetan Schools in exile with their distinct identity. The development of Tibetan children's education in exile was a historic compulsion. The schools grew literally without experience or resources, both human and material. But to everyone's surprise within a very short time the structure from kindergarten to adult education emerged. More importantly, the schools evinced a distinct identity while being modern. A great wave of sympathy from the Government of India, its people, foreign aid agencies, and above all the will power of the Tibetan people themselves, helped the schools and the community withstand all the hardships and calamities of exile.

Schools for all Children

Today, there are 82 Tibetan schools in India, Nepal and Bhutan. They fall into four categories:

1. schools managed by the Central Tibetan Schools Administration (CTSA), New Delhi, attached to the Ministry of Human Resource Development, Government of India (28 schools);
2. schools run by the Department of Education (DOE),

Tibetan Central Administration and funded by the DOE (16);

3. autonomous schools run by the Tibetan Children's Village (TCV), and Tibetan Homes Foundation (THF) (18 and 2 respectively), and
4. independent schools run by trusts or private agencies. Apart from 106 pre-primary schools, many of them in the Tibetan Children's Villages, there are 34 primary schools, 22 middle schools, 11 secondary schools leading to class 9 and 10, and 15 senior secondary schools offering schooling up to class 11 and 12.[2]

Almost all the schools have a fairly satisfactory infrastructure with resources such as science laboratories, libraries, computers and drawing facilities, as well as games and sports grounds as well as equipment for music and dance. Teachers are given in-service training to upgrade their professional skills and to teach creative methods of learning.

These efforts have been highly successful. In the space of two generations, Tibetan society in exile has moved from an overall literacy rate of 25 per cent (including the monks) to an effective literacy rate of 70 per cent. The age group 15–19 years is 97 per cent literate! The development is particularly striking in the case of women. We have no statistics relating to the period before 1959, but the figures for the exile population above 60 years of age indicate that only 2.5 per cent of women in this age group—who arrived in India as adults—can read and write. Today girls in the age group 15–19 years are just as literate as boys.[3]

It can be assumed that almost every Tibetan child in exile goes to school, if only to primary school. The challenge is the constant flow of newly arriving refugees from Tibet who have to be integrated.

---

[2]All information from Department of Education, CTA, April 2003.

[3]See Planning Council, Central Tibetan Administration, Tibetan Demographic Survey 1998, Dharamsala 2000, p. 106.

Twenty-eight schools with attached pre-primary sections are run by the Central Tibetan Schools Administration (CTSA), financed by the Indian Government and supervised by the Ministry for Human Resource Development. The total number of children in these CTSA schools is around 11,012, which is one third of the population from 5–19 years. The majority of these institutions provide for the primary and middle school level, 5 lead up to class 10, and 8 to class 12. In this article I am dealing only with the CTSA schools.

Objectives

There are two main objectives of establishing Tibetan schools in India, Bhutan and Nepal: a) to impart modern education to Tibetan children so that they are fully equipped to face the challenges of the modern world and to reconstruct Tibet's future, and b) to enable Tibetan children to preserve Tibet's rich cultural heritage, religion and identity.

Structure of Education

Today, schools at the pre-primary stage accept and take care of children aged +3 to 6. No formal teaching and learning is expected and the emphasis, especially recently, is on helping children and their parents to accept and appreciate school-readiness programmes implemented only through playway methods. All teachers in the CTSA set up, including those teaching at the pre-primary levels, are trained and have all the qualifications and skills required of the educational system. Teachers are Indians as well as Tibetans. To give an example, at the CTSA school in Mundgod there are 60 teachers including the Principal and the Rector, of these, 38 are Indian and 22 are Tibetan.

At the pre-primary stage early childhood education on the pattern of the kindergarten method is taught. Teachers are at liberty to show creativity in handling very young children with slight adaptation both in content and methodology suitable to the local cultural and traditional needs of the community. The helpers are also selected with extreme care and scrutiny by the authorities concerned. Some schools have baby rooms attached. Even today, the pre-primary schools are run free of cost for the community. Without doubt, the outstanding quality of nurses, foster parents and teachers engaged in these care centres is their sense of affection and love for children and their ability to substitute for the real parents with a true and sincere sense of caring and total involvement. We can say with pride that this sense of service comes from the faith and belief in the Buddhist religion and its principles.

Nonetheless, the playway method of nurturing and caring for pre-primary children busy in their own world has met with little appreciation from parents. Parents complain that these centres allow children to play the whole day or compel them to sleep unwillingly. Parents on the other hand want their children to learn the three R's—reading, writing and arithmetic, which for them are synonymous with education. Thus, the gap between the system and the expectations of parents still exists. This must be bridged by educating the community at large. Once the parents are convinced of the significance of the playway method and its multi-dimensional and far-reaching effects on the overall personality development of a child, it will mark a distinct shift in the history of child-care in Tibetan society. At the same time proper interaction and functional understanding between community and teachers should also be introduced.

Today primary education (class I to V) has been Tibetanised. Thanks to the pioneering work of the Tibetan Children's Village (TCV), since 1987/88 the medium of instruction for all subjects at the primary level is now Tibetan. This giant step, however, should not imply that the primary education imparted earlier through the medium of English was a failure. In any case, as regards the medium of instruction there are two schools of thought. The parents in the elite, rich and educated class prefer English as the medium of instruction. But generally speaking, this programme of Tibetanisation has received the approval of the majority of parents.

Having studied through the medium of Tibetan at the primary level, the continuity is interrupted as soon as a child reaches class VI since he/she now has to study all subjects, except Tibetan, through English as medium of instruction all the way up to senior secondary (XII standard), and of course at graduate and postgraduate levels. But whatever the ramifications, by now it seems certain that there will be no backtracking on the medium of instruction at the primary level.

From class 1–5 only two languages, English and Tibetan, are taught besides environmental studies which include social studies and general science, drawing, physical education, value education, music, dance and Tibetan cultural activities. In class 6 a third language is introduced, namely Hindi. This way the three-language formula is being implemented.[4]

At middle school level (class VI to VIII) some flexibility is envisaged in the curriculum, and in some schools, this liberty is being exercised to teach topics more relevant to Tibetan culture, history and ecology. However, at the secondary and senior secondary levels, (class IX–XII), the Indian education system and the prescribed curriculum have to be followed as the students will need recognised school leaving certificates. However Tibetan language and culture are also taught.

At secondary level (class IX and X), only five subjects can be studied as compulsory subjects—English, Tibetan, general science, mathematics and social studies which includes history, geography and civics. Besides, physical education, SUPW (Socially Useful Productive Works), dance and music are also taught.

At the senior secondary (class XI and XII), commonly known as 'plus 2 level', children have the option of choosing different streams, like arts, commerce, science, and vocational training. Science students can opt for medical and non-medical subjects

[4]In principle, Indian children learn three languages in school: their mother tongue Hindi, and one more Indian language or English (editor's note).

with or without mathematics. The Central School for Tibetans at the Mundgod settlement is the only school which offers vocational studies with the options of three streams—stenography, purchasing, and cost and accounting.

By virtue of the Indian education policy and for official recognition of the school-leaving certificates at the tenth and twelfth levels, it is compulsory for all schools to get affiliation to a Board of Education approved and recognised by the Government. Truly speaking, there is no other or better alternative system of school education for Tibetans in exile. Hence, all secondary and senior secondary level Tibetan schools in India are unilaterally affiliated to the Central Board of Secondary Education (CBSE), New Delhi, which is the apex board for examinations at the all India level. Similarly, secondary schools in Nepal are affiliated to the Nepal School Education Board.

Curriculum

Tibetan schools in India, Nepal and Bhutan generally follow a curriculum approved by the Board of Education to which the school is affiliated and which has been recognised by the government. As mentioned above, the medium of instruction in primary classes is Tibetan and from class I to V the syllabi of the NCERT (National Council for Educational Research and Training) for English and mathematics (Tibetan version) are followed. However, the textbooks for social science and general science prepared by the Educational Development and Research Centre (EDRC), TCV, Dharamsala are used in the primary classes. For the teaching of Tibetan language, history and culture textbooks, prepared by Tibetan experts under the direction of the Department of Education at Dharamsala are used from class I to XII without exception in all Tibetan schools in India, Nepal and Bhutan. Schools procure these text books through the EDRC's printing and publication agencies. The expert review committees at Dharamsala review and update the syllabus from time to time.

It is worth mentioning that Tibetan language textbooks comprise chapters on Tibetan history, religion, grammar, opera stories, poetry and lexicons, all to be taught within the seven or eight periods (35 minutes) allotted per week. Actually this has become quite a heavy load for students above class VI. Getting through the Tibetan language examination with minimum pass marks may not be difficult, but for students to achieve a high standard of language skills, the syllabus needs to be evaluated and reworked. The standard of question papers for Tibetan language in class X and XII is generally thought to be sub-standard.

Admission

Admission to Tibetan schools is open to all Tibetan children from pre-primary to class XII subject to the availability of seats. Since 1994–95 when Tibetan was introduced as the medium of instruction in the CTSA schools, local Indian children are not admitted in classes I–V. However, of late, some arrangements have been made at the local level for the admission of wards of the Indian staff. But 10 per cent Indian children can be admitted from classes VI and above. Instead of Tibetan they can opt for Hindi and Sanskrit. Generally, irrespective of any ethnic background, the minimum criteria expected for admission in class XI science stream is 50 per cent marks in aggregate with 50 per cent in science and mathematics in the class X Board exams, and 45 per cent marks in aggregate for admission in the commerce and vocational streams. For admission in the arts stream no minimum criteria are required as long as a child has passed the class X examination.

Examination Scheme

For Classes I to VIII

In general, the performance of a student for the entire academic year is evaluated by four unit tests, half-yearly and annual examinations. However, only oral tests tests are conducted for classes I and II in the subjects social science and social studies. Promotion from classes I to IX and XI to the next higher class is decided by calculating the combined weightage of four unit tests and the half yearly and annual examinations. For class V, VIII, IX and XI a common annual examination is conducted centrally by the CTSA Headquarter and evaluation work is also carried out by the teachers of other schools.

The performance of a student in subjects like drawing, physical education and music and dance, is evaluated by awarding grades from A to E. Grade E is considered below average.

Students of class X and XII appear for the All India Secondary and Senior Secondary Examinations conducted by the Central Board of Secondary Examinations, New Delhi and promotion criteria are governed by the rules framed by the CBSE from time to time.

Post School Opportunities

Limited opportunities for further studies in various colleges and universities in India and abroad are made available to students who secure 60 per cent and above in the class XII board examination. The Department of Education has succeeded in obtaining from the Government of India 17 reserved seats for Tibetan students for studies in medicine, engineering, pharmacy, technology in selected Indian colleges and universities. In addition students avail scholarship facilities from the CTSA as well as the DEO to study in India and abroad. As per the Current Status Report of the DEO, 237 scholarships have been made available between 1982–98 for students to study abroad.

Financing Education

The CTSA schools are funded by the Government of India and there are no school fees. In the six residential schools, boarding costs Rs. 1,000 per month for ten months a year. The CTSA pays these fees for 360 students, for others the Department of Education, parents, and sponsors bear the fees. The other schools under the DOE or the Tibetan Children's Villages are funded by the Tibetan Central Administration, by parents and donors.

Preservation of the Tibetan Cultural Heritage

The preservation of Tibetan culture, tradition and heritage is one of the main aims for establishing separate Tibetan schools. And, today, the services of the teachers and community towards achieving this goal have assumed a special dimension in view of the fast changing world. In this regard, the role of the Department of Education, Dharamsala has been laudable. The textbooks are replete with Tibet's history, religion, culture and traditions. The schools' annual co-curricular activities are full of Tibetan cultural events. Special posts of religious and culture teachers and music and dance instructors have been created.

There are six residential schools for 1,700 children where the staff i.e. the rector, the wardens and matrons are all Tibetan. A home-like atmosphere and environment are created; boarders learn to be self-reliant, sociable, and imbibe values of integrity, a sense of belonging and the art of living in a community. Every day, morning and evening, prayer sessions are conducted under the direct guidance of monk teachers. Every Tibetan school also conducts annual inter-house cultural dance, song, drama and skit competitions. These matches get a fillip at the zonal and central level inter-school competition in Tibetan cultural and academic activities involving debate and declamation contests held every alternative year. Special exhibitions on Tibetan culture and tradition are also being organised in schools. Talks by guest speakers, symposia and dialogues with learned and erudite lay and monk scholars are arranged in the schools blended with demonstrations of Tibetan culture and tradition. Important days like New Year (Losar), the Great Prayer Festival, and special days related to Buddha Shakyamuni's life are enthusiastically observed in the spirit of inspiration, admiration and integrity.

The teaching of music and dance has a special significance. Through this medium, and by understanding the meanings of the dances and songs, history and culture are communicated. Frequent demonstrations and exhibitions of costumes and musical instruments are held. In music and dance classes, stories and biographies of Tibet's great saints, philosophers, kings, poets and patriots are told and enacted. Jataka stories on Buddha's life are told as part of value education, and recast in the form of skits, dramas and presentations in the story-telling sessions. Calligraphy and essay competitions are a regular feature of school activities. Tours and visits to nearby monasteries and holy places are highlights of the year.

In spite of all these activities and efforts, the very vitality of transmission, appreciation and practice of Tibetan culture and tradition in our schools still falls short of fulfilling the expectations of the authorities as well as the community. The drive and interest of the younger generation towards modern rock music and Indian cinema overshadows the interest and love of Tibetan culture and tradition. Complaints of poor standard of Tibetan language, lack of interest in religious and cultural activities, rising cases of indiscipline and the formation of undesirable social habits etc. are causing concern. Perhaps, the time is now ripe to explore and adopt new ways and means to impart education on the Tibetan tradition.

Concerns and Appraisals

No doubt, the spirit of the younger generation is strong and burns with aspirations and urgency for freedom, but the challenges of today's global scenario are equally painful and perplexing. There is a strong feeling that the parents' guidance and support for children at home is not sufficient in raising their standard of academic performance and moral values. In search of a livelihood, most of the parents are compelled to move around almost half the year doing petty business like selling sweaters while children remain in the care of grandparents and aged relatives for lack of proper alternative child-care centres. This leads to dejection, demoralisation and derailment of a child's interest in studies and erratic mental and physical growth. The consequence is a high drop-out rate, a cause of great concern for all educationists. The best solution to this problem would be to open standard residential schools in the settlements for students above the class VIII. However, proper planning and staffing is a must, building on past experiences and evolving a long term vision for the future.

There is a growing trend among the Tibetan youth of today to look for quick money and luxurious lifestyles. The society in general is also getting more aware, and at times volatile in criticising the authorities and the system, though this trend in attitudinal changes is part of the democratisation process and need not be suppressed.

The lack of job placement services after the completion of schooling is a major problem. Private enterprise should be encouraged to step in. Obviously, we have not been able to utilise the multiple options of subject selections offered by the CBSE at senior secondary level, due to administrative and practical difficulties. Hence, students are left with only a few, static options in the selection of streams or subjects at the senior secondary level. This has caused a tight and imbalanced induction of students into few options of further studies, and hence to a biased overcrowding of human resources after school or university education. To cite an example, today we have a high number of graduates with B.A., M.A., and B.Com degrees, but not enough jobs. We could not afford proper planning, direction and guidance or for that matter could not take the risk of drastic changes at the appropriate stages of education because of numerous limitations. The bureaucratic conflicts and rising nepotism, pressures and pulls from higher levels are on the rise, breaking human faith and trust in the official systems.

These are but a few concerns facing the immediate present in exile. Needless to say, the awesome task of building an independent Tibet is very difficult. Our enemy is insurmountable in almost every field, and our non-violent way of struggle is no doubt fair and true, but the leadership in Beijing has absolutely no understanding of it; we have a long way to go. Ideally speaking, human hope and spirit is eternal, but the earthly body with which we are to identify at least during this lifetime as a refugee has its limitations. The younger generations will have to learn to live in the modern world, as well as be able to maintain their identity and culture. Survival as a human being may not be difficult, but survival as a refugee away from one's country is harsh. Our children today are better qualified and ask mature questions but we do not always have answers for them. Yet, the future is full of hope. Education, proper education, is the greatest weapon, and we must be awake and handle it wisely.

CHAPTER FOURTEEN

Caring for the Weakest: The Children's Villages

JETSUN PEMA

Editors' Introduction

Hidden in a forest at the foothills of the Himalayas we come upon the Tibetan Children's Village, Dharamsala. It also houses the Headquarter of all the Tibetan Children's Villages, modelled on the SOS Children's Villages in Europe. In the afternoon hundreds of children run, play and have fun on the large playground. They are all dressed alike, blue checked shirts and grey trousers for the boys, grey skirts for the girls. Two thousand five hundred children live here and study at the Village's own schools and kindergartens. We are shown into a home of a 'family' of 45 children belonging to all age-groups. They share 3 bedrooms; in the kitchen a boy about 8 years old stirs a huge pot of tea. All the children have to help the 'mother' with the cooking and the household work. In another cottage, the Kindergarten, about 20 babies, 1 to 1½ years old sit in a circle and learn how to drink from a mug. These children have been smuggled out of Tibet by their parents and now grow up in the Children's Village, where they have a better chance to receive a Tibetan education. The youngest child is only two weeks old.

The Tibetan Children's Villages (TCV) is a registered, non-profit charitable organisation for the care of orphaned and destitute Tibetan children in India. From its humble beginnings in 1960, it has become a thriving educational organisation in exile with branches extending from Ladakh in the north to Bylakuppe in the south. Today, the TCV is an integrated community with family homes for the children and schooling facilities to provide modern education alongside a good understanding of the rich cultural heritage of Tibet. After completing school education, we also provide varied opportunities for higher and vocational education depending on the children's ability and aptitude. Currently, we have over 14,000 children in our care.

The success of the Tibetan Children's Villages is mainly due to the inspired guidance of His Holiness the Dalai Lama, the dedication and selfless sacrifices of the co-workers and the kind and generous support of the Government of India, individuals, friends and organisations around the world, especially the SOS Kinderdorf International.

Background

When the fourteenth Dalai Lama moved to Dharamsala in early 1960, it was apparent that one of the most critical needs of the refugees was to care for the many children who were orphaned or separated from their families during the arduous escape from their homeland. He recognised that the future of Tibet and its people depended on the younger generation. With this in mind and out of concern for the miserable conditions under which so many children were suffering, the Dalai Lama at once assigned his officials the task of bringing these children from the road construction camps, where many refugees were working, to Dharamsala.

Initially, the children were looked after by some of the officials. But as more and more children came from the road construction camps in the Kulu Valley, in Jammu and Kashmir and other places the officials could not accommodate all of them. Therefore, the Dalai Lama entrusted the first batch of 51 children to my elder sister, the late Mrs. Tsering Dolma Takla.

Our leader requested the Government of India to assist us with housing facilities for the children. The government kindly provided an old English bungalow called Egerton Hall, which was perfect at the time.

The early days were marked by acute shortages of practically everything—food, clothing, medicine, accommodation and staff. Accommodation was our greatest concern. Children kept pouring in from the road construction camps and places where the Tibetans had initially settled. Soon news about the work of the Nursery for Tibetan Refugee Children spread among the international aid agencies notably: Swiss Aid to Tibetans, Save the Children Fund (UK), Norwegian Refugee Council, Deutsche Tibethilfe, Deutsche Welthungerhilfe and the Catholic Relief Services. And, of course, without the assistance of the Government of India and her great people, it would have been impossible for us to look after the thousands of children desperately in need of care and education.

Working against all odds, my sister directed the Nursery for Tibetan Refugee Children with inspired determination. Along with a team of co-workers she overcame all limitations and worked passionately for its success until her untimely demise in 1964 when the Dalai Lama asked me to take up this responsibility.

The efforts in the early years were mostly directed at feeding the sick and undernourished children and then sending them to various residential Tibetan schools set up with the aid of the Indian government. But the time came when these residential schools could not accept any more children. The only solution for the Nursery was to widen its scope and make provisions for school education.

Plans were at once formulated to reshape the Nursery into a fully integrated community where the children under its care would receive not only the warmth and security of a home and a mother to share with brothers and sisters, but also a good education. To fulfil these aims and objectives the Nursery was in 1972 formally registered as a charitable organisation under the

Indian Societies Act of 1860 as the Tibetan Children's Village (TCV). In the same year, it also became a full-fledged member of the SOS Kinderdorf International, Vienna. Ever since, the TCV has strengthened its contact with the SOS Kinderdorf, which continues to provide the backbone support for all the major projects of the TCV for the care and education of the Tibetan children in exile.

The mission that emerged for the TCV and which continues to inspire us is:

- to look after the physical, mental and spiritual needs of the children,
- to impart the best of modern education along with a deep understanding of the rich cultural heritage of Tibet,
- to develop a sense of national pride and identity that will enable the children to share the hopes and aspirations of the Tibetan people to return to Tibet, and
- to help our boys and girls become self-reliant, contributing members of our society and the larger human community.

Growth

The TCV grew out of sheer necessity. As the need to take care of orphans and destitute children in exile increased, it was impossible to absorb all of them in the TCV, Dharamsala. What is more, the problem of over-crowding worsened in the early 1980s when parents and relatives in Tibet brought thousands of children for better educational opportunities in exile. The communist Chinese had to relax their oppressive rule in Tibet a little and were forced to follow a more lenient policy in the 1980s. This new policy enabled children to be smuggled out of Tibet in large numbers. In order to absorb this ever-increasing exodus of children, the TCV had to expand beyond Dharamsala by starting new children's villages, schools, youth hostels, technical and vocational training centres in various parts of India. A brief on each of our projects provides an overview of our endeavours:

The Children's Villages and Schools

1. The Tibetan Children's Village, Dharamsala

The Children's Village in Dharamsala is the largest and the mother village for all TCV Projects. It has 41 homes, hostels for older children, a baby home, a hospital and four school sections—infant, junior, middle and senior. The school is affiliated to Central Board of Secondary Education (CBSE), Delhi, and offers senior secondary education in science and in the humanities. Currently we have 2,357 children in the village. The TCV Head Office, which co-ordinates all projects, is also located in the village.

2. The Tibetan Children's Village School, Patlikul

In the early 1960s, there were a large number of Tibetan refugees engaged in road construction in the Kulu Valley. The road workers had set up a temporary shed to serve as a nursery for their children while they worked. But due to lack of funds and proper management, the nursery was in a very poor condition. So in 1971, the TCV was requested to take it over. This little nursery school underwent a sea change with the construction of new dormitories, classrooms and other facilities. The school was gradually upgraded to class VIII and is now recognised by the CBSE, New Delhi. Today, it has 628 children and serves as a feeder school. There is also an Old People's Home on campus.

3. The SOS-TCV, Ladakh

The Tibetan settlement in Ladakh is one of the most remote and least developed of all the Tibetan communities in exile even today. There was a crying need to look after the children's education and welfare. Thus in 1975, with an initial grant of Rs 10,000 from the Dalai Lama and land donated by the local Indian government, my co-workers and I started a new children's village. Today, it has become an oasis in this mountainous desert with facilities for child care and education akin to the Children's Village at Dharamsala. Besides the main village and school at Choglamsar, we have 7 primary feeder schools around Leh and Jangthang. The school is affiliated to the CBSE, New Delhi, and provides education up to secondary level. Presently, we have 1,663 children living in the village or attending the school as day scholars. We also have a home for old people at Choglamsar and a small project in Jangthang.

4. The SOS-TCV, Bylakuppe

The majority of the Tibetans in India are settled in south India, particularly in the state of Karnataka. There are five major settlements with a total population of over 35,000 Tibetans. In these settlements, there were a large number of orphans, half orphans and destitute children needing immediate attention. With the overcrowding problems at the TCV Dharamsala, it was not possible to admit all such deserving children. In order to look after the children, the best solution was to establish another Children's Village in the South. With 16 acres of land donated by the settlers of the Old Settlement, Bylakuppe, a new Children's Village was opened in 1981. The funding for the village came from the SOS Kinderdorpen, Holland. Today the village has 1,049 children and the school with three sections offers education up to the senior secondary level in the commerce stream. Attached are 10 day-care centres in various parts of the settlement. Currently, we have a total of 723 pre-school children in these centres.

5. The TCV, Lower Dharamsala

As children from Tibet continued to arrive in large numbers, it was extremely difficult for the TCV to accomodate them in the main village. In 1984, we had to convert a small poultry farm in our possession into a residential school with proper facilities. As we were able to gradually absorb the children into other TCV branches, we were able to make this school cater to the needs of children with parents. It became the first Tibetan residential school fully financed by parents. Presently, it has 747 children and offers education up to secondary level.

6. TCV School, Bir

The school at Bir was first started by the Central Tibetan Administration in 1986 as an adult education centre for new arrivals from Tibet. In 1990, the TCV was asked to take over the school. We surveyed the needs of the students and formulated plans. Construction of dormitories, classrooms, a hospital and allied facilities were given due priority. On the education side, we developed a multi-pronged approach focusing on individual needs of the young adults and giving them a wide range of options—both academic and vocational—to choose from. Presently, there are 834 students in the school.

6. SOS-TCV, Bir

To ease the ever-increasing overcrowding in all TCV projects, this beautiful Children's Village was founded in 1993 with kind assistance from the SOS Kinderdorf International. It has 12 family homes and a primary school with 655 children.

7. SOS-TCV, Gopalpur

This new Children's Village started functioning in 1997 with the first batch of children arriving from Tibet. The Children's Village was constructed mainly with funds from the SOS Kinderdorf Switzerland and other SOS organisations in Europe. Today, this Children's Village has 915 children and the school is affiliated to the CBSE, Delhi. We plan to upgrade the school to senior secondary level in 2002 in the humanities stream.

8. The TCV Youth Hostel, Delhi

The TCV Youth Hostel in Delhi is a natural extension of our work. We saw the need for a youth hostel in Delhi early on because after completing school education, many of our students go to Indian colleges and universities for higher education and training. Apart from facing acute accommodation problems in these big cities, there was the visible danger of our students losing their cultural identity and moorings due to this exposure. The need for a holding environment for their further education was evident. A two-acre plot of land in the suburb of Rohini was purchased from the Delhi Development Authority and with funds from the Hermann Gmeiner Fonds the TCV Youth Hostel was built. The Dalai Lama formally inaugurated it in 1991, the International Year of Tibet. Currently the hostel houses 171 students. We also have two other smaller hostels in Bangalore and Mundgod for our school graduates. Right now, a larger hostel is under construction in Bangalore with assistance from the European Union and other friends of the TCV.

Other Projects

Vocational Training Centres

Given the large number of children in our care, we realised early on that many of our children are not born academics but have other skills and talents. The importance of catering to the various needs of our children so that they become self-reliant and contributing members of the community was foremost in our mind. In the early 1970s, we started Traditional Handicraft Centres in Dharamsala and Ladakh, where the children could learn the arts and crafts of Tibet. Over the years, these centres have played a crucial role not only in producing skilled craftsmen and women but also in preserving the traditional arts and crafts of Tibet.

The need for vocational training centres—both traditional and modern—increases with ever more children opting for vocational streams. Since there are problems in admitting our children into Indian technical institutions, we had to come up with a plan of starting our own technical training centre. We purchased land near Dehra Dun, capital of the new state of Uttaranchal in North India, and after completion of the construction, the TCV Vocational Training Centre Dehra Dun started functioning in August 2000. This project was financed by the SOS Kinderdorf International. Today, the training centre is an exciting place for our children to learn a skill which will give them a base for life. Currently, we have 130 students in the centre and they are training to become welders, turners, motor mechanics, drivers, cooks, computer experts, office secretaries, hotel managers and beauticians. We plan to add more vocations in the years to come as the training centre has a capacity for 300 students. We are very hopeful that it will play a key role in training our youth for the future. We are now in the process of getting the centre affiliated to the ITI in that region.

Further Studies

Right from the beginning, we have taken a parental responsibility for our children. Therefore, our support to the children does not end when a child leaves a village or school. Our purpose is to ensure that every child is able to stand on his/her own feet and contribute to the community when the time comes. Given this purpose, we set up an Educational Reserve Fund in the early 1970s to take care of the further education and training of our students when they leave school. Today we have 931 students under this programme, who are attending different colleges and training institutes in India and a range of career courses, depending on their ability and aptitude. We have a list of 106 different courses for our students to chose from.

The Dalai Lama has mentioned time and time again that children are the future seeds of Tibet and therefore a holistic education is vital for them. Hence our top priority has always been that the holders of Tibet's destiny are equipped with a meaningful education in all professional fields to contribute to the development of future Tibet.

As we reflect on the work of the TCV, we are happy to see so many of our educated youths doing some outstanding work within our exile community in various services—ranging from doctors, engineers, teachers, civil servants to health workers, farmers, artisans etc. And of course, many of them have become responsible parents, capable of bringing up their own children as Tibetans and good human beings. I am proud to say that many have returned to work in TCV projects. Out of the total strength of 1,159 TCV co-workers, 60 per cent are now ex-TCVians. To date, 15,000 children have gone through the TCV villages and schools. Wherever we go, we meet ex-TCVians. This gives us renewed strength and impetus to continue our work with an ever increasing sense of dedication.

Success breeds its own problems. This is the case with the TCV as well. With growing numbers of school and college graduates from various training backgrounds returning to the community, there is now a problem of finding suitable jobs for them. The exile community infrastructure and services have not kept up with the increase of educated youths. Therefore, the time has come for them to look for jobs elsewhere. This demands the ability to compete in the job market and the psychological capacity to adjust in any social setting.

To ease this crushing search for jobs to lead a meaningful life, we have now initiated a placement cell within the TCV organisation. For reasons of accessibility and easy communication we have located the placement cell in the Tibetan Youth Hostel, Delhi. As we gain experience and exposure, we are hopeful that this cell will be able to assist the youths in finding employment within and outside the exile community as time passes.

Outreach Programme

Inspired by our motto—Others Before Self—the TCV has always reached out where the need was greatest. This is amply manifested in our Outreach Programmes. We have established day-care centres in the settlements, started hostels where needed, helped the old and sick and provided support to children with parents in the form of stipends.

Though we receive many requests for the admission of children into our villages and schools, we realise the pivotal importance of child-care and love that only parents can give.

Therefore, it is crucial to support the parents of children by way of paying stipends to them and encouraging them to keep their children with them. This is working very well. Today, under this programme, we are assisting 2,258 children who live with their parents in the different settlements and Tibetan communities in India, Nepal and Bhutan. Just like the children living in our various villages and schools, all these children are also sponsored and we make sure that there is a good relationship between the sponsors and their sponsored child. We are planning to strengthen this stipend programme in the years to come so that children learn Tibetan family values besides getting an education.

The Situation in Tibet and the New Arrivals

The situation in Tibet as far as children's education is concerned is bleak, to say the least. Lack of access to proper health and education; indoctrination through the medium of instruction (Chinese) and content of the curriculum (Chinese history, politics and culture); discrimination in the form of having to study in inferior schools or having to pay higher fees, or no access to schools—are some of the examples. It all boils down to a cruel choice for the children: give up the right to education or abandon your Tibetan identity.

Therefore, thousands of children continue to flee the persecution and the lack of opportunities in their homeland. Parents risk everything to have their children, including tiny toddlers, brought to India in the hope they will receive a good education and will be brought up as Tibetans. Since the early 1980s well over 7,000 children have risked everything to journey across the Himalayas in the hope that they will receive in exile what they have been denied back home: health and education and a sense of security and well being. Surely, so many children would not have taken such a high risk for the sake of an education if the opportunities and facilities existed in Tibet. Many children escaping across the Himalayas were unaccompanied minors. The UNHCR office in Kathmandu has registered many such minors in the past few years. The children we received are indeed the lucky ones as many have been reported missing along the escape route. During their arduous journey, many children were afflicted with frostbite, others drowned trying to cross swift rivers and yet others have only succeeded after several tortuous attempts.

The TCV has to care for the children and young adults fleeing from Tibet as they cannot be sent to the Indian government-aided schools. The flow of children and youth from Tibet continues unabated. In the main village in Dharamsala alone, we had to admit over 3,500 children from Tibet. The village is bursting at the seams trying to accommodate them. The homes initially built for 25 children are now accommodating 40–50 children. The overcrowding problems are pressing in all our villages and schools because of this flow of new arrivals. Moreover, there is the constant need to assist the needy children of the Tibetan refugees who are settled in India, Nepal and Bhutan—making our work that much more urgent and necessary.

The Situation in Exile

Today the TCV are educating the third generation of Tibetans born in exile. These children have not seen their country. They might not even have heard about Tibet at first hand from their grandparents as they are no longer alive. Furthermore many of our people out of necessity live a kind of nomadic life. Due to financial compulsions they have to live in different places when they go into the sweater trade or any other petty business. Since children are the most vulnerable, they suffer the most. They are exposed to unhealthy habits and get influenced by crass cultures and habits quite alien to our way of life and values. This is having a detrimental effect in their growth and formation of values.

We are greatly concerned by this exposure and influence. And we are trying our best in our villages and schools to take necessary action so that we can counteract this influence. Of course, the best way is to give them a sound education while they are with us—an education rooted in our rich cultural heritage coupled with modern education so that when the children leave the portals of our villages and schools, they will have the necessary skills to understand the outside world and make sound judgements on their own. We are not being fanatical about it. Given our situation in exile and what is happening back home, we have no choice but to safeguard what is being destroyed in Tibet by the Chinese occupation of our country.

Education

In the field of education, our schools are affiliated to the Central Board of Secondary Education (CBSE) New Delhi, the Indian national examining body. At the secondary and senior secondary levels, our children follow the curriculum set by the CBSE and sit for the All India National Examinations because they need those certificates to gain entry into Indian training centres, colleges and universities.

Nevertheless, we use the freedom available in the primary and middle levels to design our own curriculum to suit our needs. Right from the late 60s His Holiness the Dalai Lama has been emphasising the importance of educating the children in our mother tongue, but we were not able to do anything to follow his guidance until the early 80s when we started to translate a few books into Tibetan. However, translation of other books is not sufficient.

Educational Development and Resource Centre (EDRC)

The pioneering tasks of restructuring the primary education and introducing significant changes in the middle school level in order to meet our goals started in 1985 when we established our Educational Development and Resource Centre (EDRC) at the

TCV, Dharamsala. The primary focus of this restructuring was to change the medium of instruction from English to Tibetan, to design our own curriculum, to produce all textbooks and teaching aids in Tibetan, and to start our own teacher training centre for the primary level. This is fully in keeping with the Government of India's policy that every child should receive primary education in his/her mother tongue, and this also resonates with the UNESCO Declaration of 1951 that the best medium of teaching a child is the mother tongue. This is based on strong psychological, sociological and educational reasoning.

We also realised that as we are now educating the second and third generation of Tibetans born in exile, the need to enrich and strengthen our education on the basis of our language and culture is crucial. (changes introduced with the teaching of social sciences at the middle school level—where the content is all Tibetan history—is an example) At the same time, during the formative years, it is vital for the children to experience its language, folklore, literature, music, customs, history, geography and festivals so that they grow up naturally knowing more about their homeland and its rich cultural traditions. We try to ensure that through this Tibetanisation project, we are able to give a proper education to our children.

The Tibetanisation project attempts to:

- Lay down the foundation for an effective Tibetan educational system in the future,
- Develop a new curriculum for the primary school classes in Tibetan language and to produce textbooks in all the subjects,
- Integrate Tibetan culture, history, geography, arts etc. in the curriculum,
- Strengthen interest and love for the Tibetan language and culture.

Teacher Training Centre

Along with the publication work, we realised the importance of training the teachers to implement the project successfully in the classrooms. We organised workshops, orientation programmes and meetings to change the mind-set of our teachers. We came to realise that these short-term courses were not enough. The need for a more comprehensive approach was felt, and so we came up with the idea of having our own Teacher Training Centre and established it in 1994. Over the years, many teachers have attended the 2-year intensive training programme, and we are proud to say that all our teachers at the primary level are now trained and fully qualified to teach the textbooks that are being published from the EDRC.

Mother Training Programme

Once the Teacher Training Centre was established, we used the facilities to provide training for the mothers. In our children's villages mothers have a really significant role. They are central to the growth and well being of our children. In fact they are the first teachers of the children. We give them a 3-month intensive training course in child psychology, health and hygiene, nutrition, home management and environmental awareness. Functional literacy and arithmetic are taught to the mothers who have had no schooling. A course on Buddhism and Tibetan culture is also incorporated in the training programme. To date, all the TCV mothers have gone through the training and this has proved most beneficial to our work of caring for the children.

The EDRC project with its allied services mentioned above, is a resounding success. So much so that now other Tibetan schools, including the Tibetan schools managed by the Indian Government are also switching to Tibetan as the medium of instruction at the primary level using the textbooks published by us.

Conclusion

Organisations go through life cycles. So does the TCV. As the years in exile go by, we are convinced that the work of the TCV is ever more important. In the beginning of our refugee years, the TCV was a place for the orphaned and destitute children to take shelter and regain their health and confidence. Those were the hard and trying years, with our people living in makeshift tents and moving from place to place for shelter and work. Then came the years of concentrated work to expand due to the large flow of children from settlements merging with the flux that came from Tibet since the early 80s. Now, we have been in exile for well over 41 years and our people are more settled and do realise the importance of education for their children. Today there is the added responsibility of finding placements for our school and college graduates within and outside the community.

So, though we do not have our own country, and we remain in exile, yet, due to the far-sightedness and compassion of His Holiness the Dalai Lama, education has been and is, even today, the top priority. With the changes advanced by him to democratise the community in exile, there is even more reason for our younger generation to be educated so that they will be able to judge soundly and take responsibility for the future destiny of the Tibetan people. The TCV has played a crucial role in this endeavour and of course, we will continue to serve in this respect as long as our children need our services.

Of course, all that we have achieved until now would not have been possible had it not been for the blessings and constant guidance of the Dalai Lama, the generosity of our many sponsors who are in 42 different countries in the world; and the donor agencies who have been by our side during these past forty years. Our heartfelt gratitude also goes out to the Government of India and her great people for their generosity and for being such gracious hosts to the Tibetans, who lovingly call this country their 'Home-away-from-home'.

References

Pema, Jetsun, *Tibet: My Story, an Autobiography*, Shaftesbury (Dorset) 1997.

Nawang Dorjee, Director of Education, TCV, *Tibetanisation of Primary Education.*

TCV Annual Reports, TCV Head Office Meeting Minutes, TCV Brochure.

CHAPTER FIFTEEN

Vibrant Arts

DAGMAR BERNSTORFF

In 1959, right after the flight to India, the fourteenth Dalai Lama had a very clear vision of how to preserve Tibetan heritage: history, language, art and *dharma,* the ethics of Buddhism. This leitmotif winds overtly or latently like a thread through the Tibetan diaspora, be it in the schools, children's villages, theatre, arts, handicrafts, learning and in the social life of the people. Buddhist ethics and its symbols are the foundation of Tibetan art. These principles are contained in the religious and philosophical texts based on the sayings of Gautama Buddha and commentaries of later teachers and many of these documents have been saved by monks when fleeing to India.

Very soon after his arrival in exile the Dalai Lama founded a number of institutions at several levels for the preservation of Tibetan culture. The Tibetan Institute of Performing Arts was the first one, established in 1959; the Central Institute for Higher Tibetan Studies opened its doors to students and scholars in 1967 and enjoys the status 'Deemed to be a University', since 1988; the Library of Tibetan Works and Archives at Dharamsala serves the community of scholars since 1971. The aim of the Norbulingka Institute is to foster Tibetan applied art and artisanship. And Tibet House in Delhi, founded in 1965, represents Tibetan culture not only in India, but worldwide.

TIPA, the Tibetan Institute of Performing Arts

Among the thousands of refugees, who reached India in 1959 there were many actors, musicians and dancers. Sensing the danger of their dispersal in all directions the Dalai Lama encouraged the formation of the 'Dance and Drama Society' where the artists could reassemble, pool their instruments and practice their music, their dance and *lhamo*, the Tibetan opera. 'The lively daylong operas brought colour, laughter and a reminder of home into the otherwise hopeless and dreary lives of the newly bereft refugees.'[1]

Tibetans have songs for many occasions, they sing while ploughing and harvesting, at weddings or when drinking beer. Many of these folksongs have been composed by wise men like Milarepa or by the sixth Dalai Lama; they spread Buddhist ideas in this form. Other songs praise the mountains and the river valleys and there is no dearth of love songs. There is also a tradition of 'street songs', an outlet for laypersons to voice criticism, even satire at the government.

One distinguishes three styles of Tibetan classical dance and music:

1. *Gar*, dances which were performed by young men at the court of the Dalai Lama and at formal state occasions;
2. The monastic *cham* dances with their deep symbolic meanings. Till today these dances are taught in the monasteries and performed by monks during festivals. The boundaries between monastic and secular art are however fluid.
3. *Lhamo*, the opera.[2]

The artists built a place for themselves near Dharamsala in 1960, which today is called the Tibetan Institute for the Performing Arts (TIPA). Situated on the picturesque slopes of the Dhauladar mountain-range, the buildings are decorated in Tibetan style with colourful wooden pillars and friezes. They house classrooms, practice rooms, workshops, hostels and an auditorium.[3] Presently

---

[1]Leaflet of the Tibetan Institute of Performing Arts.

[2]Ross, Johanna, *Lhamo, Opera from the Roof of the World*, New Delhi 1995, p. 4.

[3]The editors visited TIPA on 3 May, 2001.

about 150 people live and work here, actors, musicians, artisans, teachers, and students. Twenty students are admitted per year—talented children spotted in the settlements; their education takes twelve years. During the first two years the children are 'trainees' and learn the dances, the songs and how to play several instruments. They continue for another five years as 'junior artists', when they perform minor roles. But only after another five years of practice are they considered mature enough to act in major opera roles and allowed to teach. Daily life at TIPA is frugal for teachers as well as students. They live on the campus; salaries and stipends are meagre, and a canteen supplies food for all.

In order to prepare the young artists for their careers, the institute runs its own primary and secondary school, the so-called 'culture school', where more than elsewhere, a great deal of time is devoted to the arts. But a modern curriculum is compulsory as well; this grooms the students for modern life. Since 1999 twelve students have been admitted to the National Open School, an Indian institution for long distance learning, where these students qualify for higher studies. Graduates of TIPA often join the staff or become teachers in Tibetan schools; some work as Opera Masters with other dance and music groups in the settlements.

The institute needs its own workshops, e.g., a tailoring department for the elaborate costumes, shoemakers, carpenters for the props and masks and a studio for the instruments.

An old master, who has practiced the craft in Tibet itself, is in charge of the tailoring department. Asked whether there are books and documents on the costumes, he said there were none, but that he remembers everything! After the exodus many Tibetan refugees donated their ceremonial dresses to TIPA as they were no longer needed. Even today precious brocades from China, artificial silks, cords, tassles, and imitation fur are being turned into dresses, shoes, and hats and the attire of the popular snow lion.

All props like masks, swords, sceptres, jewellery are made in-house. The shoemakers produce the colourful boots made of felt, which vary according to region or status of the characters. In the studio for instruments the long horns, six-stringed lutes, flutes, fiddles, dulcimers, and drums, made of wood and goat's leather, are built and maintained. Old costumes, boots and masks can be seen in a small museum.

The centre piece of TIPA's art is *lhamo*, the Tibetan opera. Traditionally as well as today the performances are in the open air under a tent-like roof, with the audience sitting in a semi-circle. There are no props, but splendid costumes. Seeing the attire, Tibetans recognise immediately whether a king or an official, a good man or a scoundrel enters the stage. The operas are usually based on a theme taken from Tibetan history—for instance how King Songtsen Gampo courted the daughter of the Chinese emperor—or *jataka* stories, (legends about the previous incarnations of Gautama Buddha), or events in the lives of the great teachers like Padmasambhava or Tsongkhappa. 'The plot swings between the vulgar and the refined, the hilarious and the poignant, and impresses upon us the complexity of life and the co-existence of comedy and tragedy in our human experience.'[4] In the end, good always triumphs over evil. The actors spice their texts with critical commentaries and jokes on current events. They spare no one, neither high officials, nor monks and nuns, not even the state oracle.

Once a year in the spring, TIPA invites artists for the very popular *Shoton*[5] Festival, when, for a week, opera groups from the settlements come together and perform. Traditionally this festival took place in the park of the Norbulingka Palace in Lhasa, where actors and musicians from all over Tibet congregated. Their performances were open to everybody, rich and poor, young and old, men, women and children, and were presided over by the Dalai Lama himself. Nowadays the *Shoton* Festival is usually held in the month of March and coincides

[4]http://www.tibetanarts.org/opera.html

[5]*Shoton* means yoghurt, because originally the festival happened in the summer, when the meadows are green and milk is plenty.

with the *Monlam Chenpo*, the Great Prayer Festival.[6] This is also the time, when the Dalai Lama teaches publicly for two weeks.

The Central Institute of Higher Tibetan Studies (CIHTS)

The Central Institute of Higher Tibetan Studies is a research and teaching institution for Tibetology and Buddhology, as one would call it in international parlance. It is located at Sarnath, now a part of Varanasi, the place where Gautama Buddha held his first sermon after enlightenment. The aim of the institution is to teach Tibetan Buddhist tradition, research and preserve the sources and if necessary, restore them.

The CIHTS began as a department of the Sampurnanand Sanskrit University at Varanasi. Since 1977, it is autonomous, and received the 'Deemed to be University' status in 1988. It is financed by the Indian government and is accountable to the Ministry of Human Resource Development.

A brightly coloured wooden gate decorated with Buddhist symbols opens onto a park with lush tropical vegetation. Students sit on the lawns buried in their books or walk on the paths memorising texts. The two-storeyed buildings are painted in Tibetan style: red pillars and friezes contrast with pure white, the doors and window-frames are highlighted in green, blue, red and yellow. They house classrooms, the library, the administration, student hostels and flats for the teachers.

Curriculum

Four hundred students are registered at this university, among them 70 girls. About 20 per cent of the students are monks, but there are only four nuns.[7] The medium of instruction is Tibetan, therefore is not surprising that 70 per cent of the students are Tibetans. The remaining 30 per cent are Indian Buddhists from

[6]Choedon, Yeshi & Norbu, Dawa, *Tibet*, New Delhi/Wiesbaden 1997, p. 84.

[7]See chapter 18.

northern borderlands like Ladakh, Sikkim, Spiti, Darjeeling; others are Nepali or Bhutanese with a smattering of students from Mongolia and Kalmykya (Tibetan Buddhism is practised in these two countries, but the pupils often do not know the language). Some young Indians of other faiths aim at specialising in Buddhist learning. The decision to study at the CIHTS has to be taken early in life, because a precondition is the enrolment in class IX–XII of the attached high school. Professor Geshe Nawang Samten,[8] the Director, thinks that Tibetan schools do not provide adequate instruction in the Tibetan language. In the university's own high school the students get prepared for the rigours of Tibetology.

The curriculum follows the ancient Indian system of monastic education and is divided into five 'faculties':

1. Tibetan Buddhist philosophy
2. Language and Literature
3. Tibetan Medicine and Astrology
4. Art and artisanship
5. Modern science.

Fifty teachers instruct the 400 students; thus the teacher/student ratio is 1:8, which is rare in India or abroad. Seventeen professors are monks, and only they teach Buddhist philosophy. There are only two women on the staff, both Indian, who teach Hindi and English.

The courses on offer are divided into three categories: compulsory, main (*kavargiya*) and optional (*kha-vargiya*). Four languages: Tibetan, Sanskrit, Hindi, and English are compulsory. The main subject, Tibetan Buddhist Philosophy, is divided into two parts: *mulasastra*, namely historical Indian texts in Tibetan translation and *sampradayasastra*, original Tibetan texts belonging to the five Tibetan sects: Nyingmapa, Kagyupa, Sakyapa and Gelukpa and the pre-buddhist Bön religion. At the postgraduate level, the students specialise in one of the five schools. In keeping with tradition the students have to memorise

[8]Interview, 16 April 2001 at Sarnath.

certain root-texts and practise the art of dialectic discussion.[9] It is surprising that Pali, the language of Gautama Buddha's sermons, is an optional subject. Other optionals in the faculty of Modern Science are Asian History and Archaeology, Tibetan History, Political Science and Economics, but students select only one of these disciplines. Natural sciences are absent, Asian and European Philosophy are currently not offered. The languages Chinese, Japanese, German and French have a place on the curriculum, but are not being taught at present for lack of funds. It is sad to hear that Art and Artisanship is on hold for lack of a suitable teacher. It seems the Thangka painters are not trained to teach theoretical aspects, whereas the academics, well versed in the theory, do not know the technique of painting! Tibetan medicine however is being taught in theory and practice. The students assist in the campus dispensary to understand the methods of diagnosis and also learn how to mix the medicines.

The Institute follows the traditional disciplines, but unlike in the past, students are not permitted to study for ever! After five years of learning they appear for the *Shastri* exam, which corresponds to the bachelor's degree. Two years later they can obtain the *Acharya* degree, equivalent to an M.A. It takes altogether twelve years (high school included) to obtain a Ph.D.

According to Prof. N. Samten, graduates have no problem finding employment. Some of them join the faculty, others become teachers in Tibetan schools or at Indian universities.

Research and Archives

Buddhist sources are at the centre of research and archiving. The early texts in Pali or Sanskrit had originally been composed in the Buddhist centres in India. Since the seventh century, travelling scholars brought them to Tibet, where they were translated into Tibetan. In the ninth century, King Ralpachen

[9]Central Institute of Higher Tibetan Studies, Sarnath, Varanasi, *A Bird's Eye View*, p. 4, quoted as: A Bird's Eye View.

had very strict rules laid down for translation, hence they are surprisingly faithful to the originals. When Buddhism declined in India many such texts got lost, but they survived in Tibet, just as the works of the ancient Greek philosophers were preserved in Arabic translations. An estimated 5,000 Indian manuscripts, which had been listed in old Tibetan catalogues got lost. Among them there were also secular works on grammar, poetry, medicine and drama.[10]

The main emphasis of the Institute's research programme is on retranslations of such texts from Tibetan into Sanskrit and in critical editions of newly found manuscripts. Some hitherto unknown works have been discovered in the monasteries on the Indian side of the Himalayas. Thus the CIHTS makes a significant contribution to the reintegration of lost heritage in Indian philosophy and cultural history.

Many such manuscripts were carried by monks on their arduous flight to India. Hundreds of years ago the texts had been cut into woodblocks and printed on paper made of hemp and various leaves, impregnated with poison against insects; they are still very well preserved. The format of these 'books' has been inspired by Indian palm leaf texts. They consist of strips 30–50 cm long and 12–15 cm high, which are piled together and wrapped in cloth. Some of these books have colourful illuminations. With the help of the US Library of Congress these texts have been photocopied and made available for research in Tibetology and Indian philosophy worldwide.

In Tibetan Buddhism there are two major collections of documents: *Kangyur*, or basic texts, like Gautama Buddha's sayings and sermons, and *Tengyur*, or commentaries written by Tibetan scholars, explanations on *tantra*, instructions for meditation etc. Both collections consist of several hundred volumes and are available in the institute's library, in several different editions. The librarians are proud to have all essential Buddhist texts on their shelves, if not in the original, but in

[10]*A Bird's Eye View*, supra, p. 2.

copies, on microfilms etc. retrieved from various libraries the world over.

The archives are equipped with the latest information technology. Scholars compile recordings of teachings by old lamas, because—as the librarian mentioned—the young monks tend to overestimate their own state of learning.[11] A new project, funded by the Orient Foundation in Great Britain, aims at filming and recording Tibetan ceremonies to produce a CD-Rom. And soon all this will be viewable on the internet!

No doubt, the CIHTS makes major contributions towards the preservation, study and transmission of Tibetan religious and philosophical literature, not only for Buddhists and scholars in South Asia, but beyond for Buddhist studies all over the world.

The Library of Tibetan Works and Archives

The Library is at the core of all efforts to preserve Tibetan culture. The colourful building, a replica of a palace in Lhasa, is a good example of traditional Tibetan architecture. It stands on the square next to the *kashag* (the Government-in-Exile), the departments and the Parliament. A stupa in the centre is meant to ward off evil influences.

The Library contains 80,000 books and manuscripts, among them about 10,000 in European languages, and hundreds of *thangkas*, photographs and other artefacts. The institution was founded in 1971 with the aim of 'preserving and propagating the rich cultural heritage of Tibet and to counter the massive destruction it had suffered after the Chinese invasion of Tibet in 1959 and the subsequent chaos of the Cultural Revolution.'[12]

The Library is a cultural centre with a museum, a Department of Research and Translations, a Centre for Tibetan Studies and an Oral History Department. Scholars from all over

[11]Interview with Dr. Jampa Samten, Director of the Library on 17 April 2001.

[12]Library of Tibetan Works and Archives, 1987–88, p. 1.

the world do research here, finding a quiet and cooperative environment for their studies.

The first collections of books and artefacts were donated to the Dalai Lama by refugees. Today the Indian Government and numerous international NGOs finance the institution. A complex technology is needed to preserve the manuscripts, given the humid climate of Dharamsala.

The Centre for Tibetan Studies organises lectures on Buddhist philosophy and introductory courses in Tibetan language. The Publications, Research and Translations section, offers an unusual service to foreign scholars, namely a monk would assist them in finding the sources and translating them. Hundreds of researchers have benefited from this service. This Department also looks after the publications and produces about twenty titles in Tibetan or English each year, among them a *Tibetan-English Dictionary of Buddhist Terminology*. Their *Tibet Journal* reaches out to the international community of scholars.

The Museum

The Museum houses about a thousand valuable examples of Tibetan art, like *thangkas*, bronze statues, coins etc., some more than seven hundred years old. These too were presented to the Dalai Lama by refugees. For Tibetans, statues of the Buddha are objects of veneration as symbols of the person and the teachings of the founder. The method of exhibition and explanations however need more attention and application of modern pedagogy.

Oral History

Lay society hardly figures in Tibetan literature. As laymen and women were mostly illiterate, their thoughts and experiences were transmitted orally from generation to generation. The Oral History Department set itself the task of preserving this knowledge and memories of life in Tibet. Since 1976, hundreds of hours of interviews especially with older people have been recorded and transcribed.[13] There is information for instance on the history of the army, the goldsmiths of Lhasa, on the theory and practice of exorcism, and the tasks of the monk-police during festivals as well as songs the peasants sung while sowing and harvesting. One finds descriptions of clothes and of jewellery, how cooks worked, and even recipes of Tibetan cuisine. Memories of the flight have also been recorded as well as the experiences of underground organisations. Work on these recordings is very labour-intensive and funding not always easy to find.

For Tibetans the Library is a repository of sacred tradition and the faithful perambulate it, turning their prayer wheels.

The Norbulingka Institute

The Norbulingka Institute has been named after the summer palaces of the Dalai Lamas in Lhasa and evokes their architecture. As in the old capital, the institute stands at the centre of a park, the buildings seem to be more translucent than many monasteries. The difference is striking though: the park of the Norbulingka in Lhasa looks neglected and without care, several palaces are in ruins, only the summer palace of the fourteenth Dalai Lama, built in the 1950s, is a museum and therefore remains open. The second Norbulingka, however, is a place full of life and imagination.

The aim of the Norbulingka Foundation, started in 1995, is to preserve traditional forms of art, especially crafts. The ground plan follows the proportions, prescribed in the arts, of *Avalokiteshwara*, the Bodhisattva of compassion.[14] Around the Seat of Happiness Temple (*Deden Tsuglakhang*) are clustered the workshops of 300 artisans and their apprentices. From Thangka painting to metal craft, from tailoring to carpentry and printing —all traditional crafts are practised here.

---

[13]Ibid., this project was first financed by the Ford Foundation.

[14]A Bodhisattva is an enlightened Buddha, who renounces entry into nirvana in order to help human beings.

Metal craft is essential for Tibetan Buddhism as statues of all sizes are needed for temples as well as private houses—bronzes representing Gautama Buddha, Bodhisattvas, the great teachers, goddesses as manifestation of the female principle, and other iconic symbols. Colossal statues, like the 4.50 m high Buddha in the temple, are assembled from copper plates, beaten into form by hand and gilded. Smaller statues are cast using the lost wax method. This workshop is headed by Pempa Dorje, who received his training in Tibet itself.

In the Tibetan religious context *thangkas* are very important. These are scrolls with paintings of the Buddha or his incarnations, or of teachers, or abstract symbols. They are used to channel concentration during meditation in temples, monasteries and private houses. The art of *thangka* painting is a unique Tibetan contribution to the history of art and is mastered with such sophistication only by Tibetan artists. *Thangka* painting is a ritual act, open to monks as well as laypersons. The artist should be 'serene as a selfless vessel'[15] to receive the divine inspiration. The pictures are painted on cotton which has been treated with glue to avoid cracks, and the outlining and colouring follows strict iconometric rules. A completed *thangka* is considered to be a 'window to enlightenment'.

At Norbulingka, *thangkas* are not produced for storage, they are commissioned by the customers according to their wishes as they were, originally, in Tibet. Twenty-five students in different stages of training learn the art in an atmosphere of earnestness. guided by the master Tempa Chophel.[16] The training follows very strict rules and takes six years.

In another workshop the trainees learn tailoring, especially the appliqué technique. The making of traditional costumes and ritual robes is an important service for the opera and ritual

[15]Anjan Chakravarty, *Sacred Buddhist Painting*, New Delhi 1998, p. 63.

[16]The author visited a *thangka* studio in Lhasa and noticed that the young Tibetan artists used stencils and chemical colours while listening to Chinese pop music, Lhasa, 10 June 1999.

dances. Also *thangkas* are created in this technique, an art form which combines theoretical knowledge with great skill. The tailoring workshop has taken a leap into modern living and now produces clothes, bedcovers and curtains. A new craft emerged, the making of dolls in Tibetan costumes. In a small museum dolls in costumes of the different regions, classes and professions can be studied—another way of keeping the tradition alive.

The carpenters produce furniture, like chests, wooden tables and chairs intricately carved or painted in bright colours with old motifs. There is also a printing shop which specialises in screen printing for book illustrations, calendars, stationary etc.

These products and two hundred more, like toys, jewellery and notebooks are sold in the three Norbulingka boutiques or are exported, thus generating a considerable income for the institute.

The Academy of Tibetan Culture was opened in 1997. Young men and women, especially recent refugees from Tibet, study different aspects of Tibetan culture, like philosophy, history of art, poetry, and literature for six years. Compared to the CIHTS the curriculum here is more broad based and includes world history, political science and general history of art. The first batch of graduates left in 2003 and hopes to work as teachers, administrators, media persons etc.

The Literary and Cultural Research Centre was also inaugurated in 1997. Here the aim is to provide a forum for contemporary Tibetan literature. Apart from talented writers born in the settlements, a steady flow of poets and creative writers arrives from Tibet, who have had no space to articulate themselves. Ten young poets and writers live here. Apart from their own writing, they work on a Tibetan Encyclopaedia in three volumes, which is to be published in Tibetan and English as a book as well as a CD-rom.

Tibet House

Tibet House in New Delhi is a window of Tibetan Culture to the world. Its activities reach beyond the circles of Tibetologists and Buddhologists and integrates laypersons, foreign scholars and priests of other religions. Emphasis here is not only on Tibetan culture but on worldwide interdependence, universal harmony and compassion. As the Dalai Lamas said:

> We are responsible not only for our own happiness, we effect and are effected by the concerns of all others on this globe. This is the future of interdependence.[17]

Hence the emphasis of the activities of Tibet House is on the dialogue between religions and cultures, between faith and science; another field dear to the director Lama Doboom Tulku[18] is ecological responsibility from a Buddhist point of view.[19]

Library and Museum

Tibet House is home for a library and a museum. The library owns 3,000 books in Tibetan and 2,000 titles in English and other languages. The catalogue will be computerised in the near future and there are plans to build up a collection of audio and video cassettes related to Tibet. The museum is small, but contains exquisite exhibits like very valuable statues, *thangkas*, ritual objects and jewellery.

A study circle of registered members meets once a month for lectures and discussions on Buddhist philosophy, art, films etc. Tibet House regularly conducts seminars lasting several days on topics like 'Buddhist Logic' (1988) or 'Acharya Shantarakshita' (2001). Away from the busy cities in the calm surroundings of a monastery these seminars provide a unique opportunity of exchange and interaction between learned monks and academics in the fields of Tibetology and Indology.

[17]Tibet House and Foundation for Universal Responsibility, World Festival of Sacred Music, New Delhi 2000, p. 1.

[18]A tulku is a reincarnate lama.

[19]*Brochure* Tibet House, p. 1.

Exhibitions

A number of exhibitions organised by Tibet House enrich the cultural life of Delhi—for instance 'Tibetan Calligraphy' (1990) or 'Compassion and Reincarnation in Tibetan Art' (1995). The latter also travelled to Germany,[20] Austria and Switzerland. The Indian artist Kanwal Krishna witnessed the enthronement ceremonies of the fourteenth Dalai Lama: his watercolours were shown at the sixtieth anniversary of this event in 2000.[21] Every year, on 6 July, Tibet House celebrates The Dalai Lama's birthday with inter-faith recitations and tree-planting.

Highlights

Two highlights of the last decade were the inauguration of the Buddha Statue in Delhi's Buddha Jayanti Park, and the World Festival of Sacred Music. The Tibetan refugee community donated a gilded Buddha Statue to the Indian people, as an expression of gratitude and affection. The Dalai Lama personally conducted the ceremony of inauguration, an artistically choreographed ritual giving insights into the living art of monastic life. Every year Tibet House remembers this event with a lecture by His Holiness, attended by thousands of Tibetans and Indians.

The World Festival of Sacred Music greeted the new millennium in 2000. In the spirit of universal responsibility and interdependence, close to the heart of the Dalai Lama, Tibet House co-ordinated festivals of sacred music at twenty places worldwide, from Vancouver to Seoul, from Milano to Sao Paolo.

> Among the many forms in which the human spirit has tried to express its innermost yearnings and perceptions, music is perhaps the most universal. It symbolises the yearnings for

---

[20]See the catalogue: Stiftung St.Galler Museen, *Mitleid und Wiedergeburt in der tibetischen Kunst, Thangkas aus dem Tibet House Museum in New Delhi, St. Gallen 1995.*

[21]These watercolours are in the library of Göttingen University.

> harmony with oneself and with others: with nature and with the spiritual and the sacred within us and around us.[22]

Locally, city administrations, museums or cultural groups organised the festival. The crowning Finale happened in Bangalore in April 2000, where 650 artists from all over the world participated: Benedictine monks from the Netherlands, Gamelan players from Indonesia, Baul minstrels from Bengal, organists from Germany, Qawwali singers in the South Asian sufi tradition; not to forget the Tibetan flutist Nawang Kheshog, who also knows how to play the instruments of the Tuva and the Mongols and a choir of 108 Tibetan monks and nuns. The organisers did not shy away from modern popular forms of music, like spirituals or the jazz trio *Count Clovis* and the *Dharma Bums*, who interpret Buddhist ideas in their own way with songs like *Samsara* or *Winds of Karma*. The World Festival of Sacred Music snowballed and even after the official closing, festivals were held internationally, for instance in Hiroshima in 2001.

Conclusions

A well conceived mosaic of institutions preserves and transmits all aspects of Tibetan culture. Buddhist teachings as they are expressed in the scriptures are being taught and edited in the Central Institute of Higher Tibetan Studies at Sarnath. The aim is to preserve and reconstruct the existing texts and to discover new texts, hitherto unknown. The teaching at this Institute combines traditional ways of learning, like dialectical discussion, with modern methods and trains scholars and academic teachers. The Library of Tibetan Works and Archives at Dharamsala follows a similar agenda, but their courses in Buddhist philosophy are shorter and open to students of other disciplines, whereas the Library attracts Tibetologists from all over the world. The Academy of Tibetan Culture in the Norbulingka Institute draws from a broader base for their six-year courses and links

[22]World Festival of Sacred Music, supra, p. 1.

them with other academic disciplines. The Literary and Research Centre offers a forum and home for Tibetan writers.

Tibetan music, dance and opera are being practiced in the Tibetan Institute of Performing Arts and their dedicated artists see it as their mission to hand down these art forms to the next generations. Schools also teach dance and music and many settlements organise their opera groups. Last but not least, ritual dances, drumming and the blowing of the long horns are taught and performed in the monasteries.

The Norbulingka Institute fosters the Tibetan crafts and develops them further. At present *thangka* painting is only taught at Norbulingka; of course, this art form is also practiced by monks in the monasteries.

One would like to see more intensive efforts towards the study of Tibetan history, particularly the political and social aspects of lay society. Primarily all these institutions aim inwardly and help Tibetan society to find and retain their identity. But they reach out beyond the Tibetans to the small circle of international scholars and integrate Tibetan art into world culture. *Dharma* the Buddhist ethics find expression in words and symbols worldwide and unexpectedly the wishes of Gautama Buddha are fulfilled.

CHAPTER SIXTEEN

Tibetan Refugees in Nepal

MAURA MOYNIHAN

In March 1959, Tibet's young leader, the Dalai Lama, escaped from Lhasa under cover of night and sought asylum in India. Chairman Mao took swift action to consolidate Chinese control over the Tibetan plateau, and incited a mass exodus of refugees who fled the 'Land of Snows' and forged a new life in South Asia. In his biography, the Dalai Lama poignantly describes the harrowing flight from Lhasa, the regiment of Gurhka troops who rescued him at the Indian border, and the telegram from India's Prime Minister Jawaharlal Nehru, welcoming the young Tibetan leader to the land of Buddha and Gandhi. During this difficult and dangerous period in Tibet's history, the small Himalayan kingdom of Nepal also opened its border to Tibetan refugees, saving thousands of lives and preserving ancient cultural traditions which flourish today in the small Himalayan nation of 25 million people, situated between communist China to the north, and democratic India to the south.

For centuries, kingdoms in what constitutes present-day Nepal and the old theocratic Tibet were linked by trade, culture and politics. Tibet received Buddhism from the two royal brides, Princess Wen-ch'eng of China and Princess Bhrikuti of Nepal. Nepal is the birthplace of Shakyamuni Buddha, and its many Buddhist sites have been revered pilgrimage destinations for Tibetan travellers since the Buddhist faith spread across the Tibetan plateau. The small Buddhist kingdoms on the Tibet-Nepal border, Mustang, Dolpo and Lo Manthang, are precious vestiges of ancient Tibetan Buddhist culture which has been so tragically damaged inside Tibet itself. In the eighteenth and nineteenth centuries, Nepal and Tibet battled over territory, trading privileges and such matters as the minting of Tibetan coins in Kathmandu. It is a history full of drama, and well worth researching; at one point the Nepali army plundered the great monastery at Tashi Lunpo in Shigatse; at another, a furious Khampa shackled and imprisoned a Nepali who owed him money, which provoked riots in the streets of Lhasa and battle cries in Kathmandu. Despite these and other incidents, Nepalis and Tibetans are long familiar with each other's customs, and share many traditions. In the modern Tibetan exile period, the Kathmandu Valley has become the nexus of Tibetan religion and culture, with hundreds of Tibetan monasteries, schools, businesses, community centres and heritage societies, representing people from Tibet's three provinces, Ü-Tsang, Kham and Amdo. In Kathmandu's Tibetan neighbourhoods, food, clothing and dialects from Kang Rinpoche, Mount Kailash, to Eastern Lithang, mix with Nepali music, saris and topis.

Research suggests that about one million Tibetans were internally displaced during the Maoist expansion from 1949 till 1959. Due to vast distances and the harsh climate, most either surrendered or died in flight before reaching Tibet's central province, Ü-Tsang. Those who survived, journeyed on to Nepal, India or Bhutan. By late 1959 official government records numbered 85,000 Tibetan refugees in India, 20,000 in Nepal, and 8,000 to 10,000 in Bhutan. A stream of Tibetan refugees continued to enter Nepal throughout the Cultural Revolution, bringing stories of famine, mass murder and communist reforms. Today official statistics show 30,000 Tibetan refugees registered with the Nepali government, but unofficial statistics put the number as high as 100,000.

In 1959, Nepal's King Mahendra showed considerable courage in accepting refugees from Tibet, despite threats of reprisals from the Communist Chinese, who stood, armed and bellicose, at Nepal's northern border. The King granted asylum to poor farmers and high lamas alike, he built refugee relief camps along the many mountain passes that linked Tibet and Nepal, he allowed the Dalai Lama to send Tibetan representatives to Nepal to coordinate relief efforts with the Swiss Red Cross and the UNHCR (the United Nations High Commission for Refugees). In 1960 King Mahendra created Tibetan camps in Kathmandu, Solokhumbu and Pokhara, where thousands of Tibetans live to this day, without being taxed by the Nepali government.

After 1959, when Tibet was sealed behind the Bamboo Curtain, Nepal was the only country to maintain an embassy and a diplomatic presence in Lhasa. As Nepali businessmen, particularly those of the Katsura caste, of mixed Tibetan-Newari parentage, were spared attacks by the Red Guards, many Tibetans asked Nepalis to hide Buddhist sculptures and texts. The Nepali Embassy was able to secure asylum for Tibetans from Katsura families, and many children were given police escorts from Lhasa to Nepal, witnessing *thamzing* (public torture sessions) and firing squads, en route.

Indeed, the Tibetan refugees in Nepal are a unique success story, and many have earned wealth and citizenship. In Nepal, as in Bhutan, the Tibetan refugees live in a trans-Himalayan Buddhist civilisation and a Himalayan climate. Thousands of Tibetan refugees have become Nepali citizens; it is a common practice to claim Nepali parentage as Sherpas, Managbas, Mustangbas and Tamangs, and to adopt a last name such as 'Lama' or 'Sherpa'. Until the mid 1990s it was not difficult for Tibetans to obtain Nepali passports, but now refugees risk official investigation if they seek to obtain a *nagrita* status, or bonafide Nepali citizenship.

Relations between the Tibetan refugees and their hosts are as impressive an example of peaceful co-existence of distinct ethnic and cultural groups as can be found anywhere in the world. When the Tibetan refugee exodus began, the news media did not have today's facilities, neither did relief agencies, and most support came directly from the Nepali and Indian governments and individuals. With extremely limited resources, adjusting to vastly different cultures and climates in widely varied geographical zones in South Asia, the Tibetan refugees cleared forest and jungle, and created stable communites. The Nepali

Home Ministry continues to supervise the administration of Tibetan refugee activities, and allows the Dalai Lama's exile government, the Central Tibetan Administration, known as the CTA, to establish a headquarter in Kathmandu.

By the mid 1980's Tibetan carpets exports earned more foreign currency for Nepal than tourism, and employed thousands of Nepali workers, most of them poor Tamang women. A United Nations official observed:

> When I first visited Kathmandu in 1960 the Tibetan refugees were a pitiable sight, selling jewellery in the gutter, begging for food. When I returned in 1975, they were running everything.

Tibetan carpet manufacturers are Kathmandu's first modern industrialists. Many have modernised their factories, opened schools and clinics for workers, and take pride in providing dignified employment for the local populace. Even so, in the mid-1990s certain Western NGOs claimed that factories used child labour, which hurt exports to Germany and the United States, along with an over-saturation of the market. 'The heyday of the Tibetan carpets was a wonderful time in Nepal,' says Phuntsok Tenzing, who ran a carpet factory in Bhaktapur for twelve years. 'We were making money, creating jobs. Now that times are hard it's easy to use Tibetans as scapegoats. It's a shame, because we have deep ties with the Nepalis.'

If there is a centre of the Tibetan refugee world in Nepal, it is Boudhanath, the Great Stupa, where Padmasambhava, Guru Rinpoche, prophesised the restoration of the Buddha Dharma after the fall of the old Tibet to a modern conqueror. Boudhanath, once a small Tamang village encircling the great seventh century stupa, is now a teeming Tibetan city, with monasteries, schools, businesses, restaurants, a few discos and a bowling alley. The Tibetan world of Boudha is a dazzling example of the richness of the Hindu-Buddhist tradition of tolerance and plularism. Nepal granted sanctuary to many great Tibetan scholars and lamas who were educated in the old Tibet, and carried rare Buddhist and Bönpo traditions into exile. Dharma teachings and seminars throughout Nepal attract Western and Nepali students, and notably, many Chinese patrons from the mainland, Hong Kong and Taiwan. Tibetan lamas exchange and receive gifts and visits from Nepali politicians and royals, and all Tibetan monasteries bear a photograph of the Nepali King next to the requisite portrait of the Dalai Lama.

While Nepal allows Tibetans religious and economic freedom, political activities must be handled with discretion. Young people often complain about restrictions on public demonstrations, though many Tibetans understand Nepal's delicate position. 'We're allowed to have a fully Tibetan life in Nepal,' says a Tibetan hotel manager in Kathmandu. 'That's rare for refugees, and we're lucky, so we can't risk it with political statements and actions. We can do that in India.' Nevertheless, Tibetan exile publications and organisations abound in Nepal. The streets of Boudhanath, and Svyambhunath (Kathmandu's other great stupa, near Jawlakhel, and the first Tibetan settlement given by King Mahendra), are filled with posters and flyers in Tibetan, debating a range of issues. The Tibetan exile calendar is filled with new holidays and events, notably 10 March, Tibetan Martyrs' Day, commemorating those killed during the Lhasa Uprising of 1959; 6 July, the Dalai Lama's birthday; 2 September, Democracy Day, when in 1960 the Dalai Lama proclaimed a democratic constitution for Tibet, and since 1989, Nobel Peace Prize Day, celebrating the Dalai Lama's prestigious award. Losar, Tibetan New Year, is observed with solemn ritual and festive dancing in large gatherings. In all of these events, Nepali friends and neighbours join the Tibetans, Nepali officials participate in official ceremonies and give their blessings.

Success poses new problems for Tibetan exiles. A majority of Tibetan exile youth are skilled, multi-lingual graduates, thanks to the Tibetan school system, a gift to the Dalai Lama from Jawaharlal Nehru. (Many young Tibetans are better educated than their Nepali peers). With the strain between old and new values and the economic and political pressure to assimilate and adapt, it is increasingly difficult for refugees to sustain a purely Tibetan identity. 'My blood is Tibetan but my home is in Nepal,' says Tashi, whose parents fled to Pokhara in 1960. 'I've never been to Tibet, and now, I don't think about going to Lhasa. I dream of New York City.'

After forty years in exile, more Tibetans seek the advantages of Nepali or Indian citizenship over the increasingly marginal status of refugee. A Tibetan refugee identity card prohibits a Tibetan from obtaining employment in hotels and businesses in Nepal. After the 1999 highjacking of an Indian Airlines jet from Kathmandu to Kandahar, Afghanistan, Tibetan refugees are not permitted to travel by air in or out of Nepal. Said a young Tibetan journalist based in Kathmandu; 'For our parents, there was a lot of pressure from the community to stay refugees, to make a statement. For us, the pressure is economic, and refugee status holds us back.'

The post 9/11 collapse of global tourism has hit Nepal hard, and the Tibetan camps in trekking destinations such as Solokhumbu, near Everest, and Pokhara, near Annapurna, no longer earn money from tours, hotels and handicrafts. Thus more Tibetan exiles are migrating to Kathmandu in search of employment. Life in the camps holds less and less appeal for talented young people who have been educated. Nepal has few opportunies for higher education, so India and the West are the preferred destination for those seeking work outside a family business.

In the early 1980s, China built a 'Friendship Highway', linking Lhasa with Kathmandu. Premier Deng Xiaoping relaxed restrictions on culture and religion, and for the first time since 1959, the Chinese issued thousands of travel permits for pilgrims to travel to Bodhgaya, India, where in 1985, the Dalai Lama conducted a Kalachakra Puja.

The opening of Tibet allowed for a second refugee exodus, a small but steady stream of about 3,000 to 5,000 a year. As the perilous route on foot through mountain passes prevents many escapees from reaching the Tibet-Nepal border, thus it is impossible to obtain solid figures on the number of refugees who turn back or die in flight. From 1986 to 2002 an estimated 50,000 Tibetans have taken refuge in India and Nepal, increasing the exile population by more than 18 per cent. Some research puts the figure as high as 60,000, although solid figures are difficult to obtain, as all refugees do not register with the Central Tibetan Administration or the UNHCR. Every year hundreds of Tibetan businessmen, monks, lamas and pilgrims also visit Nepal with Chinese passports, and many return to Tibet. But a campaign of religious persecution inside Tibet is draining students, pilgrims and teachers from Tibet's monasteries, which have for centuries functioned as the traditional centres of education, craftsmanship and local administration. About 44 per cent of new arrivals are Buddhist monks and nuns; 30 per cent are children seeking placement in an exile school. The remainder are lay adults.

This new exodus has strained the resources of the Tibetan exile economy, which exists in a decentralised network of small settlements without sufficient land or jobs to support a burgeoning population influx. Most new arrivals first travel to India to meet the Dalai Lama, the principle motive for escape. Many find it difficult to adjust to the heat and the crowds of India, and migrate back to Nepal, looking for work where the Tibetan language is spoken. Of new arrivals, 85 per cent are from Kham and Amdo, and many find that Nepal offers both opportunities and obstacles. 'I was scared when I first got here,' says Tsedup, a young man from Chamdo. 'The food, the people, its's so strange. But the Tibetans here have a lot of power and freedom, so I hope I can stay.' The new arrivals present a political and social dilemma for the CTA in Nepal. Nepal does not want to appear to be encouraging a new refugee passage from Tibet, the CTA must maintain good relations with the host government, and it cannot obtain refugee identification papers for all newcomers.

The language and manners of the new arrivals are markedly different from the exile Tibetans, and relations between the two groups are often tense. 'The new arrivals are not like us,' says the wife of a CTA official:

> They are more rough, more Chinese. We think we are real Tibetans. But we've also become more Indian and more

> Nepali, we watch Hindi films, we eat rice, not tsampa. Maybe we don't try to understand them enough, and we forget our parents were once poor refugees too.

Several new arrivals have started businesses, entered monasteries, found Western sponsors, but many live in extreme poverty on the fringes of the exile economy. There are concerns that some new arrivals are spies for the Chinese government, sent to investigate and destabilise the exile community. There have also been isolated incidents of murder and rape by new arrivals, but whether this constitutes a Chinese policy is questionable.

On the evening of 1 June 2001, during a family dinner at Narayanahiti Palace in Kathmandu, Nepal's Crown Prince Dipendra murdered his father, King Birendra, (Mahendra's son), his mother Queen Aishwariya, his sister, brother, other members of the royal family, and then killed himself. Nepal was traumatised, Nepal's neighbours were shocked and saddened. Tibetans especially mourned King Birendra's death; he had maintained the generous policy towards Tibetan refugees established by his father. The Nepali royals live in a ritualised, medieval, arcane world, and yet when a democratic revolution arose in Nepal in 1990, King Birendra co-operated with democratic reforms, unlike his neighbour Deng Xiaoping during the Tienanmen Square protests. But in the past decade, Nepal has had over ten governments, all inefficient, corrupt and unresponsive to the populace. In the mid 1990s a violent Maoist insurgency emerged in Western Nepal. What began primarily as a caste war in a bitterly impoverished, remote area beyond Annapurna, has spread throughout the country. Some Tibetans speculate about a Chinese hand behind the Maoists. However, when Chinese Premier Zhu Rongi visited Kathmandu in May 2001, he publicly declared Chinese support for 'quelling the Maoist insurgency', which provoked humorous commentaries in Tibetan exile publications. There is strong evidence that the Nepali Maoists are funded by Naxalite movements in India's North Eastern states. Neither India nor China have much to gain by seeing Nepal swallowed by civil war; in the years since the flight of the Dalai Lama, Nepal has been the sole buffer state between India and China. Asian diplomats say, publicly and privately, that China and India have agreed to 'co-exist' in Nepal. While India is Nepal's largest foreign aid donor and sole source of petrol and other essential commodities, China has increased its investments and raised its profile in Nepal in recent years. Chinese engineers are expanding the 'Friendship Highway' and developing projects along the Tibet-Nepal border. Many new organisations in Kathmandu promote 'China-Nepal Friendship', Chinese trade fairs, academic conferences, cultural shows and tourism. As one diplomat observed: 'The Chinese don't need to support the Maoist rebels to strengthen their power in Nepal; they're doing it with investments, not guerillas.'

Political instability and economic downturn fuel civil unrest, and so Nepal's Tibetan refugee community, which prospered for four decades, finds itself vulnerable. 'Anyone who can get to the West is trying to get out' said Norbu, who fled to Nepal as a child in 1963, and is now the owner of a Tibetan art gallery in downtown Kathmandu. 'Every Tibetan refugee in Nepal could go to India tomorrow, to join the Dalai Lama. Sadly, we think about that more and more.' After the flight of the Karmapa Lama through Nepal in January 2000, Tibetan cultural and religious activities have been strictly curtailed by Nepali authorities, clearly in response to pressure from China. In December 2000, Nepali riot police, equipped with guns and truncheons, stormed the Namgyal Middle School which adjoins the Refugee Transit Camp, to close a Tibetan children's cultural performance. When the Chinese Defence Minister visited Kathmandu for eight days during Losar, the Tibetan New Year, in 2001, Tibetan Buddhist gatherings were officially banned. King Birendra had for decades managed to pacify the Chinese while protecting the Tibetan community in Nepal; whether King Gyanendra will be as skilled or as inclined to manage such delicate diplomacy remains to be seen.

The Tibetan refugee settlements were not intended to be permanent communities and the Nepali camps established by King Mahendra are becoming old age homes for the pioneer generation of Tibetan refugees who followed the Dalai Lama into exile. They are precious repositories of the vanishing world of the old Tibet, and they are a testament to the humanitarian traditions of the host nation. Those of us who have worked for years in the Tibetan diaspora which extends across the Indian subcontinent have a special respect and admiration for the people of Nepal; a small, landlocked country that defied the Red Army in 1959 and in doing so, gave Tibet to the world.

CHAPTER SEVENTEEN

Women: Emancipation in Exile

TSERING NORZOM THONSUR

All over the world women have always been referred to as the 'weaker sex' and positioned lower down the scale in a male-dominated society. We have been witness to testimonies of women being mistreated, burnt to death and sexually abused. The history of atrocities against women range from the foot-binding system in China where girls' feet were bound from birth, the belief being that a tiny foot would later fetch a good husband, to the situation in India where parents have to pay large amounts of money to find a good match for their daughters. In Muslim countries one can find women clad in veils covering their face or even their whole body so that men other than their husbands cannot see them. And one can never forget the traditional practice of genital mutilation of girls in Africa. Even today such practices continue in some places irrespective of the influence of modern education and a contemporary lifestyle.

Thanks to the women's movement and support from right thinking men and women all over the world, women have improved their status. Today, after decades of struggle, career women excel in public affairs, economics, health services and education and at the same time manage their families. Some of them, albeit few, are placed in high positions on a par with men.

Tibetan women, however, are known for the liberal status they enjoy in their society. It can be said that an understanding of the role of Tibetan women may be an inspiration to women in other countries.

The Status of Tibetan Women in Traditional Tibet before 1959

Sir Charles Bell, in *The People of Tibet* has remarked on the liberal status of Tibetan women during Tibet's independence. He stated:

> When a traveller enters Tibet from neighbouring China or India, few things impress him more vigorously or more deeply than the position of the Tibetan women. They are not kept in seclusion, as are Indian women. Accustomed to mix with the other sex throughout their lives, they are at ease with men, and can hold their own as well as any women in the world.[1]

Tibetan women have enjoyed considerable social and economic freedom and always been recognised for their qualities of strength, emotion and capacity for hard work. They had the freedom to do anything they could. Show Lobsang Dhargay, a former government official, confirmed this fact in an interview:

> Women shared equal responsibilities as men in most aspects of social life, and some were very influential politically. Tibetans have an old saying: even a nun can become the ruler of Tibet if that brings happiness to the land. This proverb symbolises the general spirit of religious, social and political freedom of our old Tibet.[2]

However, one must understand that this generalised description ignores many of the provincial variations as well as the rural/urban differences in Tibetan society.

Traditionally the position of Tibetan women was, and continues to be, remarkably progressive when compared to their counterparts in the rest of the world. However, life in Tibet was also ruled by its own customs and practices and was therefore by no means perfect. Due to their strong faith in religion and their geographic isolation from the rest of the world, people did

---

[1]Bell, Charles, *The People of Tibet*, Oxford 1928, p. 147, 156.

[2]Oral History Project, LTWA.

not enjoy modern education and democratic participation. Educational facilities and modern amenities were available only to people who could afford them. The standard of living also varied greatly between rural and urban areas.

In urban areas like Lhasa, Shigatse and Chamdo, people enjoyed a better lifestyle vastly different from the rural areas of the far northeastern and western areas. Nomads and farmers mainly dominated those rugged territories. People and especially women had to lead a life that was very harsh and difficult, hence women in Amdo and Kham were strong and tomboyish in nature. Some popular women from these areas were known for their leadership qualities during the resistance movement against the occupying Chinese forces.

Lhasa was the seat of the Tibetan government where the Dalai Lama lived in the Potala Palace and most of the government servants were also stationed there. A large number of noble families lived in Lhasa on their estates. The men were either government employees or businessmen and the women stayed in their homes taking care of the family. Traditional practice in Tibet was to employ only men to serve the government in various capacities in the *kashag* (Cabinet), the *tsongdu* (Assembly) and in other institutions. Tibet did not have any female government servants. It is not known why this practice prevailed but it is believed that it was not because of any discrimination but rather a tradition that only men could work in government service and women should accept the responsibility for the family. Sayings like 'Though I am the head of hundred men, my leader lives at home' and 'Men are the guardians of the courtyard and women, the pillar of the house' reflect the importance and respect given to women in Tibet. Women were the guardians of the house and responsible for the well-being of the family.

According to W.D.Shakabpa, the approximate population of Tibet was around six million of which 48 per cent were nomads and 32 per cent were traders and agriculturists. Monks and nuns formed about 20 per cent (18 per cent monks, and 2 per cent nuns). Before 1949, both men and women were engaged in an economy of agriculture, dairy products and trade. Women contributed extensively to farming, producing dairy products and to marketing.

In central Tibet, wives of the rich and of officials did not have to do hard work; instead they supervised the servants at home and the estates when their husbands were away. But in southeast and northeast Tibet, women had to work very hard and at the same time manage their household chores, particularly in rural areas where the population mostly comprised of either farmers or nomads. In nomadic and farming families, both men and women worked side by side looking after the animals. Chores such as milking the female yak (*dzo*), churning butter and making cheese were the responsibility of the women. Weaving woollen blankets and making dresses out of animal skins and wool were also women's skills. Besides the wool business, paper-making was also popular in Tibet, and it was a cottage industry handled by women. This paper was used in all government offices and religious institutions.

The kind of work done by women also varied according to the social class to which they belonged. But one thing was common between all classes of women: they all had considerable responsibility for the well-being and progress of the family. Tradition and culture played a vital role in the lives of the Tibetan people, who were religious and conservative. Only a few aristocrats and businessmen had contacts with the outside world and were acquainted with modern culture. Tibetan custom demanded that women respect their men and never overshadow them. Women from a young age were taught to be polite and faithful to their men. Culture and moral values had a great impact on the daily lives of women in Tibet, they voluntarily took a back seat in society, and this had nothing to do with gender discrimination per se. Women always treated the husband as the head of the family and gave him due respect. In a family food was usually served first to the father of the house and then to the rest of the family members.

Women in Tibet were not subjected to harassment or abuse because of their gender. They were regarded as equal partners in most of the areas except in some parts of Amdo in northeastern Tibet. Tsering Dolma Gyalthong, who was born and married in Tibet, remembers:

> Women were not included when the men had discussions and it would be an insult for a husband if his wife sat in a group of men during meetings or discussions. It was felt that women were good at family work.[3]

She herself was a wife of a businessman from Amdo, and worked as hard as her husband; she also ran a business to help the family. It was not unusual for women to go out and run a business.

In the Kongpo region women were given a lot of importance. The lineage of the family followed the matriarchal system and the mother of the family owned the property. Tharlam Dolma Changra, the Principal of the Central Tibetan School at Bylakuppe, remembers hearing from her mother and relatives that women enjoyed a good position in their region. In her interview she stated:

> We were from a very rich family and had large estates and servants. My mother looked after the whole housework and supervised the servants when she visited the estates. My father was the leader of the region where we lived and worked for the Tibetan government.[4]

It was said that girls always stayed at home after marriage to head the family and the property, and sons married out.

Marriages were usually arranged. Widow remarriage and divorce were common and women did not suffer any social stigma after a divorce or in widowhood. Usually members of both families settled a divorce, with property and children divided equally: sons given in custody to the father and daughters to the mother. Tibetans practiced monogamy, polygamy and polyandry. Polyandry was mostly popular among the nomads where a wife was married to two or three brothers of the same family. This

[3]Interview 6 March 2001.

[4]Interview 7 March 2001.

practice was followed in order to avoid the distribution of family wealth outside the family. In nomadic families as well as among traders the men were often absent for long periods. It was also not uncommon for a man to marry two or three sisters. The size of families was large, women gave birth to up to fifteen children since family planning or sterilisation was considered a sin and against religious ethics. Infanticide and abortions were never heard of or practised. People believed it was their karma and they were destined to give birth to the number of children they had. The girl child was not considered to be a burden like in India nor did parents have to pay dowry. It was only a voluntary practice to send a share of the property to the bride if the family could afford it.

Education was available for children of all classes and was not strictly a class privilege. Most of the popular schools were in Lhasa and schools in villages and towns were often built by traders and villagers. However, the illiteracy rate was high in traditional Tibet. This might be because the farmers and the tradesman kept their children with them to help in their work and did not send them to schools.

Also a large percentage of the population were nomads. In the towns, children were often not formally sent to schools but were taught at home by private teachers or by monks belonging to the family. In return the teachers were paid in small gifts and in kind. There were two forms of schools, those for lay children who were taught Tibetan history, literature, arithmetic and accounting and those in monasteries and nunneries for children destined to become monks and nuns, where the emphasis was on religious studies.

Traditionally women had fewer educational opportunities. Not many girls were sent to schools since it was felt that educating women was not necessary because traditionally only men were employed in government jobs. There were a few schools in Lhasa, which enrolled girls from aristocratic and rich families. Tsering Dolma Gyalthong, a former President of the Tibetan Women's Association, recalls:

I was sent to school by my parents because we came from a rich family and they felt sending me to school would help me in my future. I studied in the Tatong School in Lhasa, which had nearly a hundred students. There were a few girls from noble families. Myself and another girl—we were the only two students from ordinary families who went to school.

The people of Tibet were very religious and their day-to-day life was permeated with Buddhist practices. Every good and important work had to be initiated with a religious prayer and ceremony and there were many revered and knowledgeable monks and nuns who commanded respect from the laymen for their spiritual powers. Hence it was a question of prestige for one son or daughter to join monastic life. The parents provided their share of food and necessities. In fact, for both men and women, leading a religious life was accepted as an alternative choice to marriage.

Eminent Tibetan Women

Tibet has seen some great women who sacrificed their lives for the cause of the Tibetan freedom struggle. Women were known for their qualities in the field of religion, medicine and the battlefield. Unfortunately, only few recorded testimonies are available about the lives of these great women.

The Samding Nunnery on Lake Yamdrok was a famous nunnery, which had the only woman incarnation in Tibet: Dorje Phagmo. She was the abbotess of the famous nunnery and was recognised for her mystical powers. The story goes that during the Mongol invasion in the thirteenth century, fearing rape and assault of her nuns, she changed herself into the form of a large sow and the nuns into piglets. The approaching Mongols were surprised to see only pigs in the nunnery. After the nuns changed back into human form, the Mongols were so amazed by the miracle that they converted to Buddhism.

There were also a few women who studied Tibetan medicine and treated the sick. Many of them either learned medicine from their parents who were practitioners, or were sent to medical schools where they studied medicine. The late Dr. Lobsang Dolma, a famous medical practitioner in India, was well known for her accurate diagnosis and medication. She acquired her medical skills at the famous Chokpuri Medical College in Lhasa.

Women were also known for their artistic talents and there were many singers who sang about the lives of great epic kings like Gesar and also performed other popular stories.

Women have been known for their active role in the resistance movement even before 1959. In the 1930s Chime Dolma, a member of the Gyari family in Nyarong became the Chieftainess and revolted against both the nationalist and communist Chinese and was later executed by the nationalists in 1939.

In 1956 Dorjee Yudon, the wife of Chieftain Gyari Nyima in Upper Nyarong, inspired the whole region of Kham when she led her warriors against the invading Chinese soldiers. She and her husband, along with their men, led an attack against the Chinese soldiers stationed in the castle of the Female Dragon in protest against the merciless killing of a family of Dorjee Yudon's village.

It would be right to conclude that during the first half of the twentieth century, women in traditional Tibet were far more liberated and enjoyed greater freedom compared to their counterparts in other parts of the world. Though Tibet was a semi-feudal society one must also acknowledge that so was the socio-cultural situation in other parts of the world at that time. Given the nature of life before the Chinese occupation, women were not obliged to lead their lives within certain parameters. They had the freedom of choice.

Status of Women after the Occupation of Tibet

Although China's constitution guarantees women equal rights with men, in *practice* there is a great deal of discrimination. This is true in China as well as in Tibet where women have been victims of state-organised abuses and violence. Similarly after the occupation, Tibet was guaranteed autonomy and freedom, yet in practice the people were subjected to suppression and their lives were under total control by the Communist regime.

During the invasion of Tibet by Chinese military forces, women played a vital role in leading the national movement against the occupation. Today the stories of these brave women serve as inspiring examples to the younger generation. Women and nuns still continue to take an active part in the freedom struggle of our country and many have been imprisoned for their beliefs.

In occupied Tibet, women are subjected to double discrimination: primarily as Tibetans and then as women. As Tibetans, they are victims of occupation, arbitrary arrest, torture, violation of freedom of speech and assembly, restrictions on freedom of religion, and on freedom of travel.

As women they are subjected to the denial of reproductive rights, forced birth control, abortions and sterilisation against their choice. It is estimated that between 4–20 per cent of the Tibetan population is no longer able to reproduce, with many thousands more subjected to other forms of contraception. Increasing the number of Chinese settlers in Tibet and decreasing the number of Tibetan inhabitants through birth-control policies is a systematic policy of the communist regime in Beijing.

The plight of Tibetan women who escape from Tibet and their vulnerability to sexual exploitation and violence has been documented by various independent sources. Most of these women start on their hazardous journey either because of a well-founded fear of political persecution, or to seek educational and religious freedom and better social and economic opportunities outside Tibet.

The Road to Freedom: A Death-defying Journey

Since the occupation of Tibet by Chinese military forces, thousands of Tibetans have escaped from Tibet and continue to do so each year by travelling over rough mountains, high passes and dangerous terrain. For these Tibetans, the journey to freedom is a perilous one, and often results in the loss of lives on the way. Women and children suffer the most during these difficult journeys. Besides the fear of being arrested by Chinese military personnel, they travel with fear for life and property. Often half way through the journey, the tired travellers find themselves short of food and have to go hungry for days. There have been cases when Tibetans have been exploited by their guides who charge a lot of money and desert them in the middle of the journey resulting in arrests at the border of Nepal. As they cross the high mountains, they face numerous health risks, such as hypothermia, frostbite, injuries and starvation. In many cases, frostbite has resulted in the amputation of hands and legs, causing scars for life.

At the border women are often subjected to rape; such experiences have proved very traumatic for women and children who are innocent victims. It is indeed a 'near death' experience for each person who escapes and makes the painful journey to freedom. In spite of these difficulties, women and children continue to escape every year.

Tibetan Women in Exile

In exile, women have adapted to the demanding role of working both within and outside the house to supplement the family income. It is now fully accepted that wives and mothers work to supplement the family income. The Tibetan people have managed to keep the refugee community intact and most important of all have been successful in preserving their identity and culture. In fact, the community has been known as one of the most successful refugee communities in the world by observers. In 1995, the United Nations' Friends recognised the Tibetan refugees as one of fifty exemplary communities. Part of the credit goes to the Tibetan women for their vital contribution to the success of the community in exile.

Life in exile has brought both positive and negative influences to the community structure. People have adapted to a new system of governance based on democratic principles and to modern education. The positive influence of life in exile has mainly been modern education, which was available in Tibet only within limited parameters. Today all Tibetan children in exile have the opportunity of attending schools run by the Tibetan and Indian governments. Education and modern culture have taught Tibetans to be self-reliant and build strong foundations for their future role in Tibet. Women are no exception and have equal opportunities to attend schools and educational institutions and have accordingly excelled in many fields. Many women are employees of the Central Tibetan Administration's offices and are successful in their respective careers. If women are talented and excel in society, their talents are recognised by the public; they often seek election to the Assembly as members or even as cabinet ministers.

Tibetan women have been very quick to adapt to the new social life in exile and have contributed in the fields of social welfare, community building, economics and the political struggle of Tibet in particular. Tibetan women have established themselves as a strong force in assisting the Tibetan Government-in-Exile through social and political activities and are the backbone of the refugee community.

Life in exile has given Tibetan women an opportunity to work with international women's groups and attend various conferences and meetings related to women, raising the problems of Tibetan women in the international community. Participating in these international gatherings has enhanced the outlook of the Tibetan women's perspective on women's issues and taught them to work on a variety of issues concerning women in the global village. This has also helped to bring the Tibet issue in focus in the international community from a woman's point of view.

Today Tibetan women comprise one-third of the work force in the Central Tibetan Administration. The status of Tibetan women was given a further boost in 1988, when a Tibetan woman was appointed as Representative of His Holiness the Dalai Lama overseas. Further, the election of a Tibetan woman as a Cabinet Minister in 1990 was a step in the right direction. In 1995 again, two women, Rinchen Khando Choegyal and

Yankyi Samkhar Dashi were elected as ministers (*kalon*) in the Cabinet. There are also many women who are doctors, nurses, lawyers, social workers, educationists, computer specialists, administrators, and performing artists. However, women do not face any sexual harassment or problems at their workplaces. Even if it did exist it is very rare that such cases are discussed or brought to the notice of the community.

A gradual yet distinct increase in the number of women in the administrative service has been observed over the years. Women successfully run some of the finest institutions of education for refugee children. There are many women who are highly qualified teachers working in different Tibetan schools. It is a matter of pride that the principals of two different but large schools, the Tibetan Children's Village, Lower Dharamsala, and the Central Tibetan School, Bylakuppe are capably run and headed by Tibetan women.

The late Rinchen Dolma Taring established the Tibetan Homes Foundation in Mussoorie, a residential and educational institution for orphaned and destitute Tibetan children. Jetsun Pema, the Dalai Lama's younger sister, became the President of the Tibetan Children's Villages (TCV), Dharamsala, which provides homes, and education to orphaned children.[5] Today she is still the driving force behind the success of the Tibetan Children's Villages.

The effective literacy rate of the Tibetan population was 74.5 per cent in 1998; it is most remarkable that women among whom there was a literacy rate of only 2.5 per cent before 1959 have made a big leap in education, the young generation shows a literacy rate of 97 per cent for both boys and girls.

The *Charter of the Tibetans In-Exile* (1991) provides women with the equal right to exercise their franchise. Women can stand for elections in the local and national assemblies. Although women in the past received less representation in the Assembly of Tibetan People's Deputies, the major reforms encouraged by

[5]See chapter 10b.

the fourteenth Dalai Lama in Article 37 of the Charter for Tibetans In Exile ensures a minimum of six female members in the Assembly. With the encouragement and opportunities that Tibetan women have received from all sectors of the Tibetan community in exile, women parliamentarians have played a major role in shaping the political and socio-economic destiny of the society.

The Eleventh Assembly was composed of 46 members, of whom nine were women. In fact, women candidates from the province of Amdo (northeastern Tibet) and Ü-Tsang (central Tibet) received the maximum votes from their respective constituencies. The Twelfth Assembly saw an increase of women members to eleven. Women parliamentarians have proved to be very strong, efficient and capable. The current thirteenth Assembly has ten women members out of 46 deputies and this only proves that women have been efficient and their contributions in Parliament are being duly recognised.

Women all over the world suffer discrimination, violence and exploitation and the struggle has been for more equal partnership and women's rights. Fortunately Tibetan women have not been subjected to these inequalities and do not spend their energy struggling for equality within their society. Women in exile have, therefore, always believed that their first priority is the struggle for national survival and the return to their occupied homeland. They have been a strong force in instilling in the younger generation a sense of patriotism and belonging to the community. It has been a challenge for Tibetan women in exile to spearhead the role of preserving the identity and culture of Tibet, while at the same time struggling to maintain their livelihood. In his speech to the Fourth General Body Meeting of the Tibetan Women's Association on 1 April 1994, the Dalai Lama referred to women as

> ...indeed, mother is a lama, from whom we gain our first instruction to the wholesome quality known as compassion. The dharma teacher comes later. The quality of the foundation built by the earliest lama, mother, will determine

whether the future lama's teaching on compassion will make any impression on the child or not....

Family life in exile has changed and couples have adapted to nuclear families and produce fewer children due to economic reasons, marry later, and face insecurity about their future. Yet, people have the choice to decide freely on the number of children they wish to have, unlike in present Tibet. The majority have also adopted monogamy, though, polygamy and polyandry are also practised. Widow remarriage and divorce are common and not considered taboo. However, lately there has been an increase in divorce cases and this could prove to be disastrous to the society. There is no system of marriage counselling, and only parents and relatives act as counsellors. This kind of community support has proven successful in some cases.

Women's Empowerment

Tibetan women play an important role in the freedom struggle while in exile. Women are organised as a force through the Tibetan Women's Association (TWA). The TWA is the only women's organisation in exile and undertakes many activities to empower women. It was founded in March 1959 during the uprisings at Lhasa and has a membership of over 10,000 women and 38 regional branches both in India and abroad. It aims at providing social welfare assistance to the needy, such as single parents, nuns, the handicapped, the sick and the elderly. The TWA wants to ensure that Tibetan women have access to adequate educational information, health care, family planning and childcare. It aims at preserving and promoting religion, culture and identity, by providing educational lectures related to health care, human rights and democracy, environment preservation and it conducts political programmes to highlight the struggle of Tibet. One of the most successful projects initiated by TWA is the Tailoring Project, which assists women and young girls from disadvantaged families as well as new arrivals from Tibet. The women are provided eighteen months of training and on completion of the programme, are self sufficient in tailoring and are able to take orders for stitching clothes. The TWA also initiated the Tibetan Nuns Project to assist nuns who have escaped from Tibet.

The Tibetan Women's Association continues to play an important role in the national struggle against the illegal occupation of Tibet and represents the continuation of the women's movement that was started by the women martyrs in 1959. H.H. the Dalai Lama in an exclusive interview to TWA on 20 July 1995 prior to the Beijing Conference said:

> I think a great contribution has been made by women both inside Tibet and outside Tibet. Outside Tibet, women are participating more forcefully, and effectively at various levels in many fields, and also...are very active in social activities especially in education...so there has been a great contribution made.

But living in exile has also had a negative impact on the Tibetan people and women in particular. Adaptation to modern lifestyles and culture has diluted the traditional values and morals of the Tibetan people. While there has been progress in society, people also witness the ugly side of global marketing and liberalisation. Younger Tibetans are vulnerable and face problems in adjusting and balancing traditional and modern lifestyles. Some of the Tibetan youth may be on the verge of losing their identity and goals due to the distractions of a colourful lifestyle.

Unemployment is the biggest social problem faced by the youth and the frustration that they experience could lead the younger generation to resort to various degrading means of survival. Many Tibetans have acknowledged this. Furthermore, social problems like inadequate health care are also a great threat to the development of the society. Due to changes in food habits and climatic conditions, many infectious diseases have been a cause of worry. Poverty and psychological problems have also been a major reason for such diseases. Dolkar Lhamo, the President of the Tibetan Women's Association, Dharamsala, agrees that many women from Tibet (recent arrivals) are burdened with abdominal and gynaecological problems as a result of various contraceptive measures they were forced to adopt in Tibet.

The continued arrival of new refugees has been a cause of both joy and anxiety. With the increase in unemployment and poverty, finding sufficient space in the schools and religious institutions has been a challenge for the Tibetan government and the community. Dolkar Lhamo the President of the TWA has been quoted as saying:

> The biggest problem we face at the moment is not being able to provide proper establishment to the new arrivals from Tibet. Although the Government-in-Exile has been doing the best it can, many still find problems in establishing themselves, finding appropriate jobs and earn a basic living. Many come to us for help and we act as facilitators and support them by approaching various departments and institutions to find jobs or any necessary social support. As a result many young Tibetans approach western tourists in Dharamsala in the hope of finding some future abroad.[6]

The sense of being 'stateless' has always haunted the Tibetans both psychologically and physically. All the Tibetans in India and Nepal carry identity certificates issued by the Indian or Nepali governments. When travelling to foreign countries Tibetan women have always faced problems at airports in the form of interrogations. This has been very humiliating to our dignity and one always feels that this would not be the case if Tibet were independent. Apart from the difficulty of Tibetans not being the citizens of the host country, they have to live within certain restrictions and cannot function independently whether it be in finding jobs, organising activities or any other social work.

Challenges for the Future

Tibetan women have been the backbone of the society in exile

[6]Interview 10 July 2001.

and have played an active role in the freedom struggle. They have been a strong force behind every task and have often won applause. Women have established a major position in preserving our culture and identity in exile for the past many decades.

However, with the influence of modernisation in the host countries where Tibetans live (both in India and abroad), the younger generation is vulnerable to the changing circumstances, and there is a great threat to the dilution of Tibetan culture and heritage. The older generation is slowly disappearing and with the continued destruction of culture and religion in Tibet by the Chinese communist regime, there is every reason to fear the loss of Tibet's rich culture and heritage. It is in this respect that there is a challenge for the women in exile to work harder towards the preservation of the society's rich identity and culture.

The fourteenth Dalai Lama announced in his 'Guidelines for Future Tibet's Polity and Basic Features of its Constitution' (1992) that the existing administration and Government-in-Exile will cease to exist and no officials will continue with their authority once Tibet has gained autonomy. It is the Tibetans in Tibet who will govern the future Tibet. It is inevitable that these people who have lived under a communist rule for decades will not have the experience to govern and will certainly need assistance. Thus, women need to plan ahead and accordingly educate the exile community on the importance of democratic principles and practices.

Women entrepreneurs could also contribute to the revival of the country's economy by inviting joint ventures from outside countries. All the women and the educated position holders in exile can play a vital role by using the experience gained in exile in the restructuring and rebuilding of Tibet.

Women should also sustain the gender identity they have been able to maintain and promote the empowerment of women. They have felt that there is gender discrimination in Tibetan society but it is minimal and therefore women have always been mindful in prioritising the issue of the national struggle. It is in this vein that gender sensitisation programmes should be addressed when the national struggle is achieved. Meanwhile women should also be more vocal and take an active part in public life and social work. The TWA President supports the view that women should be encouraged by everyone in the community to come out of their stereotypical role and work actively for the cause of Tibet. Because Tibetan women and girls are somewhat shy, they tend to stay behind and do not expose themselves to public life. This could be misinterpreted as a lack of ability and efficiency.

Pema Dechen, a former Vice-President of the Tibetan Women's Association, mentions in an article 'Emancipation Through Education', that women should have the courage and determination to fight for their rights if these are denied. She accepts that women enjoy equality in the society but there are some problems caused by the attitudes of 'orthodox women' and 'conservative men'. Education is the key to bringing about change.

Women need to participate in women's conferences globally and continue to network with international women's groups. Similarly, more women's organisations need to focus on specific issues like democracy and women's rights, adult literacy, career counselling, family counselling, specialisation in planning and development works. They could organise think-tank groups with spin doctors who would assist the future government with image building, or a focus group that would train political experts and analysts.

There has been a shortage of information on Tibetan women and except for a few biographies of well-known women, which have been recorded by non-Tibetans, not much has been heard. Many documents need to be recorded on life stories of prominent women in Tibet and in exile who have contributed to the society lest the people forget about the life of notable Tibetan women.

Conclusion

Tibetan women enjoy great freedom and lead contented lives. It would be appropriate to conclude that Tibetan women in exile have gained significant importance and a high profile due to the changing circumstances. However, it must be emphasised here that it would be wrong to assume that women were ill-treated and could not have progressed in pre-1959 Tibet. In fact, during the first half of the twentieth century, poverty and inequality was prominent in most parts of the world and other countries also had room for improvement in the betterment of the society. Tibet was no exception, and accordingly the Dalai Lama initiated democratic reforms in 1959, which unfortunately could not be implemented due to the occupation.

The status of Tibetan women could prove to be a positive model for their sisters in other parts of the world. Until the national struggle is achieved, Tibetan women should and will continue to work for the national cause. They will be the voice of the suppressed people in Tibet, as well as enhance their position in society. Advancement and empowerment are two important issues, which not only improve the lives of the women in particular but also the society at large. One can only end with the saying that 'you need two hands to clap'.

References

Bell, Charles, *The People of Tibet*, Oxford 1928.

Butler, Alex: Organizing From Exile: The Experiences of Tibetan Women and Palestine Women, *Tibetan Review*, Volume 34 January–February, 1999.

Butler, Alex, *Feminism, Nationalism and Exiled Tibetan Women*, Delhi 2003.

Cheng, Nein, *Life and Death in Shanghai*, Flamingo, 2000.

H.H. the fourteenth Dalai Lama: Guidelines for Future Tibet's Polity and the Basic Features of the Constitution, 1992.

Dechen, Pema, 'The Oppression and Resistance of Tibetan Women' in: Kelly, Petra K., Bastian, Gert and Aiello, Pat (eds.) *The Anguish of Tibet*, Berkeley, Cal. 1991.

Dhargay, Lobsang Show, former official of the Government of Tibet (1959), Interview: 1999, Oral History Project, Library of Tibetan Works and Archives, Dharamsala.

Lemdha, Pachen, *Sorrow Mountain: The Remarkable Story of a Tibetan Warrior Nun*, London 2000.

Tenth Panchen Lama, *Poisoned Arrow-The Secret Report of the Tenth Panchen Lama*, Tibet Information Network, London 1997.

Patt, David, *A Strange Liberation: Tibetan Lives in Chinese Hands*, New York 1992.

Planning Council, Central Tibetan Adminisration, *Tibetan Demographic Survey 1998*, Dharamsala 2000.

Planning Council, Central Tibetan Administration, *The Integrated Development Plan I (1992–1997)*, Dharamsala 1994.

Saklani, G., *The Uprooted Tibetans in India: A Sociological Study of Continuity and Change*, New Delhi 1984.

Shakabpa, W.D. Tsepon, *Tibet: A Political History*, New York 1984.

Tibetan Women's Association, *Plight of the Tibetan Women—Information Kit*, Prepared for the Fourth World Conference on Women, Beijing, 31 August–15 September, Dharamsala, 1995.

Tibetan Center for Human Rights and Democracy, *Enforcing Loyalty. Annual Report. 2000. Human Rights Situation in Tibet*, Dharamsala, 2001.

Tibetan Central Administration, *Tibetan Women: Oppression and Discrimination in Occupied Tibet, National Report on Tibetan Women.* Report for the Fourth World Conference on Women, Beijing 1995.

Tibetan Women's Association, *The Trek to Freedom: Tibetan Women and the Refugee Experience*. A Report for the Fourth World Conference on Women, Dharamsala 1995.

Tibet Information Network, *Social Evils: Prostitution and Pornography in Lhasa*, TIN Briefing Paper No: 31, 1991.

Tsomo, Tsering, *Family Planning Policies in Tibet: A Threat or a Necessity?* Report to the Second Asia Regional Workshop on Elimination of Violence Against Women, Kathmandu 1996.

Tung, Rosemary Jones, *A Portrait of Lost Tibet*, New York 1987.

Tibetan Women's Association, *Genesis of the Tibetan Women's Struggle for Independence*, Dharamsala n.d.

CHAPTER EIGHTEEN

Tibetan Nuns: New Roles and Possibilities

KARMA LEKSHE TSOMO

In the early years of the Tibetan diaspora, female renunciants were extremely few in number and rarely known outside of their own communities.[1] Until recently, almost all prominent Tibetan religious figures, both in Asia and the West, have been male. Over the last decade, however, the situation of Tibetan nuns has changed, often quite dramatically. As the number of nuns has expanded, so has their access to educational opportunities and their visibility both in Tibetan society and internationally. Since 1959, nuns in exile, like nuns in Tibet, have been active in the political sphere as outspoken proponents of self-determination for Tibetans. Increasingly, nuns are seeking higher education and taking part in both local and international conferences, training programmes, and public events. If the current trajectory of educational advancement continues, before long, nuns in the Tibetan Buddhist tradition will be eligible to obtain the highest academic distinction, the *geshe* (*dge bshes*)[2] degree. A

[1]Tibetan terms used to denote nuns include *tsünma/btsun ma*, *getsülma/dge tshul ma*, *chömä/chos ma*, *ane/a ne* (also used for a fraternal aunt), *jomo/jo mo* (also used for a female head of household), and *jetsünma/bje btsun ma* (also used for laywomen of high religious or social status). Reflecting the improved social status of nuns in recent years, the term *chöla/chos lags* has been gaining currency in Tibetan exile communities as a respectful form of address for nuns.

[2]At the first occurrence, Tibetan terms are given in two forms: first, the phonetic pronunciation, and, second, the Tibetan spelling. Thereafter, the phonetic form is used.

combination of factors has contributed to the changing circumstances of Tibetan nuns in exile. As new opportunities open up, nuns are acquiring the knowledge, skills, experience, and confidence required to emerge as leaders at this critical juncture in Tibetan cultural and political history.

Buddhist Nuns in Tibet

In Tibetan Buddhist cultures, renunciant women have always occupied a recognised and respected place, and in all classes of society, women with serious interests in religious matters have had the option of remaining unmarried and embracing religious life. Some of these women lived lives of celibacy and simplicity in their family homes, some took up residence in secluded retreats, huts and caves, while others gathered together in convents and small religious communities nestled in the mountains. Rugged nuns with cropped hair and wine-colored robes prostrating and praying along traditional pilgrimage routes were a familiar sight. Supported in their spiritual pursuit by donations from the laity of roasted barley flour (*tsampa/tsam pa*) and coins, the nuns constituted a strong thread in the Tibetan religious fabric.

Tibetan texts include the biographies of a number of revered female saints—Mandarava, Yeshe Tsogyal, Niguma, Nangsa Obum, and many others. These female exemplars of enlightened realisation were available as role models, confirming Buddha Shakyamuni's assertion that enlightenment is possible for all living beings, regardless of gender. Jetsun Lochen Rinpoche, Ayu Khandro, and Samding Dorje Palmo are among the many renowned nuns in recent Tibetan history who deserve mention. Jetsun Lochen Rinpoche was renowned for her renunciation and her miraculous powers as well as her teachings, ritual practices, and guru devotion. Humble and unheralded, realised female practitioners such as Dharamsala's Yeshe Drolma (Ani Gomchen) leave their mark on Tibetan religious life even today.

The feminine is vividly present in Tibetan ritual practices. The fasting practice of Avalokiteshvara, known as *nyungne* (*smyung gnas*),[3] which is especially popular among Tibetan nuns, traces its origins to an Indian princess who became a fully ordained nun, Gelongma Palmo. Pilgrimage sites associated with such eminent female religious figures as Yeshe Tsogyal and Machig Labdrön, as well as the lives of contemporary female recluses, have served as sources of inspiration for women as well as men throughout Tibetan history. Indeed, the practice of *chö* (*chod*), which involves a visualised offering of one's body for the welfare of others, is traced to Machig Labdrön. In Buddhist tantric rituals, visualisation of oneself as an enlightened female 'meditational deity' (*yidam/yi dam*) is a daily meditation practice for men and women alike. Although nuns may be requested to perform the rituals of female deities more frequently than monks, and indeed may feel a strong affinity for these rituals, the praises to the twenty-one emanations of Tara are recited daily in the monasteries of all Tibetan Buddhist schools. These embodiments of enlightenment in female form symbolise the immanent possibility of spiritual achievement for nuns and laywomen, as well as for monks and laymen. Although it is rare for a woman to be recognised as a *lama* (*bla ma,* spiritual teacher) or *tulku* (*sprul sku,* reincarnate *lama*), both in Tibet and in Tibetan refugee society, women function as diviners and oracle healers in equal or greater numbers than men, especially at the village level.

Aspiring to the Spiritual Life

Like Tibetan Buddhist monks, Tibetan nuns follow the monastic discipline set forth by Buddha Shakyamuni in the sixth

[3]The *nyungne* fasting practice combines supplication to Avalokiteshvara, the bodhisattva of compassion, with prostrations, meditation, repetition of prayers and mantras, and the observation of eight precepts for a period of two days. On the first day, practitioners take one vegetarian meal at noon and liquids throughout the day. On the second day, no food or liquids, including water, are taken for a 24-hour period. A detailed description of the *nyungne* ritual is beyond the scope of this article.

century BC. Most nuns enter religious life motivated by a sincere interest in the *Dharma*, and usually with the permission of their parents. Parents are less likely to encourage a daughter than a son to enter the religious life, but generally will not oppose such a decision if their daughter is determined. The social status accorded a nun is lower than that of a monk, and opportunities for religious education are fewer. The chances of recognition as a *tulku* are practically nil for a nun, but monastic life is regarded as highly meritorious, and the ordination of a family member—male or female—is thought to benefit the entire family, even up to seven generations.

Young women who aspire to become nuns do not view marriage and family as an attractive option. Some have observed the sufferings that women experience in childbirth and the hard work they endure to support their families. Although some girls are orphans or are placed in nunneries by their parents due to poverty, most enter religious life by choice, believing *Dharma* practice to be the most beneficial use of a human life. Among nuns recently arrived from Tibet, the motivation to practice *Dharma* is especially strong, not only because many have been denied the freedom to practise religion as they wished, but also because some have been persecuted for their beliefs. Because of societal preconceptions about women's capabilities, nuns may doubt their own potential to become teachers, abbesses, reincarnate lamas, or enlightened beings. Still, they are strongly motivated to practise in order to ensure a better future rebirth and progress spiritually on the path to enlightenment. Whatever their reasons for becoming ordained, nuns are more keenly aware than ever of the value of education in achieving their religious objectives.

Contemporary Tibetan nuns take the practice of their faith very seriously. Becoming a nun signals a new life, with a new name, a new way of dressing, and a new approach to life. Although ties with family and society are maintained to varying degrees, the goal of spiritual liberation takes precedence over worldly concerns. With intense devotion, nuns 'purify the stains' of their previously created unwholesome actions and 'accumulate merit' through study, meditation, and a variety of devotional practices that include prostrations, water bowl offerings, prayers, mantras, molding small images (*tsatsa/tsa tsa*) out of clay, and circumambulating sacred sites. Tibetan nuns in exile continue these practices with full energy, just as generations of their sisters have done before, even as they assume a host of new roles.

From Humble Beginnings

Today there are an estimated 1,290 Tibetan nuns living in exile in India and Nepal as a result of the Communist takeover of Tibet. According to Tibetan Government-in-Exile records, 916 of these nuns live in nunneries established in exile, while 374 nuns live in private dwellings.[4] The flight of nuns from Tibet has occurred in two main waves: the first wave consisted of those who fled in 1959 or soon thereafter; the second wave consisted of those who fled more recently, including 402 nuns who arrived in India and Nepal between 1989 and 1993.[5] The latter wave of refugee nuns has filled existing Tibetan nunneries to overflowing and prompted the establishment of several new nunnery projects. While they await resettlement, newly arrived nuns are eligible for a monthly stipend of Rs 50 given by the Department of Religion and Culture in Dharamsala. Free medical treatment is provided in local clinics, as are rehabilitation services for those who have been imprisoned and tortured.

Although nuns and nunneries are being revived in some parts of Tibet today, their existence and well-being there are precarious, always subject to the controls and unpredictable policy shifts of the People's Republic of China. The number of nuns who escape is far fewer than the number of monks, due to the hardships and obvious risks of the journey. Nevertheless, it is safe to say that the majority of Tibetan nuns ordained since 1989 were born in Tibet rather than in exile. Despite a lack of adequate facilities, educational opportunities, and support for

---

[4]Http://www.tibet.com/govt/refugees.html.

[5]Ibid.

nuns, as well as a host of new career opportunities that are now opening up for women in general, young Tibetan women continue to opt for the religious life, motivated by religious devotion and a commitment to preserving their Tibetan cultural identity. Nuns, both in Tibet and in exile, have been leaders in the campaign for Tibetans' rights to self-determination. As Chinese control tightens in Tibet, nuns have become more keenly aware than ever that their cherished Tibetan Buddhist heritage stands a better chance of survival in exile than inside Tibet itself.

During the initial phase of emigration (1959–66), very few nuns managed to escape from Tibet. For example, in 1984 among the residents of Karma Drubgyu Targye Ling, a refugee nunnery located in Tilokpur, near Dharamsala, only eight had been nuns in Tibet, while the others were born in exile. One of the earliest communities of nuns in India, which was founded by the acclaimed nun Jetsun Dolma in the Tibetan settlement of Puntsokling in Orissa, had dwindled by the year 2000 to only two elderly nuns from Tibet. Within the Tibetan exile diaspora, the largest concentrations of nuns are centred around Dharamsala, Darjeeling, Kathmandu, Mundgod, and Bylakuppe.

The educational backgrounds of Tibetan nuns vary considerably. Some have had little or no secular education before becoming nuns, others have completed grades 8, 9, or 10, and one nun, Sra. Lobsang Dechen, who now heads the Tibetan Nuns Project, holds a bachelor's degree in education. In Tibet, young nuns usually receive their education at home or in the nunnery. Senior nuns tutor younger nuns daily in Tibetan grammar and Buddhist texts. Morning and evening, the young students memorise prayers and passages from the texts, while their teachers listen, correct, and guide their progress. This system of the older generation mentoring the younger generation continues in exile. Increasingly, Tibetan nuns born in India or Nepal have attended school, while those born in Tibet frequently have not. The task of equalising these disparities and providing remedial education to compensate for deficiencies falls primarily to the nunneries; over the last fifteen years the quality of religious studies programmes for nuns have improved markedly.

The most significant changes for nuns have been in the field of religious education, particularly the introduction of philosophical studies. At nunneries such as Samten Ling in Manali, philosophical texts are studied in intensive three-month courses that alternate with longer periods of retreat, whereas at nunneries such as Jangchub Chöling in Mundgod and Jamyang Chöling in Dharamsala, philosophical studies form the core of the nuns' activities. The introduction of philosophical studies (*tsenyi/mtsan 'nyid*) has led to the inauguration of annual intermural debate tournaments modelled after the Jang Kunchö tradition of the great Tibetan monastic universities. As a consequence of this new emphasis on philosophy and debate, it is anticipated that within a few years nuns will become eligible to receive Tibet's prized scholastic distinction, the *geshe* degree. Access to philosophical studies and the opportunity to obtain this degree are two criteria for gauging gender equity in Tibetan Buddhist society.

In theory, Buddhism is egalitarian, affirming that all sentient beings have the potential to achieve perfect enlightenment. Because the goal of Buddhism is the transformation of consciousness, and consciousness has no gender, there should be no impediment to women's equal participation in Buddhist practice. This egalitarian ideal is, however, not always realised in actual practice in Buddhist societies. Although women's spiritual practice is admired and encouraged, a female rebirth is generally regarded as the result of an inferior stock of merit, a view which can be traced to Buddhist texts. Women are stigmatised as the seducers of men, although the reverse is mostly the case. In Tibetan society, women were rarely awarded the title *lama* (religious teacher) and girls were seldom recognised as *tulkus* (recognised reincarnate *lamas*). Until recently, it was assumed that women were more suited to prayers and rituals, and less capable of higher religious studies. Fortunately, the academic achievements of nuns in recent years have corrected these misconceptions.

Many factors lead young women to enter religious life. Occasionally, girls join the nunnery inspired by relatives who are monastics. More frequently, they are motivated by a sincere wish to practice *Dharma* and liberate themselves from the sufferings of worldly existence (*korwa/skor ba*, Sanskrit: *samsara*). As small children, girls see firsthand the hardships of labour-intensive household work, the sufferings of their mothers as they give birth, and the problems and distractions in the practice of *Dharma* that usually arise within a family. Later in life, after their husbands have died and their children have grown, Tibetan refugee women may become nuns known as *genchö/rgan chos.* For many women, monastic life represents security, community, and an alternative to worldly involvements. For most, it represents freedom from household constraints and the ideal environment for the pursuit of virtue.

Beginning in the late 1980s, a new wave of refugees began to arrive from Tibet, due to a relaxation of Chinese restrictions on visiting India. It is estimated that more than 150,000 people arrived to attend the Kalachakra ceremony with His Holiness the Dalai Lama, held in Bodhgaya in February 1987. Among the new arrivals were many young people who, frustrated by restrictions on the practice of religion in Tibet, were inspired to become ordained as monks and nuns. Among the younger generation of nuns who came from Tibet, each had a story. Some had escaped to India and Nepal as a result of religious or political persecution. Some had travelled from Tibet in the company of like-minded friends with the dream of seeing the Dalai Lama and, after meeting him, receiving teachings, and experiencing the climate of religious freedom in exile, decided to seek ordination. Others were encouraged by their parents, who advised their daughters that it would be beneficial to become a nun and, in some cases, even brought them to the border. A few, after fulfilling their dreams of meeting His Holiness, faced an uncertain future in exile and found that becoming a nun was the most practical option for survival.

The Tibetan Nuns' Project, started in Dharamsala in 1987,

has taken an active role in providing food, shelter, and education for hundreds of nuns from Tibet. With international assistance, the project supports two nunneries which were established especially to accommodate the influx of refugee nuns from Tibet: Dolma Ling in Sidhpur and Shugsep Nunnery in Dharamsala. The Tibetan Nuns' Project has played a leading role in providing housing, education, and rehabilitation for nuns who have suffered imprisonment, torture, and sexual abuse as a result of the Chinese Communist occupation of Tibet. In addition to these efforts, the Project organises healthcare training programmes, annual inter-mural debate tournaments, and other innovative projects for nuns.

The Ordination of Tibetan Nuns

Most Tibetan nuns in exile have taken the 36 precepts of a novice.[6] In Tibet, women with a religious vocation were

---

[6]The 36 precepts are to refrain from: (1) taking a human life; (2) killing an animal or insect; (3) inadvertently killing an animal or insect through carelessness; (4) harming insects through splashing water on dry ground; (5) sexual intercourse; (6) taking what is not given; (7) lying about one's spiritual attainments; (8) falsely accusing a pure *gelong* or *gelongma* of transgressing a root precept; (9) falsely insinuating that a pure *gelong* or *gelongma* has transgressed one of the four root precepts; (10) causing disunity among the monastic community; (11) supporting a person who is creating disunity in the monastic community; (12) engaging in actions that erode the lay community's faith in the monastic; (13) telling lies; (14) accusing the monastery storekeeper of favoritism; (15) criticising the monastery storekeeper of being unfair; (16) falsely accusing a monastic of teaching for profit; (17) falsely accusing a *gelong* or *gelongma* of transgressing a precept of the second category; (18) rejecting or denigrating the monastic training; (19) concealing the vegetables with rice or rice with vegetables [in the alms bowl, in order to get more]; (20) taking intoxicants; (21) singing; (22) dancing; (23) playing musical instruments; (24) wearing ornaments; (25) using cosmetics; (26) wearing perfumes; (27) wearing rosaries and flower garlands as ornaments; (28) sitting on luxurious seats; (29) sitting on luxurious beds; (30) sitting on high (*contd.*)

ordained as novice nuns (*getsülma/dge tshul ma*)[7] by receiving the 36 precepts—a uniquely Tibetan formulation that includes the traditional ten precepts of a Buddhist novice plus additional rules of training. Some female renunciants wear the robes of a nun without having taken the novice precepts, instead observing the five precepts of a Buddhist laywoman (*genyenma/dge bsnyen ma*)[8] or the eight precepts of a transitional renunciant (*barma rabjung/bar ma rab byung*).[9] Because there are no fully ordained nuns (*gelongma/dge slong ma*, Sanskrit: *bhikshuni*) to administer the precepts, all Tibetan nuns receive the novice precepts from fully ordained monks (*gelong/dge slong*, Sanskrit: *bhikshu*). Unlike the Theravada tradition, this practice enables Tibetan women to receive novice ordination and become members of the monastic community; at the same time, it leaves the selection and ordination of nuns entirely up to the monks, and limits nuns to novice status indefinitely.

Some Tibetan lamas, including H.H. Dalai Lama, encourage nuns to receive full ordination, while other lamas seem to discourage it, expressing doubts about the purity of the Chinese

---

(*contd.*) seats; (31) sitting on high beds; (32) eating after midday (unless sick, travelling, or it disturbs one's meditation); (33) handling gold, silver or precious jewels; (34) wearing laypeople's clothing, ornaments, or long hair; (35) not wearing the robes of a Buddhist monastic; and (36) showing disrespect or disregard for one's monastic teacher.

[7]The ten precepts taken by a male or female novice (*getsül or getsülma*) include the five precepts of a Buddhist layperson (except here, the fourth precept entails refraining from sexual activity altogether), plus to refrain from: (6) singing, dancing, and entertainments, (7) using ornaments and cosmetics, (8) using high or luxurious seats and beds, (9) handling gold and silver, and (10) taking untimely food.

[8]The five precepts taken by a Buddhist layperson (*genyen* or *genyenma*) are to refrain from: (1) taking life, (2) taking what is not given, (3) telling lies, (4) sexual misconduct, and (5) taking intoxicants.

[9]The eight precepts include the five precepts of a Buddhist layperson except, here, the fourth precepts entails sexual abstinence), plus to refrain from: (6) singing, dancing, entertainments, ornaments, and cosmetics; (7) using high or luxurious seats or beds; (8) taking untimely food.

gelongma lineage or implying that nuns are incapable of keeping the greater number of precepts that full ordination entails.[10] Approximately fifty nuns in the Tibetan tradition (including nuns from Bhutan, India, Nepal, Tibet, and western countries) have received full ordination to date. A total of ten Karma Drubgyu Targye Ling nuns (from Bhutan, India, Sikkim, and Tibet) received the precepts of a fully ordained nun (*gelongma*) in Hong Kong in 1983 and 1986. Eleven nuns from the Sisina Nunnery in Bhutan received full ordination in Hong Kong in 1995 and another nine nuns from Ladakh, Nepal, and Darjeeling received the ordination in Bodhgaya in 1998. In addition, western nuns of the Tibetan tradition have become fully ordained in Hong Kong, Korea, Taiwan, Paris, Los Angeles, China, and Bodhgaya, starting with the English nun Khechog Palmo (Freda Bedi) in 1972.

As far as is known, the lineage of fully ordained nuns (*gelongma*) was never transmitted to Tibet from India. Although there is mention in the Tibetan texts of individual Tibetan lamas who conferred full ordination on women, there is no evidence that these ordinations were recognised by the government or by the religious hierarchy. Because there were no fully ordained nuns in the Tibetan tradition to perform the ordination, nuns have traditionally received their novice precepts from fully ordained monks (*gelong*). Tibetan monks reason that this is permissible, since the precepts for a Buddhist novice are identical for nuns and monks.

Nuns in the Tibetan tradition shave their heads and wear robes identical to those of a monk. The robes, symbolising renunciation, are an adaptation of the patched garments worn by Indian Buddhist monastics, but have been adjusted slightly

[10]Nuns in the Dharmagupta lineage of monastic discipline observe 348 precepts. This lineage, followed in the Chinese, Korean, and Vietnamese traditions is the only surviving lineage of full ordination for Buddhist women. See Karma Lekshe Tsomo, *Sisters in Solitude: Two Traditions of Buddhist Monastic Ethics for Women*, Albany, N.Y.: State University of New York Press, 1996.

over the centuries in response to the Tibetan climate and the availability of materials.[11] The robes include a maroon lower garment (*shamtab/gsham tab*), a maroon shawl (*zen/gzen*), a maroon vest (*dönka*), and a yellow outer robe (*chögu/chos gos*) which is worn on ceremonial occasions. Accessories, including an underskirt (*meyog/smad gyog*), shirt (*ngullen/rngul len*), and belt (*kerag/sked rags*), are generally yellow, orange, or red in colour. Fully ordained monks and nuns are entitled to wear a patched *shamtab* and an additional yellow robe with 25 strips of patches (*namcha/snam sbyar*), which is worn on special ceremonial occasions. Although it was not common practice for nuns in Tibet to wear the *chögu*, in response to a directive from H.H. Dalai Lama in Dharamsala in 1987, this robe is now typically worn by nuns in the Tibetan tradition.

Many Tibetan nuns are interested in receiving full ordination, but are hesitant to express their aspiration and seek ordination until the extant lineage of *gelongma* ordination (available in the Chinese, Korean, and Vietnamese traditions) is accepted as valid by the Tibetan government. H.H. Dalai Lama has stated that he personally hopes that the *gelongma* lineage can be established within the Tibetan tradition and has given permission for nuns to travel to other countries to receive the ordination, but has said that he, as an individual *gelong*, does not have the authority to rule on this important matter. To expedite the acceptance of full ordination for women among senior Tibetan *lamas*, he has repeatedly called for an international congress to discuss the issue in the hopes of reaching some consensus.[12]

Until such consensus is reached, the majority of Tibetan nuns seem content to receive the novice ordination, reasoning that the ten precepts of a novice are sufficiently difficult to observe. Some also dismiss the importance of full ordination, or assert that becoming a *gelongma* is only a matter of status, which is irrelevant to Dharma practice, even though *gelong* ordination is

[11]For example, the ochre dye used by Indian Buddhists was rare and costly in Tibet, whereas the maroon dye was widely available.

[12]See chapter 6.

clearly important and relevant for monks. If the *gelongma* ordination were available within the Tibetan tradition, many nuns would surely decide to take it, but at present it is necessary, although inconvenient and expensive, to travel abroad to receive *gelongma* ordination. Both monks and nuns often express the view that, 'It is easy to take the *gelongma* precepts, but very difficult to keep them purely.' Because *gelongmas* take more precepts than *gelongs*, it is assumed that they are more likely to break them. Although a full-fledged transgression of the precepts requires the intention to break them, not merely an accident, many nuns seem hesitant to take on additional precepts or even to discuss them. Yet until full ordination is available to both nuns and monks, the Tibetan tradition cannot be said to be fully egalitarian.

Because the *gelongma* lineage was never established in Tibet, there are three possible ways that the lineage can be established in the Tibetan tradition today. The first is to introduce the lineage by way of the Chinese, Korean, or Vietnamese traditions, where the lineage exists and is flourishing. The second is to organise a *gelongma* ordination in which Tibetan *gelongs* alone confer the precepts, without the participations of *gelongmas.* Although the texts of monastic discipline (Sanskrit: Vinaya) require that the ordination involve the participation of ten *gelongs* and ten (or, in the Tibetan, twelve) *gelongmas*—and such an ordination is certainly the ideal—*gelongma* ordinations by *gelongs* alone are frequently held in the Chinese, Korean, and Vietnamese traditions and their validity is rarely questioned. The third possibility is to organise a *gelongma* ordination that combines traditions, a procedure which is not discussed in the monastic texts. For example, such an ordination could be administered by a quorum of Tibetan *gelongs* and Chinese *gelongmas* acting together, or by a quorum of *gelongs* and *gelongmas* from a variety of traditions acting together. From the perspective of monastic law, the implications of an ordination that combines traditions have yet to be fully explored. For example, what lineage of precepts would be conferred in such an ordination? What version of the ordination procedure should be used, and which language?

Before making a decision about whether to introduce the *gelongma* lineage into the Tibetan tradition, Tibetan monks and scholars have called for research in three specific areas: (1) a comparative study of the *gelongma* precepts contained in the Tibetan and Chinese texts, (2) a comparative study of the procedures for *gelongma* ordination contained in the Tibetan and Chinese texts, and (3) verification of the extant lineages of *gelongma* ordination that have been transmitted uninterruptedly since the sixth century BC when Buddha Shakyamuni first instituted the lineage in India. The two comparative studies have been completed.[13] A determination therefore rests on the latter issue. Since it is impossible to either prove or disprove the uninterrupted transmission of the lineage, the lineage will either be disqualified on the grounds that the ordination has not always been conferred by a full quorum of *gelongs* and *gelongmas* or it will be accepted as valid on the grounds that Buddha Shakyamuni originally gave the ordination without a full quorum of *gelongs* and *gelongmas*. Proponents argue that the benefits of recognising the *gelongma* lineage far outweigh the imperatives of monastic law, not only for women and Buddhism but also for society at large.

New Attitudes and Institutions

Historically in Tibet, there have been far fewer nuns than monks, and monasteries for nuns have been fewer, smaller, and less adequately supported than those for monks. Since coming into exile, however, the situation of nuns has begun to change.

[13]A comparative study of the *gelongma* precepts in Tibetan and Chinese has been published in Karma Lekshe Tsomo, *Sisters in Solitude: Two Traditions of Buddhist Monastic Ethics for Women*, supra. English translations of the Tibetan and Chinese *gelongma* ordination procedure have been completed, but have not yet been published.

Although very few nuns were able to escape to India and Nepal, and the early years were particularly difficult for nuns, in the last twenty years there has been a conscientious effort to improve conditions for Tibetan nuns, with special emphasis on traditional learning.

A number of factors have contributed to the increased prominence of nuns in Tibetan exile society today. One factor is wider access to secular education, which has raised the educational qualifications of women in general. Another is greater public access to Buddhist teachings by H.H. Dalai Lama and other renowned teachers, which women and men alike are free to attend. Yet another factor is the changing perception of women's capabilities as conveyed through the media, through personal contacts with Buddhist practitioners and women from other countries and cultures, and through the encouragement and financial support nuns have received from abroad. The most significant gains for nuns have been in the field of education.

The establishment of educational institutions such as the Tibetan Children's Village, Tibetan Homes, and the Central Tibetan Schools have made secular education for girls more available than ever before and raised the academic standards and expectations among women, both lay and ordained. Systematic and sustained religious instruction for nuns remains limited, but is becoming more widely available. In Tibet, although public teachings were open to all, Buddhist studies programmes at the three largest monastic universities (Drepung, Ganden, and Sera, all now reconstructed in south India) were restricted to monks. Over the last fifteen years, since nuns in India and Nepal have begun to study philosophical and ritual texts seriously, the perceived barriers to women's full participation in all aspects of Tibetan intellectual life have begun to ease. For a time, female students were permitted to enrol in the Central Institute of Higher Tibetan Studies at Sarnath, and two nuns received Master's degrees there, but for about a decade during the 1980s, no female students were admitted. The doors have since opened again, but while many nuns wish to study at this prestigious institute, only eight female students—nuns or laywomen—are admitted every other year.

The new roles that nuns play today are not always innovative; one major success has simply been to gain access to opportunities that monks already enjoy. Nuns today participate in the *Mönlam* (Great Prayer Festival), study philosophical debate, construct sand *mandalas*, perform sacred dances (*cham/'chams*), join in Buddhist-Christian dialogues, and chant at Free Tibet Concerts and other public gatherings. Some of these opportunities also represent potential sources of revenue for nuns. Other nuns have travelled abroad to study, attend conferences, or receive full ordination as *gelongmas*. As nuns have become better educated, they have developed new attitudes towards their roles and their potential. They have gained greater confidence in public affairs, in negotiating government channels, and in dealing with potential donors.

Monasteries and Retreat Centres

The establishment of new monasteries and retreat centres are among the many achievements of Tibetan nuns in exile. Geden Chöling, Karma Drubgye Thargyeling, Jamyang Chöling, Dolma Ling, Shugsep, and Tashi Chöling are among the nunneries that have been established in and around the Dharamsala area since 1976. Nunneries established further afield include Jangchub Chöling in Mundgod, Karma Chökhor Dechen in Sikkim, Samten Ling in Manali, Samdrup Darjeeling in Darjeeling, Samten Tse Retreat Centre in Mussoorie, Tsogyal Shedrub Dargyeling in Bylakuppe, and Sakya Centre Nunnery and Drigung Kagyu Samten Ling in Dehra Dun. New and reconstructed nunneries have also grown up in Nepal. Nunneries in and around Kathmandu include Nagi Gonpa, Keydong Thukche Chöling, Khachö Ghakhyil Nunnery, Nyingma Payul Women's Retreat, Thrangu Tara Abbey, Trangu Nunnery, and Kari Nunnery. In the mountain regions of Nepal, there are also many nunneries; Thubten Chöling Monastery in Solu Salaria, with over a hundred nuns, is one of the largest. Untold numbers of nuns live independently in private homes, caves, and small retreat centres throughout the Himalayan region.

As Tibetan nuns established new monasteries in exile, they also assumed an expanded range of roles and responsibilities. The Karma Drubgye Thargyeling (Mahayana Buddhist Nunnery) was first established in a small cottage in Dalhousie, in 1962, by the English nun Khechog Palmo.[14] Now located two hours from Dharamsala, in Tilokpur, it is home to more than eighty nuns. Ganden Chöling, established in Dharamsala in 1974 by two nuns from Nechung Ri Nunnery near Lhasa, has grown to almost 150 nuns. The Jamyang Chöling Institute began as a literacy project for Tibetan nuns in 1987; it now has sixty nuns at two locations in Dharamsala and six outreach programmes located throughout the Himalayan region. The Dolma Ling Nunnery, started near Dharamsala specifically to address the influx of new arrivals from Tibet in the late 1980s, has grown from 105 nuns in 1991 to 160 in 2001, and offers classes in general education and crafts, in addition to Buddhist philosophy. Two large nunneries in Karnataka, south India, also offer systematic study programmes in Buddhist philosophy: Jangchub Chöling, a Gelug nunnery in Mundgod, has over 100 student nuns, while Tsogyal Shedrub Dargyeling, a Nyingma nunnery in Bylakuppe, has over 200. All of these projects began with only a few residents and expanded rapidly to accommodate increasing numbers of women interested in monastic life. All face continual challenges finding financial support to maintain their programmes.

Nuns assume the responsibility of establishing and maintaining their own nunneries. Finding land, constructing buildings, and establishing education projects are the primary concerns of most Tibetan nunneries, especially at the beginning. In Tibet nuns concentrated primarily on ritual and contemplative practices; in exile nuns may choose from a wider range of pursuits. In addition to meditation, prayers, and ritual,

---

[14]Havnevik, Hanna, *Tibetan Buddhist Nuns: History, Cultural Norms and Social Reality*. Oslo, Norwegian University Press, 1989, p. 85.

they have greater access to the study of philosophy, debate, Tibetan grammar, foreign languages, medicine, history, and literature, and to practical training in such areas as health care, ecology, accounting, communications, and computer skills. Several nuns have been trained at the Tibetan Medical Institute and are now practicing physicians in the Tibetan settlements; others are still pursuing their studies. As nuns gain greater access to education and training, they acquire knowledge, practical skills, and self-assurance that makes them more effective in their traditional roles as ritual specialists, meditators, spiritual mentors, and counselors, and to venture into an expanded range of new roles as teachers, lecturers, translators, health care providers, administrators, and community development workers.

By and large, Tibetan Buddhist nunneries are self-defined, self-governing, and self-supporting. Independent of external controls, the nuns are free to select their own leadership, create their own monastic regulations, determine their own curriculum of studies and schedule of practices, and enter into agreements, associations, and teaching relationships in accordance with the wishes of their membership. Within the nunnery, there are multiple hierarchies related to age, monastic seniority, education, official monastic duties, as well as to the wealth and social status of one's family, which operate simultaneously and fluidly in different situations. In external relations, the nuns and the nunnery as an institution operate within a variety of contexts and in relationships to other social, political, and religious hierarchies. As their standards of education and training improve, nuns as individuals and as institutions also improve their status within these distinct but mutually interwoven hierarchies.

Although Tibetan nunneries are largely self-governing, they may designate a male lama as their abbot or spiritual director, and simultaneously one of their own nuns as 'head nun'. Generally speaking, daily monastic organisation is directed by the head nun, whereas the nuns look to the lama for spiritual guidance, practical advice, and final administrative decisions. The pattern of parallel and cooperative leadership between a nunnery's internal administration and a respected male religious figure who acts as final arbitrator has its roots in Tibet, where nuns often relied on revered male lamas for guidance. A notable exception is Karma Drubgyu Targye Ling, which selected Karma Hoser to serve as abbess of their nunnery at Tilokpur. Ever since Karma Hoser left the position to engage in extended retreat in Nepal, several nuns have shared the leadership of their community. Because Tibetan nuns stand outside traditional power structures, they are free to experiment with alternative models of organisation. Their experiments in shared leadership and consensual decision often spontaneously reflect contemporary feminist values.

Tibetan nuns in exile are recognised as full members of the Tibetan monastic community (*dge 'dun*, Sanskrit: *sangha*) and have increasingly become models for women in other Himalayan Buddhist communities. Although the closing of trade routes with Tibet since 1959 has been a major economic setback for people in the Himalayan border region, the presence of H.H. Dalai Lama in India has also been an unforeseen windfall for Buddhists in these isolated areas, giving rise to an energetic reaffirmation of their own cultural and religious identities. Buddhists from the border regions regularly attend public Buddhist teachings and ceremonies, and send their sons and daughters to study in the many Tibetan schools and monasteries that have been newly established by Tibetans in exile. As Tibetan nuns in exile have gained greater access to religious education through public teachings and Buddhist studies programmes, women throughout the Himalayan region have gradually pressed for and gained greater opportunities to study Buddhist texts, ritual, and meditation. After a few nuns from the Himalayan border regions began studying at nunneries around Dharamsala, their friends and relatives from Arunachal Pradesh, Bhutan, Kinnaur, Nepal, Ladakh, Sikkim, Spiti, and Zangskar also began to seek opportunities for religious education. Zangla Changchub Chöling and Jujik Shalgön (now Drubgyu Khachö), two nunneries in the remote valley of Zangskar, instituted Buddhist studies programmes in 1989 and 1990 respectively. Yangchen Chöling and Sherab Chöling, two new nunneries with an emphasis on Buddhist studies, sprang up soon after in Spiti. The Ladakh

Nuns Project, which aims at providing education, training, and encouragement to nuns throughout Ladakh, began in 1995.

Nunneries are dependent on donations, both from the laity in the surrounding community and from abroad. Support from the Tibetan community is earned by performing prayers and pujas,[15] especially Tara pujas, fasting practices, and rituals connected with Vajrayogini. Support from western donors is often received for specific purposes: nutrition, health care, construction, and education projects. Most nuns are aware of the discrepancies between support for monasteries and nunneries, and realise that laypeople prefer to support monks. They are also aware of societal preconceptions that a female rebirth is lower than that of a male. Most are nonetheless content with the support they receive from donors and family members, since this, to whatever degree, enables them to live as nuns and concentrate on *Dharma* practice.

The administrative structures of the monks' monasteries are generally replicated by the nuns. From among their own number, residents select a head nun, disciplinarian, chant master, storekeeper, secretary, shrine-keeper, and accountant. Nuns are more apt to regard monks than nuns as their lamas and spiritual mentors, and consequently have had little experience with assuming positions of spiritual and administrative authority. In recent years, however, they have increasingly begun to assume these roles.

New Modes of Religious Discourse

Tibetan nuns in exile are situated at a unique moment in history. They are intensely concerned with the preservation of their religion, language, and culture; at the same time, they are poised to initiate changes that will thoroughly transform Tibetan

[15] *Puja* is the Sanskrit term for a religious ritual or ceremony that may include elements such as chanting, meditation, offerings, and the recitation of prayers and mantras. *Pujas* may be performed by an individual or a group. Some are performed daily, while others are performed on a monthly or annual basis.

religious discourse. The legacy they inherit is a cherished and endangered ancient technology of mental cultivation encased in a specific cultural construct; the legacy they are poised to bequeath to future generations is a method of mental development that is accessible to all people, regardless of culture or gender.

As women participate more visibly in Tibetan religious discourse, they adapt it to their own needs, financial means, and modes of perception. For example, in contrast to the elaborate rituals and ceremonies that characterise some monks' monasteries, nuns' communities tend to emphasise more ascetic practices, such as the fasting ritual (*nyungne*), and may perform rituals less elaborately. Even though the unpretentiousness of the nuns' ritual style is partly due to their more modest financial base, it may also reflect their appreciation for the values of renunciation and simplicity that are cornerstones of Buddhism.

Despite all these changes, and a host of new opportunities for nuns, it is too early to claim that gender equality has been achieved among Tibetan monastics. Genuine equality for nuns will entail equal access to education, ordination, political representation, and resources. Equal access to secular education provides a model for constructing equal education in the religious sphere. Similarly, greater and equitable representation for women in government agencies will help ensure that the voices of nuns are heard. Although nuns have no official representation in the Tibetan Government-in-Exile's Department of Religion and Culture, concern for their welfare is growing. Once nuns gain access to equal opportunities for education and full ordination, their social status and material resources are likely to increase naturally, bringing the nuns closer to parity with the monks.

With increased education has also come increased awareness of the limitations nuns face. Younger nuns have begun to notice the inequalities that exist among the opportunities that are available to monks and nuns, and to question the usefulness of gender-specific behaviours. With their considerable freedom of movement, and ability to marry and divorce and remarry, as well as work outside the home, Tibetan women in exile enjoy more autonomy than the Indian and Nepali women around them; however, women's roles and conduct are still affected by gender-related social conventions and expectations that may inhibit them from openly voicing their concerns. Yet, whether in the secular or religious spheres, patriarchal power structures can only survive if women continue to accept subordinate roles. Redefining these roles and challenging social expectations is a process that requires careful thought and awareness along with courageous action. Networking, facilitated locally through personal contacts and internationally through a variety of non-governmental organisations, has helped Tibetan nuns gain momentum for change. Throughout the sometimes painful process of social change that results from revising gender expectations, Buddhist practice can serve as a bulwark, fostering psychological growth, patience, and inner strength. For practitioners, it can provide a wealth of useful tools for developing awareness, compassion, clarity, wisdom, and pure motivation.

In Tibetan society, intensive religious practice is so highly valued that many contemplatives may neglect their physical health. For example, health surveys conducted in Dharamsala have shown a higher incidence of anaemia and malnutrition among nuns than in any other sector of the population. These findings may be partially due to inadequate daily nutrition and the rigorous fasting practices that nuns must follow to generate financial support for their monasteries. A disproportionate incidence of health problems among the nuns may also suggest that nuns tend to neglect their physical well-being and set higher standards for themselves to compensate for a perceived inferiority. An example is the rigour with which many nuns in northern India strictly maintain the monastic dress code, which stipulates that monastics should not wear hats or sleeves, even during the icy winters. In deference to the instructions of their monastic teachers, especially H.H. Dalai Lama, many nuns refrain from wearing warm clothing even in the privacy of their own rooms, in contrast to some monks who don sweaters, jackets, or even trousers in public. In conversations with nuns, many express the opinion that society judges nuns by a higher standard than monks. In their experience, people are quick to express their disapproval of a nun's misbehaviour and to criticise any infractions of monastic discipline. The positive result of higher expectations is that nuns are motivated to maintain high standards of behaviour, especially in the public eye; at the same time, nuns feel they are judged more harshly than monks, simply because of their gender.

Both the substantial achievements of Tibetan nuns and society's increased awareness of nuns in recent decades can be seen as parallel to the achievements of women in other Buddhist countries. Since 1987, Buddhist nuns and laywomen have been networking locally and internationally to share their knowledge and experiences, and create currents of change. For example, the international Buddhist women's movement, despite its meagre resources, has initiated pioneering efforts to further cross-cultural understanding and is one of the most far-reaching grassroots movements in the world today. Conferences sponsored by Sakyadhita: International Association of Buddhist Women,[16] training courses such as Life as a Western Buddhist Nun,[17] and seminars sponsored by the International Network of Engaged Buddhists (INEB), the Heinrich Böll Foundation, and other international organisations have provided nuns with access to valuable new information, skills, and insights. Nuns and laywomen in the Tibetan tradition have benefitted greatly from participating in these consciousness-raising activities. Recognising the contradictions that exist between Buddhism's theoretical

[16]The proceedings of these conferences have been edited by me and published in *Buddhism Through American Women's Eyes*, Ithaca, N.Y. 1994; *Buddhist Women Across Cultures: Realisations*, Albany, NY 1999; *Swimming Against the Stream: Innovative Women in Buddhism*, London, 2000); and *Sakyadhita: Daughters of the Buddha*, Ithaca, N.Y. 1988.

[17]The talks and teachings from this seminar have been published in two volumes: Thubten Chodron, ed., *Blossoms of the Dharma: Living as a Buddhist Nun*, San Francisco 1999 and BhikshuniWu Yin (trans. by Bhikshuni Jendi Shih, ed. by Bhikshuni Thubten Chodron), *Choosing Simplicity: Commentary on the Bhikshuni Pratimoksha*, Ithaca, N.Y. 2001.

ideals and nuns' social realities has not always been a comfortable process, but this heightened awareness has spurred many to action.

The liberating practices of Buddhism need not be confined to a complacent idealism, but can be applied to everyday social realities. By implementing Buddhism's egalitarian philosophy to help correct social injustices, the Tibetan tradition can not only avoid hypocrisy, it can also forge new directions in the contemporary application of its ancient ideals. For example, the prohibition against women entering shrines dedicated to wrathful protectors (*gönkhang/dgon khang*), rooted in pollution taboos that predate Buddhism, has been lifted in Tibetan refugee society, though it persists in certain monasteries in Bhutan, Ladakh, and Tibet.

The inevitability of change is a pivotal Buddhist teaching that has wide-ranging social implications. It is consistent with Buddhist theory to assert that, because gender roles and gender identities are culturally constructed, they can also be deconstructed. Unfortunately, Buddhist thinkers are sometimes lulled by traditional rhetoric into believing that Buddhist societies are truly egalitarian, when they are not. Arousing Buddhist societies from the slumber of complacency to effective social transformation requires individual Buddhists to act with the courage of their convictions. Social justice demands action. The gender inequities that exist in the religious sphere are only a reflection of the gender inequities that permeate every level of social discourse. The relationship between karma and gender and the effects that this theoretical relationship may have on child-rearing practices, family relationships, domestic violence, and other aspects of social development have yet to be fully explored. It makes sense that research on religion and gender be undertaken by those who are most intimately acquainted with the issues. Based on the advancements that Tibetan nuns in exile have made in the last two decades, it is reasonable to expect that they will continue to develop their unique potential—as women, leaders, religious practitioners, and agents of social change. As nuns gain access to educational opportunities, their achievements naturally erode myths about women's inferiority. Freed from the constraints of these outmoded preconceptions, nuns can get on with the urgent task of preserving Tibetan cultural identity and attaining spiritual liberation.

References

Chodron, Thubten, *Blossoms of the Dharma: Living as a Buddhist Nun*, San Francisco 1999.

Friedman, Lenore, *Meetings with Remarkable Women: Buddhist Teachers in America*, Boston 1987.

Havnevik, Hanna, *Tibetan Buddhist Nuns: History, Cultural Norms and Social Reality*, Oslo 1989.

Li, Yuchen Li, 'Ordination, Legitimation, and Sisterhood,' in: *Innovative Buddhist Women: Swimming Against the Stream*, edited by Karma Lekshe Tsomo, London 2000.

Mackenzie, Vicki, *Cave in the Snow, A Western Woman's Quest for Enlightenment*, New York 1999.

Shaw, Miranda, *Passionate Enlightenment: Women in Tantric Buddhism*, Princeton, N.J. 1994.

Tsomo, Karma Lekshe (ed.), *Buddhism Through American Women's Eyes*, Ithaca, N.Y. 1994.

Tsomo, Karma Lekshe, *Sisters in Solitude: Two Traditions of Buddhist Monastic Ethics for Women*, Albany, N.Y. 1996.

Tsomo, Karma Lekshe (ed.), *Sakyadhita: Daughters of the Buddha*, Ithaca, N.Y 1988.

Tsomo, Karma Lekshe (ed.), *Buddhist Women Across Cultures: Realisations*, Albany, NY 1999.

Tsomo, Karma Lekshe (ed.), *Swimming Against the Stream: Innovative Women in Buddhism*, London 2000.

Willis, Janice D., *Feminine Ground: Essays on Women and Tibet*. Ithaca, N.Y. 1987.

Wurst, Rotraut, *Identität im Exil:Tibetisch-Buddhistische Nonnen und das Netzwerk Sakyadhita*, Berlin 2001.

CHAPTER NINETEEN

The Spread of Tibetan Medicine

JÜRGEN C. ASCHOFF

Introduction and Overview

Tibetan medicine is a science—no question about that! Centuries of medical practice in helping the sick and suffering, clearly defined teacher-student relations, schools for teaching and learning with fixed curricula and structured examinations, hundreds of volumes of codified written material—is evidence of the scientific nature of Tibetan medicine. An internet search today for 'Tibetan Medicine' returns over 20,000 (partially redundant) sites. On the whole, these sites contain well-presented information and introductions to the fundamentals of Tibetan medicine with only a small amount—though it does exist—of random, useless information. But as much as Tibetan medicine is a science within its traditional context, it remains a science outside the system of so-called modern 'evidence based medicine', the only truly universal medical system (often also called Western or allopathic medicine) in the world today.

In order to better understand Tibetan medicine in the context of its history, of its place in Tibet, among the Tibetans in exile in India as well as in the West, I would like to start with ten basic statements.

1. What we understand as 'Tibetan medicine' is only one of several options available to the sick Tibetan. 'Classical' Tibetan medicine derives in great degree from Indian ayurveda. Important medical texts, which remain part of a physician's training, are hundreds of years old. Astrology, which was important for many centuries and has remained so even in more

recent decades, has long since been deleted from the medical student's official curriculum, both in Lhasa and in Dharamsala. Besides this 'classical' Tibetan medicine, there are so-called 'oracles' (close to shamans), and the *onpos* (close to astrologers), both of whom can help in cases of disease. Beyond the shamans and *onpos*, an ill Tibetan can turn to a 'lama as healer,' who will attempt to help or heal by means of prayer, the recitation of a mantra, or even an exorcism.

2. Tibetan medicine is a medical system within Buddhism but it is not 'Buddhist medicine'. The most important medical texts contain only a minor Buddhist admixture and can be taught and practised in complete dissociation from Buddhism. Even though this statement is a generalisation, it corresponds *cum grano salis* with reality.

3. Scientific verification of the efficacy and safety of Tibetan medications, i.e. 'evidence based medicine' with clinical trials that conform to the basic Western standard is practically non-existent. Attempts at scientific evaluation conducted in the last decades have been hampered by methodical shortcomings.

4. Today, the course of training for traditional Tibetan physicians consists of a structured, five to six-year curriculum. This course of study is offered primarily in Lhasa, where the old school of medicine was re-established in 1961, and in nearly identical form in Dharamsala in northern India, where a *Men-Tsee-Khang* (school of medicine) was re-founded in exile, also in 1961, by the Dalai Lama.[1] In addition, there is still the *amchi* system of medicine in Ladakh (though this seems to be

---

[1]There are also smaller, though still rigorous schools of Tibetan medicine in Darjeeling (Trogawa Rinpoche) with nine students (who take their examinations in Dharamsala), as well as the Central Institute of Higher Tibetan Studies in Sarnath, where lay men and women, as well as monks, are trained to be Tibetan physicians in connection with studies in Ayurveda (and therefore officially recognised by the Indian authorities). Another school is located in Bodnath/Kathmandu, currently with eleven students. A training centre in Scotland (Akong Rinpoche) has been closed. In Germany, the German Acupuncture Society (Dr. Maric-Oehler) offers in association with Prof. Pasang Yonten Arya an 'Introduction to (*contd.*)

vanishing as more and more *amchis* apply in Dharamsala for medical education). In the *amchi* system, sons receive instruction in the art from their fathers and must, after an apprenticeship of many years, demonstrate their knowledge in an examination before all the *amchis* of their district. In all of these educational centres, the areas of pharmacology and pharmacy—the gathering, purchase and processing of plant and animal products, together with the manufacture of pills—have been almost completely separated from the training of Tibetan physicians. Today, hardly any Tibetan physician manufactures his medications. Instead, he purchases them from Tibetan pharmaceutical manufacturers and centres.

5. On completion of his studies in Lhasa, the traditional Tibetan physician is legally authorised to practise medicine anywhere in China. The traditional Tibetan physician trained in Lhasa or Dharamsala is, however, prohibited by law in both Europe and America from performing medical procedures in an independent, unsupervised setting. On the other hand, it is permissible for a Tibetan physician in the West to counsel patients on lifestyle and dietary issues, so long as he does not perform specifically 'medical' diagnostic procedures or attempt to treat individual diseases.

6. The sale of Tibetan medicines in the West by either Western or Tibetan physicians obtained from Indian or Chinese manufacturers is prohibited and may result in prosecution. The sale of Tibetan medicine of Indian or Chinese origin through a European pharmacy on the prescription of a Western physician and in small quantities is permitted, provided the Tibetan preparation in question is registered and approved for sale in its

---

(*contd.*)Tibetan Medicine' (six seminars) followed by 'Basic Training in Tibetan Medicine' (14 seminars). While this programme is open exclusively to licensed physicians, the Kailash-Institut in Freiburg/Breisgau offers a course for non-physicians consisting of seminars taught by the Tibetan physician Dr. Namgyal Qusar. While these courses in Germany provide a deeper insight into Tibetan medicine, they cannot replace a course of studies occupying several years.

country of origin. Because of these limitations, the only way to legally distribute large quantities of Tibetan medicine in the West would be to actually manufacture these preparations in the West following registration with the appropriate government agencies.

7. Although I do not have the statistics to support my claim, it is my long-term experience that Tibetans in both Tibet and India, though not compelled by internal or external factors, today entrust themselves to Western scientific medicine in preference to their own traditional healers. On the other hand, Western patients seem positively fascinated with Tibetan medicine and Indian patients often consult Tibetan doctors in Delhi. Similarly, certain kinds of Tibetan medicine, particularly the Tibetan jewel pills, are held in high esteem by the Chinese in China.

8. The enormous demand for Tibetan pills, both in China and for (illegal) distribution in Western countries (several hundred tonnes annually) presents a serious danger to the delicate flora and fauna of the Himalayas. Today, cheaper or more easily accessible substitutes are increasingly being used in place of traditional ingredients in Tibetan preparations. The type and extent of this substitution is unknown, except, of course, to the manufacturers.

9. Tibetan medicines are not homeopathic. They represent an allopathic pharmacological system and some medications include highly toxic plant derivatives. The combination of numerous ingredients (the simplest pills contain about six ingredients, while the complex and complicated jewel pills consist of at least twenty-five, and sometimes as many as a hundred—ingredients) corresponds to the theoretical concepts of Tibetan medicine and assures a gentle therapy supposedly free of side-effects within the framework of a holistic treatment approach. In its present state, Tibetan medicine is not appropriate for emergencies. It knows neither surgery nor obstetrics nor immunisation.

10. There is a real danger that traditional Tibetan medicine will more or less dissolve into Western medicine. Today, many Tibetan physicians have already turned to Western methods of diagnosis. Tibetan medicines are being produced and distributed

for treatment of diseases defined by Western medicine.[2] Tibetan medicine is thus threatened with the loss of its traditional and very individual system of thought.

History and Origins

The origin of all knowledge of healing is the historical Buddha Shakyamuni in his emanation as the Medicine Buddha. On this point all Tibetan physicians agree. Figure 1 depicts along one axis the development of Tibetan medicine down to modern times, while a parallel axis shows the development of Western, so-called evidence based medicine. The documented history of Tibetan medicine begins in Tibet in the first half of the seventh century. At that time, King Songtsen Gampo (*Sroï-btsan sgam-po*) is said to have gathered to his court Indian and Chinese physicians, as well as practitioners from Persia and possibly even a Greek physician named 'Galenus' (or, more probably, someone professing corresponding ideas or knowledge). Under King Thrisong Detsen (*Khri-sroï lde-btsan*) we hear of the first ranslation of Indian medical texts into Tibetan. The foundation

[2]Over the past twenty years, five symposia or congresses have brought together Tibetan physicians and Western scientists and researchers. The first was in Venice in 1983, and was attended by Tibetan and Western practitioners. This was followed in 1996 by a symposium at the University of Ulm (Germany), entitled 'Tibetan Medicine, East meets West—West meets East', and by a larger congress, the 'First International Congress on Tibetan Medicine' in November, 1998 with 1,600 participants in Washington, D.C., which concentrated on psychology, psychotherapy and life-style issues. To start the new millennium, there was the '2000 International Academic Conference on Tibetan Medicine', which took place in Lhasa in July, 2000. This was attended by about 300 Chinese and Tibetan participants, together with about 30 'foreign experts'. The latest conference was held 2003 in Munich bringing together and into discussion Tibetan, Ayurvedic, Yunani and TCM doctors from around the world, to exchange views with representatives from the Western medical system.

of Tibetan medicine was and remains the Indian Ayurvedic system of medicine and not—as is today sometimes claimed by the Chinese—the traditional Chinese medicine (TCM), which makes up at most ten per cent of Tibetan medicine.

The most important Indian Ayurvedic medical text that has been included in the *Tengyur* (the 'Collection of Commentaries') is the *Astangahrdayasamhita,* composed by the seventh-century Indian physician, Vagbhata. Surprisingly, however, the subsequent development of Tibetan medicine has, in fact, been based less on the *Astangahrdayasamhita* than on another text that has not been included in the *Tengyur,* the famous *Gyüshi,* the 'four treatises' or 'tantras'. This work, for which a partially surviving Sanskrit text is known, appears to have been set down in writing by the famous Tibetan physician Yuthog Yontan Gonpo the Younger (*gYu-thog Yon-tan mGon-po,* 1112–1203). Numerous commentaries and sub-commentaries on the *Gyüshi* have subsequently appeared, forming a considerable part of Tibetan medical literature.

A special characteristic of Tibetan culture is represented by the 'lines of tradition', or the paths of transmission of specific knowledge or skills. It is crucial to list the most important persons who have influenced the development of Tibetan medicine down to the twentieth century. Beginning in the eighth century, these include historically documented individuals whose knowledge has been committed to writing in the form of extensive manuals and medical texts that have survived down to the present day. Of these, about ninety per cent exist only in the original Tibetan, only a very small portion having been translated into any Western languages:

- Nagarjuna 'Mahayana'—author of the second century AD (not identical with the 'alchemist' of the same name who lived in the seventh or eighth century).
- Vagbhata (seventh century)—author of the *Astangahrdayasamhita-nama.*
- Chandranandana—fourth generation of the Vagbhata lineage.

- Padmasambhava—the great guru from Uddiyana.[3]
- Vimalamitra.
- Yeshe Tsogyel (eighth century)—the first prominent female figure in Tibetan culture and medicine.
- Yuthog Yontan Gonpo the Elder (708–833)—son of a famous family of physicians.
- Chagdum Namkye Kyebu Melha (eleventh century).
- Yuthog Yontan Gonpo the Younger (1112–1203)—presumed author of the *Gyüshi,* the 'four medical tantras'.
- Dangti Jampal Zangpo (thirteenth century).
- Orgyenpa Rinchenpal (1229–1309)—responsible to a great extent for the development of effect and very special Tibetan medicines which are based on the use of mercury and its 'detoxified' application. He has been long known in India as Rasasiddhi.
- Rangchung Dorje—the third Karmapa (1284–1339).
- Jangdag Namgyal Dagzang (1394–1475)—founder of the Jangpa tradition of medicine (the competing parallel tradition was the Zurkharwa).
- Zurkhar Nyamnyi Dorje (1439–1475)—the most famous physician of the Zurkharwa tradition.
- Rin-chen-rgya-mtsho, 'Brong-rtse Lha-btsun (fourteenth century).
- Gongmen Konchog Deleg (fifteenth century).
- Burtshowa Yonten Gyamtso (born in 1516).
- Digung Rigdzin Chökidagpa (1595–1659).
- Darmo Menrampa Lozang Lhödag.
- Desi Sangye Gyamtso (1653–1705)—founder of the Chakpori 'medical school' in Lhasa, which existed until 1950. He was a powerful and important personality and was responsible for the medicine *thangkas* and important medical texts (see bibliography).

---

[3]Padmasambhava, according to current Western opinion among scientists, should not be considered an historical person but rather a traditional 'figure' uniting numerous ideas of his time in the sense of a 'doxocographic crystallisation'.

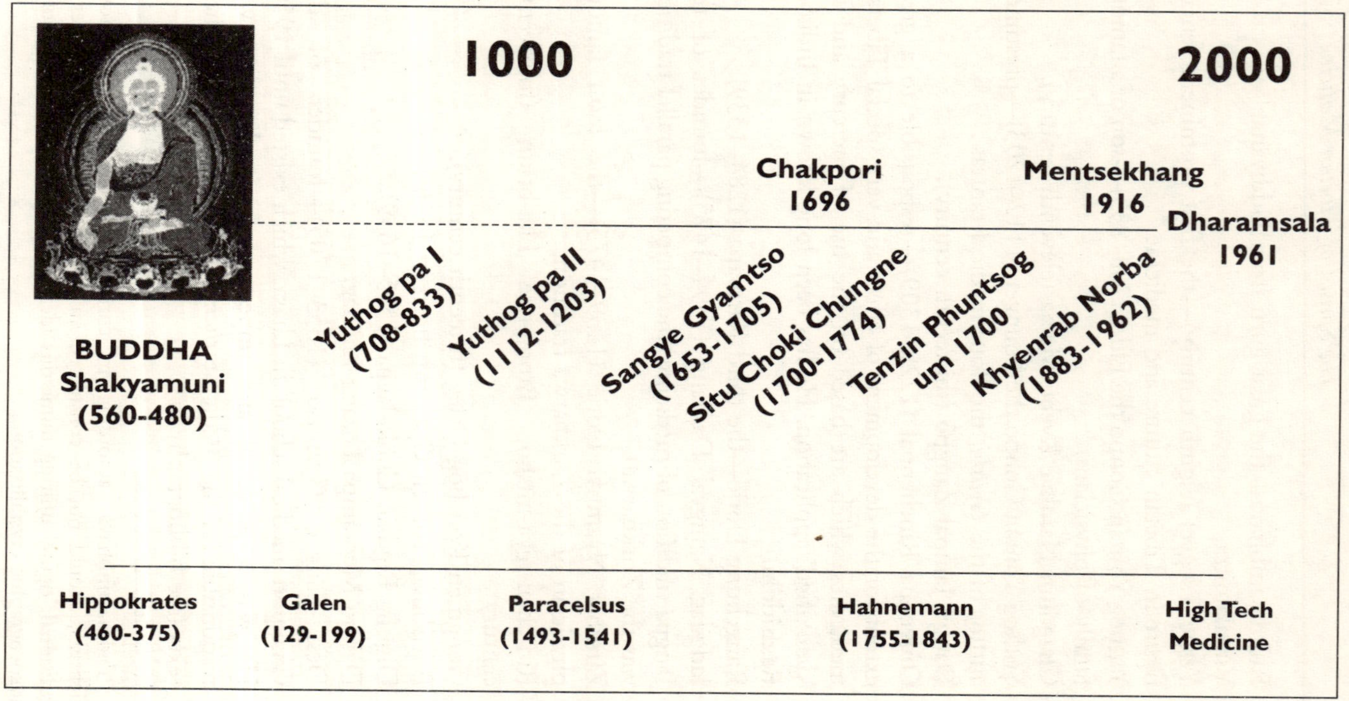
1000
2000
BUDDHA
Shakyamuni
(560-480)
Yuthog pa I
(708-833)
Yuthog pa II
(1112-1203)
Chakpori
1696
Sangye Gyamtso
(1653-1705)
Situ Choki Chungne
(1700-1774)
Tenzin Phuntsog
um 1700
Mentsekhang
1916
Khyenrab Norba
(1883-1962)
Dharamsala
1961
Hippokrates
(460-375)
Galen
(129-199)
Paracelsus
(1493-1541)
Hahnemann
(1755-1843)
High Tech
Medicine

- Situ Chöki Chungne (1700–74)—he composed important medical texts, including one concerning the jewel pills, the *Dngul chu btso bkru.*
- Deumar Tenzin Phuntsog (about 1700)—author of two important, as yet untranslated medical texts, the *Dri med shel gong* and *Dri med shel phreng* [*Principles of Tibetan Pharmacology* and *Materia Medica*].
- Karma-nges-legs-bstan-'dzin, Si-tu Dbon (eighteenth century)—author of famous medical texts.
- Jamyang Khyentse Wangpo (1820–1912).
- Kongtrul Lodöthaye (1813–99).
- Ju Mipham Gyamtso (1846–1912)—a gifted physician and teacher.
- Kyenrab Norbu (1883–1962)—Based on his recommendation, the thirteenth Dalai Lama approved and initiated the foundation of the new Men-Tsee-Khang, an institute for medical training and teaching for both monks and laity in the centre of Lhasa.
- O-rgyan Bstan-'dzin Rgya-mtsho (from Kong-po, nineteenth century).
- Karma Choe-'phel (born in Snye-mo in 1930).

Secondary Literature

An easily accessible introduction to Tibetan medicine is available in the secondary literature that has appeared in German and other European languages. A similar overview appeared as early as 1900 in Heinrich Laufer's *Zur Kenntnis der tibetischen Medizin* (reprinted in Fabri Verlag, Ulm, 1991). An insightful study of the development of Tibetan medical literature can be found in W. A. Unkrig's introduction to Korvin-Krasinski's book, *Die tibetische Medizinphilosophie* (1953). Finally, in the last ten years, numerous Western and a few Tibetan authors have written on various aspects of Tibetan medicine. These include Fernand Meyer, whose *Gso-ba rig-pa—Le système médical tibétain* (Paris, 1981) has also been translated into German as *Einführung in die tibetische Medizin*

(Lüneburg, 1991). Other useful works include Egbert Asshauer's *Heilkunst vom Dach der Welt* (Freiburg i.B., 1993, several editions) or *Gesundheit durch Harmonie—Einführung in die tibetische Medizin* (Munich, 1990 and later editions) by Yeshi Donden, for many years the personal physician of the fourteenth Dalai Lama. For other important publications, see the bibliography at the end of this chapter.

None of the works mentioned above, however, provides so insightful a representation of the conceptions of the Tibetan physician concerning the functions of the body and the equilibrium of these functions as does Cyrill (Johannes) von Korvin-Krasinski in his book, *Die tibetische Medizinphilosophie.* This book is, however, so comprehensive and at the same time complex that only a few will probably read it with pleasure. This gap is filled by Wladimir Badmajeff, a Russian-Polish physician, whose rather brief *Chi Schara Badahan* (reprint: *Lung Tripa Bäkän. Grundzüge der tibetischen Medizin*, Ulm, 1994) outlining the beliefs of the Tibetan physician concerning the holistic viewpoint of body and soul remains valid today.

Tibetan Works on Medicine: Original Texts and Translations

Although only a few Tibetan medical texts have been translated into Western languages, their study affords a much deeper insight into Tibetan medicine than that provided by the secondary literature. It will rapidly become apparent that a great many publications with partial translations and commentaries have centred on the *Gyüshi*, the basic or standard text in Tibetan medicine.

1. The first tantra (*rTza-rGyud)* or root tantra (Sanskrit *Mûla Tantra*) has been translated by Jhampa Kelsang, *The Ambrosia Heart Tantra,* with notes by Yeshi Donden (Dharamsala, 1977). This first tantra makes up the first volume of a complete English translation of the *Gyüshi* in 15 volumes, which was begun by

V.D. Dash in Delhi in 1994. The latest volume to appear is Volume VII, published in spring, 2001.

2. Of the second (*bShad rGyud*) or explanatory tantra (Sanskrit *Akhyata Tantra*) about half has been published as Part II of the *Ambrosia Heart Tantra* (see above).

3. The third tantra (*Man ïag rGyud*) or *Oral Instruction* (Sanskrit *Upadesha Tantra*) consists of 92 chapters of which very little has been translated to date. The chapters on gastroenterological problems (colics, representing essentially chapter 49 of the third tantra) have been translated into Russian by B. D. Badaraev and co-workers (Ulan-Ude, 1976) and from Russian into English by Dr. Stanley Frye (Dharamsala, 1981). Three chapters on Tibetan psychiatry (chapters 77, 78 and 79) have been translated by Terry Clifford (York Beach, 1984), and the chapter on epilepsy has been published in a critical parallel translation by R. E. Emmerick (Groningen, 1987).

4. The fourth tantra (*Phyi-ma rGyud*), the *Notes and Supplements* (Sanskrit *Uttarà Tantra*) has also been partially translated. This includes primarily the texts concerning pulse diagnosis that have been translated into English. For example, Yeshi Donden has translated selections from the first chapter (Dharamsala, 1980), to which R. P. Steiner has added four additional selections on pulse diagnosis (Garden City, 1987–89).

The sheer volume of works concerning the *Gyüshi,* however, shows at the same time that a certain stagnation, expressed in the repeated reaching back to an ancient work, many centuries old, still forms the basis of Tibetan medicine. With the possible exception of Ayurveda, it can be said for essentially all traditional systems of medicine that modern, scientifically oriented development of these systems practically does not occur. Perhaps, such further development may not even be desirable: for example, in the last few decades, such 'further development' for traditional Tibetan medicine (as well as for traditional Chinese medicine) has only been attempted in the form of the blending in of Western medicine without any effort to 'evaluate' the essence of traditional medicine to determine its efficacy. This blending together leads inevitably to a loss of the special, holistic, philosophical nature, which is a very fundamental element of every traditional system of natural healing.

Efficacy and Treatable Diseases

All relevant Tibetan publications claim—and all practising Tibetan doctors refer to their empirical knowledge—that Tibetan medicine offers this or that remedy for this or that disease. It is, however, never described and no effort is ever made to validate whether beyond the time factor—diseases often resolve spontaneously over weeks or months––a given Tibetan medicine exerts either a specific or unspecific (by promoting a cure) salutatory influence beyond a simple placebo effect. One exception is Padma 28. This preparation stems from the Badmajeff family tradition and is taken from the Mongolian-Tibetan treasury of medicines. It is a herbal preparation and has been licensed to the Swiss Padma AG. Its origin in Tibetan medicine cannot be denied but it has been modified in order to comply with European guidelines. Besides the work on Padma 28 a few publications have analysed the prophylaxis of migraines using the jewel pill, Rinchen Jumar 25. This preparation has also been modified in cooperation with Dr Tashigang.[4]

In figure 2, I have attempted to present the structure of Tibetan medicine in a simple diagram. It is based on the three life energies, namely, *lung* (wind, spirit), *tripa* (fire, light) and *bäkän* (water, earth). The equilibrium of these three life energies engenders harmony and health, while disturbance of this equilibrium results in disease. The Tibetan physician works and acts on the basis of questions posed to the patient, pulse diagnosis, inspection of the tongue and urine evaluation to establish the differential diagnosis.

Classical medications used in Tibetan medicine such as the jewel pills, which, besides vegetable and animal products, contain

[4]Published in Aschoff/Rösing, Ulm 1996. See bibliography.

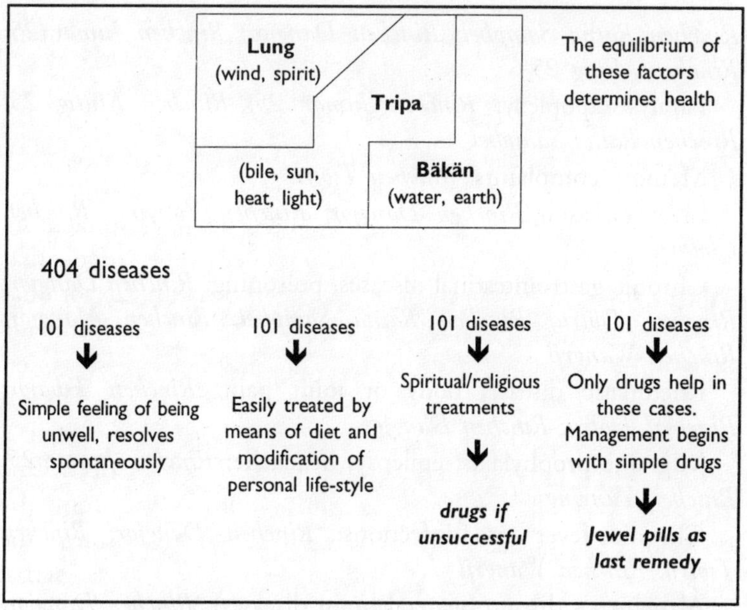

metals, minerals and precious stones, and represent a class of preparations specific and peculiar to Tibetan medicine, are considered to be wonder drugs for the treatment of numerous diseases. Using as an example these most differentiated of all Tibetan preparations, we will show in a very practical light how Tibetan physicians employ the ten jewel pills available today for treatment of specific disease entities recognised in the West and now adopted by Tibetan medicine.[5]

Long, healthy life (i.e. prophylaxis): *Rinchen Dangjor; Rinchen Tsotru*

Strengthening of the immune system (general immunity): *Rinchen Dangjor; Rinchen Ratna Samphel*

Cancer: *Rinchen Ratna Samphel; Rinchen Tshajor*

Altitude sickness: *Rinchen Ratna Samphel*

Psychosomatic/psychiatric diseases (Diseases of civilisation):

[5]Comprehensive information on Tibetan jewel pills can be found in J.C. Aschoff, T.Y. Tashigang: 'Tibetan Precious Pills'; see bibliography.

Rinchen Ratna Samphel; Rinchen Dangjor; Rinchen Jumar 25; Rinchen Mutig 25

Paralysis/apoplexy: *Rinchen Jumar 25; Rinchen Mutig 25; Rinchen Ratna Samphel*

Memory complaints: *Rinchen Tsotru*

Liver diseases: *Rinchen Dangjor; Rinchen Yunying; Rinchen Chakril*

Chronic gastrointestinal diseases, poisoning: *Rinchen Dangjor; Rinchen Tsotru; Rinchen Ratna Samphel; Rinchen Mangjor; Rinchen Wangril*

Rheumatic disease, body or joint pain: *Rinchen Tshajor; Rinchen Tsotru; Rinchen Dangjor*

Migraine prophylaxis, epilepsy, headache: *Rinchen Jumar 25; Rinchen Yunying*

Chronic fever and infections: *Rinchen Dangjor; Rinchen Tsotru; Rinchen Wangril*

Alzheimer's disease (general brain diseases): *Rinchen Dangjor; Rinchen Jumar 25*

All diseases of the eyes: *Rinchen Chakril*

Hypertension: *Rinchen Ratna Samphel; Rinchen Mutig 25*

Food poisoning: *Rinchen Mangjor; Rinchen Chakril; Rinchen Yunying*

Allergies: *Rinchen Dangjor*

Vascular disease, arteriosclerosis: *Padma 28* (not a jewel pill but rather a simpler Tibetan medicine approved and manufactured in Switzerland).

What can we say about this list? First, the target symptoms addressed by Tibetan pill medicine are not those of acute diseases but rather the chronic and long-term disorders of both Asia and the West. These include illnesses belonging to the three main groups of diseases responsible for a great proportion of human suffering, namely gastrointestinal diseases, joint and connective tissue pain and general, unspecified disorders of mood, i.e. psychosomatic disorders in their broadest context. It also shows, however, how difficult it is in the context of such long-term diseases, whose spontaneous natural course is marked by significant fluctuations in severity, to demonstrate true therapeutic success in terms of 'evidence-based medicine'.

Tibetan Medicine in Tibet Today[6]

The following statistics concerning the present state of Tibetan medicine in Tibet and the neighbouring provinces of China were reported during the International Academic Conference on Tibetan Medicine held in Lhasa in July 2000. Traditional Tibetan medicine is practised in 57 hospitals, probably including a number of outpatient clinics. Between 500 and 600 traditional Tibetan physicians work in Tibet and neighbouring regions and about 20 per cent of the population of Tibet utilises traditional medicine exclusively. The official *Catalogue of Medications for Basic National Healthcare* includes 35 preparations drawn from the treasury of traditional Tibetan medicine. In addition, more than 200 Tibetan preparations have been granted a so-called 'trading permit' authorising their sale in China. Based on this permit, foreign importers can obtain these drugs for sale in the West, as, for example, in Germany, where they can be provided on prescription in small quantities to individual, private-pay patients. In response to market demand, about 30 pharmaceutical factories are devoted exclusively to the production of Tibetan medicines, one of which, the Pharmaceutical Factory in Lhasa described below, dumps about 500 tonnes (!) of pills onto the market annually.

The Training of Traditional Tibetan Physicians in Lhasa

The first medical college in Lhasa was founded as early as 1696

[6]Both in Tibet and for Tibetans in exile, hospitals and physicians of the Western type (evidence-based medicine, high-tech biomedicine) are certainly of much greater importance than traditional medicine, particularly in all cases of acute disease, for surgical procedures, trauma, life-threatening conditions, obstetrics and immunisations.

by Sangye Gyamtso (1653–1705), regent of the fifth Dalai Lama, and stood on the Iron Mountain opposite the Potala Palace. Called Chakpori, this famous medical school was an institution similar to a monastery in which Buddhist monks were trained as physicians. Laymen, on the other hand, had practically no chance of being educated there. It was first destroyed at the time of the Chinese invasion and later levelled by the Red Guards during the Cultural Revolution.

To meet the needs of contemporary Tibet, the College for Traditional Tibetan Medicine was founded in Lhasa as a state educational institution in 1989 and offers a six-year curriculum for the training of Tibetan physicians. For the first four years, with the exception of short clerkships, there is practically no contact with patients. Besides anatomy and physiology, as described for hundreds of years in the *Gyüshi* and its commentaries, anatomy in the Western sense is presented by instructors of Western medicine. Prerequisite for admission is the certificate of school completion valid throughout China. Of the 300 or so applicants, 30 students are selected and admitted each year. The students are exclusively drawn from the laity: lamaist monks, who are educated in the monasteries and complete a totally different preliminary education, do not receive a certificate of school completion. The proportion of male to female students is about one-to-one.

The curriculum includes learning by rote of the first, second and fourth tantras of the *Gyüshi* during the first year. The second and third years are occupied by the study of the corresponding commentaries. The third tantra is so complicated and, in long passages, so 'confused', that students are not required to learn it by heart. The fifth year consists of practical courses in both the Men-Tsee-Khang and in a hospital. Following the fifth year of studies and a state examination, the graduate receives the official title of a physician for traditional Tibetan medicine, but is not yet permitted to treat patients unsupervised. The government sends these young physicians to various places throughout the country where they work for two or three years as residents under the supervision of an experienced physician. The best are granted their wish—to practise in Lhasa.

The Men-Tsee-Khang in the Centre of the City

The new clinic in the immediate vicinity of the Jokhang in the centre of the old city of Lhasa is connected directly to the old Men-Tsee-Khang. Its staff sees about 500 ambulatory patients daily. All patients pass through the admitting section and a brief chart containing written data is created for each person. Next to admitting on the ground floor is a pharmacy where patients can purchase the medications prescribed by the physician. While patients pay for their drugs, diagnosis and treatment by the physician is free of charge. The two-storey building is divided into about 20 different departments and treatment rooms. These are closed off by curtains and are accessible to all patients. The patient can also approach the physician of his choice for initial consultation. In the case of older, experienced or renowned physicians, 10 to 20 persons can be seen in the packed rooms. They wait their turn and, as is usually the case in Asia, no one concerns himself with issues of privacy: everyone sees and hears whatever goes on around him.

The Factory for Tibetan Medicines

The Pharmaceutical Factory is located in a suburb of Lhasa. It was founded in 1962 and has been extensively modernised in the last few years. It employs more than 100 technicians and workers who put in a seven-hour day. Saturdays and Sundays are free. The factory produces about 200 preparations using over 500 different ingredients. The factory is an economically independent enterprise supplying all required medications to the Men-Tsee-Khang and to physicians throughout Tibet. It is a successful enterprise, as are the other thirty pharmaceutical manufacturing sites in Tibet.

When you visit Dr. Lobsang Dorje, the vice-director of the factory, in his apartment on the grounds of the factory, he will show you a scientific collection of photographs he took of the plants and raw materials used in traditional Tibetan medicine. Over many years he has very professionally photographed these materials and medicinal plants, including where they grow, their different names and how they are harvested. He has compiled a collection of several hundred photographically documented ingredients. Both the director and vice-director are faced with the same challenge: attracting and training competent successors. The students of the medical college, several of whom I met at the factory, only spend 14 days here for a clerkship. The ones I saw appeared fairly uninterested in the production of medications. They all wish to become physicians, not pharmacists.

Tibetan Medicine in Exile: Practise and Training

The Men-Tsee-Khang was re-opened in Dharamsala in exile, in 1961. Today, it has forty branches, mostly in the Tibetan settlements in India and Nepal, with a foreign centre in Amsterdam. These centres are in great demand, particularly by the Indians and Nepalese. For example, in the Men-Tsee-Khang in Delhi-Nizamuddin, a total of 94,540 patients were seen in the year 1997/1998. This is double the number seen in Dharamsala (42,111 patients). Only 10 per cent of patients are Tibetans. The Men-Tsee-Khang, together with its branch centres, employs 104 physicians, about one-third of whom are women. The treatment, in principle, is free. Patients, able to do so, make donations. Very low prices are charged for medications, but special concessions are made for monks, nuns and students. Treatment by mail is also offered and about 2,000 patients make use of this service annually.

As in Lhasa, the study of Tibetan medicine in Dharamsala requires five years. Graduates receive the title of *sMan-pa-Kachupa.* Every year the school admits 25–30 students selected from several hundred applicants. Astrology can also be studied in a curriculum of the same length, though last year, only seven students matriculated. The department of astrology, which includes eight astrologers (one of whom is a woman), can create horoscopes and produces amulets, calendars etc. Attached to the institute is a pharmaceutical department in which 170 different medications are produced. Some of the ingredients are grown on farms, while, due to concern for the environment and the surrounding Indian population, animal products are being replaced with plant alternatives. Like Ayurvedic drugs, Tibetan medicines are not registered. This prevents their export into countries of the European Union. The physicians, however, travel throughout the world and pass on their knowledge and the treatment methods of this alternative medicine.

Conclusion

We can report that, both in Tibet at the College for Traditional Tibetan Medicine in Lhasa, and at the Men-Tsee-Khang in Dharamsala in northern India, physicians for traditional Tibetan medicine are being trained in a rigorous programme conforming fully to traditional educational guidelines. Outside India and China, however, as is the case with physicians for traditional Chinese medicine, diplomas from these institutions are not considered equivalent to the M.D. degree (completed university/medical school education in Western medicine); hence, traditional Tibetan physicians cannot legally practise medicine in the West.

Tibetan medicine understands the concepts of health and disease less from an organ-based concept than under the holistic aspect, meaning that changes in lifestyle and dietary measures play a predominant role in treatment. Only when these measures are ineffective does the physician prescribe pills. Tibetan medicine certainly represents a science and a cultural treasure that deserves protection. It uses a holistic approach to treat diseases and ailments, first instituting changes in lifestyle and diet, only then turning to medications, which are also gentle and have few adverse effects. Several large groups of diseases of civilisation come into consideration for treatment with Tibetan medicine and may, in fact, be more effectively treated than with

Western high-tech medicine. There has not yet been, however, a full evaluation conforming to the standards of 'evidence-based medicine'.

The greatest danger for Tibetan medicine is its fusion with the Western medical system, which, in an age of globalisation, free media, the internet and exotic tourism, is probably impossible to control. The most important challenge to those in positions of responsibility is to maintain the traditional core of Tibetan medicine and to set the boundaries separating it from Western medicine as a traditional system of healing.

References

Aschoff, Jürgen C., *Annotated Bibliography of Tibetan Medicine*, Kommentierte Bibliographie zur tibetischen Medizin, Dietikon/Ulm 1996.

Aschoff, Jürgen C., Ina Rösing (editors), *Tibetan Medicine 'East meets West, West meets East*, Proceedings of the International Symposium University of Ulm/Germany, 19/20th July 1996. Ulm 1997, 2nd edition 1999.

Aschoff, Jürgen C., T.Y. Tashigang, Jacob Maier, Clinical trial in Migraine Prophylaxis with Jumar 25, in: Aschoff, Jürgen C., Ina Rösing (editors): *Tibetan Medicine 'East meets West, West meets East'*, Proceedings of the International Symposium University of Ulm/ Germany, 19/20th July 1996. Ulm 1997, p. 21–38.

Aschoff, Jürgen C., T.Y. Tashigang, *Tibetan 'Precious Pills: The Rinchen Medicine. A Tantric Healing System with Great Benefits, Some Problems, Many Secrets*, Ithaca N.Y. 2001.

Badmajeff, Wladimir, Lung Tripa Bäkän. Grundzüge der tibetischen Medizin. Neuausgabe der deutschen Übersetzung 'Chi Schara Badahan', mit einer neuen Einführung von Dietrich von Engelhardt. Um ein Vorwort, Inhaltsverzeichnis, einige Anmerkungen und eine Bibliographie zur tibetischen Medizin ergänzt durch den Herausgeber Jürgen C. Aschoff, Ulm 1994.

Choedrak, Tenzin, *Ganzheitlich leben und heilen. Der Leibarzt des Dalai Lama über Vorbeugung und Therapie von Krankheiten.* Mit einer Einführung hg. von Egbert Asshauer, Freiburg i.B./Basel/Wien 1994.

Clifford, Terry, Tibetische Heilkunst. Die Einführung für westliche Leser in eines der ältesten ganzheitlichen Heilsysteme. Mit einem Vorwort des Dalai Lama, München 1986. (Original: *Tibetan Buddhist Medicine and Psychiatry. The Diamond Healing*, York Beach, Maine 1984).

Donden, Yeshi, *Health through Balance. An Introduction to Tibetan Medicine*, Ithaca, N.Y. 1986.

Finckh, Elisabeth, Grundlagen tibetischer Heilkunde. Nach dem Buche Gyüshi. 2 Bände. (Schriftenreihe: Asiatische Heilkunde — Forschung und Praxis) Uelzen 1975 (Band 1)/1985 (Band 2).

Finckh, Elisabeth, *Der tibetische Medizin-Baum*. Texte und Illustrationen, Uelzen 1990.

Jork, Klaus und Gerke, Barbara, Tibetische Heilkunst, in: *Alternativen in der Medizin. Behandlungsformen zwischen Wissenschaft und Empirie*, p. 205-220, Stuttgart 1993.

Korvin-Krasinski, Cyrill von, *Die Tibetische Medizinphilosophie. Der Mensch als Mikrokosmos*. (Mainzer Studien zur Kultur- und Völkerkunde. 1), Zürich 1953. 2nd edition 1964.

Kusar, Namgyal, *Tibetische Medizin und Ernährung* (Original: Namgyal Qusar, *Mèdecine tibétaine et alimentation*), München 1997.

Meyer, Fernand, gSo-ba Rig-pa. *Le système médical tibétain*. Editions du Centre National de la Recherche Scientifique, Paris 1981, reédition 1987, 1988.

Meyer, Fernand, *Eine Einführung in die Tibetische Medizin*. Ursprung und Praxis, in: Dokumentation der besonderen Therapierichtungen und natürlichen Heilweisen in Europa (Hrsg. Zentrum zur Dokumentation für Naturheilverfahren e.V.), Halbband 2: Weitere Medizinsysteme, p. 1043-1052, Lüneburg 1991.

Namkhai Norbu, Entstehen und Leben. *Abhandlung zur tibetischen Medizin*. Aus dem Tibetischen übersetzt von Enrico Dell'Angelo, Arcidosso 1983.

Sangye Gyamtso, *Klassische tibetische Medizin*: Illustrationen der Abhandlung Blauer Beryll von Sangye Gyamtso (1653–1705), [Red. Yuri Parfionovitch … übersetzt und bearbeitet von Thomas Geist…]. 2 Bände, Bern/Stuttgart/Wien 1996.

Schüttler, Günter, *Die letzten tibetischen Orakelpriester. Psychiatrisch-neurologische Aspekte*, (Forschungen zur Ekstase. Monographien und Expeditionsberichte), Wiesbaden 1971.

Taube, Manfred, *Beiträge zur Geschichte der medizinischen Literatur Tibets*, (Monumenta Tibetica Historica. Abt. I: Scriptores. Band 1.), St. Augustin 1981.

Unkrig, Wilhelm Alexander, Von der Heilkunde und den praktischen

Lebensregeln des Lamaismus, chapter 18 in: Wilhelm Filchner, *Kumbun Dschamba Ling. Das Buch der hunderttausend Bilder Maitreyas. Ein Ausschnitt aus Leben und Lehre des heutigen Lamaismus*, pp. 362–375, 519–528, Leipzig 1933.

Vogel, Claus, *Vagbhatas Astangahrdavasamhita*. The first five chapters of its Tibetan version (Abhandlungen für die Kunde des Morgenlandes XXXVII, 2) Wiesbaden 1965.

III

Planning the Return to Tibet

CHAPTER TWENTY

Rebels: The Tibetan Youth Congress

TSETEN NORBU

The Early Days

One of the most positive aspects of life in exile is that education has been made accessible to most young Tibetans.[1] The educated young people have spontaneously introduced new ideas and styles into Tibetan society. And they have founded the youth movement as part of the Tibetan freedom struggle. The birth of the Tibetan Youth Congress (TYC), the Tibetan Communist Party, the Tibetan Youth Association in Europe (TYAE) have led to new patterns of interaction among Tibetans, especially young Tibetans and changed their role perceptions.

In schools, teachers would start their lessons with: 'You students are the future of Tibet' and end with the definition of the DRA (the enemy), NYEN (i.e. Tibetan People) and GON[2] (the saviour i.e. His Holiness the Dalai Lama). When I was a young student in school in the mid-1970s, I attended the sessions and meetings in open meadows on wet ground as a member of the newly founded Tibetan Youth Congress in our settlement in Nepal. And today fortnightly meetings are still held to discuss the aims, objectives and programmes of the Tibetan Youth Congress. TYC members who attend these meetings come from different segments of society, from families of teachers, farmers, staff of the settlement offices and ordinary Tibetans. The meetings are indeed a representative voice of all Tibetans

[1]See chapter 13 for a detailed analysis of the Tibetan schools in exile.
[2]TCV Textbook class 9.

from different walks of life and different parts of the exile community. Regular meetings are followed by different activities in the respective areas either in the form of demonstrations, cultural programmes, sports, etc.

In some settlements in India, youths are engaged in physical exercise including pseudo-military drill and practice with wooden guns in addition to the regular activities. The 'broomstick brigade'[3] of college students in New Delhi, who cleaned the dirty lanes of Majnu-ka-Tilla[4] or the buildings of schools in places like Nainital, Gangtok and Delhi are examples of the wide range of activities of Tibetan youths in those days. And Samdhong Rinpoche's experiments of the Bal Sabha at that time is a legend of a bygone era. When Samdhong Rinpoche[5] was the principal of the Tibetan School at Dalhousie in the late 1960s and early 1970s he created a kind of students' council called the Bal Sabha. This Sabha elected its own executives and engaged in many extracurricular activities including debates. The founding of the Tibetan Youth Association in Europe (Verein Tibeter Jugend in Europa, see chapter 21) has given a new direction to the Tibetan youth in that part of the world.

The founding of the Tibetan Communist Party in the 1970s was a very controversial exercise and prompted numerous angry discussions in all sections of society. The discussion topics usually ranged from why do we need a Gunten Tang (communist party) when we have suffered and fled from the Chinese? to Does this bunch of young Tibetans want to enslave us once more under a new Gunten Tang? and so on. The questions and the apprehensions were genuine but then at that time large parts of the student communities in South Asia were fascinated by Marxist doctrines and most of the youth in this part of the world are still influenced by leftist ideas. How could young Tibetans be an exception while studying in the same

---

[3]See Tibetan Youth Congress Silver Jubilee Book, Dharamsala 1995, p. 54.

[4]Majnu-ka-Tilla is a Tibetan quarter in Delhi.

[5]Samdhong Rinpoche is the author of chapter 24.

environment? As expected the Communist Party of Tibet had an untimely death even though it had some of the most brilliant Tibetans as its members.

The Birth of the Tibetan Youth Congress

The educated Tibetan youth felt the need to use their newly-acquired knowledge for the betterment of the Tibetans and Tibet. To achieve the full synergistic effect of their collective power they felt the need for a new platform from where they could rise and challenge the Chinese might together. This vision was given shape with the formation of the Tibetan Youth Congress in 1970.

Four energetic Tibetans, Tenzin Geyche Tethong, Lodi Gyary, Tenzing Tethong and Sonam Topgey pooled their energies to create a representative youth organisation. They made all efforts to gather delegates from Tibetan settlements in India, Nepal and Bhutan. The Dalai Lama was the guest of honour for the inaugural congregation, and as the final outcome the Tibetan Youth Congress was launched. A total of 315 delegates from 35 different places representing 63 areas took part in this event.[6] The eight-day meeting was attended among others by the *kalons* (ministers) and other high ranking dignitaries besides the Dalai Lama. The birth of the Tibetan Youth Congress on 7 October 1970 was a milestone in shaping the future youth movement.

The goals[7] of the Tibetan Youth Congress are:

a) to work under the leadership of the Dalai Lama for the common good of the government and people of Tibet,
b) to unify the forces without consideration of localities, religion and class,
c) to imbibe the religious precepts and conventional Tibetan good manners amongst youths, considering the richness of the Tibetan culture and carry on its tradition and

[6]Compilation of TYC's GBM and AGM Resolutions, 2000, p. 3.
[7]Ibid., p. 220.

d) to fight for the complete independence of Tibet (sic) as the definitive goal cherished by the Tibetans in as well as outside Tibet even by sacrificing oneself.

Efforts were made to strengthen the organisational structure of the TYC in terms of membership and regional chapters. The branch organisations in each of the settlements and areas are called Regional Working Committees (RWC). And the individual members are enrolled there in their own areas. Individual members as well as the RWC pay annual fees to the Central Executive Committee (Centrex) of the TYC at Dharamsala. The Central Executive Committee and the RWCs collect additional financial resources when needed.

Today the Tibetan Youth Congress has over 15,000 members worldwide, spread over four continents with 73 Regional Chapters. The General Body Meeting (GBM) is the highest policy-making authority of the TYC. It meets once in three years. The participants are the Central Executive Committee (Centrex), the Presidents and the General Secretaries of all the RWCs plus one representative participant for every 50 ordinary members per chapter. The General Body Meeting will deliberate all relevant political questions. This body is empowered with the authority to amend the constitution besides deciding on all important matters or reviewing decisions from time to time. The GBM further decides on the activities for the coming three years. The elections for the Central Executive Committee (Centrex) members are held at the end of every GBM and their terms are fixed for three years. They cannot be re-elected for more than two consecutive terms. The Dalai Lama is always the guest of honour and the sessions are concluded after six days. The next GBM will evaluate the progress on resolutions of the previous one. The annual Working Committee Meeting (WCM) of the TYC is convened on a rotating basis in different Tibetan settlements in India. This offers young Tibetans an opportunity to see the workings of the TYC with their own eyes as they are allowed to attend the meetings as observers in their respective areas. The annual Working Committee Meeting decides on the calendar of activity for that year as well as on other policy matters. Based on the resolutions of the GBM and the WCM, the Central Executive Meeting (Centrex) formulates programmes and activities in line with those resolutions. The Centrex also directs all Regional Committees in their activities and guides them whenever necessary. It oversees the activities of all the chapters in addition to formulating policies at the centre.

The Tibetan Youth Congress steers clear of petty sectarian and regional political pushes and pulls. As a matter of policy, we involve ourselves only in issues that are national in dimension and participate in activities that will have repercussions on our national struggle. Our involvement and activities aim at attaining freedom for the Tibetan people and re-conquering Tibet—our fatherland.

The activities of the TYC within the Tibetan community, in the international arena and our relationship with Tibet have earned us a cherished place in the hearts of Tibetans in and outside Tibet. This kind of support has given us strength and energy to constantly work together with the Tibetan people. The TYC's organisational expansion in the last three decades is a reflection of the people's faith in us. This is accompanied by an increase in its activities and financial spending. Today the TYC plays an active role on national as well as international platforms, raising the issue of Tibet. Its outreach and activities at national and international levels including its connective relationship in Tibet have a positive effect on the Tibetan Freedom Movement itself. Keeping our stand clear and respecting the views of others, we are able to command respect and guide the youth movement giving it momentum and direction. Our regular programmes and actions have given the youth a new sense of responsibility.

Some of the first tasks undertaken were building up the organisation and social work. Our members and Regional Working Committees are now engaged in different activities like demonstrations, campaigns, organisational debates and mass mobilisation in four continents namely Asia, Europe, North America and Australia. All the chapters must carry out the fixed programme of activity in a given time frame, as well as the specific actions demanded by the resolutions of the WCM and GBM. All these activities must be supported by adequate resources that are collected from the Tibetans themselves. Ours is an organisation dependent solely on the Tibetans for both human and financial resources.

Within Tibetan society, we are engaged in encouraging democratic practices among ourselves so that once we return to Tibet, we will be able to galvanise our society towards democracy. The democratic experience of the Tibetans in exile is only a few decades old. It needs to be practised in order to develop mechanisms that can work and govern our society. Only a democracy can offer equal opportunities to all sections of our society for the improvement of their lives. Keeping the Tibetan people informed about the political happenings in and outside Tibet is very important. Appropriate actions and campaigns follow this up.

The Tibetan Youth Congress has been instrumental in founding numerous Tibet-related organisations like the Himalayan Action Committee on Tibet, the Tibetan Women's Association and other Indo-Tibetan organisations. It has played a key role in giving shape to the only existing Tibetan political party—the National Democratic Party of Tibet.[8] The TYC has played a proactive role in democratisation, advocacy and information dissemination. The publication since 1974 of the magazine *Rangzen* (Freedom) spreads information both in English and in Tibetan. The Centrex members visit every corner where Tibetans live. These frequent visits enable us to mingle with the people and receive feedback that will ultimately guide us to formulate correct policies and actions in the coming months. Today when you look at the who's who of the Tibetan Government-in-Exile, many of the *kalons,* secretaries, members of parliament etc. have graduated from the ranks of the TYC. This is another contribution to society.

[8]Tibetan Youth Congress Silver Jubilee Book, supra, p. 24.

We have come a long way since our first major hunger strike programme in the 1970s. This was followed by numerous peace marches, the storming of the Chinese Embassy in New Delhi, signature campaigns, the Boycott Olympics 2000 programme, a hunger strike unto death in New Delhi and Geneva as well as numerous other programmes. Mr. Lobsang Jinpa, the then President of the TYC, visited Tibet as a member of the fact-finding mission in the early eighties. Another President Lhasang Tsering visited Europe at the time when the Dalai Lama announced the 'Strasbourg Proposal' giving our perspective on the issue. Similarly Tsewang Phuntso was in jail at Monte Carlo during the voting of the Boycott Olympics 2000. I myself led the International Union of Socialist Youths (IUSY) delegation to the 55th session of the UN Commission on Human Rights in Geneva in order to raise the issue of Tibet and to lead the hunger strike there. The TYC has participated in numerous national, international and UN sponsored conferences and raised the voice of Tibet at all the appropriate occasions. As member of the IUSY and the World Fellowship of Buddhist Youths (WFBY), we have continuously participated and raised the issues of Tibet at appropriate forums. On many occasions we were able to get resolutions on Tibet adopted.[9]

Youth Organisations in Occupied Tibet

Though I was asked to write about the exiled Tibetan youth in South Asia, it would be unfair on my part to neglect the youth activities in occupied Tibet. The resistance of Tibetans against the Chinese aggression from the early days of the occupation to the 1959 uprising and the heroic challenges throughout the Cultural Revolution to date symbolise the Tibetan freedom struggle. The fight against the Chinese by organised and other methods are an important chapter in the modern history of Tibet. Numerous underground groups have fought the

[9]See IUSY Congress Resolutions, Kathmandu 1996.

oppressors during and after the uprising. Many of those events are recorded and are an inspiration. The 1980s[10] opened a new chapter in the Freedom Struggle when the Tibetans took to the streets of Lhasa and asked the Chinese to leave Tibet. Renewed peaceful demonstrations after 1987 have drawn international attention and focus on the Tibetan issue once again bringing it centrestage. The participation of the Tiger Dragon Youth Organisation of Tibet in the eighties and the Youth Organisation of Tibet today play a key role in moulding the opinion of Tibetans in occupied Tibet and creating awareness on issues and happenings inside Tibet. These organisations have repeatedly called on world leaders and the UN to take up the issue of Tibet in order to find a lasting solution. Petitions were forwarded to the UN Headquarters at New York and the UN Human Rights Commission through foreigners and also through us. It is another matter that this has fallen on deaf ears. The active resistance of the Tibetans in Tibet has challenged the Tibetans in exile to be more proactive in this part of the world.

I still remember vividly how a Tibetan *tangyon* (a high-ranking official and member of the communist party), during one of my missions to Tibet explained to me that in the 1970's he was eager to be given an assignment at the Tibet-Bhutan border. He wanted to take revenge for the Bhutanese cruelties and inhuman treatment meted out to the Representative at the Tibet Office at Thimpu and to other office bearers. Hot irons were run on the bodies of the then Representative and the news of this cruelty had a terrible effect on the minds of the Tibetans. Another young Tibetan told me that if the Tibetan guerilla movement could have planned a massive incursion exercise during the Cultural Revolution, the Tibetans in Tibet would have been ready to rise against the Chinese. This also indicates the lack of statesmanship, far-sightedness, planning and strategy on our part. At that time we had a huge guerilla

[10]Scientific Buddhist Association, Tibet the Facts, London 1990.

network, we knew that there was famine in most parts of Tibet. And we knew that suppression had crossed all limits. Even when we had the resources, we could not visualise and act on the wishes of Tibetans in Tibet and take the risk that was worth taking. And we should not repeat this mistake again because opportunities will not wait. Either one must be able to seize the opportunity or create one.

Leadership and the Youth

When I look at the history of other people and nations that struggled like us to gain freedom, I find one thing very distressing. Look at India, for example. If one turns the pages of the Indian freedom struggle, one can find numerous leaders besides Gandhi and Nehru who had the vision as well as the courage to sacrifice at the altar of the nation. These leaders have moulded and shaped the Indian freedom struggle and inspired the entire Indian youth. Now have a look at our own freedom struggle and try to find a role model leader. Apart from His Holiness the Dalai Lama, we have to fumble over the next few names of potential leaders. When I say leaders I mean those who can carry all the Tibetans with them, who can be role models and who are listened to by all the Tibetans and still have the potential to be statesmen. I often say we failed to produce leaders except His Holiness the Dalai Lama. This vacuum has discouraged the youths to follow any example. It is time for all the middle level leaders to prove their strength and be an example for the coming generations. The emphasis should be on producing leaders not just bureaucrats.

Youth that May have Failed

Working in the Tibet Office at Kathmandu in the eighties and receiving newly arrived Tibetans from Tibet was exciting. During an informal chat in the evening, I recall one of the refugees telling us how impressed they were with the youth delegation that had visited Tibet. Another added that the youths were well qualified, energetic and appealing. They were all praise for this delegation. They said that these youths would surely guide Tibet into independence. Years later, when some of them revisited Dharamsala, the comments were disheartening. They said that their hopes had been shattered. These exile youths could really have made a difference. But today when they look at the Tibetan Government-in-Exile, only one out of the entire youth delegation is serving in the government.

In fact if one looks at the youths of the sixties and seventies, they had the education, exposure, motivation and training. They were in a position to serve our Fatherland. Yet hardly any one of them could withstand the harsh climate of the Tibetan polity or the dangers of bureaucratisation. And most of them failed to pass the leadership tests that led to universal acceptability. The career-oriented thinking of the youths and sectarian considerations have eaten into society and its structure. The idea of sacrifice is gone and this will continue without a fundamental change in the thinking of the youths. And this change is not forthcoming because there are no footsteps to follow. More than forty years in exile and we still remain a society where leadership flows and stops at Dharamsala.

Youth and the Future

As the saying goes, the youths hold the future. The older generation of leaders was driven by motivation and sacrifice and dedication to His Holiness the Dalai Lama. The new generation is driven in addition by career considerations. And that is a major limitation. A freedom movement has no place for individual considerations.

To produce qualified, capable and selfless leaders for the movement is as much the need of the hour as it is the responsibility of the system to produce them. And lack of it will wear out the whole machinery of the movement. Motivation and sacrifice must not be substituted by career considerations.

Challenges Ahead

From the early days of 1959 to the 60s, the efforts of the Tibetan government were directed toward solving the pressing needs of food, clothing, shelter and hygienic living conditions for the rush of new arrivals. This was followed by the effort to offer free education to all children and youth of school-going age. Therefore, the efforts of the leaders at that time were to offer short-term solutions. In fact it is natural for the leaders of that time to concentrate more on the pressing daily needs of the people. The time has changed. Tibetans have, with the blessings and hard work of the elders, created a better life for themselves. This means they are far better off now in terms of economic, educational and social conditions. And this should make the leaders think about long term solutions to the Tibetan problem and prepare themselves accordingly. While solving daily problems is important, it should not be so energy-draining as to affect the momentum of the struggle itself.

Our leaders should reassess their goals. Now it is time to give more consideration to the long-term strategy for challenging the enemy. This demands competence, integrity, sacrifice and above all statesmanship. A radical change in the functioning of the cabinet and other political cells is critical. If we continue to spend most of our time, energy and resources on the problems of the settlements and the exile community, then we are knowingly or unknowingly neglecting the struggle for the freedom of Tibet. So our slogan should be to challenge and defeat the enemy and stop quarrelling within. The bureaucratic mindset and regional squabbling has been hindering the long-term strategies of the freedom struggle. Most of our leaders have become bureaucrats and all the bureaucrats of the world have the same inbuilt limitations since they are working within the limits of the rules and regulations. Leaders need vision and the courage to take risks when taking difficult decisions. The bureaucratic mindset usually is to think for the coming five or ten years. But Tibet needs leaders who can at least foresee the next fifty years. Generally a leader who has emerged from the masses can acquire vision and will have the confidence to take decisions, even risks. The culture of part-time politics should be discouraged.

Inverse Democracy

The Dalai Lama has blessed us with democratic governance.[11] Whether it is the promulgation of the 'Future Constitution of Tibet', the present 'Charter of the Tibetans-in-Exile' or the recent address regarding the direct election of the Chief *kalon*[12] by the Tibetan people—all are initiatives by the spiritual and temporal leader himself. Have the leaders and the people failed to live up to his expectations? Is it the failure on the part of other functionaries who have a say within the formal system and keep themselves engaged in calculating the result of combinations and permutations?

This is why the Dalai Lama has time and again reminded us and guided us on the path of democracy. We find ourselves in a unique position where we have been endowed with democracy. But the effectiveness of democracy has been dissipated. People fail to cherish its importance. And leaders have metamorphosed into mere bureaucrats. I would like to see it the other way round in a real sense.

A democracy not well fought is not well understood and underserved. Rather it has, in our case, ill served its purpose. Since democracy has been presented to us, the feeling of being accountable to the people is not given too much importance. In a hard-earned democracy, people value it. Here we fail, may be because we have not paid the price.

Need for Political Parties

When you take the vow to become a monk, you need to preserve your celibacy. You can't do away with it as long as you are a

[11]See chapter 7.

[12]Ibid.

monk. A democratic society needs political parties. You cannot have democracy without political parties. Since we do not have political parties our cabinet and our parliamentarians do not have clearly defined pledges to be carried out in the next 5 or 10 years. For example, many of our settlements do not have safe drinking water. In a party system, the parties will pledge in their manifestos that they accomplish drinking water access to all settlements in the next five years. Similarly the manifestos will portray their visions for the next ten, twenty or thirty years. During the next elections, voters will scrutinise the candidates' accomplishments. But in our system, one can seek election to the Assembly for five years and stay there for the entire period without saying a word and still go back to the electorate.

Responsible Tibetans need to think and see beyond the next five years, not about who will become members of parliament and who will be the future *kalons*, but focus on the long-term interest of and the struggle for the future of society. Our system lacks a platform for potential leaders to develop their skills. It also lacks a youth development scheme where the youth movement could play a decisive role in the political process.

The Tibetan system of education produces a large number of high school and college graduates each year. Those who fail to find a place in government service will stray here and there. As per government statistics, only ten per cent of the school graduates will have the opportunity for scholarships.[13] With a youth policy, these young Tibetans could be put under a scheme and be productive. They could be qualified for exile as well as Tibet. If we don't act and aim at Tibet, merely managing the settlements will not lead us to Tibet. It is time to outgrow that limitation and target our enemy. When we think of our enemy we fight in unison. When we think of the exile community, then we engage ourselves in all those regional, sectarian and religious considerations.

---

[13]Planning Council, Integrated Development Plan–II (1995–2000), Central Tibetan Administration, 1994, p. 133.

The Need for Statesmanship

Most of the world's leaders and statesmen are products of difficult times in the history of their respective country. A difficult period offers challenges as well as provides opportunities. Churchill and Nehru, Mandela and Arafat, Gandhi and the Dalai Lama are some of the examples. And today's Tibetans are bestowed with those unique challenges and opportunities. In order to accept the challenges one needs courage, determination and the ability to deal with difficult situations.

The lack of long-term planning, bureaucratic management of politics and part time politics are the major shortcomings in our system. To challenge and defeat our enemy, we need to spend more time and energy to correct these shortcomings. By offering a clear policy direction accompanied by a chain of programmes for the masses, one would lessen the divisive forces within society. The lack of a clear policy direction creates a vacuum in society. This will encourage sectarian, regional, religious and other groups to fill the vacuum. Our past experiences have shown us that those are harmful and unproductive tendencies. We certainly need to learn from past mistakes.

One simple example could illustrate this. During the time of the Tibetan Youth Congress' hunger strike in New Delhi in 1998, Tibetan society was mired by two events that were the talk of the town: a conflict among the people from Kham and the Shungden controversy. When the momentum of the hunger strike picked up from days to weeks to months, all those controversies died a natural death. The talk of the town was 'hunger strike, hunger strike and hunger strike'. Tibetans from all over the world would call my mobile number in order to enquire about the hunger strikers or to congratulate us on the movement, but hardly anyone could continue the conversation. After saying a few words they started to sob and the call stopped there. This hunger strike has in fact roused all the living souls of Tibet leading to the martyrdom of Thupten Ngodup[14] who burnt himself in a flame of freedom.

---

[14]See TYC Statement, 29 April 1998.

Acts of solidarity came from occupied Tibet as well. At least two groups of couriers have given us messages of support from Tibet in person. And one additional message has travelled all the way to Pakistan to London and back to New Delhi. All these acts have shown that Tibetans are ready to rise at every available occasion. I felt at that time that it is the leadership has failed Tibet, not the Tibetan people.

The concept of youth sub-culture is a part of the emergence and growing importance of the large-scale ideational culture in the second half of the last century. It indicates a state somewhere between separation from and integration with the dominant culture of a society. Broadly speaking a youth culture is neither clearly separated from adult conventions nor is it fully with and integrated in the latter.[15]

Researchers on youth cultures document varying styles and patterns of youth behaviour. The most familiar one is alienation and rebelliousness. This has been the focus of research on the contemporary world-wide phenomenon of youth unrest as the consequence of a generation gap. Summing up various findings, David Matza points out three forms of rebelliousness. These are, delinquency, radicalism and bohemianism. All these forms of rebelliousness have a special appeal to young people. Each form of rebelliousness is in some sense a threat to the stability of a system, though each may threaten different aspects of it.

The Tibetan youths of today are born and brought up in a foreign land and there are problems attached to this. They are as much influenced by their inheritance as by the local environment. Juvenile delinquency is not the problem of young Tibetans, though bohemianism may be. However a little more radicalism may even be desirable. And leadership must come from within the Tibetans themselves. Our enemy is in the north and that is where we should direct all our efforts. The West is too far away and being too dependent on the West might render us ineffective. Our future policy-makers should embody all these

[15]Coleman, J., *The Adolescent Society,* Glencoe, Inc. 1961, p. 147.

aspects while formulating and rejuvenating the struggle within the minds and bodies of the Tibetans.

Postscript

Kalsang Phuntsok Godrukpa, President of the Tibetan Youth Congress since 2001 on the policies of the TYC (Interviewed by Dagmar Bernstorff on 28 March 2003)

DAGMAR BERNSTORFF: Mr Phuntsok, how do you see the role of the Tibetan Youth Congress in the political process of the exiled Tibetans?

KALSANG PHUNTSOK: One of the main objectives of the TYC has been a commitment to democracy, a democratic system in the exiled community. From the very beginning, the TYC has been involved seriously and very actively with democratisation and also voiced the necessary changes that are needed. In fact the direct election of the Prime Minister by the Tibetan people was a demand of the TYC a few years ago. It was done very very vociferously and the result we see today, although the credit goes to His Holiness for being very liberal. Even today there are many demands which the TYC has raised. For instance we like to see the election of the Members of Parliament on the basis of the exiled population and not only of the provinces in Tibet. Tibetans are very fond of saying that 'Ah, we are very different from the rest of the world'. That is not necessarily good. It is helpful to have representatives from the provinces and from the religious sects, but it is also very very important to have a real representation of the voters.

D.B.: As far as I know the TYC does not accept the Dalai Lama's middle path of autonomy for Tibet within China. How do you see the future of Tibet?

K.P.: Well, that is very true. His Holiness has made two very striking, important declarations, one is the 'Five-point Peace Plan' in the United States in 1987, the TYC has accepted that, and then the Strasbourg Proposal 1989, where His Holiness said that he is ready to accept a kind of autonomy. The TYC has not accepted this. We made it very clear that our legitimate goal is Independence. Tibet was never part of China, there is no reason why we should give up to-day. That is number one. Number two, the autonomy which His Holiness is seeking with China is a very sincere gesture from his side, but we know that there will not be any reciprocity from the Chinese. China will never have the intention, unless and until there is some big change in the present structure of the Chinese government. If China becomes a democratic system then changes will come. But looking at China today the expectations that the Chinese will give any consideration for the Tibetans are not based on any logic. There is no sincerity. So this is one area where the TYC will never ever come to an agreement. We believe in Independence.

D.B.: But how do you want to achieve Independence? By international pressure?

K.P.: No no, to be very frank, nobody has a solution. But it is a wrong understanding and wrong notion in the minds of the Tibetan people as well as outsiders that achieving independence will be very difficult, a very big task, next to impossible, but seeking autonomy and living within China is something that is easier and feasible. We don't look at it that way. For us it is the other way: Independence is achievable. It is feasible. It could happen any time even without China's serious participation. Even if they don't want it, it might happen. History proved it. Think of Russia, of East-Timor…small nations seem to carry it eventually…but our effort must be there.

D.B.: The Dalai Lama thinks that this struggle for liberating Tibet should be based on non-violence. Do you think that is feasible?

K.P.: That is perfectly feasible.The TYC has not deviated from this principle from the very beginning. But I am unable to get a perfect definition of what is 'violence', what is 'non-violence'. All our policies are based on His Holiness' philosophy, we accept that violence will not serve any purpose, it is not a choice at all.

But where we differ is, for us there can be other options

besides non-violence. We are not saying there is only non-violence, we say violence is something that is not acceptable to the whole world but there can be many combinations. We are not talking about ends and means, we are just talking about justification of actions. In Buddhism lots of things depend on the intention. If the intention is good then the action is not the most important aspect. If you go by Buddhist philosophy you can go to any extreme.

CHAPTER TWENTY-ONE

Between Cultures: Young Tibetans in Europe

WANGPO TETHONG

Late one night, at a recent Tibet event in a chic gallery in Zurich, a well-known Swiss filmmaker asked a young Tibetan about his impressions of Hollywood's films on Tibet. The young man explained that he especially liked Martin Scorsese's movie *Kundan*, and that he imagined Tibet exactly as it was portrayed in the film. Obviously, the Tibetan was too young to know the Tibet of the 1940s and the 1950s from direct experience, but the film had reinforced the way he had pictured his homeland.

What components make up the image Tibetans in the West have of their native country? Is it the credibility and appearance of authenticity achieved by a few artistically-arranged stereotypes? The answers to such a question can open the way to a better understanding of the political concept of Tibet among young Tibetans in exile.

It would be presumptuous to generalise or make final pronouncements of any kind. The 'average Tibetan' does not exist, just as the 'average Swiss' or the average 'European youth' does not exist. The children of the first generation of Tibetan exiles, born in the West in the 1970s or 1980s, were raised in a political environment completely different from the environment in which young Tibetans, who recently immigrated to Europe from India and Tibet, were raised.

A young Tibetan growing up in a Swiss mountain valley has little in common with the young Tibetan who may have made a name for himself or herself in the London fashion scene, or a young Tibetan in Boston who may soon be completing his or her University degree. It would be wrong to see Tibetan youth as a uniform group and completely distinct from their host countries' peer groups. Young Tibetans share the same personal career ambitions as their western counterparts, and all are very much a part of a global youth culture.

Nonetheless, discussions with young Tibetans confirm the fact that they do consider Tibetan culture as one of the most important elements in establishing their identity. At the same time, it is evident that due to a rapidly globalising world, cultural and regional characteristics change their meaning away from a common national identity.

In the case of Tibet, both for outsiders as well as many Tibetans, national or ethno labels have projected a Tibet that has little to do with reality. However, what does exist are the invisible ties of culture and history, and the experiences of Tibet's recent political fate. These are not the results of marketing fads, or dreamlike projections, but a reflection of reality. Even if the willingness to accept the political and cultural legacy of Tibet varies among the Tibetan youths growing up in Europe, it can be assumed that their concept of what that inheritance entails has some commonalities.

Unlike any other immigrant group in Europe, the Tibetans have received and continue to enjoy a lot of goodwill. They are generally thought to be religious, modest, nature-loving, very spiritual, and opposed to violence of any kind. And, they are universally and rightfully recognised as victims of the Chinese invasion of their country. One can say that this has made it easy for young Tibetans to identify with Tibet. But the empathy from the outside world can also take on a very possessive and distorted view of Tibet and the Tibetans, and they are often required to put such exaggerated views in their right perspective with considerable confidence and bluntness.

The main focus of this article is on the state of political consciousness among young Tibetans, and more specifically on how they see themselves. An exhaustive analysis of this issue should be undertaken in the wider context of cultural identity and the impact of external influences that are changing it. This could be a challenging task for future enquiries. At this point, however, the remarks above should suffice to lay the ground for a reflection on the situation of Tibetan youth.

Anyone who has taken part in a demonstration organised by Tibetans in exile knows that the number of young Tibetan participants is always relatively high, and that they are usually engaged, creative and original in the way they express their political goals. When asked about their motivation, they talk eloquently about the current difficult situation in Tibet and their personal obligation to help the people in their homeland.

And if you continued the conversation further and asked them about their political convictions or if you asked them to describe their image of political Tibet, you will get answers that will help your understanding of Tibetan youth.

Among the youth, there generally exists a rather homogeneous picture of Tibet's history that has wide gaps in crucial phases. The territory of political Tibet is usually bigger than it really was at any time during the last 300 years; from Ladakh in the west to Dartsedo in the east, often described in terms of the three provinces of Amdo, Kham, and Ü-Tsang. But if you enquired where the local power centres of the state were located and how they were organised, you would get vague answers. Some young people have only dim recollections of lectures on the Tibetan system that dealt with the unusual linkage between political and religious leadership.

However, on certain aspects of Tibetan history, more precise opinions are expressed. Despite the social backwardness of Tibet in the past, most people will refer to 'the old Tibet' as a happy country. They blame the former Tibetan aristocracy, a group that nowadays enjoys the least social esteem, for the backward conditions that ultimately led to the loss of their homeland. The highest regard is usually reserved for the reincarnated lamas, especially those from their own region. And there is some understanding that the period between the death of a Dalai Lama and the political coming of age of his successor is deemed to be a time of crises by most Tibetans. And lastly, their aim for Tibet is outright *rangzen*, which means independence.

Vague but vivid images of Tibet's past can be found in songs, letters to the editors, and in articles in Tibetan youth magazines, and it would be very enlightening to explore these matters further. The individual Tibetan youth might not be aware that many of these images were born in the fifties and sixties and gave rise to a new Tibetan nationalism. These powerful images from the early years of exile retain their influence and are closely connected to the political ideas promoted in the exile community up to the present day. The political mindset of the young Tibetans can, therefore, only be understood in the context of the history of the Tibetan community in exile.

The phenomenon of Tibetan nationalism is nourished by older traditions as well as newer sources. Its rise can be explained by recent events in Tibetan history and by the example of independence movements in the third world at the beginning of the sixties. To my mind, there are four distinct elements that constitute Tibetan nationalism, elements which did not exist before the Chinese invasion of 1950:

1) The cultural and political differentiation from China, with a strong focus on Tibetan culture and Tibetan Buddhism at its core.
2) The unity and equality of the three regions of Tibet, and the unity among the different religious groups, with the goal to create an egalitarian society in an independent Tibet.
3) The Dalai Lama as a symbol of the Tibetan struggle for freedom,
4) The experiences of the uprising against the Chinese between 1956 and 1959, and the ensuing glorification of the resistance organisation and its leaders.

A number of exile Tibetan organisations in India are more or less devoted to such an agenda. Most of them were founded in the sixties or at the beginning of the seventies, and some, like the Tibetan Youth Congress, have regional branches in Europe.

Among the Tibetan exiles, Tibetan nationalism—and national unity as the central pillar of this ideology—did not generate undivided enthousiasm. The opportunity to take part in political decisions had to be systematically extended to all social classes. Democratisation by participation can be seen as a side effect of the larger political agenda. Members of the former ruling elite viewed with suspicion new groups, or people formerly occupying marginal political power, now gaining importance in exile. At the same time, regional leaders of the Tibetan border areas saw the newborn ideology just as another means to exert dominance over a minority. This movement created numerous conflicts of interests. On the other hand the beneficial effect was that many traditional patterns of political reasoning had to be abandoned.

The formation of a Tibetan national identity, with a clear perception of one's own history, coupled with the development of a specific self-consciousness of an exiled people, had a great impact on the every day life of the Tibetan community in exile. It is obvious that during the first two decades of exile, and in part even today, there existed a certain amount of 'bunker' mentality, and a tendency to tabooise certain issues pertaining to some periods of our history and their political and social questions. The resistance within the Tibetan community to openly deal with a truthful analysis of the Tibetan society before 1959 is understandable, as is the danger to follow a line of reasoning that would be close to the Chinese view and propaganda of traditional Tibet. There was also the great fear that the fragile newly gained unity would be endangered by such openness.

The pressure of living in exile produced a distorted and somewhat idealistic image of our own past among the youth. This is especially noticeable in popular literature and in the performing arts. Young Tibetans were incessantly told that they were not only the future of the Tibetan people, but that they also had to act at every moment as respectable cultural ambassadors of a nation. The line between youth and adulthood became blurred, and so it was possible that a person, actually over thirty years old, could feel that he or she still belonged to the youth. Youth was not defined by age but by the ability to fulfil specific criteria of responsibility.

Separated by oceans and continents, these trends within the Tibetan exiles on the Indian sub-continent did not seize the Tibetans in Europe with the same intensity. This can also be explained by the fact that the Tibetans in Europe and in North America do not live in concentrated groups but are scattered all over. They do not have institutions such as schools and settlements that allow for a real community, and the economic centres they depend on have not been designed exclusively for them.

In the Indian subcontinent the situation is different because the Tibetans have their own micro community systems. These ideas have found expression in the public talks of the Dalai Lama, in schoolbooks and in the way public festivities are celebrated. Some of the public gatherings or celebrations have little in common with authentic Tibetan culture; often it is a strange mixture of a political meeting, a Tibetan ceremony, with elements of popular folk dance performances, in the style popularised by the Chinese army in Tibet in the 1950s. Many of the younger Tibetans who remember little or nothing of Tibet, have adopted these new public political expressions as a substitute for Tibetan cultural life. These concepts mildly influenced the Tibetans in the West.

The most influential forums where the political identity of young Tibetans was formed were the youth organisations. In Europe and especially in Switzerland, where the largest group of Tibetan exiles in Europe live, the most important organisation is the 'Tibetan Youth Association in Europe' (TYAE). In the beginning, the focal points of discussions were about questions of integration, of Tibetan identity, and how to preserve it. Some younger Tibetans still face severe personal problems in dealing with these issues, sometimes even drifting into drug dependency and crime. A group of Tibetan youth, originally taken in by Swiss families and adopted, face substantial problems in preserving their identity. Many of them have lost the Tibetan language and some feel they belong neither to the old nor to the new environment.

Only a few young Tibetans are not involved with the TYAE, which one of the founding members described as follows:

> The biggest Tibetan youth organisation in the West plays an important role as mediator in the interactions of different societies, between a Tibetan defined private sphere and the Swiss public. The youth organisation understands itself to be a self-help organisation. It has to try and foster the national cultural identity of its members through youth oriented political and cultural work. On the other hand, the organisation has to advance the social contact and further the cultural interaction between Swiss and Tibetans through public events.[1]

When the first generation of young Tibetans emerged in Switzerland, a great deal of community responsibility was placed on them, but some members of the older generation found this to be problematic. They did not question the political power that was being entrusted, but rather the competence of a younger generation of Tibetans influenced by their European environment; their competence as cultural interpreters of the past, and as representatives of the Tibetan people to the outside world in explaining their views on Tibet. But worse, in the eyes of many elders, some of the youths were carrying issues and debates that were taking place in the outside world into their community, such as the generational conflict that had shaken the West at the end of the 1960s although, because of innate Tibetan moderateness, in somewhat muted and less intense ways.

In the autumn of 1987, unrest broke out in Tibet. In a review of the events then, *Junges Tibet* reported:

> Uprising in Tibet' declared the title pages of all the big newspapers. For the first time the news on TV showed pictures of violent conflict between Tibetan demonstrators

[1]Gyaltag, Gyaltsen, Uberleben in der schweizerischen Diaspora zwischen Selbstbehauptung und Anpassung, in *Junges Tibet* Nr. 1, 1997.

and Chinese police in Lhasa. The Tibetans in Europe were completely unprepared for those events.[2]

Overwhelmed and euphoric that an uprising against the Chinese overlords had finally begun, the Tibetan youth in Switzerland started a flurry of activities. Never before or after this period were the demonstrations and meetings charged with such emotion and earnestness. In those years there were no problems in motivating people, nor was it difficult to find participants for political happenings. Many youths were highly excited about taking part in demonstrations for the first time. There were small run-ins with the police, and for the first time, the seemingly gentle Tibetans experienced tear gas, ripped clothes, and police dog bites which were accepted as marks of distinction and treated like trophies.

In the 1990s, parallel to the democratisation of the exile community, the youth organisations and their protagonists began to lose their dominant role. This was primarily the result of age; many of the former activists had reached adulthood, withdrawn into private life, or had taken over other functions within the Tibetan community. Second, a conflict of different Tibetan cultures in exile emerged. On one side stood the Tibetans who were largely integrated into a western society and wanted to bring their experiences into the Tibetan world. They had an action-oriented view of politics and were not able to grasp the significance of the changes that had taken place in the course of the democratisation in the larger exile community, mainly on the Indian subcontinent. And on the other side was a growing number of Tibetans who had emigrated from India in the early 1980s, and who, like the majority of the exiles, represented a conservative worldview in which Tibetan nationalism and traditional Tibetan values were key components. The major changes which they had experienced in the mainstream Tibetan community gave them an excuse to see themselves as 'true Tibetans' as opposed to the western-assimilated Tibetans. As a result, a number of western Tibetans, among them many liberal

---

[2]Tethong, Wangpo, Beatles oder Stones, in *Junges Tibet* No. 1, 1995.

and active individuals, grew frustrated and withdrew from public life.

The political developments in Tibet after 1989 required exile Tibetans to respond with a concrete answer to the situation. However, there were hardly any experienced political activists or groups in the community who were able to find a powerful counter strategy to the Chinese policy in Tibet. Much time has been wasted on futile discussions of how the Chinese can be convinced by diplomatic means to come to the negotiation table. Like the rest of the community, the youth also got confused by the debates of the political leaders. Instead of putting the political struggle on a foundation of sober analysis and political principles that are rooted in our historic experience, outdated Indian influenced concepts like *satyagraha* and *ahimsa* were discussed at length with no real consequences. It follows that the gap between spiritual rhetoric and the needs of *realpolitik* is widening.

Where is the Tibetan youth in Europe today? After more than forty years in exile, the original importance of the youth in the community has diminished. Their former role as the political avant-garde and mediator with the outside world has also been reduced.

Today's adult generation is able to master their day to day life without depending on their children. And the young people move in circles that don't necessarily consist of Tibetans. Many young people have severed their ties with the exile Tibetan community and the only contact they have with Tibet is through their parents. In the political arena the situation is similar. There is an air of normalcy with no real sense of crisis any more with regard to Tibet.

The structure of today's Tibetan youth in Europe is more complex than in the 1970s and1980s, because of the influx of new Tibetan families from India. And recently the number of Tibetans emigrating directly from Tibet to Europe has also increased. These people have to overcome the same initial problems their countrymen faced when they first arrived. Among the second generation Tibetans there are many children whose parents work and live as unskilled labourers in factories and occupy the lower ranks of the social hierarchy in the countries where they are settled. A new phenomenon are young people who grew up in sheltered lower middle class homes. Overall, however, the level of education in general has improved. The number of Tibetans with school, college, or even university degrees is moving up, on par with those in their host countries.

Among these, one meets a great number of politically engaged youth, and the number of young women who are in some way involved has visibly increased. It is remarkable that these young people are mostly the children of first generation exiles, and not, as one would expect, Tibetans who recently fled from Tibet. Opinion polls support this theory. For many of the newest arrivals, education and establishing roots in the new society takes priority. If asked about the possibility of returning to Tibet, their answers show traces of frustration and disillusionment. But if one poses the same question to a Tibetan youth, who has grown up in Europe, the answer quite often surprisingly is 'Yes, I can imagine returning to Tibet'.

One can conclude that for a Tibetan exile in Europe, the increasing loss of the Tibetan language or lack of childhood memories of Tibet do not seem to be a barrier towards the formation of a Tibetan consciousness. On the contrary, the fascination with a lost homeland only seems to be increasing. And the images of Tibet that dwell in the minds of the young Tibetans have the tendency to become unimpeachable the more their lives diverge from the real Tibet.

References

Junges Tibet, magazine of the Verein Tibeter Jugend in Europa, discontinued since 1998.

Gyaltag, Gyaltsen, *Die tibetische Familie im Wandel und Spannungsfeld zweier Kulturen*, Rikon, Zurich 1990.

Gyaltsen, Kelsang und Gyaltag, Gyaltsen, *Jugend im Exil*, hg. Verein Tibeter Jugend in Europa (commemorative issue), Zurich 1980.

Tethong, Wangpo, *Der Wandel in der politischen Elite der Tibeter im Exil, Integrations und Desintegrationsprozesse in der politischen Führungsschicht 1950 bis 1979*, opuskula tibetana, Rikon, Zurich 1980.

CHAPTER TWENTY-TWO

Tibet's Future—Options for Self-Governance

EVA HERZER

Despite fifty years of brutal Chinese occupation, the Tibetan people's aspiration for freedom remains strong and very much alive. Although not one state recognises Tibet as a separate country, Tibetans refuse to accept China's rule, which has resulted in the continuing destruction of Tibetan culture, religion, language and an ancient traditional way of life. The passage of time has a way of cementing the status quo in people's minds, and many in the international community believe that the annexation of Tibet is a fait accompli which, given the power imbalance between Tibet and China, is irreversible. Yet, Tibetans, now in their third generation in exile, have not lost hope that they will regain control over their homeland. They take strength from Buddhist philosophy, which teaches that nothing is permanent or static, that everything is in fact impermanent. A look at recent world history certainly seems to confirm this teaching, whether we look to the reunification of Germany, the collapse of the Soviet Union or the recent independence of East Timor, all developments which before their occurrence appeared highly unlikely, if not utopian.

In pressing forward with their struggle, Tibetans are faced with two extremely challenging questions. First, what future political status are Tibetans prepared to accept? This question requires an examination of whether Tibetans will only accept full independence or whether their goals for self-governance can be met through an autonomous arrangement. In case of the latter, as will be discussed below, careful consideration must be given to the substance and form of such an autonomous status. These issues are currently the subject of fervent debates within the exile community and the source of much disagreement. The second question is how Tibetans can achieve their goal in the light of the political realities in China, the political power imbalance between Tibet and China, the status of international law and the current international political climate. This article will attempt to provide a framework for the discussion of these issues, which are of vital importance for the people of Tibet, the survival of their culture and the rule of law in general.

In addressing these questions, it is important to clarify, at the outset, that Tibetans do not come to the international community with only a morally justified claim, begging for mercy. Rather, notwithstanding current political realities, they are entirely within their legal rights to seek independence or any other form of self-governance. This is an important reality because it makes the Tibetans' request for self-governance not only an issue which the international community might want to support out of compassion for the Tibetan people, but one the international community must take on if it wants to support and enforce the rule of international law, rather than the law of force. A brief summary of the Tibetans' legal claim is therefore in order.

From an international legal perspective, Tibetans are entitled to make decisions regarding their political future based on two separate rights, the right to territorial integrity and the right to self-determination.[1] The right to territorial integrity is the right of a sovereign nation to retain control over its territory. In other words, this is what is sometimes referred to as Tibet's historical right or claim. Thus, if Tibet can show that it was sovereign prior to the Chinese invasion, then it is entitled to continued

[1]A detailed discussion and legal authorities can be found in *The Case Concerning Tibet,* written by the International Committee of Lawyers for Tibet, Berkeley, USA, and published by the Tibetan Parliamentary and Policy Research Centre, New Delhi 1998.

and future sovereignty, which means it has the right to decide on its future political, social, cultural and economic status. While Chinese and Tibetan history is intertwined in several significant ways, many scholars, including the International Commission of Jurists, have come to the conclusion that Tibet's historical claim to sovereignty is valid and that Tibet, if it so chooses, is entitled to have its sovereign status restored. Other scholars, many politicians and of course China, disagree with that conclusion. China claims that Tibet became a part of China at the time of the Mongol (thirteenth century) and Manchu (eighteenth century) invasions during which both China and Tibet were, in different ways, under foreign rule or influence. However, common rule by one invader does not legally establish a unification of the invaded countries. If it did, national boundaries all over the world would look quite different today. Most serious scholars of international law agree that Tibet was a sovereign nation, minimally, from 1913 until 1949, when it was invaded by China. This alone is sufficient to conclude that China's military annexation was unlawful and that Tibetans have the right to territorial integrity.[2]

Tibet's second legal pillar is the right to self-determination. This right is separate from Tibet's territorial, or historical claim. In other words, even supposing Tibet was a legitimate part of China in the past, Tibetans today have the right to self-determination. The right to self-determination is anchored in the very first article of the United Nations Charter and is a right which applies to peoples, not individuals. There is no genuine dispute that Tibetans are a people, which under international law is defined as a group of people with a common historical tradition, a racial identity, a shared culture, linguistic unity, religious affinity, a territorial connection and a common economic life. The Tibetan people's right to self-determination has been explicitly recognised by the United Nations General

---

[2]A detailed discussion of the historical claim is beyond the scope of this article but can be found in *The Case of Tibet*, supra note 1, p. 5. See also chapter 2 of this book.

Assembly, in 1961 and 1965, when the UN called on China to respect the Tibetan people's right to self-determination. Tibetans thus stand on firm legal ground when they insist on the exercise of their right to self-determination.[3]

The potential problem with the right to self-determination is that the law is not settled as to the scope of its implementation. When a people wishes to implement its right to self-determination by seeking full independence and a state does not want to give up control over the territory claiming the right to territorial integrity, a tension is created which must be resolved. Some scholars argue that a people who have the right to self-determination may choose any option, including independence or complete secession. Others argue that the right only extends to self-determination within the framework of the state. However, this dichotomy can be resolved by looking at the underlying principles of international law and by balancing the legitimacy of the state's assertion of its territorial integrity claim and the people's request for independence or secession. A careful analysis of the tension between the Tibetan people's right to self-determination, including the right to choose independence, and China's claim to territorial integrity leads to the conclusions that this tension must be resolved in favour of Tibet for several reasons. First, territorial integrity can only be invoked by legitimate governments conducting themselves in compliance with the principles of equal rights and self-determination of peoples.[4] A state's legitimacy derives from satisfaction of its duties to its citizens which include the duty to protect the population, to promote the economic cultural, social and spiritual welfare of the people it governs, to promote respect for human rights and fundamental freedoms and to promote self-determination and equal rights. When a state does not promote these interests but instead represses the people, destroys their culture and economically exploits them, it loses legitimacy

[3]For legal authorities see *The Case of Tibet,* supra note 1 p. 46.

[4]World Conference of Human Rights: The Vienna Declaration and Programme of Action, 1993.

as a government and cannot prevail on its claim of territorial integrity. Second, the tension between Tibet's right to self-determination and China's claim to territorial integrity must also be resolved in favour of Tibet because China, in violation of the norms set forth in Article 21 of the Universal Declaration of Human Rights, deprives the Tibetan people of their right to democratically elect their political representatives. Lastly, the Tibetans' right to self-determination should be enforced as against China's claim to territorial integrity because doing so will advance the fundamental values of the international community by creating a demilitarised buffer zone between China and India, the world's most populous states. Therefore, from a legal point of view, Tibetans must be allowed, by virtue of their right to self-determination, to freely choose their future political status.

There are at least three basic options for Tibet's future political status: Independence, on one end; total integration into the Chinese state, on the other end, or Tibetan self- governance through an autonomous arrangement within the Chinese state ('the Middle Way' approach advocated by the fourteenth Dalai Lama). While some Tibetans in Tibet are occasionally quoted in the Chinese press in favour of Tibet's total integration into the Chinese 'motherland', there appears to be no support for that option among Tibetans who are free to express their wishes without fear of imprisonment or other official reprisals. The option of independence, however, enjoys tremendous support in the Tibetan community. Most Tibetans agree that independence would be the best solution. Independence, however, faces huge obstacles. These obstacles are not legal but political. China is adamantly opposed to Tibetan independence. Tibetans, numbering less than six million do not have the physical power to win an outright confrontation with a nation of over 1.2 billion people. On the international level, China wields considerable power as a member of the UN Security Council and as a potential market for western business. As a result, there is no discussion on Tibetan independence in the halls of the United Nations. That topic is practically taboo among UN officials and diplomats. Tibetans have not been able to convince even a single government to support their quest for independence. At the United Nations most political leaders do not even have the courage to discuss China's human rights record. Interestingly, even those countries who would have everything to gain from Tibetan independence remain silent at best or explicitly recognise China's claim to Tibet. India, for example, which has had longstanding border disputes with China and would greatly benefit from a demilitarised Tibetan buffer state refuses to support an independent Tibet. It fears China's retaliation if India were to support Tibet. Yet, despite these realities, many Tibetans, including the Tibetan Youth Congress, promote independence as the only acceptable solution. They insist on their rights and believe that anything short of independence would irreparably harm the future of Tibet. They distrust any joint arrangement with China, and for good reason, given the violation of the 1951 17-Point Agreement and China's most reprehensible record in Tibet. What has been notably lacking, though, in the independence campaign is a clear strategy or work plan addressing the overwhelming political obstacles to independence. This is not surprising, in light of the political realities, which make Tibetan independence, at least in the foreseeable future, a goal most difficult, if not impossible, to achieve. Nevertheless, many Tibetans feel very strongly that the current barriers to independence do not justify a solution short of independence. Advocates for independence are therefore prepared to wait until conditions in China and in the international community have changed sufficiently to allow for an independent Tibet.

The third option in exercising self-determination is an autonomous arrangement between Tibet and China, or in the Dalai Lama's words, an arrangement for 'genuine self-governance', short of independence. The Dalai Lama first proposed such an arrangement in 1987 in an address to members of the United States Congress.[5] In 1988, he elaborated his

---

[5]*Legal Materials on Tibet*, Second Edition (1997) p. 123, International Committee of Lawyers for Tibet, Berkeley, CA 1997.

proposal for an autonomous arrangement in an address to the European Parliament in Strasbourg, since referred to as the 'Strasbourg Proposal'.[6] He clearly recognises that Tibet is legally entitled to independence, but is prepared to compromise because he feels that time is running out for Tibetans since the deterioration of Tibetan culture, after fifty years of occupation, is progressing at a rapid rate. The Dalai Lama is concerned that waiting for the historical changes, which may be necessary to bring about independence, may take too long and may come too late for the survival of Tibetan culture. He therefore developed a pragmatic approach which addresses some of the current political obstacles. His proposal for autonomy resonates with the late Deng Xiaoping's comments that everything is negotiable except independence. It promotes, the Tibetan leader believes, China's goals for unity and stability, while providing significantly for Tibet's self-rule, and thus preservation of the Tibetan culture, religion, language and way of life. It is also a proposal which has gained substantial support from governments and politicians around the world. Negotiations for autonomy is a demand, which is much easier for governments to support than independence because it promotes peaceful conflict resolution and does not challenge state sovereignty, which governments are very reluctant to do. So far the efforts of the Tibetan Government-in-Exile to garner international support for such negotiations has resulted in resolutions calling for such negotiations, passed by many parliaments, including the US Congress, the Canadian Senate, the Australian Senate, the European Parliament, the German Bundestag, the Parliament of Liechtenstein, the House of Representatives of Belgium, the Chamber of Deputies of Luxembourg and other parliamentarians around the world.[7] The President of the United States, as well as other heads of governments, have discussed the need for

[6] *Legal Materials on Tibet*, note 5 supra p. 127. See appendix at the end of this chapter.

[7] For governmental and non-governmental resolutions in support of Tibet see *Legal Materials on Tibet*, note 5 supra.

negotiations directly with the Chinese leadership. The US administration appointed a special Tibet co-ordinator whose mandate it is to promote such negotiations. While such efforts are very positive signals for Tibet, they have not yet resulted in convincing China to enter into negotiations with the Tibetan Government-in-Exile. Even though there have been some negotiations about beginning negotiation, Chinese preconditions have prevented this. China seeks a statement from the Tibetans that Tibet was never independent and that Taiwan is a part of China. The Tibetan response has been that it is willing not to talk about the past, but not to lie about it. On the issue of Taiwan, the Tibetan leadership believes that this is an issue for the Taiwanese, not the Tibetans to address. The Tibetan Government-in-Exile hopes that increased and more effective international pressure on China will lead to the latter's agreement to enter negotiations without pre-conditions. While international pressure has grown significantly in the past ten years, it has not yet been strong enough. The US and the EU, for example, have expressed their concerns over human rights violations in Tibet and have pressed for negotiations, but have been unwilling to draw political or economic consequences when China failed to agree to negotiations. On the other hand, when US business interests are harmed by copyright violations, the US moves swiftly and effectively toward trade sanctions, and as a result very quickly obtains Chinese cooperation and compliance. Why the difference? Businesses insist on effective state action. They will not accept less. Civil societies around the globe, on the other hand, do not insist on human rights law compliance as a condition for normalised political and economic international relations. The current state of affairs is well-summarised by a quote in the *New York Times* from a US State Department Official in 1999 who, while describing talks between Madeleine Albright and her Chinese counterpart in Beijing, said: 'Human rights was prominent but not dominant.' The challenge for Tibetans thus is to achieve an international political climate in which human rights are dominant, not just prominent. They must convince entrepreneurs and governments that their objectives in China are furthered if China abides by international law and that it is therefore in their best interest to pre-condition cooperation and joint ventures on a solution to the Tibetan issue.

The delay in negotiations, regrettable as it is, may be a blessing in disguise because it allows the Tibetan community the time to thoroughly discuss its options and decide what options are acceptable to the majority of at least the exiled Tibetan community, which is free to express its opinion without fear of reprisals. This is especially important because few topics evoke stronger and more heated reactions in the Tibetan community than that of autonomy. This, of course, is not a surprise given that Tibetans have suffered unspeakable human rights violations and cultural destruction in the so-called Tibet Autonomous Region (TAR), where Tibetans have minimal rights to govern themselves in theory and virtually none in practice. Autonomy, however, can take many different forms and the self-government or autonomy proposed by the Dalai Lama in his 1988 Strasbourg Proposal would provide for Tibetan control over most matters affecting Tibet.

If autonomy can take such different forms, what then is autonomy? Self-government of a people (such as the Tibetans) within the framework of a sovereign state is generally referred to as autonomy.[8] Despite the fact that well over forty autonomous arrangements have been created in the twentieth century, the term 'autonomy' has no generally accepted meaning in international law. This is not surprising, since one autonomous arrangement can be completely different from the next. Autonomy is a vague, if not meaningless concept, unless and until it is defined, on a case by case basis, as a particular distribution of governmental powers between two governments. The government of the people who seek self-government, usually

---

[8]For a detailed discussion of autonomy see *Tibetan Autonomy and Self-Government: Myth or Reality*, a compilation of papers on this subject, published by the Tibetan Parliamentary and Policy Research Centre, New Delhi 2001.

referred to as the autonomous government and the government of the sovereign or larger state, often referred to as the state government. Some of the major governmental powers which must be addressed in the drafting of an autonomous agreement are the power to control cultural affairs, education, the official language, national symbols, health and social services, the economy, taxation, natural resources, environmental policy, transportation, postal and telecommunication systems, law and order, administration of justice, currency and monetary policy, determination of citizenship, foreign policy, defence, passports and visas, customs, border control and immigration, as well as political rights. In deciding whether an autonomous arrangement will meet a particular people's needs, it is necessary to carefully examine the distribution of these governmental powers between the autonomous government and the state government. Depending on this distribution of powers, an autonomous arrangement can provide for actual or virtual independence, as it does in the case of Liechtenstein and Andorra, or virtual subjugation, as it does in the case of the present Tibet Autonomous Region.

The task for Tibetans, therefore, is to examine carefully which governmental powers must be under Tibetan control if an autonomous arrangement is to meet the needs of the Tibetan people. This process of analysis is well on its way. In November 1999, Tibetan ministers, parliamentarians and leaders met in New Delhi with international law experts to discuss the legal and theoretical framework for a possible autonomous arrangement between Tibet and China.[9] The conference was based, in part, on a study conducted by the International Committee of Lawyers for Tibet, which examined 34 autonomous arrangements around the world.[10] It provided the Tibetan leadership with vital information on how governmental powers have been divided,

---

[9]This conference was financially supported by the Friedrich Nauman Foundation.

[10]*Forms of Autonomy*, International Committee of Lawyers for Tibet, Berkeley, CA 1999.

successfully and unsuccessfully, in other currently existing autonomous arrangements. The conference was also attended by exiled Chinese scholars who provided their impressions of the Chinese view of autonomy. A summary of these proceedings and copies of the papers presented are available from the Tibetan Parliamentary Research Centre in New Delhi in the form of a book titled *Tibetan Autonomy and Self-Government: Myth or Reality*. This conference led to further explorations within the Tibetan Government-in-Exile which is now preparing itself for negotiations with China. In September of 2000, the International Committee of Lawyers for Tibet and the Tibetan Parliamentary Research Centre held two three-day workshops for Tibetan teachers and settlement officers from India and Nepal on the issue of autonomy with the aim of empowering participants to hold autonomy workshops in their respective communities throughout India and Nepal. These workshops were intended to support the democratic process within the Tibetan community by encouraging a well informed discussion at the community level on the various forms of possible autonomous arrangements.

What forms then could an autonomous arrangement between Tibet and China take? An answer to this question requires both an examination of what governmental powers Tibetans need to control in order to secure their most important interests and what legal structure the arrangement would take. As to the first issue, the Dalai Lama stated his goal when he announced his 1988 Strasbourg Proposal, which seeks a Tibetan government, which 'will have the right to decide on all affairs relating to Tibet and Tibetans', except for certain aspects of foreign policy and defence.[11] Whether this goal is achievable, and whether this should mean that Tibetans would exercise all governmental powers which directly affect them, is subject to debate upon closer examination. In analysing the ramifications of various distributions of governmental powers it may be helpful to

[11]See also the Interview with the Dalai Lama in chapter 6.

Tibetans to examine how other peoples' autonomous arrangements have dealt with these issues.[12] Yet, it is important to note that autonomous arrangements do not lend themselves to being copied wholesale because the interests and needs of each situation are different and must be addressed accordingly. It is therefore necessary that Tibetans carefully analyse the potential consequences of the allocation of each and every governmental power. While a thorough analysis is beyond the scope of this article, some of the issues, which Tibetans must decide, and their treatment in other autonomous arrangements, are discussed below.

There is little debate over some governmental powers, such as the power over cultural affairs. Cultural preservation lies at the foundation of almost every struggle for self-determination. The power over cultural affairs is the only governmental function over which each and every autonomous government examined in the study conducted by the International Committee of Lawyers for Tibet ('the study') has control. In some cases, however, such as the present Tibet Autonomous Region (TAR) and Xinjiang Uighur Autonomous Region, this control is a matter of right, but not of practice, because all governmental matters are ultimately in the hands of the Communist Party and thus the central government of the Peoples Republic of China. The case of Tibet is one of the starkest examples of the disastrous consequences when a people lose control over matters affecting their own culture. There is little doubt that Tibetans would not consent to an autonomous arrangement, unless it provided for Tibetan control over all matters affecting the Tibetan culture.

Another area of utmost importance for the preservation of a culture and a people's identity is control over education. Most autonomous governments insist on controlling education in order to guarantee survival of their people's cultural identity and

[12]See Forms of Autonomy, note 10 supra, for a detailed discussion of the distribution of governmental powers in 34 selected autonomous arrangements. Detailed information regarding all autonomous arrangements discussed in this article can be found in that publication.

of their native language. For example, the Swedish speaking Aland Islands, an autonomous province of Finland under the 1991 Act of Autonomy for Aland, administer their own schools, where instruction is in Swedish, with English as a second language. Finish is offered as an optional language. Several examples underscore the importance of providing sufficient second language instruction, especially in remote regions, so as to open post-secondary school educational opportunities to students. In Micronesia, an associated state of the United States under the 1982 Compact of Free Association, education is within the exclusive jurisdiction of the autonomous government. Students are taught in each of the applicable Micronesian languages and English is required as a second language. Due to the geographical isolation and the low quality of some of the English instruction, many Micronesians graduate without proficiency in English. Because relatively few books are available in the Micronesian languages, educational levels remain low and students are not adequately prepared for a college education, which is only available abroad. Similar considerations may be relevant for Tibet.

Language is a key component of cultural identity and control over the official language is often critical to effective self-governance. In some autonomous arrangements the state's language is the sole official language. In the TAR, for example, the official language is Mandarin, which constitutes an effective barrier to participation in governmental affairs for many Tibetans. In other arrangements, the language of the people is the only official language. This is the case in Kashmir where the official language is Urdu. Similarly in Quebec the official language is French even though the rest of Canada is English speaking. In some cases, such as the Aland Islands, the people's language is the official language, but translation from and into the state's language is available for certain official business. A number of autonomous arrangements provide for several official languages so as to meet the needs of the people and the state. Such arrangements are found in Hong Kong, the Cook Islands, Micronesia, Belgium, Greenland, Scotland, Tatarstan, Catalonia, the Basque Country and Puerto Rico. Strong arguments can be made for and against these various arrangements for an official language and Tibetans will have to prudently examine their ramifications.

Whether social services and healthcare should be solely controlled by the Tibetan autonomous government requires careful consideration. In many autonomous arrangements, health care and social services are provided by the people's autonomous governments. For example, Hong Kong, Liechtenstein, South Tyrol, Kashmir, Tatarstan, Scotland, San Marino, Puerto Rico, the Netherlands Antilles, Basque Country, Catalonia, Andorra and Gibraltar all have exclusive control over these functions. While health care and social services are inherently internal affairs issues, in many cases they are a function of the state, in part, for financial reasons. An unsuccessful example of people's control over health care is found in Zanzibar which has insufficient funds to adequately provide for its population's needs. As a result there have been outbreaks of epidemics due to lack of potable water and inadequate sewage and electrical systems. In Quebec, on the other hand, health care is within the autonomous government's jurisdiction, but Quebec has transferred responsibility for health and social services to the Canadian federal government because the financial burden was too large for the autonomous government. Similarly, the Faroe Islanders have chosen to share that power with the Danish government in order to benefit from its technology and financial resources. For Tibetans, the decision of whether to seek sole or shared control will not be an easy decision because, on the one hand, the delivery of health care and social services has serious cultural consequences and, on the other hand, China currently has superior financial resources which could, but certainly have not to date, substantially benefitted the Tibetans.

One of the most crucial decisions in the creation of any autonomous arrangement involves control over the economy because development of and control of the economy is essential to building a financial base for self-governance. Many autonomous governments have sole or substantial control over their economy. The study shows that there is a high correlation between an autonomous government's degree of economic control and the health of the economy, on one hand, and the level of self-governance exercised by the autonomous government on the other hand. For example, Tatarstan controls its own economy. Its oil reserves and strong military industry positioned Tatarstan to successfully negotiate a bilateral treaty with the Russian Federation, which guarantees to Tatarstan substantial powers of self-governance not enjoyed by other members of the Russian Federation. Economic power can also be successfully shared. In Quebec, for example, intra-provincial business is controlled by Quebec, while inter-provincial trade is controlled by the federal government. Lack of a viable economy leads to dependency in many other areas, as demonstrated by the case of the Navajo Nation. The issue of economic control is closely linked to the control over natural resources. This is especially so in an area like Tibet which is very rich in natural resources. Natural resources are the main source of actual or potential wealth for many peoples. By the same token, many states desire full access to these resources and it is often difficult to persuade states that it is in their best interest to allow an autonomous government control over natural resources. However, the economic viability of the autonomous people is generally in the state's best interest. State concerns over potentially unsound management of natural resources can be addressed through joint regulation of natural resources linked to international standards and best practices. The decision over natural resources will be an especially difficult one for Tibet and China. Tibetans, on the one hand, need control over these resources for their future economic well being and they also have strong spiritual beliefs which require protection of certain natural resources. China, on the other hand, has massively exploited Tibetan natural resources and is unlikely to agree to complete Tibetan control, given the prevalence of many vital raw materials and mineral deposits on the 'roof of the world'.

A related issue of great concern to Tibetans is that of control over the environment. Sound environmental policies are essential for a sustainable economy and for all beings within a territory. These policies are therefore of great importance to the autonomous people as well as to the larger state because ecological devastation knows no boundaries. This power can be held by one entity, or it can be shared. Some autonomous arrangements, such as the Interim Agreement for Palestine, provide for adherence to international environmental standards and joint environmental impact assessments. Joint control is therefore not necessarily counterproductive, so long as it is tied to specific international standards. In the case of Tibet, there are strong links between environmental protection and spirituality. While exploitation of certain natural resources may be environmentally sound by international standards, it may be in violation of Tibetan spiritual beliefs when sacred sites are involved. For these reasons and because of China's past and current devastation of many aspects of the Tibetan environment, many Tibetans feel very strongly that an autonomous arrangement must assign the power to control the environment and natural resources to the Tibetan government.

The power to tax is also linked to the control of the economy and government services. Some autonomous governments may levy taxes with respect to matters within their jurisdiction, while states often reserve the powers to tax on matters of state-wide interest. Another related issue is that of power over the monetary system and currency. Most peoples use the currency of the state. However, as with postage stamps, currency may be of symbolic significance. Some peoples have a separate currency which may be used interchangeably, at the same value, with the currency of the state, which controls the monetary policy. This includes the Holy See, Scotland, Liechtenstein, Gibraltar and the people of the Cook and Faroe Islands and the Netherlands Antilles. Hong Kong has its own currency which is independent of the Chinese currency. In today's globalised economy, there is a trend toward elimination of separate currencies, as evidenced by the emergence of the Euro. Tibetans could benefit from a careful economic analysis of the consequences of different decisions affecting taxation and currency.

Also relevant to the economy is the power over transportation. This power can also be of strategic and military importance. State participation in transportation may be beneficial to an autonomous government which lacks necessary financial and technological resources. However, issues of ultimate control over transportation must be considered very carefully because transportation and population influx often go hand in hand, an issue of particular importance for Tibet. Another power of strategic and military significance is that over the postal and telecommunications systems. While most autonomous governments have chosen not to control these systems which are expensive to run, some exceptions exist. Hong Kong, the Cook Islands and the Netherlands Antilles, for example, control their own postal and telecommunications systems. San Marino and Italy share a postal union but San Marino issues its own stamps which are collectors' items due to their small circulation and thus a major source of income. This may be an interesting source of revenue for Tibet to explore.

Control over policing is essential, especially when the relationship between the people and the state has historically been hostile, as is the case in Tibet today. China has granted that right to Hong Kong, which has exclusive jurisdiction over law and order within its territory. Given the high level of police abuse in Tibet today, it is difficult to imagine that Tibetans would accept anything less.

In most autonomous arrangements, ultimate judicial control rests with the state. Only Micronesia, Andorra and Liechtenstein have an independent judiciary of their own with complete jurisdiction over all civil and criminal matters. Some autonomous governments have their own judiciary which is linked in various ways to the state. While Puerto Rico, for example, has its own court system based on Spanish law, rather than the English law on which the US judicial system is built, the US retains some control by allowing final judgments of the Puerto Rican court to be appealed to the US Supreme Court. In Hong Kong, judicial powers are vested in an 'independent' judiciary based on English common law. Hong Kong's judiciary, however, is not truly independent since the decisions of its highest court are reviewable by China's National People's Congress. In some arrangements jurisdiction is divided. For example, the Inuit, under the 1991 Nanavut Land Claim of Canada, have control over the trial and appellate courts, while the Canadian Supreme Court has final appellate jurisdiction. In negotiations for judicial powers consideration must be given to the quality of the judicial system of the state and to the traditional judicial system of the autonomous people. In other words, the legal system's process, its neutrality and its independence from political forces may be of more importance than the issue of who controls it. The Tibetan proposal for an autonomous Tibet foresees a democratically governed Tibet. China's judiciary is highly political and in practice is not independent and will therefore most likely not be compatible with a democratically governed autonomous Tibet.

A very important power is the power to control foreign affairs. Foreign affairs powers can be held exclusively by the autonomous government, by the state or they can be shared. While there is often an assumption that all foreign affairs powers are matters of exclusive state concern, the study shows that foreign affairs powers can be successfully divided and shared. The interests of the state and the autonomous governments can best be met if foreign policy powers are divided in a practical manner, so as to give the state and the autonomous government those foreign policy powers which complement the other governmental powers they hold. Autonomous governments which enjoy a high degree of internal self-governance have a substantial interest in participating in matters of foreign policy which affect their areas of self-governance. By the same token, a state may have little interest in an area of foreign policy that is related to a governmental function within the control of the autonomous government. Thus, for example, where the state has no involvement in the economy of the autonomous people, it may have little interest in the power to enter into trade treaties affecting the autonomous territory. San Marino, Liechtenstein, the Cook Islands, Micronesia, Andorra and Tatarstan, are all economically strong entities and enjoy the highest level of control over foreign policy within the entities studied. Liechtenstein, for example, is a sovereign state, but through an autonomous arrangement has authorised Switzerland to conduct most of its diplomatic affairs. However, it retains ultimate power over its foreign policy. Some autonomous arrangements provide for limited participation of the autonomous government in foreign policy matters. In Hong Kong foreign affairs powers are vested in China. China nonetheless has authorised Hong Kong to conduct certain external affairs on its own in accordance with the Basic Law. Thus, under the name of Hong Kong China, Hong Kong may develop, maintain and conclude relations and agreements with foreign states and international organisations in the areas of trade, shipping, communications, tourism, monetary affairs and culture. Hong Kong is a distinct member of a number of international organisations, including the World Trade Organisation, the International Monetary Fund and the Asia Pacific Economic Co-operation. The Dalai Lama's Strasbourg Proposal would allocate foreign affairs powers similarly. It would grant foreign policy powers to China, except as to those matters which affect Tibetan self-government in the areas of religion, economy, education, culture, tourism, science and sports.

A decision will also have to be made as to who controls customs, borders and immigration of foreign citizens. In the great majority of autonomous arrangements, the state controls, assumes these powers. These powers, though, can be exercised jointly or can be divided between the state and the autonomous government. While Canada, for example, has power over borders and customs on Inuit land, the Inuit may exclude non-Inuits, Canadians and foreigners from entering their territory. Canadian military exercises require Inuit agreement. Special attention must be paid, particularly in the case of Tibet, to internal immigration and to residency requirements because internal immigration can have a profound impact on culture and can lead to cultural destruction.

In virtually all the autonomous arrangements studied the power of defence is within the exclusive jurisdiction of the state. This may not be appropriate for Tibet because Tibetan leaders seek a demilitarised Tibet. In the Dalai Lama's words, they seek to establish a 'sanctuary of peace', which would provide a buffer zone between the world's two most populous nations, China and India. The spiritual and temporal leader proposed a regional peace conference to set up such a sanctuary of peace and in the interim proposed a partial demilitarisation.

As can be seen from the diversity of power sharing agreements mentioned above, the division of governmental powers is clearly a very complex matter, which requires careful consideration. It is a process, which is, of course, also very dependent on the power balance between the negotiating parties. It is the first and most important task in shaping an autonomous arrangement. Also very important, however, is the legal form which a potential autonomous arrangement between China and Tibet could take. Two forms favoured by many Tibetans are federation and associated statehood. China is more likely to want an autonomous province status for Tibet. Autonomous provinces are created by the larger state, which authorises a local government to control local affairs subject to the centralised authority of the state. The degree of autonomy in such arrangements can be slight or more substantial, but it always involves considerable state involvement. Such arrangements usually do not allow the autonomous people to terminate their relationship with the state. In an associated state relationship, the autonomous people or smaller entity is linked to a larger state and has substantial self-governance, with little participation by the larger state. Usually either party may dissolve the relationship unilaterally. These arrangements, based on consent and mutual benefit, are often symbiotic. For example, Micronesia is of strategic importance to the US, while its virtually non-existent economy makes the association very attractive to the islanders. An associated state relationship results in virtual or actual sovereignty and it is therefore questionable whether such an arrangement is politically achievable for Tibet.

Another model is that of a federation where two or more parties enter into a constitutional framework with a central or federal government and several provincial governments. Governmental powers are divided between provinces, or component units, and the federal government. Often this division of power is set forth in the federation's constitution. A classic example of a federation is the United States. The success of a federation depends on a number of factors. First and foremost, the federation must be based on the consent and authority of each entity or people involved. Second, in order to avoid overreaching by the stronger governments within the federation, a successful federation requires a supreme constitution which can only be amended, by consensus or majority consent of all constituent units. The constitution must clearly delineate the division of power among the governments within the federation. Lastly, the federation must have an independent supreme court to interpret and enforce the constitution and to decide disputes between the various governments of the federation. A federation would provide China with an excellent and face-saving framework for resolving conflicts on multiple fronts. Tibet, Inner Mongolia, East Turkestan, other ethnic peoples under Chinese rule and the various Han Chinese provinces could all form a federation of co-equal members. A federation could also provide a solution for the longstanding conflict between China and Taiwan. Such a solution would provide for the unity and stability of the region, which China seeks, while enhancing its economic viability and preserving its cultural diversity. Prominent members of the Chinese democracy movement, including those who oppose Tibetan independence because they, like the Chinese government, fear the deterioration of the Chinese state all together, support the creation of such a federation. They see it as a viable vehicle for democracy and national unity. While it is unlikely that China would agree to the creation of such a federation at the present time, it is not unrealistic to expect that such an arrangement could be a future possibility if the democratic forces in China gain the upper hand.

Possibilities for a future Tibet are thus many. However, genuine self-governance for Tibet will not become a reality until either changes take place in China's political landscape or until the international community levies effective pressure on China.

China's economy is very dependent on exports, which makes it vulnerable to effective international pressure. Given the Western business lobbies' insistence that their governments do not alienate China, such international pressure, however, is unlikely to emerge unless civil societies around the world require that their governments and businesses stop working with China until China negotiates a political solution for Tibet. Tibetans must garner support not only in the west, but also from governments in Asia, Africa and South America, many of which are members of a UN voting block known as the group of 77, which routinely supports China's positions. The Tibetan struggle will need to develop the prominence and fervour, which toppled the South African anti-apartheid regime. It is up to each one of us to mobilise our societies and insist that our political representatives and the businesses we support condition their interaction with China on China's willingness to negotiate the implementation of the Tibetans' right to self-determination. Human morality, justice and international law all support the Tibetans' demand for self-determination. Ultimately a victory for the rule of law in Tibet will be a victory for non-violent conflict resolution in general. It will be a much-needed antidote to the rule of force, which has characterised so many recent political conflicts. As state governments and citizens all over the world attempt to find ways to prevent terrorism, it is imperative that those struggling non-violently are more strongly supported than ever. A violent response to terrorism will only feed more violence. What is needed today is effective insistence on successful resolution of political conflicts through peaceful means. The international community could make Tibet a highly visible model for creating peace through self-determination, if it persuaded China to negotiate a mutually acceptable political solution, with the Tibetan people.

References

International Committee of Lawyers for Tibet, *The Case Concerning Tibet*, published by the Tibetan Parliamentary and Policy Research Centre, New Delhi 1998 (also available at www.tibeticlt.org).

International Committee of Lawyers for Tibet: *Legal Materials on Tibet*, Berkeley, CA. 1997 (also available at www.tibeticlt.org).

International Committee of Lawyers for Tibet', *Forms of Autonomy*, Berkeley, CA, 1999.

Tibetan Parliamentary and Policy Research Centre, *Tibetan People's Right of Self-Determination*, New Delhi 1996.

Tibetan Parliamentary and Policy Research Centre, *Tibetan Autonomy and Self-Government: Myth or Reality?* New Delhi 2000.

International Commission of Jurists, *Tibet: Human Rights and the Rule of Law*. Geneva 1997.

Hannum, Hurst, *Autonomy, Sovereignty, and Self-Determination*, University of Pennsylvania Press, Philadelphia, VA. 1996.

UNESCO Centre of Catalonia, *The Implementation of the Right to Self-Determination as a Contribution to Conflict Resolution*, Barcelona 1999.

van Walt van Praag, Michael, *The Status of Tibet—History, Rights, and Prospects in International Law*, Westview Press, Boulder, CO. 1987.

Sisk, Timothy D., *Power Sharing and International Mediation in Ethnic Conflicts*, United States Institute of Peace, Washington, D.C.1996.

Appendix

Address to the Members of the European Parliament

by His Holiness the Dalai Lama

Strasbourg, 15 June 1988

We are living today in a very interdependent world. One nation's problems can no longer be solved by itself. Without a sense of universal responsibility our very survival is in danger. I have, therefore, always believed in the need for better understanding, closer cooperation and greater respect among the various nations of the world. The European Parliament is an inspiring example. Out of the chaos of war, those who were once enemies have, in a single generation, learned to co-exist and to co-operate. I am, therefore, particularly pleased and honored to address this gathering at the European Parliament. As you know, my country—Tibet—is undergoing a very difficult period. The Tibetans—particularly those who live under Chinese occupation yearn for freedom and justice and a self-determined future, so that they are able to fully preserve their unique identity and live in peace with their neighbors.

For over a thousand years we Tibetans have adhered to spiritual and environmental values in order to maintain the delicate balance of life across the high plateau on which we live. Inspired by the Buddha's message of non-violence and compassion and protected by our mountains, we sought to respect every form of life and to abandon war as an instrument of national policy.

Our history, dating back more than two thousand years, has been one of independence. At no time, since the founding of our nation in 127 BC, have we Tibetans conceded our sovereignty to a foreign power. As with all nations, Tibet experienced periods in which our neighbours—Mongol, Manchu, Chinese, British and the Gorkhas of Nepal—sought to establish influence over us. These eras have been brief and the Tibetan people have never accepted them as constituting a loss of our national sovereignty. In fact, there have been occasions when Tibetan rulers conquered vast areas of China and other neighboring states. This, however, does not mean that we Tibetans can lay claim to these territories.

In 1949 the People's Republic of China forcibly invaded Tibet. Since that time, Tibet has endured the darkest period in its history. More than a million of our people have died as a result of the occupation. Thousands of monasteries were reduced to ruins. A generation has grown up deprived of education, economic opportunity and a sense of its own national character. Though the current China leadership has implemented certain reforms, it is also promoting a massive population transfer onto the Tibetan plateau. This policy has already reduced the six million Tibetans to a minority. Speaking for all Tibetans, I must sadly inform you, our tragedy continues.

I have always urged my people not to resort to violence in their efforts to redress their suffering. Yet I believe all people have the moral right to peacefully protest injustice. Unfortunately, the demonstrations in Tibet have been violently suppressed by the Chinese Police and military. I will continue to counsel for non-violence, but unless China forsakes the brutal methods it employs, Tibetans cannot be responsible for a further deterioration in the situation.

Every Tibetan hopes and prays for the full restoration of our nation's independence. Thousands of our people have sacrificed their lives and our whole nation has suffered in this struggle. Even in recent months, Tibetans have bravely sacrificed their lives to achieve this precious goal. On the other hand, the Chinese totally fail to recognise the Tibetan people's aspirations and continue to pursue a policy of brutal suppression. I have thought for a long time on how to achieve a realistic solution to my nation's plight. My Cabinet and I solicited the opinions of many friends and concerned persons. As a result, on September 21, 1987, at the Congressional Human Rights Caucus in Washington, DC, I announced a Five-Point Peace Plan for Tibet. In it I called for the conversion of Tibet into a zone of peace, a sanctuary in which humanity and nature can live together in harmony. I also called for respect for human rights and democratic ideals, environmental protection and a halt to the Chinese population transfer into Tibet.

The fifth point of the Peace Plan called for earnest negotiations between the Tibetans and the Chinese. We have, therefore, taken the initiative to formulate some thoughts which, we hope, may serve as a basis for resolving the issue of Tibet. I would like to take this opportunity to inform the distinguished gathering here of the main points of our thinking. The whole of Tibet known as Cholka-Sum (U-Tsang, Kham and Amdo) should become a self-governing democratic political entity founded on law by agreement of the people for the common good and the protection of themselves and their environment, in association with the People's Republic of China.

The Government of the People's Republic of China could remain responsible for Tibet's foreign policy. The Government of Tibet should, however, develop and maintain relations, through its own Foreign Affairs Bureau, in the fields of religion, commerce, education, culture, tourism, science, sports and other non-political activities. Tibet should join international organisations concerned with such activities.

The Government of Tibet should be founded on a constitution of basic law. The basic law should provide for a democratic system of government entrusted with the task of ensuring economic equality, social justice and protection of the environment. This means that the Government of Tibet will have the right to decide on all affairs relating to Tibet and the Tibetans.

As individual freedom is the real source and potential of any society's development, the Government of Tibet would seek to ensure this freedom by full adherence to the Universal Declaration of Human Rights, including the rights to speech, assembly, and religion. Because religion constitutes the source of Tibet's national identity, and spiritual values lie at the very heart of Tibet's rich culture, it would be the special duty of the Government of Tibet to safeguard and develop its practice.

The Government should be comprised of a popularly elected Chief Executive, a bi-cameral legislative branch, and an independent judicial system. Its seat should be in Lhasa.

The social and economic system of Tibet should be determined in accordance with the wishes of the Tibetan people, bearing in mind especially the need to raise the standard of living of the entire population.

The Government of Tibet would pass strict laws to protect wildlife and plant life. The exploitation of natural resources would be carefully regulated. The manufacture, testing and stockpiling of nuclear weapons and other armaments must be prohibited, as well as the use of nuclear power and other technologies which produce hazardous waste. It would be the Government of Tibet's goal to transform Tibet into our planet's largest natural preserve.

A regional peace conference should be called to ensure that Tibet becomes a genuine sanctuary of peace through demilitarisation. Until such a peace conference can be convened and demilitarisation and neutralisation achieve, China could have the right to maintain a restricted number of military installations in Tibet. These must be solely for defence purposes.

In order to create an atmosphere of trust conducive to fruitful negotiations, the Chinese Government should cease its human rights violations in Tibet and abandon its policy of transferring Chinese to Tibet.

These are the thoughts we have in mind. I am aware that many Tibetans will be disappointed by the moderate stand they represent. Undoubtedly, there will be much discussion in the coming months within our own community, both in Tibet and in exile. This, however, is an essential and invaluable part of any process of change. I believe these thoughts represent the most realistic means by which to re-establish Tibet's separate identity and restore the fundamental rights of the Tibetan people while accommodating China's own interests. I would like to emphasise, however, that whatever the outcome of the negotiations with the Chinese may be, the Tibetan people themselves must be the ultimate deciding authority. Therefore, any proposal will contain a comprehensive procedural plan to ascertain the wishes of the Tibetan people in a nationwide referendum.

I would like to take this opportunity to state that I do not wish to take any active part in the Government of Tibet. Nevertheless, I will continue to work as much as I can for the well-being and happiness of the Tibetan people as long as it is necessary.

We are ready to present a proposal to the Government of the People's Republic of China based on the thoughts I have presented. A negotiating team representing the Tibetan Government has been selected. We are prepared to meet with the Chinese to discuss details of such a proposal aimed at achieving an equitable solution.

We are encouraged by the keen interest being shown in our situation by a growing number of governments and political leaders, including former President Jimmy Carter of the United States. We are also encouraged by the recent changes in China which have brought about a new group of leadership, more pragmatic and liberal.

We urge the Chinese Government and leadership to give serious and substantive consideration to the ideas I have described. Only dialogue and a willingness to look with honesty and clarity at the reality of Tibet can lead to a viable solution. We wish to conduct discussions with the Chinese Government bearing in mind the larger interests of humanity. Our proposal will therefore be made in a spirit of conciliation and we hope that the Chinese will respond accordingly.

My country's unique history and profound spiritual heritage renders it ideally suited for fulfilling the role of a sanctuary of peace at the heart of Asia. Its historic status as a neutral buffer state, contributing to the stability of the entire continent, can be restored. Peace and security for Asia as well as for the world at large can be enhanced. In the future, Tibet need no longer be an occupied land, oppressed by force. unproductive and scarred by suffering. It can become a free haven where humanity and nature live in harmonious balance; a creative model for the resolution of tensions afflicting many areas throughout the world.

The Chinese leadership needs to realise that colonial rule over occupied territories is today anachronistic. A genuine union, or association can only come about voluntarily, when there is satisfactory benefit to all the parties concerned. The European Community is a clear example of this. On the other hand, even one country or community can break into two or more entities when there is a lack of trust or benefit, and when force is used as the principal means of rule.

I would like to end by making a special appeal to the honourable members of the European Parliament and through them to their respective constituencies to extend their support to our efforts. A resolution of the Tibetan problem within the framework that we propose will not only be for the mutual benefit of the Tibetan and Chinese people but will also contribute to regional and global peace and stability. I thank you for providing me the opportunity to share my thoughts with you.

CHAPTER TWENTY-THREE

Support for Tibet Worldwide

ALISON REYNOLDS

> In the struggle for public opinion on the issue of Tibet, our adversary is an organised international anti-China force.
> *Zhao Qizheng, Minister of Information, State Council, People's Republic of China, describing the Tibet Support Movement, June 2000.*

> To be pro-Tibet is not to be anti-China, but rather pro-justice.
> *His Holiness the fourteenth Dalai Lama, 24 October 2002, New Delhi.*

The Tibet support movement consists of a widespread and diverse mix of more than 300 organisations on five continents. With a few notable exceptions, the majority of these were established in the late 1980s, as a response to a period of uprising and crackdown in Tibet which coincided with the country being opened up to foreign tourists. Amongst the exceptions to this is the Tibet Society of the UK, which claims the honour of being the oldest Tibet Support Group and was established in 1959 after the failed Tibetan National Uprising.

A number of individuals who were instrumental in establishing Tibet campaign organisations were present in Lhasa in 1987. These included Robert Barnett who was a founder, along with the Tibetan academic Tsering Shakya, of the Tibet Support Group UK—a former name of the Free Tibet Campaign. John Ackerly, now President of the International Campaign for Tibet and for many years its Director, was also in Lhasa during this period. These individuals witnessed first hand the brutal way in which Tibetan protests and demonstrations were crushed; and a number of individuals organised themselves to gather photographs and documentary evidence which they smuggled out of the country to the media. The Tibetan uprisings of the late 1980s and the experiences of these individuals are well-documented in such books as *Sky Burial* by Blake Kerr, a travelling companion of Ackerly's.

Although many of the so-called Tibet Support Groups (TSGs) are a hybrid of campaigning and relief work, around 150 are solely 'political' campaigning organisations, i.e. their work is dedicated to bringing about a change in the political status of Tibet. The majority of these advocate independence as the primary goal of a process of political change for Tibet.

The TSGs are scattered across the world, but with particular concentrations in India, where the largest Tibetan exile community resides, Western Europe and North America. However, TSGs have also been established in such diverse locations as Central and South America, Eastern Europe and Japan.

These groups strategise and organise to some degree, via an e-mail list-serve through which information and ideas are exchanged and developed, and more recently through the establishment of the International Tibet Support Network (ITSN). ITSN has around 120 member organisations that are represented by the regional election of 24 Steering Committee members. The Steering Committee has two co-chairs, including myself. ITSN aims to develop campaign strategies on priority issues, determined by consensus, and construct action plans, which members can adopt to whatever degree they feel is possible or appropriate, based on their resources and the cultural and national political context in which they operate.

Many TSGs are very small, run by dedicated volunteers, most of whom have been involved in supporting Tibet in some way for fifteen years or more. However, there are now around half a dozen organizations that have one or more full-time members of staff.

The Free Tibet Campaign is one such organisation. Established in 1987, the Free Tibet Campaign stands for the rights of the Tibetan people to decide their own future. It campaigns for an end to the Chinese occupation and for the Tibetans' fundamental human rights to be respected. The Free Tibet Campaign exists to educate the public about the situation in Tibet and put pressure on governments, inter-governmental organisations, such as the UN and, increasingly, corporations for change. Its work is carried out at two levels, on two scales: national and international, public and political. Its activities include public awareness raising events, demonstrations, lobbying, letter-writing and media work.

The Free Tibet Campaign has carried its message and its influence to people all over the world. In June 1997, representatives of the campaign were active in Hong Kong, where they flew the Tibetan flag on the eve of the hand-over, taking the opportunity to highlight the contradiction between Britain's acknowledgement of the passing of the colonial era, and China's continued occupation of Tibet.

In October 1999, in an extraordinary series of events, the Free Tibet Campaign made sure that Tibet was at the top of the public agenda during President Jiang Zemin's State Visit to the UK. The image of a lone protestor attempting to unfurl a Tibetan flag as the Chinese President rode down the Mall with Her Majesty The Queen was splashed across the front pages of almost every newspaper in the country. Simultaneously, public outrage began to build as news emerged that the Metropolitan Police had been apprehending other protestors and confiscating Tibetan flags and placards, despite the fact that supporters of the Chinese President were permitted to retain and wave Chinese flags. The tone adopted by the police towards demonstrators throughout the visit evoked media ire, and the campaign became something of a cause celèbre. Underlying it all was the undeniable sense that the handling of the visit was politically motivated. Jiang Zemin was known to be highly sensitive to protest about Tibet.

In a famous outburst earlier that year, he told the Swiss Parliament that they had 'lost a good friend' when they failed to shield him from demonstrators. Although the Foreign Office and the police denied colluding to protect the President, Chinese officials were seen on television cameras appearing to direct police officers during Jiang's visit to Cambridge, and there was no doubt that police officers had been briefed to recognise, and remove Tibetan flags. A supporter of the Free Tibet Campaign hung a Tibetan flag from his riverfront balcony on the day that Jiang Zemin was due to sail downstream to Greenwich. During the course of the morning, police officers visited the supporter's apartment block and tried to persuade the doorman to give them access to the offending flat so that they could take the flag down. In the months that followed, the Free Tibet Campaign successfully challenged the legality of the Metropolitan Police's handling of demonstrations. In the High Court the following May, the Police admitted that its officer's actions had been unlawful. The Free Tibet Campaign exposed the sensitivity not only of the President to protest, but the fear the British government had of souring relations with China.

One of the most rewarding outcomes of the work of TSGs such as the Free Tibet Campaign has been the early release of a number of Tibetan political prisoners. These include, in 2002, Ngawang Choephel, an exiled Tibetan ethno-musicologist, who had been serving an eighteen-year sentence for 'spying' and 74 year-old Takna Jigme Sangpo, who had spent much of the previous forty years in prison, for such 'crimes' as putting up posters calling for Tibetan independence. In October 2002, a young nun by the name of Ngawang Sangdrol, who had been serving a sentence totalling 21 years, was released after nine years' imprisonment. Ngawang Sangdrol was born into a family of activists. She was first arrested in 1992 for taking part in a small pro-independence demonstration: she was held for nine months, but not sentenced. In 1995 she was sentenced following another demonstration in the Barkhor area of Lhasa. During her time in the Drapchi Prison she continued to be politically active, and her sentence was increased on three other occasions: for recording of Tibetan nationalist songs with 13 other nuns; for not co-operating with a 'patriotic re-education' campaign in the prison, and shouting 'Free Tibet!' when she was made to stand outside in the rain as punishment; and for being perceived as a ring leader when there were major disturbances in the prison in May 1998, despite the fact that the protests were started by political prisoners.

The Free Tibet Campaign and other TSGs, as well as human rights organisations such as Amnesty International, have worked hard to raise the international profile of political prisoners such as Ngawang Sangdrol. Major letter writing campaigns by individual supporters have greatly enhanced these efforts. The effect of this campaigning has been that Chinese leaders, who recognise that there is political capital to be made by releasing high profile prisoners, particularly before important summits with the United States, have identified Tibetans as being at the 'top of the list' for release. Following her release from prison in October 2002, Ngawang Sangdrol remained living under very restrictive conditions in Lhasa, without access to sophisticated medical attention which was required to determine whether she had suffered permanent damage from the numerous beatings and torture that she endured in prison. In March 2003, as a conclusion to a worldwide campaign, Ngawang Sangdrol was permitted to travel to the United States.

But the Free Tibet Campaign does not only work on civil and political rights. The basis for its campaigns being the Universal Declaration for Human Rights, this means that social, economic and cultural rights are also included. Economics are playing an increasingly important role in the future of Tibet. In June 1999,China refocused its strategy on economic development as a means of consolidating political control, and the 'Western Economic Development Plan' was launched. This ambitious plan included the construction of a railway line from Gormo (or Golmud) in Amdo (Qinghai Province) to Lhasa, and the exploitation of natural gas reserves in the Tibetan plateau's Tsaidam Basin. Other aspects of the Plan affect the troubled occupied territory of East Turkestan (Xinjiang)—the homeland of the Turkic speaking Uighur people in the far northwest of China.

Campaigns by TSGs have been effective in highlighting the political motivation behind this strategy, and successful in depriving China of investment capital with which to carry out its ambitious developments. Following action by US campaigners, US$ 7 billion was wiped off the expected revenue from the flotation of shares in the state-owned Chinese energy company PetroChina, which offered 10 per cent of its holding on the New York stock exchange in March 2000. More than one fifth of that share offering was bought by the British Company BP, which became the largest foreign shareholder in PetroChina. In April 2001, the Free Tibet Campaign and its partner TSGs, together with the Sudan Lobby (which was protesting BP's link, through PetroChina's parent company, China National Petroleum Corporation, to human rights abuses in the Sudan) brought a shareholder resolution to BP's Annual General Meeting. Although the resolution was not passed, it received the backing of shares with a market value of Pound Sterling 3.8 billion, greater than BP's investment at the time in the whole of China. Since 2001, BP has become involved in providing solar panels to remote villages in western Tibet.

One of the greatest tests of China's apparent willingness to engage with western governments to improve its human rights record will be the 2008 Olympic Games. In 1994, Free Tibet Campaign was part of a successful effort to prevent the prestigious 2000 Olympic Games being granted to Beijing, on the grounds of China's appalling record on human rights. The campaign was not so successful in 2001, when Beijing was granted the 2008 Games, but many observers regarded this decision as a fait accompli—rumour suggested that the International Olympic Committee (IOC) promised Beijing that the next time it submitted a bid for the Games, it would be granted. As the IOC admitted when it announced Beijing's victory, there was only one issue on the agenda—human rights. François Carrard, the Executive Director of the IOC, famously described the Committee as having taken 'a bet' that the Games would be a force for good in China. Chinese officials representing the Beijing Games promised that there would be complete media freedom in 2008, although this statement was later qualified as referring to the reporting of sports only. Now, almost two years after this statement was made, there has been no progress towards media freedom, and the whereabouts of Chinese individuals who were arrested for protesting against Beijing's bid for the Games, remain unknown.

The relationship between the Tibetan Government-in-Exile and the Tibet campaign groups is often questioned. All non-governmental organisations (NGOs) are, or should be, precisely that—organisations that are independent of all governments. Their role in society is an important one: they exist to promote alternative ideas and to give a voice to those who do not have one. NGOs thrive in democracies; some are very successful in achieving their objectives, others less so. In a dictatorship or one party state, such as China, NGOs may be non-existent or its members persecuted.

Many TSGs work in partnership with organisations that are promoting democracy in China, as there is no doubt that a free China will be to the advantage of Tibet. TSGs should also work hard to ensure that governments, particularly those with bilateral dialogues on human rights with China, advocate building civil society in China, and promote a better understanding of the role of NGOs.

China often blames the Tibetan Government-in-exile for the activities of the TSGs, and also seeks to control the TSGs indirectly by applying pressure on the very Tibetan Government-in-exile. The Chinese Government has so far failed to accept or understand that the Tibetan Government-in-exile does not and cannot dictate the activities of the TSGs nor, since it is building democratic structures in exile, should it wish to.

With the release of political prisoners and more positive signs that China is willing to talk to representatives of the Dalai Lama, there is evidence that the TSGs are becoming increasingly effective and successful, but there is a long way to go. The motivation of those who have chosen to become involved in the Tibet support movement is to alleviate the suffering of the Tibetan people living under Chinese occupation, and until that suffering is a thing of the past, Tibet support groups will not cease in their endeavours.

The views expressed here are not necessarily those of the Free Tibet Campaign.

CHAPTER TWENTY-FOUR

Education for Non-Violence

SAMDHONG RINPOCHE

The twentieth century is considered by many as one of tremendous achievements in the fields of science and technology. Man reached the moon and the revolution in information technology reduced this globe to a 'village'. But, the twentieth century also witnessed two World Wars, declared and undeclared wars, civil strife and terrorism. All over the world, fundamentalisms are growing to the point where no one appears to be safe. The holocaust of Hiroshima and Nagasaki is unforgettable evidence of the horrific scale of the human power of violence, as well as the will to use it.

A small isolated nation called Tibet remained unnoticed by the rest of the world. Its people were absorbed in peaceful and spiritual activities, and did not imitate their neighbours in the pursuit of material growth. But Tibet could not escape being a victim of twentieth century violence when it was forcefully occupied by the Chinese People's Liberation Army in 1951. This occupation resulted in perpetual violence on the Tibetan Plateau upto this day. Initially it went unnoticed by the rest of the world, hidden, as it was, behind the Chinese iron curtain. One third of the people of Tibet were killed or died as a result of that occupation. Tibetans could not themselves remain peaceful either under such provocation and reacted quite violently for a number of years.

His Holiness the fourteenth Dalai Lama's consistent teaching of compassion has ultimately transformed the Tibet Freedom Movement in exile as well as in Tibet into a non-violent movement. In my view, this has not been an easy task, and it is no small achievement to have restrained the Tibetan people from using violence for the last forty years.

Guided by the fourteenth Dalai Lama, the Tibetan leadership now has the vision to establish a non-violent society as soon as Tibet obtains genuine autonomy and the freedom to shape its own affairs. Many intelligent people assume that creating a non-violent society in the postmodern age is just an utopian ideal and cannot be realised in a pragmatic world. Yet others believe that the reason for this false assumption is mental conditioning and indoctrination by a violent lifestyle. If one individual can become non-violent, then many others can too. So why should not a community or society become non-violent if earnest efforts are made? In order to create a non-violent society, the education system, both formal and informal, needs to be oriented towards imparting non-violence as an integral part of instruction

What is Non-violence?

Today, the concept of non-violence can be interpreted in many ways. The word 'non-violence' is used in various contexts—from religion to politics, and from art to economics—but each person has a different understanding of its inherent sense.

The concept of violence is diverse, hence the concept of non-violence is also diverse. People generally take violence to mean a direct and manifest action, such as killing or inflicting injury. But indirect harm like structural exploitation is not taken as violence; therefore the common understanding of non-violence is simply the absence of killing or injury to others. Often non-violence is overly simplified and interpreted as merely non-action or non-reaction. To have a correct understanding of non-violence it is necessary to define violence clearly and comprehensively.

In the Indian tradition, the teaching of compassion and non-violence, or *ahimsa*, stems right from Vedic times, but the ancient Indian concept of non-violence was limited in scope. For example, religious war, elimination of evil forces, self-defence or defence of weaker beings, and a number of other violent acts were justified and sometimes even recommended. The most comprehensive philosophy of non-violence was preached by Gautama Buddha and by Mahavira the founder of the Jain religion. In these traditions no form of violence is justified whether in defence of religion or of the self. The Buddha's teaching of *ahimsa* emphasised the intention and mindset of a person. Mahavira on the other hand, placed greater emphasis on action. He taught the monks to walk on bare feet and cover their nose and mouth with a piece of cloth to protect them from killing even small insects. He tried to teach the practice of *ahimsa* to the greatest extent that was humanly possible.

However, in ancient and medieval times, non-violence was largely confined to the individual—in the practice of religion and spirituality. No one had ever thought of or preached the applicability of total non-violence in social, political, and state affairs before Mohandas Karamchand Gandhi. Even during his lifetime there were slight differences between modern western pacifism and Gandhian *satyagraha.*

Gene Sharp, in his *Gandhi as Political Strategist,* classifies the various kinds of principled non-violence into six major types:

1. Non-resistance
2. Active reconciliation
3. Moral resistance
4. Selective non-violence
5. *Satyagraha*
6. Non-violent revolution

According to him, these are listed in order of increasing activity; there is no strict separation between these types. Many non-violent activities may not exactly fit into any of them. But this classification system should be viewed simply as a tool to facilitate understanding of the phenomenon, a tool that is neither perfect nor final, but may be useful. A brief definition of each of these types of non-violence follows.

1. Non-resistance

This is largely followed by some of the Christian sects who adhere to the principle of 'resist no evil'. Literally, during times of oppression, they simply hold on to their beliefs and follow them, ignoring evil, and accepting suffering as a part of religious duty.

2. Active reconciliation

This group favours the use of good will and reconciliation not only towards outward action, but also to personal reconciliation and improvement in one's own life before attempting to change others. This method is practiced by the Quakers and similar sects.

3. Moral resistance

This group believes that evil should be resisted, but by non-violent, peaceful and moral means. They emphasise individual moral responsibility, individual refusal to participate in any evil, such as war, slavery etc., and at the same time they encourage the individual to act against evil, by speaking, writing, preaching and non-violent direct action, by education, persuasion, individual examples, etc.

4. Selective non-violence

The believers in selective non-violence would refuse to participate in select violent conflicts. For example, they may refuse to participate in international warfare, but they might choose to use violence in other situations to accomplish certain desired objectives. They do not believe in total non-violence, but in many particular situations they use non-violence as a better means to achieve their desired goal.

5. Satyagraha

Satyagraha is the most perfect form of non-violent resistance. Developed by M.K. Gandhi, it is based on the ancient Indian tradition of non-violence and the more contemporary non-violent civil disobedience movement adopted by David Thoreau and others. The term '*satyagraha*' was coined by Gandhi himself after seeking various suggestions through a newsletter. It literally means 'to insist upon truth'. This principle is applicable to all kinds of actions for one's own spiritual practice, as well as for individual or collective social actions against injustice, exploitation, or unjust domination of any kind. In one's own spiritual practice it means to hold on to truth as understood by oneself, and not to compromise under any circumstances, however difficult and inconvenient it may be. In social action it means to insist upon truth as justice, and refuse to accept or succumb to any kind of injustice committed by anyone, including the State, the law, or individuals, but not to react or revolt by violent means. On the contrary, it means readiness to accept suffering of any kind, punishment, torture, coercion, or pressure, rather then accepting or tolerating injustice. This method is most in consonance with the teachings of the Buddha, and the most perfect way of practicing non-violence in an individual's spiritual life, as well as in social action or national movements.

6. Non-violent revolution

Gene Sharp states that 'non-violent revolution' is the most recent type of principled non-violence. It is still very much a direction of developing thought and action rather than a fixed ideology and programme. 'Non-violent revolutionaries' believe that the major social problems in today's world have their origins at the roots of individual and social life and can therefore be solved only by a basic, or revolutionary change in individuals and society.

Among the believers in this approach there is general recognition of four aspects of a non-violent revolutionary programme: (1) the improvement by individuals of their own lives; (2) gaining the acceptance of such principles as non-violence, equality, cooperation, justice, and freedom as determining values for the society as a whole; (3) building a more egalitarian, decentralised, and liberal social order; and (4) combatting what is regarded as social evils by non-violent action.[1]

This categorisation of six different types of principled non-violent action is quite comprehensive, though not exhaustive.

According to Sharp, this approach has mixed origins and has been developing since 1945 in various parts of the world. It appears to be an ideal practice of non-violence for social change, but in the international scenario it does not seem to have evolved much during the last five decades.

Among these six types of non-violent action, Tibet's commitment to non-violence is most similar to Gandhi's '*satyagraha*'. The most important aspects of non-violent action preached by the Dalai Lama correspond with the essence of Gandhian thought and practice.

In my view, non-violence can be classified into two types: (1) Non-violence as conviction, as religious faith and (2) non-violence to be used strategically as a preferable alternative to violence, but not as an object of faith.

People who engage in the first type of non-violent action do not resort to violence under any circumstance; but those who engage in the second type may resort to violence if they think it is strategically more appropriate. For the people of Tibet, under the spiritual and temporal leadership of the fourteenth Dalai Lama, non-violence is their conviction and the object of their faith. They would never indulge in violence even if doing so would be a more effective strategy to resolve their problems. Hence, they require intensive education and training on how to apply and sustain non-violence.

According to Buddhist teachings, violence means any action or cause of action that (1) derives from negative emotions such as hate, greed, or ignorance; and (2) results directly or indirectly in immediate or subsequent harm to any other living being. Non-violence does not mean simply absence of violence or remaining inactive. Non-violence is the wilful restraint from

[1]Gene Sharp, *Gandhi as Political Strategist*, Boston, 1979, p. 221.

violent action or cause of action and springs from positive emotions such as compassion, kindness, and wisdom. Therefore, the cultivation of a compassionate, non-violent attitude in a person's heart and mind is the key to non-violent action. Such cultivation of attitudes requires lifelong education, training and practice.

Need for a System of Education in Non-violence

In the present civilisation, education is often merely seen as passing information from one to another. Such information can be gathered from various sources, and does not require learning from a human being, from a lineage, or wisdom tradition. The present corpus of modern education, particularly the education in science and technology, does not instill peace and non-violence. Instead, it inculcates powerful ambitions for short-term material gain and creates competition. Such education encourages narrow nationalism, regionalism, and racism; thus humanity is divided on the basis of colour, caste, creed, race, language, religion, nations, and so on, creating unnecessary conflict and hostility. Other major causes of violence include economic disparity and environmental degradation. The scale of violence and destruction has increased to such an unprecedented extent that the very survival of the globe is threatened. So there is ample evidence that the modern educational system has not only totally failed to reduce violence in any form, but has actually helped to increase it. Therefore, a system of education in non-violence needs to be evolved.

What is education?

According to Buddhist teachings, education, (*shiksha*) leans on a holistic approach for total development and transformation of the individual. It is a three-fold process of awakening, which begins from moral and physical discipline or *shila*; concentrated and contemplative training of the mind or *samadhi*; and of wisdom or *pragya*. The stages in this awakening process are to be practised sequentially and also interrelatedly. Opposed to the mere passing on of information, this process awakens the virtues and intelligence of the human mind by eliminating the hindrances and ignorance temporarily created by mental deficiencies which prevent it from perceiving things as they are, with no distortion. Jiddu Krishnamurti's favourite phrase for purposeful education—'flowering in goodness and awakening of intelligence'—is a perfect description of Buddhist education.

In order to bring about this purposeful education, it is necessary to combine sensitivity, intellect and spirituality. That can only happen if the learning acquired from information is processed by one's contemplation and critical examination. Whatever is learned from books, or a teacher, or from any other means, is borrowed knowledge. Until one contemplates upon it, analyses it, and arrives at a realisation from one's own self-examination—whether the content obtained from the information is based on truth or falsehood—it is not reliable knowledge. Realisation from one's own contemplation will not be borrowed knowledge, but a self-realisation that has the authenticity of self-knowledge. After having such a realisation, then concentrated meditation upon it will gradually provide the direct perception of the truth. And that perception brings about a really educated mind, or a mind that evolves through true education, and is not a creation of false propaganda or brain-washing. Such an educated mind will not know the boundaries between the self and others, nor will it make a person violent. Only this kind of education will make it possible to reduce violence and inculcate non-violent behaviour. Unless the entire existing system of education is transformed in a positive way, education in non-violence cannot be imparted.

Subjects of education in non-violence

Non-violence cannot be taught as one of the many subjects in a formal syllabus. Today, many people think that adding another subject and textbooks on topics as moral values, the environment, or non-violence, means education in those subjects. This implies that all other subjects—such as mathematics, social sciences, arts and crafts, literature, and languages—have nothing to do with moral values, the environment, non-violence, and so forth. That is the basic error from which the majority of educators have not been able to extricate themselves. Values and morals are not to be taught as a separate subject. The entire learning process, and whatever is taught as part of formal or informal education, has to be oriented towards morals and ethics, and a holistic teaching and learning system should be part of the transformation of the students' whole being—body, mind, spirit and vision. Therefore, what is important is not the choice of subjects, topics, or textbooks. What is important is the method and orientation of the teaching-learning process. When this process touches the heart and spirit of the students, thus helping to transform their whole being, then positive education, including education in non-violence, is possible.

To impart education in non-violence at a national level, the following factors have to be taken into account:

- quality of teachers,
- identification of subjects to be emphasised,
- teaching method and orientation,
- cultural, social, and political environment,
- integration of physical, intellectual, emotional, social, and spiritual elements, and
- evolving appropriate educational systems and programmes on the basis of the above-mentioned factors.

Quality of teachers: The success of education in non-violence will depend entirely on the quality of the teachers. Until teachers become non-violent persons, they will not be able to teach non-violence whatever the extent of their academic qualifications. The training of teachers will be the key factor for effective education in non-violence. The selection of candidates as prospective teachers and their all-round training in education in non-violence should have top priority. Therefore, any nation or organisation aspiring for education in non-violence, will have to make every possible effort and invest the necessary time and resources to produce well qualified teachers.

Identification of subjects to be emphasised: Today many people think that education in non-violence is something different from the usual secular education, and many classify it as religious or moral education, a domain exclusive of all other subjects. This is a misconception. Religious education, if imparted in the right way, may help the teaching of non-violence. But in the present day scenario, a number of so- called religious educators (though these are actually not true religious educators) create more dogma, fundamentalism, intolerance and hate. This kind of negative education imparted in the name of religion should be avoided at all cost. On the contrary, rational and secular subjects should be emphasised. To make a person's temperament rational and reasonable, logic is one of the most important subjects. Traditional Indian logic— particularly Buddhist logic—should be emphasised as a primary and basic subject for education at all levels.

Similarly, those subjects that help to eliminate any kind of blind faith or irrational dogma should be highlighted. Various treatises on subjects of equality among beings, love and compassion, caring for others, tolerance, forgiveness, patience, generosity, service, selflessness and sacrifice for the sake of others should be preferred. These texts may be drawn from religious canons or ethical teachings, but everything should be based on reasoning, not on faith or commandments.

Teaching method and orientation: The teaching method is extremely important for education in non-violence. Well-prepared teaching methods and teaching aids should be used to encourage the free and unconditional thinking power of the learners. The teaching-learning programmes must be oriented to dispel the conditioning of the learners' mind, and awaken their power of discrimination and reasoning. When students begin to believe, without questioning, whatever they are taught, their inquisitiveness and freedom of enquiry is diminished. The student should actually be stimulated to a genuine self-examination and be empowered to enquire into the truth.

The teaching method and orientation must evolve in such a way that the negative tendency of competition should not arise at all in the minds of the learners. The basic error in modern education is that it makes people violent by encouraging a sense of competition right from childhood. From pre-school to advanced studies, comparison and competition become the basic thrust for learners. The system of reward and punishment perpetuates this. False concepts such as 'healthy competition' or 'free and fair competition' totally mislead people. The basic objective of competition has always been victory over others. So, in reality, no competition can be healthy, or free and fair. In today's world, competition is one of the biggest sources of direct as well as structural violence. Only when the spirit of competition is eliminated, can students be trained in the non-violent way of life.

The teaching method and orientation should also be a tool to overcome the misconception that there are numerous situations where violence becomes indispensable. Today, this misconception is pervasive in the majority of so-called educated people. The power of discrimination and reasoning must be inculcated in the minds and hearts of the younger generation in order for them to realise that there *is* a non-violent solution to every problem—a solution that is more effective and lasting than a violent one. The superiority of non-violent and cooperative solutions over violent and competitive ones will thus become a reality in their minds and hearts.

The whole education system should be oriented towards realising these insights through a rational mind. In addition, a sense of contentment and recognition of the importance of sustainable material growth for the purpose of happiness and well-being should be inculcated through a holistic education. If the education method and orientation is improved in such a way, then every part of the learning process will become an education in non-violence.

Cultural, social, and political environment: For imparting an effective education in non-violence, the cultural, social and political environment is immensely important. Fortunately for the people of Tibet, we already have a non-violent Buddhist cultural environment. With a slight reorientation and dispelling of corruption that infiltrated over time, it may not be difficult to recreate a congenial cultural environment. In this age it is not easy to have a non-violent social environment. But the fourteenth Dalai Lama has proposed to turn the Tibetan Plateau into a zone of *ahimsa* (see chapter 6). His vision is not only to make Tibet peaceful for Tibetans, but to develop it into an example and a place for universal education in non-violence.

If the Tibetan Plateau could eventually be developed into a zone of *ahimsa* as envisaged by the Dalai Lama, it would offer a congenial social environment for education in non-violence. But at the same time, we must remember that merely declaring a region as a zone of *ahimsa* and making it free from military personnel and weapons, may not be sufficient to have the desired social and political environment for education in non-violence. Society should also be free from structural violence and a violent economic system. It would therefore be necessary to develop social, political, and economic systems that are free from such structural violence, invisible exploitation, and unending competition among human beings. This means it will be necessary to dissociate the Tibetans from the harmful forces of globalisation and economic competition, which tend to make man greedy, consumerist and exploitative.

Gandhi constantly opposed indiscriminate industrialisation and an open-market trade system. His ideas of *gramswaraj* (village self-rule) and constructive programmes provide a foundation to build a non-violent human society. But unfortunately, free India could never implement these ideas. The socio-economic structure of pre-1959 Tibet was very close to the Gandhian *gramswaraj* ideals. If given the opportunity of avoiding foreign interference, Tibet could go through a wonderful transformation simply by changing the superstructure of land ownership and the money-lending system, and slightly reorienting the ancient co-operative system of work. Thus Tibet could become a perfect self-sufficient community in accordance with the ideals of *gramswaraj*. Even today, after more than fifty years of communist dictators' misrule, Tibet has still a better potential to build a self-sufficient society.

Another difficult task would be to have a congenial political atmosphere for education in non-violence, which would demand the evolution of a genuine democratic system. Tibetans, as a nation, are committed to this. They are not simply committed to democracy; the intention is *genuine* democracy. But this would not be an easy task, because most democratic models available in today's world don't allow genuine rule by the people. In fact direct democracy like in Switzerland would be preferable to representative democracy with its elements of competition, imposition of the majority views on the minority and influence of powerful media.

Genuine democracy, or true rule of the people, can materialise only when each individual achieves a culture of self-rule and self-sufficiency. As long as the division between the ruler and the ruled exists, a true people's rule cannot be established. Gandhi's definition of *swaraj* (self-rule) is not a rule of self over others, it is the self controlled by oneself. A genuine democracy, or people's rule by consensus, would be the best political background for an education in non-violence. Tibet, a small nation without much cultural, language or ethnic diversity, can easily achieve such a genuine democracy.

Integration of physical, intellectual, emotional, social and spiritual elements: The demerits of the modern education system include instruction that is oriented to professional specialisation and watertight compartmentalisation that can never transform an 'educated' person into a wholly developed individual—an integrated entity. Specifically, the individual's physical, intellectual, emotional, social, and spiritual aspects are not integrated, and have lost their interrelationship, creating modern human beings with fragmented personalities. Education in non-violence should be an effective instrument to integrate all these different aspects for a holistic transformation of a person through a well-conceived and planned education system.

Physical well-being or physical fitness, including prevention and cure of diseases, should be based on a non-violent medical system such as traditional Tibetan medicine, ayurveda, naturopathy, reiki, acupuncture, acupressure, homeopathy, and so on. The ancient Chinese system of physical exercise and the ancient Tibetan system of *yoga asanas* must be encouraged. Physical exercises based on military training or violence-oriented aggressiveness should be avoided. The concept of health based on neutralising feelings of hate, greed and ignorance should be taught. Right from a young age people must be made aware that intolerance is a major cause of many diseases.

Similarly, all intellectual pursuits must be based on reason and rationality. How to deal with emotions on the basis of spiritual insights and philosophical understanding must be made an integral part of the education system.

Spirituality should not be confined only to the old and invalid, or to be pursued by a few, such as monks or nuns, who are completely withdrawn from the mainstream of society. Spirituality should be made an integral part of the education and learning process, and each individual must have the right to access it, and get the opportunity to practice it. A system of education must be evolved that is born out of spiritual and moral principles, having the potential of developing each individual's physical, intellectual, emotional and social capacities in a holistic manner. Only then can an effective education in non-violence be possible.

Evolving appropriate educational systems and programmes on the basis of the above-mentioned factors: For an effective education in non-violence, there must be appropriate formal and informal educational institutions and programmes on the basis of the principles discussed above. In the pre-1950s, Tibet, as a nation, was a centre of learning. Its position in the world was unparalleled, and it produced the largest quantity and finest quality of scholarly literature, and the highest number of spiritual practitioners who have attained the most elevated spiritual levels.

There are two basic types of literary works: (a) those translated from other languages, and (b) those written originally in Tibetan. The people of Tibet invented and developed their script and grammatical rules as recently as the seventh century A.D., and started to produce literature with a small population—at any point in time not more than six million. Within the relatively small period of around 1,300 years, Tibetans have produced one of the largest bodies of literature in the world. It is amazing, and sometimes it appears to me that the whole nation must have been engaged all the time in the production of literature. The highest, subtlest, and most original philosophical works were produced by Tibetan scholars.

But some people are critical and hold a contrary view. In their view, Tibet remained a most backward country until the twentieth century and had a very low literacy rate when the Chinese occupied it. Such criticism needs to be objectively examined without bias. It cannot be denied that there were at the time of the Chinese occupation, no adequate formal educational institutions for all children and youths, particularly in the lay community. Although formal education was largely confined to monasteries and nunneries for the ordained, there was an informal education system. In almost every village there were priests, ayurvedic doctors, officials, and elders who taught young people reading and writing. As a result, many bright youngsters did get incentives and opportunities for formal education and higher studies.

The system of informal education, as well as the system of transmission of knowledge as an inheritance, played a most important role for the people of Tibet in the past, more so than formal educational institutions. This system was deeply rooted in the spiritual relationship between teacher and disciple, which makes the education holistic and unfragmented. By passing down the knowledge through the lineage, the system of informal education has been preserved.

In future, we cannot refuse universal formal education, as well as building adequate educational institutions such as schools, colleges and universities. But, with regard to education in non-violence, we must give equal importance to both the informal and formal education systems. The informal education system must not be neglected and discarded. In particular, proper treatment of pre-school age children at home by parents and relatives will lay a solid foundation for non-violence education.

Spiritual instruction from individual teachers from time to time, as Tibetans enjoyed in the pre-occupation period, should be re-established. Informal community education could also be administered in arts, handicrafts, agriculture, songs, dances, music, and story-telling in the tradition of the Lama Mani, a nomadic storyteller. These apparently insignificant and unorganised ancient customs played a great role in the past in shaping the morals of Tibetan society, which must be recognised and revived again.

As far as the formal education system is concerned, the nation's education policy must rest on equality, genuine democracy, protection of ecology and the environment, self-sufficiency, contentment and, above all, non-competitiveness. Comparison between success and failure should not be the yardstick of evaluating the results of education. On the contrary, human minds flowering in goodness should be the objective as well as the yardstick for evaluating education. Respect for others, equal respect for every religion, and refraining from economic exploitation of other human beings as well as other sentient beings must be given top priority in the curricula of the formal education system. An atmosphere of logic and reasoning must be created. Scientific education should be limited to the minimal requirements, and each scientific subject must be balanced by instruction in morals and ethics, so as to avoid the chance of misusing the scientific and technological knowledge for violence and exploitation.

The structure of the formal education system need not be too rigid, but it may be roughly organised as follows: five years of basic or primary school, three years of middle school, and four years of high school. Then higher education and universities can be developed compatible with those of other countries. Just after completion of middle school, all students should undergo six months of intensive training for the application of non-violence in social, economic, and political life. Without this training, no one should be allowed to engage in a craft of any sort or in higher education. Appropriate laws may be passed to make this training compulsory for every citizen. This system would be in contrast with many other nations' systems of universal military training after schooling.

After completion of this training in non-violence, the majority of students would undergo two years of vocational training, so that they may start to earn a living. This training must be carefully chosen, well oriented for right living and a non-violent way of life. Only selected students who aim at university and higher education should continue with high school.

Periodical training camps, workshops, symposia and related activities should be organised for education in non-violence also for adult groups. Such specially structured courses must be conducted from time to time, particularly for local community leaders, members of state legislative councils, the national parliament and the judiciary, police personnel, and central and state government servants. Special emphasis should be given to short-term annual in-service training courses in non-violence education for teachers, which are compulsory and a requirement for tenure and promotion.

Whenever any situation arises in the Tibetan community that triggers off violence, the matter must be examined immediately, the cause of violence eliminated and possible preventive measures adopted. These should be publicised for the people's benefit. Such findings should also serve as an input for the educational curriculum.

The few points mentioned here contain only some of the aspects upon which more elaborate systems and methods for education in non-violence could be researched into and developed. In this limited space I cannot discuss all the points exhaustively, but the ones included here can be considered as indicative for the amplification of a comprehensive scheme for education in non-violence.

CHAPTER TWENTY-FIVE

The Commitment of the Friedrich Naumann Foundation

HUBERTUS VON WELCK

To secure freedom worldwide and in every sphere of society is the aim of the Friedrich Naumann Stiftung, the German Foundation for Liberal Policy. It is committed to realising human rights and human dignity, the basis for freedom to flourish. In South Asia, the Foundation has been working towards the strengthening of democratic structures and the implementation of human rights. In doing so, it helps to create a broad, firm political base for economic and social reforms.

Against this background of strengthening human rights, rule of law, protection of minorities and support for the development of democratic structures, the Foundation entered into co-operation with the Tibetan community in exile way back in 1991. The Foundation's partner here is the Tibetan Parliament-in-Exile, the Assembly of Tibetan People's Deputies. Initial deliberations on closer co-operation resulted in the identification of the following areas as requiring greater support:

- The gradually emerging process of democratisation which commenced in exile calls for more intensive support and implementation to ensure its success.
- Political awareness in the Tibetan refugee community needs to be heightened by civic education, thereby strengthening the Tibetans' ability to appraise political developments and determine their future path to freedom.
- As followers of the Buddhist faith, the Tibetans do not believe in armed struggle to regain their motherland, Tibet.

Rather, they stand committed to a peaceful, non-violent campaign under the leadership of the fourteenth Dalai Lama, with the objective of recovering their freedom, particularly in the religious and cultural spheres. This distinctive aspect of their struggle should, time and again, be brought to the attention of the international community in order to secure international support for the Tibetan cause.

- A group of well-qualified Tibetan leaders must emerge, actively involved in the democratisation process and capable of assuming leadership responsibilities.

On the basis of this analysis, the Tibetan Parliament-in-Exile and the Friedrich Naumann Foundation agreed to cooperate in the following areas:

- Civic education programmes which impart to the exiled Tibetans a clear sense of direction for their political debate, particularly on the non-violent struggle and enable them to make their own active contributions to securing freedom. These programmes have to be followed up by relevant publications.
- Support for developing a vibrant, assertive democracy backed by corresponding institutions.
- Training Tibetans to equip them with the knowledge and experience to assume political functions even in an international environment.
- Expanding and intensifying local, regional and international support for the Tibetan cause.

In order to effectively assist in the realisation of these goals, it was proposed to set up an institution to implement programmes and efficiently conduct seminars and conferences. Accordingly, the Tibetan Parliamentary and Policy Research Centre (TPPRC) was founded in 1992 and assigned the following tasks, among others:

- Providing support to the process of democratisation and its institutionalisation in the Tibetan society in exile.

- Strengthening the Tibetans' chosen path of peace and non-violence in seeking to return to their homeland.
- Assisting Parliament and Government in working out perspectives for Tibet's future.
- Preparing studies on how to design parliamentary procedures in accordance with Tibetan culture.
- Creating a data bank on Tibet for research purposes.
- Preparing analyses of current political issues for the Tibetan Parliament.

The Research Centre is headed by an executive director responsible to the Governing Council which has as its members the Chairperson of Parliament and the Deputy Chairperson, the Prime Minister *(kalon tripa)*, the Minister of Information and International Relations as well as the Minister of Education. The Private Secretary to the Dalai Lama, the executive director of the TPPRC and the Representative of the Friedrich Naumann Foundation are also members of the Council. The Council meets twice a year and decides on the framework and the priorities for the Centre's activities and also approves the annual budget.

During the ten years of its existence the TPPRC carried out a comprehensive programme of civic educational activities with the active support and guidance of the Friedrich Naumann Foundation. Listed below are some areas of activity with concrete examples:

- Seminars, discussions, colloquia, opinion polls—often in collaboration with regional or international academic or cultural institutions—on topics relating to the Tibetans and their desire to return to Tibet. The results of these interactions are published as reports, monographs and books.
- Studies on the working of democratic institutions, their procedures and modes of functioning and how to adapt them to the Tibetan tradition.

  Parliamentary sessions are recorded and reports compiled to be distributed to all Tibetan settlements worldwide. In this way every Tibetan has the opportunity to follow the work of his/her representative in parliament. In the process s/he is informed within a short passage of time about the topics, questions, as well as critical interventions and subsequent parliamentary decisions and votings. Since the Members of Parliament are not elected from constituencies, and therefore direct constituency work is not possible, the TPPRC regularly organises information-gathering visits by parliamentarians to the Tibetan settlements in Nepal and India. In doing so it ensures that communication between the Tibetan people and their representatives is maintained, enabling a feedback on problems and topical developments which give an input to questions and discussions in Parliament. By organising information meetings in the Tibetan settlements, the TPPRC encourages the founding of local assemblies to strengthen self-government and thereby assist familiarisation with democratic structures and procedures.

- Events dealing with the historical, political, legal, social, economic and cultural developments in Tibet and their present status.

  Workshops are held to deliberate on topical questions such as the relationship between China and Tibet as well as India. Journalists, university teachers, civil servants and the general public in India constitute the target group.

- Training programmes for parliamentarians and members of the cabinet on topics such as 'public accountability', 'constitutional systems and parliamentary work', 'procedures and practical functioning of a parliamentary democracy'.

  After elections and before or after parliamentary sessions seminars are organised to assist parliamentarians in carrying out their work. In the course of these workshops parliamentary proceedings and motions are discussed in detail so that the Members learn to handle the instruments at their disposal with confidence.

  In 1994, a group of Tibetan Deputies were invited for an information-gathering trip to the Federal Republic of Germany, giving them the opportunity to get acquainted with the work of parliaments in Germany, of interacting with their fellow-parliamentarians there, and reporting on their own situation.

Parliamentarians and members of the government may participate in seminars of the Friedrich Naumann Foundation's International Academy for Leadership (IAF) in Gummersbach and benefit from the wide choice of programmes on offer.

- Seminars for opinion leaders from Tibetan settlements, schools and local parliaments on current political issues and perspectives for the Tibetan freedom movement.
- Training programmes for students and pupils, representatives of youth organisations and associations, on political developments on the one hand and on communication, executive skills, organisation, management as well as strategies for non-violent campaigns on the other.

Thus information programmes for young people were conducted in 1992 and 1993 where an introduction to the political system in exile was given and visions for future development on the basis of the provisional constitution (Charter of the Tibetan People in Exile) were discussed.

- Conferences and symposia on the concept of Tibet's autonomy as a natural concomitant of the right to self-determination and the possibilities of its realisation.

Two seminars were held in 1994 and 1996 where Tibetans and international experts dwelt at great length on the right to self-determination in international law and its effects, implications and possibilities for Tibet. The presentations and conclusions of these seminars were subsequently published.

It is not independence that the Tibetans demand from the People's Republic of China, but religious and cultural autonomy. In November 1999, the TPPRC organised a conference on 'Tibetan Autonomy and Self-Government: Myth or Reality'. The autonomy so far granted by China does not for the most part go beyond the nomenclature: 'Tibet Autonomous Region'. The conference examined various models for autonomy existing worldwide, from Greenland to South Tyrol. These models stand testimony to a vast range of autonomy arrangements which have in the meantime proved their viability in practice.

Drawing on the results of this conference, texts for educational programmes have been prepared reaching out to Tibetan opinion leaders such as teachers and functionaries in the settlement and to acquaint them with various autonomy options and apply these specifically to a future Tibet. In the course of interactions the seminars witnessed lively and exciting discussions which did not exclude the requirements of the Chinese.

- Information programmes and photo exhibitions on Tibet, the Chinese invasion, life in exile and prospects of autonomy for Tibet.
- International conferences in collaboration with Tibet Support Groups, with the objective of strengthening international solidarity.

The second international conference of Tibetan Support Groups was held in 1996 in the parliamentary hall of the 'Wasserwerk' in Bonn—then serving as the seat of the German Bundestag (the Parliament). The participants, representatives of Tibet Support Groups worldwide, worked out an action plan focussing strongly on the campaign strategies of various groups and improved coordination between them. Using the conference as a pretext, the Chinese government closed the office of the Friedrich Naumann Foundation in Beijing.

Four years later, in May 2000, Berlin played host to the third international conference of Tibet Support Groups in the Legislative Assembly of the Land of Berlin. It was at this conference that the 'International Network for the Support of Tibet' was established with the aim of effectively coordinating the work of Tibet support groups worldwide and continuously updating the action programmes for religious and cultural autonomy.

The Friedrich Naumann Foundation is the only organisation which has over the years been consistently supporting the Tibetans in exile on their path to democracy and in their political struggle for human rights, freedom of religion and the preservation of their unique culture in their homeland.

Dr. Otto Graf Lambsdorff, Chairman of the Friedrich Naumann Foundation, visited Dharamsala in October 2001 to learn first hand about the progress and results of the cooperation between the two partners. As a keen observer of developments in the exiled Tibetan community, he was impressed by the level of democratisation, believing it to be surprisingly advanced. The direct election of the Prime Minister (*kalon tripa*) in 2001 not only confirmed this process of democratisation but also strengthened it further. Graf Lambsdorff is of the opinion that only very few communities in exile have so resolutely pursued democratisation. He pledged the Foundation's continued support for the Tibetans' non-violent campaign for their rights, with the aim of reaching a negotiated understanding with the People's Republic of China.

References

Bhattacharjea, Ajit, *Tibetans in Exile—A Democratic Vision*, TPPRC, New Delhi 1994. Reprinted 1997.

Dulaney, Andrew G., Cusack, Dennis M. and van Walt, Michael, *The Case Concerning Tibet: Tibet's Sovereignty and the Tibetan People's Right to Self-Determination*, TPPRC, New Delhi 1998.

Gupta, S.P. and Ramachandran, K.S., *History of Tibet*, TPPRC, New Delhi, 1995. Reprinted 1997; Chinese Edition, New Delhi 1997.

Indian Press on India-Tibet-China Relations, TPPRC, New Delhi 1997.

Mehrotra, L.L., *India's Tibet Policy*, TPPRC, New Delhi 1996, Reprinted 1997.

Mehrotra, L.L., *Bharat ki Tibet Niti, Mulyankan evam Vikalp*, TPPRC, New Delhi 1999.

Rinpoche, Ven. Samdhong, *Tibet—A Future Vision*, TPPRC, New Delhi 1996; Tibetan Edition, New Delhi 1997.

Saran, Shankar, *India, Tibet and China: An Agonising Reappraisal*, India Tibet Friendship Society, New Delhi 1996.

Saran, Shankar, *Fifty Years After the Asian Relations Conference*, TPPRC, New Delhi 1997.

Saran, Shankar, *Bharat-Chin Sambandh aur Tibet: Ek Purnvichar*, (Hindi) TPPRC, New Delhi 1998.

Saran, Shankar, *Tibet Samasiya*, (Hindi *Statements by Atal Bihari Vajpayee*), TPPRC, New Delhi 20003.

Sharp, Gene, *The Power and Practice of Non-Violent Struggle*, translated by Shastri, Pema Tsewang into Tibetan, TPPRC, New Delhi 1999.

Shiromany, A.A., *The Spirit of Tibet—Universal Heritage—Selected Speeches and Writings of His Holiness the Dalai Lama*, New Delhi 1995.

Shiromany, A.A., *The Spirit of Tibet—Vision for Human Liberation—Selected Speeches and Writings of His Holiness the XIV Dalai Lama*, TPPRC, New Delhi 1996.

Shiromany, A.A., The Political Philosophy of His Holiness the XIV Dalai Lama—Selected Speeches and Writings, TPPRC, New Delhi 1998.

Tibetan People's Right of Self-Determination, TPPRC, New Delhi 1996.

Tibetan People's Right of Self-Determination—Brief Summary, TPPRC, New Delhi 1997.

Tibet's Parliament-in-Exile, TPPRC, New Delhi 1996, Reprinted 1999.

Tibetan Autonomy and Self-Government: Myth or Reality?, TPPRC, New Delhi 2000.

Tsomo, Tsering, *Tibet Since the Asian Relations Conference*, TPPRC, New Delhi 1998..

World Press on Panchen Lama—Selections from Press Reports, TPPRC, New Delhi 1996.

About the Contributors

Jürgen C. Aschoff is Professor of Neurology at the University of Ulm, Germany. He has been a regular visitor to the cultural region of northern India and Tibet for the past thirty years and has been doing research on Tibetan medicine since 1990. He is the author of several books and articles on Tibetan medicine.

Dagmar Bernstorff studied Political Science, Sociology and History at the Universities of Munich, London and Freiburg. She taught International Relations and Political Science of South Asia at the Universities of Munich and Heidelberg. She has written and published extensively in these areas. She now lives in New Delhi.

Michael von Brück is Professor at the Institute of Protestant Theology and Comparative Religions, University of Munich. He studied Protestant Theology and Comparative Religions at the Universities of Rostock, Regensburg, Munich and Madras.

Victor Chan was born in Hongkong and now lives in Canada. He is a member of the Institute of Asian Research, University of British Columbia, Canada. He is President of the China-Tibet Initiative, a Canadian organisation for the furthering of relations between Tibetans and the Chinese.

Gyaneshwar Chaturvedi, PhD, retired as Professor of Political Science at St. John's College, Agra University in 2003. He studied at Agra University and at the School of Oriental and African Studies, University of London. He writes extensively on identity formation, xenology and Hindu fundamentalism.

Joachim Glaubitz is Associate Professor for International Relations at Munich University. He studied Sinology and Japanology at Leipzig and Hamburg and has taught International Relations at the University of Munich since 1973.

Gyaltsen Gyaltag was born in Lhasa and fled to India in 1956. The Pestalozzi Chidren's Village at Trogen, Switzerland, gave him shelter in 1969. He studied to become a primary school teacher and later read Psychology and Education at Zurich University. He taught at the Pestalozzi Children's Village from 1986–91. From 1991–95 he was the representative of HH. the Dalai Lama in the Tibet

Office in Zurich, where he looked after relations with the EU and the UN. Gyaltsen Gyaltag passed away in 2002.

Eva Herzer, is an attorney and mediator in the San Francisco Bay Area. She is currently the UN Observer for and Chairperson of the International Law Committee of the National Association of Women Lawyers in the USA. She is also a member of the first Steering Committee of the International Tibet Support Network, an umbrella organisation of over 130 Tibet support groups from around the world.

Karma Lekshe Tsomo, PhD, is Assistant Professor of Theology and Religious Studies at the University of San Diego, USA. An American bhikshuni practising in the Tibetan tradition, she is President of Sakyadhita: International Association of Buddhist Women and Director of the Jamyang Foundation, an initiative that has provided educational opportunities for women in the Indian Himalayas since 1987.

Maura Moynihan is a writer, musician and painter. She spent part of her teenage years in India. Maura studied at Harvard University and at the Corcoran School of Art in Washington D.C. As a consultant for Refugees International, she spent many years in Nepal, working with Tibetan refugees. In 1997, she testified on Tibet to the US Senate Foreign Relations Committee.

Dawa Norbu, PhD, is Professor of International Relations in Central Asia at the Jawaharlal Nehru University in New Delhi. He fled from Tibet with his parents in 1959 and later studied at St. Stephen's College, New Delhi and at the University of California, Berkeley. Dawa Norbu was also the editor of the *Tibetan Review*.

Tseten Norbu was born when his parents fled from Tibet. He studied at Tribhuvan University, Kathmandu, Nepal, and in Japan and the Philippines. He worked in the Reception Centre and in the Tibet Bureau at Kathmandu. He was President of the Tibetan Youth Congress from 1995–2001.

Tsering Norzom Thonsur is a Member of the Assembly of Tibetan People's Deputies, elected for a second term in 2001. She was born in India and grew up in the Mundgod Settlement. Tsering Norzom studied at the University of Mysore and holds a diploma in Systems Management and Laboratory Technology. She was President of the Regional Tibetan Women's Association at Mundgod from 1980–90 and is a member of the board of the Tibetan Women's Association.

Jetsun Pema is President of the Tibetan Children's Villages. Younger sister of the Dalai Lama, she was born in Lhasa and went to school in India. She completed her studies in England and in Switzerland. In 1964, the Dalai Lama entrusted her with the management of the Tibetan Children's Villages. Jetsun Pema is the first woman to be a member of the Kashag, the cabinet, and held the education portfolio from 1990–1993. Her autobiography *Tibet: My Story* was published in 1996 and has been translated into ten languages.

Tsewang Phuntso heads the Liaison Office of the CTA for Latin America, in New York. He holds an M.A. in Sustainable International Development from Brandeis University, USA. He was President of the Tibetan Youth Congress from 1990–1995. He worked in various capacities in the Tibetan Central Administration, till 2001 as Joint Secretary in the Ministry of Information and Broadcasting and edited the Report 'Tibet under Communist China: 50 Years'.

Alison Reynolds is Director of the Free Tibet Compaign and co-chair of the International Tibet Support Network, an independent membership organisation campaigning in support of the rights of the Tibetan people to freedom.

Tsepak Rigzin is Principal of the Central Tibetan School at the Mundgod Settlement since 1992. He attended Tibetan schools at Kalimpong and Simla and studied Buddhist Philosophy and Tibetan Literature at the Institute of Buddhist Dialectics, Dharamsala from 1975–1981. From 1981–1992, he worked in the Research and Translation Section of the Library of Tibetan Works and Archives, Dharamsala. He is a member of the Commission for 'Tibetan National Education Policy'.

Samdhong Rinpoche, Kalon Tripa (Prime Minister) of the Kashag was born in Tibet as the fifth incarnation of Samdhong. He studied Buddhist philosophy at the Drepung Monastery in Lhasa and after his flight to India, at the Gyuto Tantric Monastery in Dalhousie. From 1981–2001, he was Vice-Chancellor of the Central Institute of Higher Tibetan Studies at Sarnath from 1981–2001. The Dalai Lama nominated him member of the XIth Assembly of Tibetan People's Deputies in 1991 and he was the Chairman of the Assembly till 2001. In the same year, he was directly elected by the Tibetan people in exile as Prime Minister.

Thupten Samphel is Secretary of the Department of Information and International Relations, CTA. He studied History at St. Stephen's College, New Delhi, and Journalism at Columbia University, New York. Thupten Samphel is the editor in chief of the *Tibetan Bulletin*. He writes frequently for the *Tibetan Review, Hindustan Times, Tribune, China Report,* etc. and corresponds for the Bureau of the Associated Press in New Delhi.

Gerald Schmitz studied Law and Sinology at Bonn University. He worked for several years as lawyer at Braunschweig and is now a judge at Göttingen. He has published several articles on Tibet from the point of view of International Law.

Sherab Gyatso is English and has been ordained as a monk in the Tibetan tradition since 1986. From 1987–99 he studied at the Institute of Buddhist Dialectics, Dharamsala, where he became the institute's first-ever foreign graduate.

For the past seven years he has taught at the Lotsawa Rinchen Zangpo Translator Programme, training foreign students as interpreters.

Tenzin Gyatso, the Fourteenth Dalai Lama was confirmed as the incarnation of the Thirteenth Dalai Lama in 1939 and received the traditional education of a Buddhist monk. At the time of the Chinese invasion in 1950 he was enthroned as the spiritual and secular head of the Tibetans at the age of sixteen. In 1959 the Dalai Lama fled to India and formed the Tibetan Government-in-Exile. He was awarded the Nobel Prize for Peace in 1989. His numerous publications on Tibetan Buddhism and the status of Tibet include his autobiography *Freedom in Exile* (1998, 3rd edition), and *The Political Philosophy of His Holiness the XIVth Dalai Lama* (1998).

Wangpo Tethong, son of Tibetan refugees, was born in Trogen (Switzerland). He studied History and Law at the University of Zurich. From 1986–1990, Wangpo Tethong was a board member of the Association of Tibetan Youth in Europe. He co-founded the Student Study Circle for Tibet. Wangpo Tethong edited the Tibetan-German paper '*Böd Shon*' (Young Tibet) from 1990 to 1997. He is the elected President of the Swiss-Tibetan Friendship Society since 2001. Wangpo served as Secretary and Press Liaison of the Green Party in the Kanton of Zurich and is currently Press Officer of Greenpeace, Switzerland.

Penpa Tering was born in India and grew up in the Bylakuppe Settlement. He was elected to the XIIth Assembly of the Tibetan People's Deputies in 1996 and subsequently to the XIIIth Assembly in 2001. He is Executive Director of the Tibetan Parliamentary and Policy Research Centre (TPPRC) in Delhi since 2001.

Tsering Tsomo is a Member of the Assembly of Tibetan People's Deputies since 2001. She holds an M.A. degree in Geography from the University of Kentucky, USA. Tsering Tsomo worked in the Department of Information and International Relations of the CTA as Head of Women's Problems and later of Environment and Development. She was also Managing Director of the Tibetan Parliamentary and Policy Research Centre (TPPRC) from 1997–2001.

Kunchok Tsundue holds a doctorate in Geography from the University of Bochum in Germany. He is Secretary of the Planning Department, CTA. He had a major responsibility in the conducting of the Tibetan Demographic Survey in 1998 as its Technical Officer.

Hubertus von Welck is Director of the Regional Office, South Asia of the Friedrich-Naumann-Stiftung in New Delhi, India, since 1998. He studied Public Administration at Konstanz University and participated in an interdisciplinary course on Problems of Developing Countries from 1977–1978. Hubertus von Welck joined the Friedrich Naumann Foundation in 1979 and represented the foundation in Zimbabwe in the 1980s. He headed the Personnel Department of the foundation from 1989–98 before moving to New Delhi.

Index